ABOUT THE AUTHOR

Trish always fancied herself a writer, but she dutifully picked gherkins and washed dishes in a Chinese restaurant on her way to earning herself an economics degree and a qualification as a chartered accountant instead. Work took her to Canberra where she promptly fell in love with a tall, dark and handsome hero who cut computer code, and marriage and four daughters followed, which gave Trish the chance to step back from her career and think about what she'd really like to do.

Writing romantic fiction was at the top of the list, so Trish made a choice and followed her heart. It was the right choice. Since then, she's sold more than thirty titles to Harlequin with sales in excess of seven million globally, with her books printed in more than thirty languages in forty countries worldwide.

Four times nominated and two times winner of Romance Writers of Australia's RuBY Award for Romantic Book of the Year, Trish was also a 2012 RITA finalist in the US.

You can find out more about Trish and her upcoming books at www.trishmorey.com and you can email her at trish@trishmorey.com. Trish loves to hear from her readers.

The Trouble With Choices

TRISH MOREY

mira

First Published 2018
First Australian Paperback Edition 2018
ISBN 9781489257796

THE TROUBLE WITH CHOICES
© 2018 by Trish Morey
Australian Copyright 2018
New Zealand Copyright 2018

Published by
Mira
An imprint of Harlequin Enterprises (Australia) Pty Ltd.
Level 13, 201 Elizabeth St
SYDNEY NSW 2000
AUSTRALIA

® and TM (apart from those relating to FSC ®) are trademarks of Harlequin Enterprises Limited or its corporate affiliates. Trademarks indicated with ® are registered in Australia, New Zealand and in other countries.

A catalogue record for this book is available from the National Library of Australia www.librariesaustralia.nla.gov.au

Printed and bound in Australia by McPherson's Printing Group

MIX
Paper from responsible sources
FSC
www.fsc.org   FSC® C001695

To Gavin,
Happy 30th anniversary to my favourite hero.
Thank you for our four gorgeous girls, the laughs along the way,
and for being there through thick and thin.
All my love,
Trish xxx

1

Sophie

Nan started playing 'Here Comes the Bride' on the organ up front, while the words going around and around in Sophie Faraday's head marched to a different tune.

I'm just not that into you.

Sophie swallowed against the lump in her throat. A fine time for Jason to realise that little fact, the night before her brother got hitched. Tears pricked at the corners of her eyes, but she wouldn't cry, not now, not when she was about to walk down the aisle at Dan and Lucy's wedding. Even if she had blown five hundred dollars on a spa suite at Mount Lofty House, where she'd now be spending the night alone.

Five hundred dollars!

She lifted her face to the blue sky and breathed deeply. Oh God, don't cry! If she started now, she'd never stop.

She blinked hard as Siena started down the red carpet, barely registering the oohs and aahs over how grown up her ten-year-old niece looked today in her lilac-coloured junior bridesmaid gown. A gentle puff of spring breeze, the air sweetly scented, sent white cherry blossom drifting over the congregation, their petals landing on shoulders and in hair.

And even from the depths of her own personal hell, Sophie had to hand it to Dan and Lucy. It was genius to get married in the orchard in springtime. It was the perfect venue for a wedding. So beautiful. So utterly romantic.

So unlike Jason.

Sniff.

What had he told her when she'd asked him why? That she was too demanding. Too needy.

Of course she'd been needy!

She'd needed him to get on that plane and arrive back in Adelaide from his fly-in-fly-out job like they'd arranged. She'd needed him to be her sexy, loving partner today, to pull her against him and tell her how much he'd missed her these last three weeks they'd been apart. She'd needed him to smile down at her and laugh at her jokes like she was the only woman alive.

Most of all, she'd needed not to be dumped the night before her own brother's wedding.

And that somehow meant she had a problem?

Siena reached the front and peeled off to the left, and Beth was the next to follow her daughter down the aisle. The organ kept right on pumping out the notes and Sophie watched her sister as if on autopilot.

Three months they'd been together. Three months and four days to be exact since Jason had seen her profile on the dating site, HEA.com, and messaged her, wanting to meet up on his next break. The start of a beautiful relationship, he'd told her as he'd gazed into her eyes the very first time they'd met, he was sure of it.

And she'd believed it was, meeting every break since, bar one, until that beautiful relationship had crunched to a sudden halt less than twenty-four hours ago.

So much for happy-ever-after-dot-com. More like happy *never* after, the way her luck was going.

She gripped the posy in her hands that much tighter, imagining her fingers wrapped around Jason's throat right now. He might have waited until after the wedding. Could have left his 'I'm just not that into you' speech for another time. Surely he could have pretended to be into her for just one more day, not to mention one more very expensive night?

Five hundred dollars!

'Sophie!' her older sister Hannah hissed behind her. 'Get going!'

She snapped to with a start, saw Beth already at the front and everyone looking expectantly her way. Even Nan missed a couple of notes because she was looking over her shoulder. Crap!

She took off too fast and wobbled on her heels. *Whoa,* she thought, clutching onto her posy like a lifeline and using all of the pause before the next step to steady herself. Maybe she shouldn't have downed that last glass of champagne. Or the one before it, for that matter. But then, it was a day for celebrating.

Not to mention a day for drowning her sorrows.

Still, it wouldn't be a good look if she fell flat on her face during the bridal procession. She almost snorted at that, though snorting would hardly be a good look, either. But at least now she didn't have to force a smile. The mental image of herself face-planting into the red carpet during the wedding march saw to that.

Wagner's famous processional sounded through the valley, and the soft air rippled the silk of her gown and sent another sprinkle of cherry blossom raining down onto the proceedings, as Sophie methodically—meticulously—put one foot in front of the other, and slowly made her way forward. By the time she got near the front without disgracing herself, her confidence was building and she was grinning in triumph. Dan was frowning a little, but that was no surprise—he was her older brother after all, and he'd have found something to be annoyed about—probably Nan missing those notes. She sent him a wink, and only then noticed the best man standing beside him, almost missing her next step. Because Nick Pasquale, she couldn't help but notice, had scrubbed up well for the occasion, so well she almost hadn't recognised him. She added a few more watts to her smile and aimed it in his direction in appreciation.

There was definitely something sexy about a man all gussied up for a wedding.

Hello …

The lightbulb smacked her right between the eyes, her realisation sparking a new resolution.

Stuff Jason!

Because this was a wedding and there had to be lots of eligible men here, and all of them dressed up for the occasion. Not Nick, of course—he'd always treated her like a little sister, and she had a spa suite going begging and wasn't planning on being treated like anyone's little sister tonight—but it was a wedding and she'd dropped four kilos in the last month, and she was a pretty hot-looking bridesmaid if she did say so herself. And if she couldn't get a shag at a wedding when she was a bridesmaid and looked this good, she really was hopeless.

Fired up with her new resolve, she winked at Beth as she took her place alongside, but her sister was staring into space, lost in her thoughts, Siena in front of her busy plucking at her unfamiliar skirts.

So when Hannah arrived, Sophie grinned at her instead. Now there was only Kate, Lucy's friend and matron of honour, to walk down the aisle before the bride made her entrance. Before long, the formalities would be over with and Sophie could get stuck into the serious business of finding herself a suitable candidate for the night.

She caught Hannah peering strangely at her before glancing back over her shoulder down the aisle. Leaning closer, she whispered, 'Are you okay?'

'Yup,' Sophie said, 'never better,' and Hannah was already straightening, seemingly convinced, except Sophie hiccuped and Hannah must have caught a whiff of alcohol because her eyes opened wide in disbelief.

'Oh God. Please tell me you're not drunk!'

This time she did snort, just a little, because the idea was so ridiculous. Of course she wasn't drunk. A little tipsy maybe …

'How could you be so stupid?' her sister hissed.

'What's wrong?' whispered Beth, who'd suddenly decided to pay attention.

'Sophie's drunk.'

It was Beth's turn to look appalled. 'What?'

In front of them, Siena turned, her big brown eyes blinking up at the three sisters. 'What are you all whispering about? Who's drunk?'

'Shhhh,' Sophie said, putting a finger to her lips, loving how it would be damn near impossible for anyone to tell if she was slurring that, while her twin sisters either side glowered at her. Then, Kate took her place at the front, and Sophie welcomed the new arrival with another grin and shrugged at the question in the other woman's eyes, as if she didn't know what was going on. Meanwhile, the collective gasp behind them told her that the bride was on her way.

Saved by the bride, Sophie thought, thoroughly amused by her own wit. What was Hannah's problem? Clearly, she couldn't be *that* drunk. She turned to watch the woman who would soon be their sister-in-law, and swayed a little as she did, earning herself another glare from Hannah in the process. She raised her eyebrows and grinned back, before the approaching bride snagged her attention.

Because wow, what a bride. Lucy looked amazing as she walked down the aisle on the arm of her mother. Dressed in a cream-coloured lace sheath over a miniskirt, and with cherry blossom artfully woven into a circle on her head, Lucy had never looked happier or more gorgeous. The bridesmaids had all helped Lucy get dressed and played fetch for the hairdresser and makeup artists, who had arrived early in the morning, but none of them could take one shred of credit for how radiant she looked right now. It was all down to Lucy herself, and the love that shone from her eyes and radiated from her smile.

The love she felt for Dan.

Sophie sighed wistfully. And to think her crazy brother had let Lucy walk away when last cherry season was finished and risked losing the love of his life forever.

Sophie glanced over at her big brother, saw his eyes similarly full of admiration and love, and wanted to hug him right then and there for putting this right. Getting Lucy back had been like a magician pulling a rabbit from a hat, and now marrying her—well, that was no cheap trick. That was pure magic.

The pair reached the front, and if the look Lucy and Dan exchanged wasn't enough to melt the most cynical of hearts, it sure was enough to peel back the fog of alcohol and let back in the pain of Jason's betrayal. Sophie choked on a sob, once again fighting back the tears. Was it so unreasonable to want the same kind of love for herself? Was it so unreasonable not to want to wait until she was a crusty thirty-seven years old like her brother to find that special someone to share her life with?

No, it damned well wasn't.

The organ music faded away and Nan took her seat next to Pop in the row behind. It was birdsong that played the accompaniment while the celebrant welcomed everyone. A simple service, Lucy and Dan had planned. Short and to the point, with just the important bits included to share with family and friends.

It wouldn't take long and then Sophie could get stuck into the serious business of man hunting. She needed to mingle and check out who else was on the guest list she'd paid only lip service to before today.

And then she felt a familiar pressure and found another reason for hoping the ceremony wouldn't take too long. She crossed her legs under her gown and pressed her thighs together as inconspicuously as possible. Because all that champagne was doing more than just kicking in.

Right now, she really needed to pee.

2

Beth

Beth Faraday watched Lucy take her place by Dan's side, and swallowed back a lump in her throat. Lucy looked utterly stunning in her gorgeous lace wedding dress. *Every girl should wear a wedding dress once in her life*, she remembered her mother telling her, through lips loaded with half a dozen dress-making pins, her hands busy pinning seams in the ivory satin, while Beth had held up her arms, feeling like a fraud.

And, as it turned out, Beth *had* worn that wedding gown once, to the church where she and Joe were to be married. She'd been determined to wear the dress by then, although she'd dispensed with the veil and added a black sash around her expanding waist.

It wouldn't have been right to have worn a veil to a funeral.

She blinked away the scratchiness in her eyes, never more grateful that Dan and Lucy had decided to get married here, in the orchard, rather than the little church on the top of the hill where generations of locals had been christened and married and, ultimately, farewelled.

Where Joe had been farewelled.

The celebrant's words washed over her, words of love and union and what it meant to be married, words that once would have been spoken for her.

A movement right in front distracted her—Siena, tugging at the side seam of her bodice. She smiled softly at her daughter, whose dark-brown eyes would never let her forget Joe, even though Siena would never know him, and not for the first time, she thought how unfair it was. Siena should have a father. She and Joe should be bringing her up together. Instead, Siena was stuck with just her, and both Joe and their daughter had missed out on so much.

Too much.

'I do,' said Dan, and Beth blinked dewy eyes to attention, as it was Lucy's turn next to answer the big question.

'I do,' the bride repeated a few moments later, as a puff of breeze sent another flurry of petals scattering over them all.

God, so very beautiful, and the lump in Beth's throat grew so large it squeezed tears from her eyes. Bittersweet tears, both happy and sad, for the things that were and for the things that could have been.

Siena pulled at her bodice again, where the seam bit into her waist, and Beth cursed herself that she wasn't half the dressmaker her mum was. Siena was growing up so fast, she should have known to allow an extra centimetre each side.

A neatly manicured hand flashed out, fingers applying a firm rap against the girl's shoulder, and her daughter stilled and turned rigid. Beth stiffened with it. Bloody Hannah! Beth peered beyond an oblivious Sophie, who looked like she was in some kind of pain, to her older-by-ten-minutes sister, who was now smiling smugly, her focus one hundred per cent on the words of the vows being exchanged.

Oh yeah, Beth thought, Hannah would be hearing some more words later, too. She just hoped she might pay them the same attention.

3

Hannah

The celebrant looked to the best man. 'May I have the rings, please?'

Hannah Faraday smiled. Such a lovely service, in spite of her stupid sister getting herself tanked—what was that about?—and her niece jiggling around like a tea bag in a cup. It was lucky she was there to keep this wedding on track.

The celebrant coughed into his curled hand. 'The rings,' he prompted, leaning closer, 'please?'

Nick Pasquale came to with a jolt, and started flapping at his pockets. Hannah rolled her eyes. God, was nobody else paying attention to this ceremony? She looked sideways at her sisters, to see if they shared her frustration, only to see Sophie looking like she was gritting her teeth, and Beth for some reason scowling right at her, and thought, apparently not.

The rings were retrieved, and the wedding got back on track, and Dan and Lucy made their vows to share their lives and to love each other as long as they both shall live.

'I now pronounce you husband and wife,' said the celebrant, and Dan and Lucy shared their first kiss as a married couple, to the cheers and applause of the assembled guests. For the first time today, Hannah experienced a momentary pang of wistfulness. Marriage was so far off her radar it wasn't funny, but every other wedding or so, she was reminded why, and she found herself wondering, *Why me?*

And then the moment would pass in a flood of rationality. Marriage was for a different kind of person, for romantics and the ones who wanted to raise a family. For people like Dan and Lucy, who were clearly made for each other. Not even close to being a number-one priority for practical people like her, already busy with their lives and careers.

The newlyweds started making their slow way back down the aisle and she fell in behind Kate. Fifteen minutes had been allowed for congratulations before the wedding party and family were due to assemble in a nearby spot in the orchard, where Dan's gleaming nineteen-sixty-nine Triumph Spitfire was prepped and ready for photographs. Strictly speaking, it was Kate's job as matron of honour to organise the bridesmaids, but Hannah was sure Kate wouldn't mind if she pulled rank on this one. Hannah was older, after all. She'd ensure the bridesmaids were there on time and didn't keep anyone waiting.

Except that Sophie disappeared the second the formalities were over, and Beth and Siena looked like they were going to do the same thing. 'Where are you going?' she called to Beth. 'We've got photos coming up.'

'Going to touch up my makeup, actually,' Beth said. 'You got a problem with that?'

Hannah blinked at the hostile tone. *Actually*, she did have a problem, given they were supposed to be gathering soon for photos like the plan said, but Beth hadn't waited for her answer, and Hannah figured that maybe touching up her makeup was code for having a word to Siena about what standing still meant. At least that might explain her snippy tone.

She turned to where she'd last seen Kate only to find her gone too, absorbed into the crowd. Typical.

So, it was no surprise to Hannah that she was the first to arrive for the photographs at the allotted time, given she seemed to be the only one to pay more than lip service to their responsibilities. Oh, she could excuse the bride and groom for taking their sweet time to get to the designated spot in the orchard. Lucy and Dan would have to run the gauntlet of the sea of guests wanting to congratulate them, but that didn't excuse everyone else.

The photographer strode up, his big camera bag slung over his shoulder, a camera in one hand, a tripod in the other. He nodded to her in acknowledgement, and then swung the bag down onto the ground and got to work changing lenses and checking the light.

'They're all hopeless,' she said, smoothing her skirts. 'Everyone knows photographs are supposed to be happening now.'

He smiled as he screwed on a new lens, bagging the other one. 'It's okay. No rush. They'll get here.'

Hannah sighed as she turned to see if anyone else was coming yet, only to find that, no, nobody was. In fact, nobody looked close to coming anytime soon. One side from the crowd still gathered around Lucy and Dan, she could see Nan and Pop deep in conversation with a group of local orchardists, while Beth was chatting to the post-office lady and clearly totally oblivious to Siena, who was now running around playing chasey with another child—while in her flower-girl dress and before photos of all things. What was her sister thinking?

Finally she spotted Kate, her own new husband with his arm looped around her shoulders, while the best man, Nick Pasquale, looked on. She clucked her tongue. Nick, who looked sensible enough, but who'd been daydreaming about God only knows what during the ceremony because he'd had to be asked twice for the rings.

Hopeless.

But if all that wasn't bad enough, there was Sophie, who looked like she was heading for the bar. Bloody hell, that was so not going to happen. Hannah tossed off a quick, 'I'll just go round everyone up,' over her shoulder to the photographer as she set off, marching back to where the guests were still milling around Dan and Lucy.

It was just lucky for them that somebody was taking this wedding seriously.

4

Sophie

The photos were almost done, and Sophie felt drained from the effort of smiling. On the plus side, it had been so long since she'd had a drink, she was feeling less tipsy by the minute. She watched as the photographer shot off a few extra snaps of Dan and Lucy in front of the car—he'd asked everyone to wait to make sure he had what he needed before he let them all go, and then the sun had moved, the light dappled and golden, and he'd gone back to work again. Now Sophie stood to one side of the group, barely aware of the conversation going on between the rest of the bridal party, lost in her own thoughts while she watched the photographer do his stuff.

'Now, Lucy,' the photographer said, as he had Dan standing behind her, his arms around her waist. 'Look up at Dan. Dan, look down.'

Click. Click. Click.

'Lovely. Let's see a kiss …' Dan obliged, leaning down and kissing his bride, both of them unable to stop smiling. 'Perfect, keep it going.'

Click. Click. Click.

Sophie sighed as she gazed at the picture of true love playing out before her. If she wanted love like that for herself, she was going to have to start being more selective. No more dickhead boyfriends. No more believing a guy's bullshit 'forever' stories because she wanted them to be true. She was going to find herself a man who'd be her partner for life. Someone who'd love her the way Dan loved Lucy.

No, forget selective, she was going to be a whole lot more ruthless. *Starting tomorrow.*

Because tonight she just needed a stopgap. Someone to share a five-star hotel room with so she wouldn't feel like she'd blown all that money for nothing.

She looked over her shoulder to the party already in progress, the reception well underway, a DJ set up near the dance floor currently belting out John Paul Young's 'Love is in the Air', and right this minute she wasn't just hoping JPY was right. She was counting on it.

A waiter arrived, bearing a tray of drinks, heading for Sophie first because she was closest. 'Don't give her anything alcoholic,' ordered Hannah from a distance. 'She's had enough.'

'Do you have older sisters?' she asked the girl as she reached for a glass.

'No.'

'Take my advice, keep it that way,' she said conspiratorially as the hand that had been hovering over the water picked up a glass of the sparkling wine instead, and not because she particularly wanted it, but because she knew it was guaranteed to annoy the older sister who was now marching her way towards Sophie with Beth hot on her heels.

'Somebody has to watch over you,' Hannah said, glaring at the flute in Sophie's hand, 'don't they, Beth?'

'Do they? You know, I've been meaning to tell you, Han, you're wasted as a vet,' said Beth, reaching for a glass of bubbles herself. 'You should have been a policewoman.'

'What do you mean by that?'

'You're so bloody bossy.'

Sophie would have laughed, but the look of abject horror on Hannah's face told her that would be a very bad idea.

'I am not!'

Beth gave an unladylike snort. 'Yes, you are.' She looked around to see where her daughter was, seeming relaxed when she found her happily still playing chasey. 'Look at the way you ticked off Siena during the ceremony. I saw what you did, you know.'

'Well, somebody had to do it.'

'No, you didn't. You're not her mother.'

'Clearly, her mother wasn't paying attention. Siena was fidgeting.' Hannah turned to Sophie. 'She was fidgeting, wasn't she? You must have seen it.'

Sophie shrugged and cast a glance over at the dance floor. She didn't want to get involved in a bitch session between her sisters, not if they were both too busy to pick on her. Besides, she had more important things on her mind—like that group of men hovering to one side of the dance floor looking like they were lacking in female company. 'I didn't notice.'

'Oh, that's right,' said Hannah. 'You were too drunk to notice. God only knows why you need another one, but don't listen to me. And take it from me, Beth your daughter was jumping around like a jack-in-the-box.'

'That's garbage. Her seams were digging into her waist. She was uncomfortable, that's all.'

'Well, she stayed still after I tapped her on the shoulder. All she needed was someone to give her a little bit of guidance.'

'What? And you don't think I do?'

'Girls, girls,' their nan interrupted, a vision of wall-to-wall blue floral fabric, as she bustled over with Pop. 'This is a happy day for all of us, isn't it, Clarry? Don't ruin it by bickering. Not when you all look so beautiful.' She stood back and took in the sight of her three granddaughters and her great-granddaughter in their bridesmaids' gowns and gave a wistful sigh. 'Oh, I do wish your mother could have been here today to see your brother get married. What rotten luck to break her leg like that.'

'I know,' said Hannah. 'But they couldn't let her fly all the way from Zurich in a cast.'

'And Dan's going to send a movie,' Beth said, 'so she and Dirk won't miss out entirely.'

'Would either of you like a drink?' the waiter asked, offering the new arrivals the tray.

'Not for me,' said Nan, holding up her hand. 'I'll have a glass of moscato later, and Clarry here, he's on doctor's orders not to drink too much after that scare he gave us all last year.'

'I'm fit as a mallee bull,' said Pop, puffing out his chest as he looked longingly at the glasses of beer.

'Of course you are, Clarry,' said Nan, patting his hand away from the tray, 'as fit as a mallee bull who's had a heart attack and a bypass op, which is why you're on strict instructions to take it easy.'

Pop grumbled something under his breath, while Sophie kept one eye on the group of men. Who were they? Friends of Dan's? Long-lost cousins? 'Are we done here?' she asked the photographer, itching to get away and find out.

'Five minutes,' he said, holding up the splayed fingers of one hand while he looked through his viewfinder, and Sophie took no consolation in the fact that he was holding up just four. 'Just want to check I've got everything. Won't keep you.' Sophie sighed as he went back to his *click, click, click*.

'Ah, bless,' Nan said on a sigh as she watched the newlyweds posing by the car. 'Did you hear the wonderful news, Sophie? Kate's just told us she's expecting a happy event and she's only been married ten minutes herself. And wouldn't you know, she didn't want to say anything and steal anyone's thunder today, but she's just so excited, she was bursting to tell someone. Such lovely news.' She nodded in the direction of her grandson and his new wife. 'It won't be long and there'll be babies on the horizon here, too, you mark my words. High time our Dan became a father.'

Sophie, Hannah and Beth all looked at each other, all thoughts of sisterly snark forgotten, because they knew Lucy's history, that a couple of years back she'd suffered a miscarriage at nineteen weeks, and that she was terrified at the prospect of getting pregnant in case the same thing happened again. And they knew their brother had married Lucy first and foremost because he loved her and wanted to spend his life with her, not for the opportunity to have kids.

'I hope you haven't said as much to Lucy and Dan,' Hannah said, and just for once Sophie agreed with her bossy big sister. Beth, too, by the look of concern on her face.

'Why not?' Nan said with the certainty of the long lived with the equally long and firmly embedded belief. 'Every woman wants babies. It's the natural order of things.'

'Who says so?' said Hannah.

'Mother Nature,' insisted Nan with a nod. 'The birds and the bees. After all, that's why we women were put on earth.'

Hannah snorted. 'Well, I sure as hell wasn't.'

Nan refused to be fazed. 'You don't mean that, Hannah. You just haven't met the right man yet. Wait until you do, and you'll soon change your tune, believe you me.'

'No, I won't. I'm never getting married. I'm never having kids. Instead, I'm going to enjoy a brilliant career, with nobody else's undies to wash and my choice of what's on TV every night.'

'Jeepers,' said Beth. 'You make me feel jealous, and I don't even have anyone else's undies to wash. Well, apart from Siena's, that is.'

Nan reached over and patted Beth's hand. 'You'll find someone else one day, Beth, I know you will.'

'What if I don't want to?'

'You don't have to spend your entire life mourning Joe,' said Hannah.

'Is that what you think I'm doing?' Beth directed at her sister. 'You seem to forget I've got Siena to look out for. I'm not interested in another relationship while she's my first priority.'

'Which is all very noble, but it's been ten years.'

Beth guffawed. 'So says the woman who's never getting married or having a child when she was never even close! Give me a break, Han, at least I've been there. At least I've made my contribution to the world's population.'

Hannah kicked up her chin like she'd been pistol whipped, her blue-green eyes flashing with something that looked like pain. 'I was just saying—'

'Well, I don't know,' said Nan, shaking her head and looking a little lost. 'I'm just a silly old goose, of course, but in my time this is what everyone knew—women want babies—and that's what we're designed for.' Her watery eyes alighted on her youngest grand-daughter. 'Sophie!' she announced. 'You want to have children one day, I know you do. That's why you became a teacher.'

'Got to be the best contraceptive going,' said Beth dryly.

'No, Nan's right,' Sophie said, 'I do want to have kids. Not that I was planning on getting started tonight, if that's what you were hoping.'

Nan tittered. 'Well, no, it would be nice if you got married first.' The older woman looked around, frowning. 'Speaking of which, where is that nice young man of yours? I haven't spotted him yet.'

Sophie looked into her glass and sighed. Ah well, the truth was going to have to come out sooner or later. 'He's not my nice young man, as it happens,' she said, frowning when she looked over to the dance floor and saw a couple of female guests approach the group of men she'd been watching. Damn. She turned back to her family. 'Turns out, he's not very nice at all.'

'Oh, but I wanted to ask if Daphne wanted some more eggs.'

Sophie raised her eyes to the heavens, but she knew that not even divine intervention could save her now. 'Nan, I don't think Jason's mum is going to be hanging out for eggs.'

'No?' Beth's eyes narrowed. 'All you said was that Jason was late.'

'Yeah, really late as it happens. He's not actually coming.'

'He dumped you?' Hannah asked, using the superhuman sense that sisters had to drill down to the core problem through the cracks in what wasn't being said.

Sophie closed her eyes, but that was a mistake because clearly she wasn't as sober as she hoped she was becoming if the action made her feel a bit woozy, so she opened them again quick smart. 'Last night, yeah.'

'Oh, dear,' said Nan, wringing her hands, 'and just when you were getting on so well, too. What went wrong?'

She gulped, the last thing she needed was pity from a woman in a blue pillbox hat. 'It wasn't that serious.' At least, Jason obviously hadn't been.

Pop snorted. 'Boy must have rocks in his head, passing up a Faraday girl.'

Sophie found a tentative smile. 'Thanks, Pop.'

'No wonder you looked a bit out of sorts at the ceremony. Looked like you were about to burst into tears for a while there.'

'Don't talk rubbish, Clarence Faraday,' Nan said, slapping the back of his hand. 'Sophie was just so happy for Dan.' She turned to her granddaughter. 'Isn't that right, Sophie? Weddings always make me cry.'

'Sure,' she said, remembering that she'd been concentrating on not peeing. It was a miracle she hadn't burst. 'I'm happy for both of them.'

'Oh,' continued Nan, still shaking her head. 'But it's such a shame about you and Jason, isn't it? To think I was saving a dozen eggs for his mum.'

'Life's just full of disappointments,' Sophie said, glancing over at the group she'd been scoping. And there was another disappointment, because the women had been paired off with the men and were being led hand in hand towards the dance floor to Robbie Williams singing 'Angels'. A nice close number.

Crap!

'Not to worry,' said Nan, evidently liking that one out of three granddaughters was making the right noises. 'There's someone out there just waiting to meet you, and when you do, you'll be only too happy to have his babies.'

'Maybe. Though right now, I'd be happy to settle for a bit of …' *hot sex* '… um, romance.'

Nan tutted, stroking Sophie's arm with her gnarled fingers in a way she wouldn't have if Sophie had said what she really wanted.

'It's rubbish,' said Hannah, 'all this "women want babies" or "women need to have babies in order to be fulfilled" bullshit. It's a social construct, nothing more. As if we're all ticking time bombs and we're worthless if we don't procreate.'

Nan looked crestfallen. 'Is it? And I was so hoping for some more good news to go with the wedding.'

'It'll happen,' Sophie said with a reassuring smile, trying to make up for Hannah's sudden abrasive tone, wondering where that all came from. Hannah had always been the sensible no-nonsense sister. She'd never professed an interest in having children, but Sophie had never heard her being so vocally hostile in her opposition to the concept. 'Probably when you and we are least expecting it, too. Isn't that how it always happens?'

Nan sniffed, looking somewhat consoled by the thought. 'I hope you're right, Sophie.'

'All done,' called the photographer. 'Thank you, everyone, I won't keep you from the celebrations any longer.' The women all sighed with relief at the change of subject as a smiling Dan and Lucy joined them.

'Time to party?' Dan said, his arm around Lucy. 'I think my new bride needs a whirl around the dance floor.'

'We all do,' said Beth. 'Come on, sisters of mine, we better go circulate.'

'You two go ahead,' said Sophie, busy scanning the crowd.

Hannah scowled at her. 'You're not going off to sulk because that bozo Jason stood you up?'

'What?' said Dan and Lucy together.

'Forget it,' said Sophie, wanting to stick pins in an effigy of her eldest sister.

Not that Hannah could forget it, of course. 'Jason dumped her last night, the night before the wedding, can you believe it? Which explains why Sophie's been self-medicating on bubbles since eight this morning. It's a wonder she made it down the aisle.'

Sophie rolled her eyes. 'Thanks for that, Han. Appreciate it. *Not!*'

'It's no more than the truth.'

'Told you,' said Beth. 'Can't help herself. Bossy to her bootstraps.'

'Give me a break,' said Hannah. 'Somebody has to keep you all in line.'

'Not me,' said Sophie, 'I'm out of here. I'm going to go enjoy this wedding.' And she set off to check out the guests.

Half an hour later, Sophie was feeling far less hopeful. The speeches had been done and the cake had been cut, and from what she'd managed to scope of the guests, there weren't that many eligible men, after all. A few orchardists and sons, and friends of orchardists. A guy from the garage where Dan got his vehicles serviced. A couple of his old schoolmates, most of whom seemed to have come complete with a woman on their arm.

Sophie looked disconsolately down at the near-empty champagne flute in her hands, annoyed by the way the few available single men had been hoovered up while she'd been busy with the photos. Her hopes of finding a companion for the night were fading by the minute, the heady glow of champagne disappearing with it. If she was going to spend the night by herself, what was she worried about? There was no point being sober. She looked over at the bar.

Hello …

Her eyes narrowed, and she had to squint a little to focus. He looked youngish, but he was kind of cute, with one of those haircuts where the sides were all shaved, leaving a flop of hair over his brow. Adorable really. And if he was serving alcohol, he couldn't be that young. Nothing in her hastily configured plans to find company for the night said it had to be a guest she invited back to her luxurious hotel room. There was no harm in checking out all the possibilities …

She gathered up her long skirt in one hand in a way she knew would pull the silk closer and emphasise the sway of her hips as she walked, and sashayed over to the bar. The barman was drying a glass with a tea towel when he looked up and saw her coming. She watched as he took in her smile and her wiggle and all points in between, and she liked it when the hands on the glass stopped rotating.

She leaned one hip up against the bar. 'Hi,' she said, trying not to stare at the zit on his chin or the jut of his Adam's apple, which she hadn't noticed from further away. After all, who was she to judge?

Even she still got the odd zit and besides, it wasn't like she could afford to be too choosy.

'Um, hi.'

'So,' she said. 'I have this problem.'

He looked perplexed. 'What is it?'

'It's this glass.' She held out her flute. 'It seems to have a hole in it.'

He blinked so hard at her, Sophie could just about see the cogs turning slowly behind his eyes, before he suddenly swung into action. 'Oh, I can fix that,' he said, pulling a bottle of sparkling wine from the ice bucket to fill a new glass for her.

She took a sip of the cool bubbly liquor and gave a blissful sigh. 'I do love a man who can solve my problems.' And she could swear he was blushing. Totally adorable!

'So tell me,' she said, licking her lips before pausing as she regarded him coyly over her glass. 'Do you have a girlfriend?'

'Um. No.' Then he seemed to have thought better of it, because he added, 'At least, not at the moment.'

'Wow. That's nuts, a good-looking guy like you.' She would have cringed at her cheesy words, but bar boy was grinning and lapping it up and she thought, what the hell? 'Funny, though, because I don't have a boyfriend.'

'No way!'

She shrugged, liking the way the conversation was developing. 'Well, I did,' she said, preparing to embellish the truth in the interests of strengthening her case. 'But I found out he was two-timing me with one of my best friends and so I dumped him.'

Bar boy had all but forgotten about the glasses he was supposed to be drying. 'He wasn't good enough for you.'

She gave a wistful sigh. 'I know. But now I'm all alone.' She looked longingly towards the dance floor as couples leaned close and bodies swayed. 'I don't suppose you dance.'

He looked torn. 'Um, I can't. I mean, I can, but I'm working.'

She winked as she took another sip. 'Maybe later, then?'

His eyes skated over her like he couldn't believe what was on offer, while his Adam's apple bobbed up and down disconcertingly, and for a second she started having second thoughts. But only for a second, until he said, 'Maybe,' and half sounded like he meant it.

She laughed as she held up her glass and he topped up her wine.

Game on!

'Hey, Sophie.'

She swung her head around, her smile wide until she saw it was the best man who was coming and said, 'Oh, it's you,' and swung it right back around to the barman again. Except the barman was looking right at Nick.

'Can I get you a drink?' he asked.

'Sparkling water, thanks.'

The barman pulled a bottle from the bucket at his side and poured the last inch in the bottle into a glass, before diving around in the ice and coming up blank. 'I'll just grab another bottle. Be right back,' he said, before heading over to where the spare drinks had been stashed by the shed.

Sophie pouted, crossing her arms. 'You didn't have to send him away.'

'What's your problem? Don't tell me you fancy him.'

'And what's it to you if I do?'

'Come on, Sophie, he's about twelve years old.'

'He can't be, not if he's serving at the bar.'

'Great. So he's eighteen. I didn't figure you for a cradle snatcher.'

'Go away, Nick.'

'I'm waiting for my drink.'

'You're cramping my style.'

'Your style is barely out of short pants.'

She pushed herself off the bar and lifted her chin as she raised herself to her full height, a technique Sophie found made her pretty formidable when your opposition was three feet tall, like the kids she was used to dealing with at primary school. 'I don't recall asking for your opinion.'

Nick didn't look half as intimidated as the kids did. Damn. 'Nope, that's because this is your lucky day and I'm offering it for free—just because your boyfriend dumped you is no reason to go pick up any Tom, Dick or Harry. You might at least find yourself someone old enough to shave.'

She gave up on trying to outsize him and glared at him instead. 'Who told you I was dumped?'

'Does it matter?'

'God, is nothing sacred?'

'Sorry to keep you waiting,' said the bar boy, hurrying back and looking suspiciously from one to the other as he approached.

'Not a problem—um, sorry,' Nick said, squinting at the barman's name badge. 'What's your name?'

'Zephyr,' he said, screwing off the cap and topping up the glass.

Nick glanced sideways at Sophie, his brows heading north. 'Thanks for that, um, Zephyr,' he said, as he was handed the glass, and with one deft movement, he'd plucked the glass of champagne from Sophie's hand and substituted it with the glass of sparkling water.

'Hey! What do you think you're doing?'

'Saving you from a bigger headache tomorrow than you're already going to have.' He poured what was left of her glass out on the lawn. 'Don't you think you've had enough?'

'What are you, my mother?' She looked over his shoulder, her eyes narrowing when she saw Dan watching them, and put two and two together. 'Oh, I get it. Dan set you onto me.'

He shrugged. 'What if he did?'

'Thanks, Nick.' She plonked the water down on the table. 'It's sweet of you, really it is, but I don't need a babysitter.' She turned back to the bartender. 'Ignore my friend here, Zephyr. I'll have another glass of bubbles, thanks.'

Nick raised one hand and stopped the kid in his tracks, but it was to Sophie he directed his next words. 'So maybe you should stop acting like a baby.'

'What? How dare you?'

'Come on,' he said, grabbing her by the hand and pulling her towards the dance floor as Elvis started crooning. 'They're playing our song.'

'We don't have a song.'

'We do now.'

'Nick!'

But it was useless fighting because Nick wasn't about to let her go.

Nick Pasquale was all kinds of stupid. If he thought 'Can't Help Falling in Love' was their song, he was in cloud-cuckoo land. And if he thought she was going to let herself be babysat all night just because her brother had asked him, he could think again.

But he had a vice-like grip on her hand and a steely determination about his jaw as he towed her towards the dance floor that told her he was deadly serious and there was no way she was getting out of this without making some kind of scene. And oh, wouldn't he just love her to try that!

She refused to give him the satisfaction. Instead, she'd pretend to scamper quietly behind him and play along with this dance thing, let him think she was acquiescing, and then after a song or two, he'd relax and she'd blow him off.

Easy. Just as soon as this song was done.

Their song. What a joke. Definitely all kinds of stupid. Not to mention boorish, arrogant and completely out of line. What was it with big brothers and their friends?

He eased up his grip on her hand when he found a space on the dance floor and turned her towards him, but the hand he placed in the small of her back more than made up for any sense of impending freedom. She might as well be his prisoner. She looked over his shoulder so she didn't have to look at him, saw the smiles on the other couples swaying to Elvis, and felt the resentment building inside. Everyone else looked happy. Nobody else looked like they were having their evening railroaded by a friend of a big brother with an overblown sense of responsibility.

'So, how long have you been a member?' she asked, because he was coaxing her to move to the music and she really wasn't enjoying listening to a love song when tonight was turning into a complete shambles.

'Member of what?'

His voice sounded gruff, like he was grinding the words through that set jaw, and she especially didn't like the way she could almost feel the vibration of his voice through his grip. It was no fun being this close to someone who was behaving like such an arse.

'The fun police. You know—determined to root out and put an end to fun wherever it manifests itself.'

'Aren't you having fun?'

'Sure, you nailed it. I'm having the time of my life.'

'There you go,' he said, 'that makes two of us.'

She sniffed, and immediately wished she hadn't. He was wearing some spicy aftershave that didn't smell anything like the Lynx the Year Six/Seven boys laid on thick to impress the girls at school. This was spicier, maybe with a touch of sandalwood, and something else, something that was more difficult to pin down.

She didn't like that she couldn't pin it down. She didn't like that she liked it. Most of all, she didn't like that he hadn't stepped on her toes once.

Who knew Nick Pasquale would be so light on his feet? Talk about annoying.

Elvis faded away and Sophie saw her chance. 'Well, thanks, Nick,' she said, dropping her hand from his shoulder. 'It's been a real hoot, but I really have to—'

'Not so fast,' he said, lifting her hand back to his shoulder as the instrumental started for the next song, and if she wasn't mistaken— crap, that'd be right, it was none other than Rod Stewart with 'Tonight's the Night'. Once upon a time it had been her mum's favourite song, and now that she was older and understood the lyrics, Sophie really didn't want to think too much about why.

'You don't have to do this, you know. I'm sure there are plenty of women here tonight you'd rather be dancing with.'

'Maybe I'd rather dance with you.'

'Liar,' she said, but she let him lead her again, swaying to the gravel-over-velvet tones of Rod Stewart seducing his inexperienced lover. She swallowed back against a bubble of disappointment, thinking about the bottle of French champagne she'd ordered, no doubt already chilling in an ice bucket alongside a king-sized bed strewn with rose petals. She'd hoped tonight was the night. After Jason had bailed on their last hook-up—because he'd messaged he'd been too ill with gastro to travel (like hell)—she'd done everything humanly possible to ensure tonight was a night to remember— other than convincing Jason that he cared enough for her to be here by her side, apparently.

She sighed, letting herself lean a little closer to Nick's shoulder. There was something about his aftershave, some ingredient whose name hovered just out of reach, but if she concentrated hard enough, she was sure it would come to her in a minute or so. Another song and she'd have it, and he'd no doubt be satisfied and they could give up this pretence of wanting to dance together.

But at least it gave her something to think about while she waited for him to have had enough. He was a much better dancer than she'd have ever imagined. He was no Patrick Swayze of course, his moves were more sideways swaying than dirty dancing, but that was okay, too.

At her back he shifted his thumb a fraction and her whole body tingled. A big hand, his long fingers splayed, radiating warmth wherever they made contact. And Sophie was never more aware that just one sheer layer of silk separated them, one sheer layer that shifted with every dance move. A subtle slide of fabric against skin that made her breath catch and her flesh hum. A subtle pressure from his hand that willed her body closer and made her want to give in.

Weird.

This was Nick, her brother's best man. His best mate, who'd been set on her like a faithful dog. It was laughable.

Though he was single …

No. No. *No!*

She straightened in his arms, clamping down on that thought quick smart. Maybe she really was drunk, because this was Nick. He didn't want to be here, dancing like this, holding her like this. He was doing her overbearing brother a favour, that was all.

And she was so not going to make a fool of herself over someone who would stoop to doing something like that. As soon as this song was over, she was out of here.

The song ended and she shifted further away. 'So, are we done yet?' She hated the husky note her voice had suddenly found.

'On the contrary,' he said, 'we've only just begun.'

A sense of panic overwhelmed her. 'Look, Nick, you don't have to do this.'

'What if I want to?'

'Yeah, well, we both know that's not the truth.'

'One more dance, okay?'

And only because it wasn't too unbearable she agreed, and somehow one more dance became two, or maybe six, since she'd lost count, until she heard murmurings from the crowd. 'What's going on?' she asked, pulling her head from Nick's shoulder, from where it had no right to be. When had that happened?

'Dan and Lucy are leaving,' he said, taking her hand to lead her from the dance floor.

'What?' she said, eyes blinking her back into reality. 'Already?'

'It's eleven o'clock, Sophie. Looks like the party's over. Come and say goodbye.'

Sophie stopped and stood stock still. 'No!'

'What? You don't want to see Dan and Lucy off?'

She shook her head. How could she explain? This couldn't be happening. 'Of course I do. It's just …' She'd barely begun searching for someone to share the night with before she'd got waylaid by Nick, and now she'd wasted an entire evening, but she could hardly tell him that. 'It can't be over yet.'

But Nick was right. The DJ was packing up and they were the only couple left on the dance floor, the remaining guests milling around the newlyweds as they made their way to the waiting car. Even the guy behind the bar had disappeared.

Sophie's frustration turned to anger. As soon as Dan and Lucy departed, the guests would follow and filter away and she'd be left alone.

The long night stretched out before her. A long night in a rose-petal-strewn bed with champagne laid on and no one to share it with. A long, lonely night without the happy ending she'd been hoping for, bereft of the chance that attending this wedding with her might inspire Jason to take their relationship to a whole new level.

Stupid. So damned stupid.

'Thanks for that, then,' she snapped, as she picked up her skirts and swept past Nick, those damned tears she'd been on the verge of all night feeling like a tsunami building behind her eyes. One false move and the tsunami would burst through. Bloody Nick.

'Not the most gracious thanks I've had from a dance partner,' he said, refusing to take the hint and disappear like she wished he would. 'Anyone would think I stomped all over your feet.'

No, he'd been a good dancer. Surprisingly good when it all came down to it. So damned good that she'd completely lost track of time.

'How about we just forget it?' she said.

'Sophie?'

She turned. 'Just drop it, will you?'

He held up both hands in surrender. 'If that's what you want.'

'You have no idea what I want.' And she shouldered her way into the crowd gathered around the happy couple.

Bloody Nick.

Bloody Jason.

Bloody men!

Hannah met her threading through the crowd, took one look at her and said, 'Jeezus, what happened to you?'

She sniffed. 'Nothing.' Absolutely bloody nothing. That was the problem.

Her sister shrugged. 'Come on, then, we're supposed to be bridesmaids, we better go wave goodbye to the happy couple.'

Sophie was suddenly suspicious. 'Where've you been?'

'Nowhere. Just talking shop.'

Sophie rolled her eyes. That'd be right. Hannah was vet first, human later. Mention the word 'animal', and Hannah would forget what day it was. Sophie squeezed her way through the crowd until they reached the front and waited while the bride and groom were kissed and hugged and blessed by what looked like the entire population of Norton Summit and the surrounding districts.

She caught Dan's eye first, saw his momentary frown turn to a smile and said, 'Hey, big brother, congratulations.'

He pulled her into a hug and squeezed her tight. 'Thanks, Soph,' he said as they pulled apart. 'You okay?'

Was he asking whether she'd forgiven him for setting his best mate to babysit her, or asking whether she was still tipsy? Not that it mattered. This was no time to take her brother to task. 'All good,' she managed with a smile, and pulled him down to plant a kiss on his cheek. 'You've done well yourself this time, bro,' she said, nodding towards the glowing Lucy.

Her brother's smile said it all. 'Don't I know it?' he said as he looped an arm around his new wife and hauled her closer, pressing his lips to her hair.

'Hey, Sophie,' Lucy said, seeing her there, 'thank you so much for being my bridesmaid. I can't believe I have three sisters of my own, now. I love you guys so much!'

Sophie blinked at the moisture in her eyes as they hugged. 'We love you, too,' she said. 'Thank you for marrying our grumpy brother and putting him out of his misery.'

'Hey!' protested Dan, but he was smiling and looking down at Lucy, and she was gazing up at him with 'that' look again—the one that underscored Sophie's loneliness like nothing else. Then it was Hannah's turn to wish the newlyweds well, and Sophie allowed herself to be edged out of the way until she found herself squeezed to the back of the crowd. She stood apart thinking about what her new sister had said. 'Thank you for being my bridesmaid,' while her aching heart lodged and stuck in the back of her throat.

Sophie had been possibly the crappiest bridesmaid in history. She could have ruined the wedding. If she'd fallen flat on her face walking down the aisle—if she'd picked a fight with Nick or even with Dan because she'd thought they were out of line … But it hadn't happened and she had the rest of the night to be grateful for it. Lord knows, there was nothing else to do tonight. And she'd had such hopes for the evening. Such high, romantic and utterly pointless hopes for tonight, as it had turned out, given Jason had in all likelihood finished with her two weeks ago when he'd feigned illness. He'd just been too gutless then to tell her.

God, she was all kinds of a fool.

Dan and Lucy were making their final goodbyes. A handshake for Nick and a clap on the back for Pop, a big hug and a kiss for Nan, and everyone beaming. Everyone happy. And as the weight of the last twenty-four hours of disappointment weighed down on her, Sophie couldn't stand it anymore. Even as a flurry of cherry blossom rained down on her, she turned her back on the joyful scene.

There was a ripple of excitement behind her. A ripple that became a buzz and then a series of squeals and screams that managed to squeeze through a crack in her misery.

She heard Siena cry, 'Catch it!' and turned in time to see a sea of clamouring hands and something flying through the air over the top.

Before her brain had managed to connect the dots, a floral missile collided with her chest with a whump. Everyone clapped and cheered, and Siena jumped up and down and said, 'Yay! Sophie's next!'

Sophie took one look at the crumpled arrangement in her hands and felt her heart crumple with it. Siena was in for a big disappointment.

5

Hannah

Pop knew how to cut a rug. Or so he'd told everyone who would listen. He was doing his best to prove it on the dance floor, too, as long as the music lasted, despite his wife's futile attempts to get him to act his age and take care of his heart and sit down.

Hannah watched her grandfather bopping away to Elvis's 'Blue Suede Shoes', while Nan stood nearby remonstrating with him, trying to get him to pace himself.

'Who's winning right now, you reckon?' she asked Beth, watching on alongside, their earlier words forgotten. With the formalities over, they could all relax.

'Right now, my money's on Pop,' Beth said. 'He's got a new lease on life since that bypass op.'

'Yeah, let's just hope it doesn't kill him in the process.'

'I don't know. He seems in pretty good form tonight.'

'That he does,' said Hannah, chewing on her lip. She turned to her sister. 'Beth, you know a thing or two about medical issues, do you think Nan's okay?'

'Well, she's carrying a bit more weight than Pop is, and she isn't up to his fitness levels, by the looks, but yeah,' she nodded, 'she seems okay.'

'No, that's not what I mean. Not exactly.' She watched Pop twisting on the dance floor like he was back in nineteen fifty-five. 'You don't think she's losing it a bit? Mentally, I mean.'

'Why do you say that?'

'Just today, when she was going on about all that baby stuff. She was so adamant.'

Beth scoffed. 'Funny, I thought that was you.'

She rolled her eyes. 'Okay, so she just looked confused sometimes, like she'd lost track of where she was going.'

'Oh come on, Han, it's been a long day for a woman in her eighties. Of course she'd be tired with all the excitement, and that was before the disappointment of Sophie's bust-up. Look at it from her point of view—she'd been counting on Dan starting a flurry of Faraday marriages and she knew damn well the next one wouldn't be coming from you or me. I bet she'd already pencilled Sophie's wedding into her diary, along with her babies.'

Hannah bit her lip. 'She did sound like she was counting on it.'

'Yeah, and think about it. All that talk about women wanting babies to satisfy some deep-down biological need, from a woman who only ever had one child. She wants more great-grandchildren, that's all, she just can't come right out and say it. She has to dress it up in spin, and make it sound like we're letting the side down— without actually saying that, of course.'

Hannah had to admit that hadn't occurred to her. 'So, you otherwise think she's okay?'

'God yes, she's as canny as she's ever been.' Beth turned her head back to the dance floor and nodded. 'Jeepers, check her out now.' Hannah did, and there was her nan, grooving it with Pop and laughing her head off. 'Looking at the spark in Pop's eyes,' Beth added, 'I reckon there might be some dirty deeds going down later tonight in Summertown.'

Hannah looked at her sister, aghast. 'No amount of bleach is ever going to sanitise my brain of that image.'

Beth laughed. 'You should try sex one day, Han. You might even find you like it.'

'Who says I haven't?'

'Nobody. But then nobody said you had, so we all just assumed you were Norton Summit's oldest virgin.'

Hannah kicked up her chin, not liking the concept that her sex life, or lack of it, might be cause for speculation, though still not sure that her sister wasn't just engaged in a digging exercise. In which case, she could go right on digging because Hannah wasn't volunteering anything. 'I never realised my virginity or otherwise was a topic of local interest.'

'Come on,' said Beth, 'this is a small town filled with orchardists and primary producers, true, but even so, we're going to run out of weather talk at some stage. And if one sister can't even confide in her twin ...' Beth arched a brow, the challenge obvious.

Hannah swung her head back around to the dance floor. 'So, you're sure nothing's wrong with Nan?'

'I said so, didn't I,' said Beth, smiling at the side step. 'What's your excuse?'

Hannah scowled. 'I thought we were talking about Nan.'

Her younger sister smiled. 'Have it your way. Look, Han, I haven't seen anything to think she's losing it, any more than the next eighty-something-year-old, and I transport a lot of oldies who are.'

Hannah nodded on a sigh, relieved with the opinion of her much more medically experienced sister—at least when it came to humans, that was. There was a reason she preferred dealing with animals. They came with neither subtext nor subterfuge. 'Good to hear. In that case, I better try to prise Nan and Pop from the dance floor and get them home before we all turn into pumpkins.' She looked around at the rapidly thinning crowd. The Elvis fest was continuing, this time it was 'Always on My Mind', and even Nan and Pop seemed to be enjoying the slow number. Hannah grimaced. It didn't bear thinking about. 'What happened to Sophie, do you know? I haven't seen her for ages.'

'Washing dishes, last time I saw her. Doing penance or some such, for getting herself blind before the wedding.'

'Good thing too.'

'Oh, come on, Han. Her boyfriend dumped her the night before the wedding. Of course she was going to feel a bit shattered.'

'She didn't have to get herself pissed.'

'No, she didn't, but there was no harm done and she knows she was out of line. And which one of us hasn't ever done something we later regretted?'

Hannah just sniffed and looked away. 'I better go round up Nan and Pop.'

6

Beth

'Why can't we stay a bit longer, Mum?'

'Because we can't,' said Beth, fastening her seatbelt, her mind still busy churning over her conversation with Hannah. 'It's almost midnight and I've got work in the morning.'

'But we never stay late for anything because you're always working.'

'That's about the size of it, yeah. As soon as you can drive or you can work and give me a day off, let me know, and you can make your own arrangements.'

'Mu-um, that's like, years away.'

Beth nodded sagely. 'Believe me, I know, so until then, I'm the worker and I'm the driver, which means I'm the boss. Okay?'

Beside her, Siena gave a melodramatic sigh, crossing her arms as she slumped down low in her seat. 'I just don't know if I can wait that long.'

Beth blinked as she felt an arrow from the past pierce her straight through her heart. 'That's your father speaking,' she said quietly, as she headed out onto the windy hills road, her headlights cutting a swathe of light ahead. 'Joe could never wait for anything, either. He was always rushing in.'

'What was he like?' Siena asked, not for the first time fascinated by the man who was her father, the father she would never know.

'Well, you've seen the photos, but he had olive skin and dark hair,' said Beth, remembering back, 'and he had even darker eyes and long black lashes, and he rode a motorbike and in his leather jacket, he was sexy as hell.'

'Mum!'

'Come on, Siena, of course he was. We were teenagers and crazy in love. Where else do you think you came from, the cabbage patch?'

'We don't have cabbages,' her daughter protested with a yawn.

'Exactly. So any more questions before you fall asleep?'

'I'm not sleepy.'

'No,' said Beth with a smile, 'you're just resting your eyelids.'

'Was he looking forward to me being born?' her daughter asked, her voice as soft as the green dash lighting in the darkened interior.

Beth caught her breath. 'Yes. He was right by my side at your twenty-week scan and he was so excited. He couldn't wait to meet you.' But that was the problem. Joe found it hard to wait for anything. And this time, he hadn't.

There was no response, and as they passed under one of the rare streetlights between here and home, Beth looked over and saw that her daughter had fallen asleep, her eyes closed, her lips slightly parted. And not for the first time, Beth sent up a silent curse for all that had been lost, for the wedding that had never happened, for the family that had been torn apart before it had even got started. Her fingers curled tighter around the steering wheel as salt water leaked from her eyes.

So unfair.

Fifteen minutes later her headlights lit up the street number on the front fence that she'd fashioned herself from brightly coloured chips of tiles, and she pulled into her long driveway, thankful to be home at last. She tapped Siena's shoulder until she was awake enough to walk to bed—her daughter was far too big these days for her to carry like she'd done for so many years—and Beth had a chance to change her clothes and clean off her makeup. But in spite of tomorrow's early shift, she didn't slip straight into bed like she probably should. Instead, she felt the tug of her studio calling, and the need to create. And it wasn't just to make sense of the memories of Joe churning through her mind, because Hannah was mixed up in there, too, along with her secrets.

In her sleep singlet and shorts, she circled the mosaic-topped table on the verandah and turned on the lights in her studio, sending colour popping from the walls courtesy of myriad artworks adorning the one-time garage: a fat fish in splashes of blue and green, an eastern rosella bold and bright, and a multicoloured lantern hanging from the ceiling. Benches lined three sides of the room, with an oversized sofa on the fourth, with a long narrow table dividing the space, much of its horizontal surface filled with jars holding coloured glass or beads or fragments of tiles.

And there, in the middle of the table, lay her latest work in progress. A mother koala with her joey on her back, wedged in the fork of a gum tree. The young koala had been a regular visitor to their garden and when she'd arrived with a joey on her back, Siena had been entranced, and Beth had decided to immortalise the moment in mosaic. She'd mostly finished the tree and the grey-tan bulk of the mother koala, and was working on the detail of their sweet furry faces, the black button eyes and the enormous leathery nose.

She got to work, sorting through black pieces of tile and glass to find the perfect ones, while her brain sorted through the conversation she'd had with Hannah, the conversation that had ended with a feeling that Beth didn't know her twin half as well as she should. She understood a person wanting privacy, but this was her sister—her twin—and it was only sex. It wasn't like it was that earth-shattering.

Beth worked on, selecting fragments, discarding them, her eyes constantly weighing each piece. They'd been close as siblings. Peas in a pod, Pop had labelled them, and best friends as well as sisters through primary and high school, though Hannah had always been the boss. And then Hannah had left to study veterinary science in Perth, and Beth had missed her like crazy because the teaching degree she'd originally enrolled in meant she could stay right here in Adelaide. And then Beth had met Joe and her world had tilted towards a new kind of love.

Joe was funny and sexy and hot-blooded and passionate, and it had taken away some of the pain of Hannah living so far away. Getting pregnant hadn't been part of the plan, at least not so young, but they'd been planning on getting married one day, anyway.

And then Joe had died, and Hannah had come back not for a wedding but for a funeral.

Is that where she'd lost her bond with her sister? Because Beth had well and truly dropped the ball, quitting her studies and spending the next year in a funk, before deciding that paramedics rather than teaching was what she wanted to do, even while she was trying to care for an infant. Had she inadvertently pushed Hannah away because she'd been so absorbed in her own misery? Was this the reason Hannah was holding back now, because they didn't share the kind of bond they might have otherwise shared?

Beth yawned, and stretched her arms high above her head as she surveyed the face of the koala she'd just finished and liked what she saw. Time for bed. She would be tired tomorrow, but she'd been tired since before Siena was born. Why should tomorrow be any different?

7

Sophie

'Come on, Sophie,' said Nick. 'How about I give you a lift home.'

The party was well and truly over. Sophie had stayed back to help clean up, though it was more about making up for her earlier behaviour than any need to hang around, especially when everyone else seemed happy to let it wait until morning. But now, the chairs had been stacked and the plates and glasses washed and put away, and there was nothing left to do.

She blinked up at him as she wiped her hands on a tea towel. She'd been so busy focusing on what she was doing, she hadn't realised Nick was still here. He'd dispensed with his suit jacket and tie at some stage and rolled up the sleeves of his white shirt, accentuating the tanned olive skin of his forearms. He looked like he'd been working. He looked—good.

'Where did you come from?'

'I've been outside helping out with taking down the lighting. Figured seeing you were still here, you could maybe do with a lift home.'

'Thanks, but that won't be necessary.' It wasn't like she was going home, it's just that there was no rush to get there. Not anymore.

'Sophie—'

'It's okay, Nick,' she said, 'Dan's gone. You don't have to babysit me anymore, I won't tell.' She saw the disappointment skate across his eyes and instantly regretted saying what she had. Just because she'd had a crap day and night, she didn't have to take it out on him.

'Sorry,' she said, putting a hand to a forehead that was starting to ache. That was the trouble with drinking so early in the day—the hangover didn't wait for morning to kick in. 'You didn't deserve that. It's just … It's just that it hasn't been a really good day.' And it was going to be one very bad night.

'I know.'

She snorted. 'You don't know the half of it.'

'Well, I did force you to dance with me.'

'Yeah, well, there was that.' Though that had turned out to be one of the day's highlights. A surprising highlight, when it all came down to it, and kind of nice …

'So how about you let me make up for it by giving you a lift home.'

She grazed her bottom lip with her teeth. There was no way she was going to drive her car and it would take an age for a cab to get up here in the hills at this time on a Saturday night. Nobody knew about the booking she'd made at Mount Lofty House, and she wasn't at all comfortable with sharing the information—let alone the humiliation—with anyone, particularly this man, someone who might very well turn around and tell her brother. He knew along with everyone else that she'd been dumped, and it wouldn't take much to put two and two together and come up with loser.

'That's sweet of you, Nick, considering you don't even like me.'

'Who said that?'

'You called me a baby, remember?'

'I said you were acting like one.'

'Right.' She frowned. 'That's heaps better.'

'I never said I didn't like you.'

Had his voice just dropped an octave? Because something had sure stroked its way down her spine. 'Oh.'

'So, are we friends?'

She swallowed. 'I guess.'

'And can't one friend offer another a lift home at the end of a long day?'

She looked up at him, wondering why he'd be bothered. Just being neighbourly or because of some overblown sense of responsibility to her brother? Whatever, she was tempted to say yes, and not just because she was tired and it would save waiting for a taxi. Nick Pasquale was far better looking than she'd ever given him credit for, and far better looking than your average taxi driver. His short dark hair looked more ruffled than it had earlier and there was a distinct whiskery shadow that turned his jaw into a bold dark line. But it was the blue eyes that captured her attention. Slate blue, like a stormy sea. Why had she never noticed that Nick had blue eyes? He was Italian, surely they should be brown? Only now, they were frowning and she realised he was waiting for an answer.

'Don't you have somewhere you need to be? A babysitter you have to relieve?'

'Minnie's at Penelope's tonight.'

'Oh, but you probably have other things—'

'It's just a lift, Sophie. It's no big deal.'

'Maybe, but it's not that simple, either.'

The faint vertical lines between his dark brows furrowed and became more distinct. 'Why?'

She wavered. Letting him give her a lift to the hotel would be tantamount to admitting what a fool she'd been. 'You don't want to know. You'll think it's stupid. You'll think I'm stupid and naive and I know I am, but it seemed like a good idea at the time because I didn't know ...'

'Sophie,' he said, shaking his head, half smiling, half confused. 'What on earth are you talking about?'

'You won't laugh?'

'How do I know if I'll laugh or not? I've got no idea what you're going to say.'

'Okay, so try not to laugh and I'll tell you.'

He held up one hand and set his face to deadpan. 'Okay, I'll try my hardest.'

She swallowed and looked uncertainly up at him. 'In that case, if you really want to give me a lift, that would be nice. Except you see, I'm not actually going home ...'

He'd taken the news surprisingly well, she figured, as he turned the car onto the windy road climbing towards the hotel. At least, he hadn't laughed. Not that she hadn't noticed his eyebrows shooting north when she'd come out with Mount Lofty House.

Beside him, Sophie gazed out of the window into the inky night, the beam from the headlights illuminating the trees that lined the narrow road. 'They look like claws.'

'What do?'

'The branches of the gum trees. In the headlights they look like claws, reaching out.' She shivered, even though the night was far from cold.

'Are you all right?'

She leaned her head back against the headrest and closed her eyes, but the next two-hundred-and-seventy-degree bend to the left put paid to that. She opened them up and grabbed hold of the handle above the door. 'Yeah. No.' She took a deep breath. 'I'm okay.'

He lifted his foot from the accelerator. 'You're not going to be sick?'

She put a hand to her head. 'No. Just a bit of a headache. God only knows why I'd have one of those. It's not like I did anything to deserve it. Much.'

He smiled. 'If you can laugh at yourself, you can't be feeling too bad. You're probably just dehydrated. Drink a lot of water before you go to bed.'

'Thanks. I'll do that.' Then she gave a deep sigh as she turned back and said, 'I'm really sorry, you know, for being such a pain in the arse tonight.'

He winked over at her. 'You weren't that bad a dancer.'

She rolled her eyes. 'I was talking about before, at the bar, when you switched my drink.'

'When you were trying to pick up Zit Boy?'

'Zephyr. His name was Zephyr, remember?'

'How could I forget? And what do you remember most of all about Zephyr—apart from his ridiculous name and his bad skin, that is?'

She pulled a face. 'Yeah, okay, point taken. But I was rude to you and I'm sorry. You didn't deserve that.'

He shrugged. 'You were angry with me. You thought I was trying to spoil your fun.'

'You *were* spoiling my fun. You and that interfering brother of mine.'

'He was worried about you.'

'It was his wedding day for heaven's sake. Surely he had more pressing things to worry about than me having a couple of drinks?' She stared at him a moment before she dropped her head in her hands. 'God, my own brother's wedding day and he was worried about me. So how bad was I?'

'On a scale of one to ten?' He shrugged. 'Not that bad. Maybe an eight or nine?'

'Oh God, that bad!'

'Hey, I was kidding. You were nowhere near that bad.'

She groaned. 'But did I look drunk? Hannah said I was drunk.'

'I don't know,' he said, changing down a gear to negotiate a tight bend. 'You did seem a bit …'

She waited while he searched for the right word. Because he was trying to be polite?

'… wooden, walking down the aisle.'

Sophie let go of the breath she'd been holding. All in all, it could have been worse. 'I stumbled at the start. I was trying not to fall flat on my face.'

He nodded. 'That'd do it.'

'But that was it?'

'Well, you were a bit smiley.'

'Smiley? Aren't people supposed to be happy at a wedding?' Then she pinched her nose with her fingers. 'God, you're right. I remember now. I was so happy to make it to the front without tripping up, I was grinning like a loon. Do you think anyone else noticed?'

'No way,' he said, shaking his head. 'I was right up front, that's the only reason I noticed. I'm sure nobody else did. Nobody at all.'

Sophie looked at him, weighing up his words while he kept his eyes firmly fixed on the road. Supa Glue couldn't have kept them more firmly fixed. She leaned back in her seat. 'You're a terrible liar, Nick Pasquale.'

He shrugged and gave a wry smile. 'I've been called worse things.' He turned to her then. 'Don't worry about it, Sophie. You looked beautiful in that dress and with your hair up like that. A real knockout.'

'I did?'

He nodded. 'Still do. So stop worrying.'

Sophie leaned back in her seat and shut up, because Nick Pasquale had told her she looked beautiful. Wow. Nick Pasquale. There was a turn-up. Or was it? Her eyes fell on his hands on the steering wheel. Big hands. Long-fingered. Capable. She remembered how that hand had felt at her back, the subtle slide of his thumb against the silk of her gown, and the warm stamp of it at her lower back, and remembering made her skin tingle and her tummy flutter.

And he expected her to stop worrying? Oh boy.

The lamp-lit gates of Mount Lofty House appeared in the head-lights and Sophie sucked in a breath.

❧

'Here we are,' Nick said, pulling up outside the sandstone walls of the old one-time mansion. Everything was hushed and dark, with just a single lamp above the door turning the stone walls to a honeyed gold. Nick peered suspiciously at the imposing entrance, the doors of which were closed and at this time of night, he sus-pected, bolted shut. The entire building appeared to be slumbering. 'Will they still have someone on reception?'

'They've got a night bell. I checked all that when I dropped off my bag earlier today.' She looked at the digital display on the dash. 'Yesterday, come to think of it. Anyway, thanks for the lift.'

'No,' he said, putting the car in gear and heading for a nearby car park before she could open the door. 'I'm not leaving you alone outside a locked door in the middle of the night.'

'Really, I'll be fine.'

'I'd prefer to see you safely inside.'

'Why?' she asked, plucking up the battered bouquet from her lap with one hand and bundling the long skirt of her gown in the other. 'Are you worried I might get bitten on the ankles by a wayward koala?'

But her attempt at humour fell flat because he was already out of the car and heading for her door. He wasn't sure why she'd look so apprehensive about him seeing her inside, it was no big deal. It wasn't as though it was going to take any time. He'd have her checked in and be back in the car and out of here in under five minutes. Tops.

He offered her his arm and she took it, sliding from the car to stand in a waterfall of cobalt silk that threatened to wash away all his resolve. It didn't help that she looked so good. Curves in all the right places, and he'd done more than just admire them from a distance. It was going to take him a good while to forget the feel of her sweetly curved lower back under his hand, and the way she'd trembled ever so slightly as his thumb had stroked her skin. Her boyfriend—ex-boyfriend—had been nuts to miss tonight.

Not that it mattered to him.

Five minutes, he told himself, as they climbed the steps to the arched entrance portico, the sounds of their footsteps disturbing the hushed night air. He pressed the after-hours bell and they waited.

'It's a beautiful hotel,' she said, her voice low and a little tremulous. 'I've always wanted an excuse to stay here.'

He wasn't sure what to say to that. Something about it being her lucky night didn't seem appropriate under the circumstances, but she sounded a bit edgy and he figured she needed conversation, so he ran with, 'I guess it was a bit late to cancel.'

'Yeah, though the voucher was going to expire soon, anyway. I had to use it for something.'

'Voucher?'

'From that quiz night last year, the night before Pop had his heart attack. Our table won it, but then Lucy auctioned it and so I bid for it.'

He thought back to that evening, the cogs in his brain rewinding. His table had been narrowly pipped at the post by the Faraday clan, but there was nothing unusual about that, but the prize ...

The memories came back to him in a rush. 'Hang on, you bid five hundred dollars for that voucher.'

'I did. I won it too.'

He shook his head. 'You're telling me you've paid five hundred dollars for one night in a hotel?'

'More than that, actually, if you factor in the extras. Though it's still a bargain. You can pay heaps more than that for a night in one of the suites here.'

But whatever she'd said after 'more' was lost on him. 'You paid *more* than five hundred dollars? For one night with some dickhead boyfriend who didn't even show?'

'Come on, Nick. You're starting to sound like my brother.'

'And he'd have a point! What were you thinking?'

She sniffed and removed her hand from his elbow. 'You know what, Nick? I'm thinking maybe I should go in and register by myself, after all.'

He wouldn't mind if she did. And frankly, when it all came down to it, he was more than a little bit miffed that she'd been so willing to waste both her time and money with people who didn't deserve it. Not just the no-show boyfriend, but the kid behind the bar, whom he was pretty sure she'd been hitting on. As the no-show's replacement for the night? It didn't bear thinking about. Especially considering how she'd treated Nick, like he was public enemy number one. God, if she was chasing the likes of a kid barely out of short pants who had zits, you'd think she might at least have asked him first. Not that he would have said yes if she had, but still …

Before he could tell her that suited him just fine, the door swung open and a breathless night manager full of apologies for keeping them waiting ushered them into the softly lit lobby with an all-encompassing efficiency that blew apart any idea of getting away, and before Nick knew it, he was being handed the key to Sophie's suite.

'Enjoy your stay,' the night manager said after giving them directions.

'Thank you, I'm sure we will,' said Sophie, looping her hand around Nick's arm to lead him away, and it was just as well she did, otherwise he might have remained rooted to the spot all night. 'Come on, honey, I can't wait to see our room.'

Around them as they walked, the stately hotel slumbered on, the air hushed and softly fragrant, the only sound the ticking of a grandfather clock.

'Honey?' he whispered when they'd taken a right as instructed, and when he was sure the night manager was out of earshot.

'You'd rather I call you sweetheart?'

He grunted. 'I don't think so.'

'Then honey it is.'

He looked down at her, catching the upturn of her lips as she looked steadfastly ahead. She'd shed the air of gloom that had hung over her like a dark cloud during the wedding post-mortem in the car and there was a brightness about her since they'd arrived at the hotel. 'You're enjoying this, aren't you?'

She smiled up at him. 'You did seem a bit shell-shocked back there.'

'I was already out of here—or so I thought.'

She squeezed his arm. 'Not long and you'll be free, I promise.'

Except the brush of her body and the velvet stroke of her perfume when she'd hauled herself close to him to squeeze his arm had reminded him of how good she'd felt when they'd been dancing, and now he was wondering why he was in such a rush to get away.

Because staying longer was not an option.

A grand entry stood at the end of the passage. 'Looks pretty posh,' he said, checking the key in his hand to make sure it was the right door.

'Best room in the house,' she said beside him as he slid the key in the lock to an audible click.

'Here you go,' he said, pushing open the door for her. 'All safely delivered right to your door. My work is done.'

'Do you have to rush off?' she said, pausing in the entry. 'At least let me offer you a coffee or something.'

'Bit late for coffee for me.'

'Then come in and see what I paid for and see if it's not worth the money.'

He held up one hand. 'Hey, forget I said anything back there. What you paid is your business.'

'At least come and have a look. Don't worry, I'm not going to jump your bones or anything.'

'Well, there's a relief,' he said, as he stepped inside, but he didn't know why she had to make it sound like she was doing him a favour by not jumping his bones when she'd seemed only too keen to jump on everyone else's. It was really starting to rankle.

Then he stepped inside and forgot all about feeling miffed, because this was not like any hotel room he'd ever been in. Gentle music was coming from somewhere and lamps glowed softly either side of the private entry hall, on one side illuminating a massive bedroom and on the other, a luxurious lounge and dining room. He stepped into the lounge room because he figured it was the lesser of two evils, and drank in the high ceilings, tastefully papered walls and the olde-worlde furniture.

'Wow,' he said, because no other word came close.

'I know.' She pulled back the ceiling-to-floor drapes to the dark outside. 'There're balconies either side and views over the Piccadilly Valley, too, not that you can see anything, now. Isn't it gorgeous?'

It was. Everything was tasteful and elegant and it was no wonder it cost a bomb. A big old-fashioned stereo accounted for the music. Love songs, he realised as James Blunt started singing 'You're Beautiful', probably playing on a loop. Figured. He took a left and found himself in a bathroom four times as big as his was at home, but then it needed to be to fit in the massive spa that took up one entire corner. It looked big enough to teach Minnie to swim.

'Isn't it wicked?' she said, screwing the top off the bath gel to sniff. 'I am so going to enjoy a bubble bath tonight.'

He blinked and headed for the next door, all thoughts of innocent swimming lessons banished as visions of naked limbs and bubbles invaded his thoughts. He really did not need to think about Sophie naked in a bubble bath.

But of course he wound up in the bedroom. Enormous, like the lounge room before, with a sitting area on one end and a bed fit for a king on the other. Fit for half a dozen kings, by the looks, and strewn with rose petals, with a silver ice bucket containing a bottle of champagne set at a jaunty angle on a bedside table alongside.

He imagined Sophie, fresh from her bath, sliding naked between the sheets as rose petals scattered on the floor. And as a lump wedged thick and tight in the back of his throat, he thought, *What a waste.*

'Nice,' he managed to force past the lump, knowing that he needed to get out of there. He'd seen more than enough.

'You see! So now, tell me this suite is not worth the money.'

He fingered the bottle of champagne, taking a closer look at the neck. Of course it was French. She'd really gone for broke, all right. 'Did he know you had this room booked?'

'Who?'

He turned around, saw her testing out the mattress, bouncing up and down and grinning like a kid who'd been let loose in a toy store. 'The guy you planned all this for. Mr No-Show.'

'Jason?' She stood up, her delight falling from her face as she turned and smoothed the bed where she'd sat. 'No. He had no idea.'

'It was supposed to be a surprise, huh?'

'Yeah.'

'What a loser.'

She laughed a little at that, a fractured laugh. Before she cut it off with a swallow and blinked too quickly. 'Yeah. You said it. A real loser.'

Suddenly, her excitement and delight at exploring every nook and cranny of her accommodation was gone.

'Sophie,' he said, the change in her tugging at him as he realised it had all been an act, and the fragile, brittle facade of joy she'd carried with her into the hotel had cracked and shattered to fall and scatter like the rose petals that littered her bed.

'You should go, Nick,' she said, looking at the floor, her hands clutching her arms, her fingers biting into her skin.

He'd been on the cusp of leaving. He'd been that close to stepping back into that private lobby and out the door. Now, he had a choice to make. He took a step towards her.

'No!' she said, putting up one hand. 'I'm warning you, it's going to get messy in here any second and you really don't want to be around to witness that. Thanks for the lift. I'll see you round.'

She spun away from him and turned her head to the ceiling, clearly waiting for him to go. He heard her drag in a shuddering breath, practically willing him to walk away, and he didn't know what to do except he knew he had no choice, and that he couldn't leave her, not like this. Not when it had been his words that had tipped her over the edge.

It was instinct that propelled his feet and took him to her, pure instinct that saw his hands on her shoulders to turn her. 'Sophie,' he said, as her keening sob tore apart what was left of her composure.

'I thought he loved me,' she said, collapsing against his shoulder. 'I wanted him to love me.'

'It's okay,' he said, rocking her gently as he held her close to him, while she cried great heaving sobs. One hand stroked her hair as hot tears soaked into his shirt. 'It's going to be okay.'

'It's not okay. Jason said—'

'Forget Jason. He's a loser.'

'No,' she said, sniffing. 'I'm the loser. I'm pathetic.' She dissolved into a fresh round of tears, clinging to him, crying her heart out, while he rocked her from side to side to the sounds of his namesake, Nick Cave wondering about the existence of angels.

This Nick didn't know much about angels, and he also wasn't sure when comforting someone in distress had moved to something more carnal, but he did know a real woman when he felt one, and Sophie Faraday was all woman. He'd been carting an erection around most of the night that had her name written on it and it was all he could do not to press her sweet body hard against it.

'You're not pathetic,' he told her. 'So you made a mistake. You're human. It's allowed.'

'I drove him away. I'm hopeless.'

'You're beautiful.'

Her shuddering stopped. She snuffled against his chest. 'What did you just say?'

He hesitated. He was standing on the edge of a precipice and whether he was pushed or he jumped was up to Sophie. Either way, it was a long way to fall, but there was no going back. 'I said you're beautiful.'

Tentatively, slowly, she peeled her head from his sodden shirt, blinking up at him through red, puffy eyes and her hair stuck to the side of her tear-ravaged face, and still she was gorgeous. 'Are you crazy?'

He smiled a little at that, because she was right, but not because he was wrong. 'I think I must be.' And he dipped his head and pressed his lips to hers. Nothing more than a press, a meeting of his lips with hers, a shared breath between them, and she tasted sweet and salty, warm and achingly real.

It took every bit of restraint he owned not to push harder. She was hurting and it would be wrong to take advantage of her, especially when she'd made it more than plain that he wasn't her type. She'd probably slap his face for that and he'd deserve every bit of it, but all he knew was that he couldn't not kiss her.

Her eyes were wide and confused when he lifted his mouth away. 'You really are crazy.' She sounded slightly breathless, her voice low and husky, and the sound of it stroked his senses. Because she hadn't pulled away, and if he wasn't mistaken, she wasn't about to sling him out in disgust. But he had to know for sure, before he made more of a fool of himself than he already had.

'Tell me to go again, and I will.'

'Don't you dare go anywhere,' she said. 'At least, not before you kiss me one more time.'

He growled as he pulled her closer, the sound reverberating down through her bones to her toes and up again before lodging deep in the pit of her belly. Then his mouth was on hers and she felt a rush of heat as his lips moved over hers, and thankfully they weren't gentle this time, but urgent. Heated. Insistent.

Hungrily, she parted her lips and he accepted her invitation, and she felt the sweep of his tongue and tasted him in her mouth, reminded of dark chocolate and coffee beans, rich and decadent and masculine.

He tasted all man.

He felt all man, his lips softer than you would ever guess, his whiskered skin rough against hers, the sensations contrasting and melding in their heated breath and making her dizzy with desire, a desire further fuelled by the feel of his muscled flesh shifting under her seeking hands.

Oh God, Nick Pasquale was kissing her and she was burning up.

Nick Pasquale!

How was this even happening?

Breathless and disbelieving, she drew herself back from his kiss, and slowly, as if reluctantly, he let her go, his breathing as ragged as her own, his blue eyes looking as perplexed as she felt.

'I don't understand,' she said, panting for air as she licked lips that felt full and more sensitive than she could remember. 'This is you. You've always treated me like I was your little sister.'

He laughed slightly through his own choppy breathing, before pressing his lips to her forehead. 'Is that what you thought? I can promise you I'm not thinking big-brotherly thoughts about you right now.'

Heat flared deep in her belly. She swallowed. 'Tell me. What kind of thoughts are you having?'

'Dangerous thoughts. Reckless thoughts.' He ran his hands down the length of her spine, cupping her behind, squeezing and pressing her against his hardness. 'Thoughts I'll no doubt be ashamed of come daylight.'

His words fed into her need, the press of him an intoxication headier than any wine. In answer, she ground her hips against him. 'In that case, you better show me while it's still dark.'

A sound tore from his throat, half agony, half victory, before he pulled her closer, his hot mouth finding her throat this time, burning trails of fire under her skin that merged and raged into a firestorm between her thighs, before he swung her into his arms and tumbled them onto the rose-petal-strewn bed.

It was some time later before Sophie had a coherent thought in her head, still panting as the smouldering ashes of her body pieced themselves back together. She blinked. God, she'd needed that. But who would have guessed it would be Nick Pasquale who would make it happen?

Then again, the plans for this night had been so perfected and polished, she'd been well and truly primed to go off tonight, all she'd needed was a willing partner. She stretched and smiled luxuriously at that. She probably could have taken the Abominable Snowman to bed and still gone off like a firecracker.

Take that, Jason!

Hmm.

She settled back into her pillows. That was interesting. Funny how she could think of him now without pain lancing through her, when he'd caused her so much pain before. 'I don't think I really loved him.'

The man she'd thought slumbering next to her stiffened. 'Who?'

'Oh, sorry,' she said, not realising she'd spoken out loud. 'Jason, I mean, I couldn't have loved him, surely? Not if I can turn around and have sex with somebody else ten minutes after he dumps me and not feel bad or guilty about it. Maybe I didn't love him at all. That's mental.'

There was a pause. A sigh. 'I don't know,' he offered, his voice little more than a sleepy murmur. 'Maybe you're just in love with the idea of being in love.'

She blinked. 'You think?' But it was a question directed more at herself than at him, which would have been pointless anyway, because already she'd felt his body heavying next to hers, his muscles relaxing, his breathing slowing in rhythm with the hush of the valley around them.

And he felt warm and all kinds of wonderful beside her, but it was to his simple, if sleepy assessment that her thoughts turned—that she was in love with being in love. He was wrong of course. He was a man. What would he know?

Still, she turned the concept over and over in her head, prodding it, testing it, examining it from all angles, before discarding it again as nonsense.

It was laughable, really. All she wanted was what Lucy and Dan had. The real deal. True love. And who could judge her harshly for wanting that? Nobody, that's who.

Whereas, if she was merely in love with being in love, then surely she'd be dreaming of her perfect wedding and her perfect married, loving life and simply trying to find someone to slot into that picture? Someone who'd put her on a pedestal and laugh at her jokes and treat her like a princess?

She wasn't that shallow.

She wasn't that needy.

She swallowed, blinking into the dark.

Or was she?

Jason's charges against her rushed back in a tide that carried with it all the flotsam and jetsam of her demands and hopes and expectations that this one night together be their most magical yet. And none of it was because she loved him. She'd wanted to love him, just as she'd wanted him to love her, sure. But she didn't, and that had been made blindingly obvious the moment Nick had flushed all thoughts of Jason from her mind.

And it had all been because she'd wanted Jason to fit the fairytale picture she'd spun out of gilt thread around herself. She sighed, the gilt thread, the evidence of her naivety, figuratively unravelled and littered around her. God, she'd been so stupid.

The man beside her sighed in his sleep and rolled over. She smiled across at his darkened form. And it had taken Nick Pasquale to make her wake up to herself. There was a turn-up.

Nick woke to a feeling of supreme satisfaction cocooned in the unbeatable cushion of body heat, all of which lasted about a millisecond. His heart skipped a beat, thinking he must be imagining it. Thinking he must be crazy.

Bloody hell!

Because he realised he wasn't just crazy. He was stark raving bonkers.

For alongside him the reason for his satisfaction and warmth slumbered on, her back to him, her brown hair splayed across the pillow, and her gorgeous behind nestled into his thighs. Dangerous, he thought, as he twitched, already tensed for action. And then the light of day registered and he frowned as he reached for his watch. He hadn't meant to fall sleep.

'Bollocks!' he said, bolting from the bed, thrusting his legs into his underwear.

'Hmm?' Sophie murmured, pushing the hair from her face as she rolled over. 'What's wrong?'

'It's seven-thirty. Minnie gets dropped back at eight. I have to go.'

'Oh.' She pushed herself to sitting while he dragged on his trousers, coyly pulling the sheets up over her breasts like he hadn't spent the best part of the night getting up close and personal with them.

'Will you be okay getting home?'

'I'll catch a cab.' She tucked her knees up under the sheet as she watched him scrabbling for his clothes. 'I guess this saves us any awkward post-coital conversations, huh?'

He stopped, his hands on his belt. 'Sophie, I don't …'

'No. Don't worry, I don't want any awkward post-coital conversation, either. In fact, I actually had an epiphany last night.'

He raised his eyebrows. 'Only one? I counted at least two,' and was inexplicably delighted to be rewarded with her blush.

'I'm serious here! I had an epiphany, right after you fell asleep. I was thinking about what you said, about how maybe I'm in love with the idea of being in love, and then I got to thinking about Jason. You know, the night he dumped me he told me the reason was that I was too needy and demanding, but not only that, he couldn't even be bothered turning up the last time he had time off—he made some lame excuse instead, too gutless to tell me the truth. Anyway, I put the two together, and the more I thought about it, the more I realised you were right.'

'Sophie,' he said, 'don't go taking my word for anything. I've got a failed marriage behind me. I'm hardly qualified to give anyone advice, least of all about relationships.'

'No, you were right. I saw Dan and Lucy so in love and I wanted that for me. I wanted someone to look at me the way Dan looks at Lucy. I wanted someone I could look at that way. I wanted to be in love like that, too.'

He shrugged his shirt up over his shoulders, did up a couple of buttons and tucked the tails into his pants. 'There's nothing unusual in that. Most of us are looking for someone.' He thought about that for a second as he dived for his socks, before qualifying it with, 'At least, at some stage or other.' At least until it ended up going pear-shaped.

'No.' She shook her head, the waves in her hair bobbing wild and untamed around her face, as uninhibited as she'd been last night. He wished he was an artist in that moment, so that he could capture the contrast between her untamed hair against the creamy perfection of her skin with something more than memory.

'Even at the wedding,' she continued, 'when you told me I should stop acting like a baby—'

He dragged his attention away from how she looked and sat on the edge of the bed to pull on his socks. 'God, can you forget I said that?'

'I deserved it. I was acting like a baby. I was angry and miserable and so stupid.'

'You had just suffered a major bust-up.'

'That's no excuse and you know it. I was so selfish. All I was thinking about was me and wanting to wallow in my misery, and I could have ruined Dan and Lucy's wedding in the process.'

'But you didn't.'

'No thanks to me. Anyway, last night while I was lying here awake, I worked it out. I need to grow up.'

He thought about her breasts and her hips and how she'd felt all around him, and found it hard to keep his voice from going rough around the edges. 'I happen to have it on pretty good authority that you're already all grown up.'

'You're really sweet,' she said, although he knew damned well after last night that he was anything but. 'But no, not physically, I mean mentally. I have to get out of this mindset that just because I'm the baby of the family, I can go on acting like one forever.

And if I'm going to fall in love with someone, it's going to happen. I have to stop trying to force it and wanting every relationship to be "the one".'

He grunted, tying his shoelaces. On the scale of morning-after conversations, this one was turning out to be far closer to comfortable than awkward. 'Sounds fair.'

'I think so. And meanwhile, I'm going to celebrate being single. I mean, it's not the end of the world being single, is it? It's not some illness that has to be fixed. Beth's single and she's okay and so is Hannah, and they're both twenty-nine. And look at you, you're single and you don't look like you're about to slash your wrists.'

'Hey, I've been married once already, remember.'

'Sure, but you don't look like it bothers you.'

'Well, it's different. I have Min to think about.' He glanced at his watch—Min, who will be dropped off in precisely twenty-one minutes. By Penelope, who would just love to catch him wearing last night's wedding threads.

'So, I'm going to be footloose and fancy free and stop thinking every time a guy so much as looks at me that he wants to marry me and that we'll both live happily ever after.'

This was good, he told himself as he dived for his jacket and scanned the room for his phone or his keys or anything he'd missed. At least he didn't have to worry about Sophie waiting for him to call or thinking that last night actually meant anything, even though he'd be lying if he said he wouldn't mind a replay.

He looked at her, propped up in the bed with her bare arms around her sheet-covered knees, looking so pleased with herself for coming up with a personal plan of action and looking utterly gorgeous in the process that he was kind of sorry she had, even if it was for the best. 'I have to go,' he said, resisting the temptation to walk over and give her a kiss goodbye, because that would completely send the wrong signals. Better just to walk out. If she wanted anything more, she'd have to ask for it, and the way she was talking, that wasn't on the cards.

'Catch you later,' she said, which was his cue to leave, no obligation and completely guilt free. He had his hand on the doorhandle when he heard a hesitant, 'Nick …'

His breath caught, and he turned his head to see her teeth worrying a bottom lip that already looked like it had gone some hard yards and felt a stab of guilt. He really should have shaved last night. 'What is it?'

The confidence she'd woken up with had all but disappeared, and now she looked uncertain. 'You won't tell Dan about this, will you?'

Not likely! He was pretty sure Dan didn't have bonking his sister in mind when he'd asked him to look after her. But he simply said, 'I won't if you won't.'

'Ha. Don't worry, *nobody's* going to hear it from me.'

Right. That put a full stop to the affair, right there. He forced a semblance of a smile to his lips and nodded. 'Then we're good.'

He was halfway out the door when he heard, 'Oh, and Nick?' This time he didn't turn around.

'Yeah?'

'Thank you.'

8

Beth

Beth couldn't rid her nose and mouth of the metallic tang of blood. She slammed her locker door shut in the change rooms, wishing she could as easily slam away the taste. She was used to the blood, more than used to it given her job as a paramedic. What she could never get used to was the fact that sometimes, despite their best attempts, despite fighting tooth and nail, things didn't always end well. She would never get used to the fact that this very moment, someone was getting a visit from a couple of policemen—from strangers— calling to ask them to sit down and making sure they did, before they told them that their son, or father or husband wouldn't be coming home tonight.

She rested her head between her forearms on the locker door and banged her forehead against the metal.

Bang. Bang. Bang.

Get over it, she told herself, *get a grip*, knowing that she should, because this was what she did. This is why she'd dropped teaching to become a paramedic. Except there was no getting over it, no getting a grip, because this was the worst of them all.

A motorcycle crash and the rider had died at the scene.

They weren't supposed to die.

God, as if yesterday's wedding hadn't been reminder enough of what she'd lost. Now, the metallic taste in her mouth mocked her as the memories flooded back: of her mum, knocking on her bedroom door only to tell her, her face bleached of colour, that she had a visitor; of her nan leaning against the kitchen bench staring blankly over the boiling kettle while Joe's dad stood in the middle of the lounge room looking shattered.

Her blood had run cold as her mum and Nan had sat her down between them on the sofa, each of them holding one of her hands, while Joe's dad had explained that his wife was too unwell to come, all the while avoiding her eyes as he stared through his tears at the baby bump that was now so heavy in her lap. He told her she should be the first to know after them, but they couldn't tell her over the phone.

And Beth had already worked out what he was going to say before he'd said it, and still she hadn't been able to make any kind of sense out of the words. All she'd been able to do was wail and wrench her hands from the others' grip so she could surround her unborn child in her arms and hug her baby bump. Hard.

She slammed her head into her locker one more time and breathed deep before slumping onto a bench, her head in her hands. Oh God, when would it stop?

'Beth,' a colleague said, putting a hand on her shoulder as he recognised her distress if not the root cause of it. 'We did all we could. We can't save them all.'

'I know,' she conceded, breathing hard, but that didn't make it any easier.

He gave her shoulder a squeeze and she smiled up her thanks, even though he had no idea why it hurt so much.

But then nobody knew. Nobody understood.

That Joe's accident had been all her fault.

9

Hannah

Hannah wiped down the examination table after her final vet consultation of the day, the smell of disinfectant overpowering the myriad other distasteful smells she'd encountered during the long working hours. Already, she was contemplating the joys of walking through the door to the adjoining flat she called home and putting her feet up with a nice glass of sauvignon blanc, a treat she usually reserved for a Friday evening. But then, today felt a hell of a lot more like a Friday than a Monday.

Then again, yesterday had felt a whole lot like a Friday, too.

She was tired after the big wedding, she told herself, that was all. Worn out because that long day had been followed by another with several hours spent helping out at a native animal shelter. Yesterday she'd mucked out four kangaroo shelters and laid out new straw before spreading the old muck over the refuge's front garden for mulch. No wonder she was tired.

And Nan thought she should be lusting after having babies. Ha! Because she had so much time for looking after babies, of course.

And Nan had such a bee in her bonnet about it, poor Lucy wouldn't hear the end of it now that she was married to Dan. Only Nan was bound for disappointment on that score, too, given that Lucy was so hesitant to try again in case she miscarried once more. Twenty weeks. She could well understand Lucy's reluctance to want to go through that a second time, to be permanently watching the clock and waiting for something to go wrong.

Hannah stopped wiping, checking her bench to make sure she hadn't missed anything. No, with both Lucy and her out of the running, and Beth so insistent that she'd done her bit with Siena, it was all down to Sophie to supply additional Faraday progeny. Not that that was going to happen anytime soon, given she'd just been dumped.

Just try telling Nan that, though, with her 'It's what women were put on God's green earth for' manifesto. When Hannah knew for a fact that it wasn't. There had to be more than that and she was going to prove it.

She heard a knock on her door before it opened a crack. 'Sorry, Doc,' said the vet nurse, 'I know I told you we were done, only we've got an orphaned joey, just brought in.'

'Another one?' Hannah said, because there'd been three orphans last week, but native animal emergencies were never turned away, whatever time of day or night. 'Show them right in. Oh, and Verity, you better grab us a pouch and liner.'

By the time Hannah finished washing her hands, the nurse was back. 'This is Declan Cummins,' she said, ushering in a tall man bearing a jumble of towel in his arms, before handing Hannah the soft cloths and pulling the door shut behind her.

'Nice to meet you,' she said automatically, her eyes firmly fixed on the bundle he was carrying. Judging by the size of the towel, it wasn't a very big joey inside. 'Let's take a look at what you've got, then.' She peeled back a corner and peered into the folds to see a set of frightened eyes looking up at her, the joey's hind legs bucking in protest at the sight of yet another stranger. 'It's okay, sweetie,' she crooned to the animal, covering it up again to make it feel more secure.

'Will it be all right, do you think?'

'Well, it's got fur,' she said, encouraged by the discovery, because the younger and furless 'pinkies' were always a lot more work. 'That's a good start. Here, put it down on the table and I'll have a closer look.'

He did as she asked, his movements surprisingly gentle. Big hands, she noticed absently, that looked like they'd be more at home wielding a chainsaw, and yet here they were treating the bundled-up infant with immense tenderness. She asked him to keep one of those hands to steady it in case it startled and tried to jump, as bit by bit she peeled away the towel, being as gentle as she could. It was important not to stress the tiny orphan any more than necessary, though she knew by the way its heart was frantically beating that it was terrified, and little wonder. It had already suffered what must have been a shocking collision before being thrown to the road, only to then be plucked from its mother's pouch, and now to suffer the indignity of being poked and prodded by a stranger. She kept her eyes on her patient while she asked the question, 'You're quite sure the mother's dead?'

'One hundred per cent,' he said, as Hannah methodically examined the tiny creature, all long legs and tail, with big eyes and the softest grey fur. 'There were two of them and they sprang from nowhere, thinking they could cross in front of the car. I slammed on the brakes and the first one made it. The second one …' He shook his head. 'I stopped and checked. I was about to drag it clear of the road when I saw something move, and I found the lil' tacker still tucked inside, though its mam was well gone.'

Her eyes flicked up at the music in his voice, for the first time curious about the man who'd brought in the animal. He was taller than she'd realised, with sandy hair and a whiskered jaw peppered with white, and a nose that looked like it might have been broken at some time in the past between a pair of dark eyes. Eyes that were watching her just as intently as she was assessing him. She blinked and returned her attention to the joey. So, the man was Irish, that was hardly reason to gawk. 'It wasn't attached to the teat?' she asked, delicately checking the animal's mouth, back to business. 'You didn't have to pull it off?' Because this man probably had no idea how wrong that would be.

'No. It was like getting hold of a handful of spaghetti, to be sure, but it came out easy enough once I had hold.'

She smiled at that, imagining the trouble his big hand must have had to make head or tail on the joey. And because she found no damage to its mouth, she believed him. Good man.

'So where did it happen?' she asked, reaching for her small digital scales.

'Over at Norton Summit, up near Moores Road. I've got a few acres over that way.'

Not just a visitor passing through, then. She let that surprise drift quickly by and nodded, satisfied, as she weighed the joey. She then rolled it into the soft fleece liner and the pouch the surgery volunteers sewed up for just such a purpose, and held it to her chest to keep it warm. After an initial struggle the joey settled, but she was too experienced to be fooled into thinking it would all be plain sailing from here. 'I'll get someone out to mark the body, so people know it's been checked.'

His brows tugged together, bringing her focus back to his eyes, which she realised were more than dark, they were the deepest shade of blue. 'I didn't know to do that, but I'm happy to. Save anyone else the trouble, seeing I'm out that way already.'

'Would you? Even better. Use spray paint to mark it with a cross, in case anyone else is wondering. I'm sorry for the mother, but apart from the shock, this little one looks to be fine. Thanks for bringing it in. I'll see that it's well looked after.' As soon as she found some-one who could fit in another infant joey to care for. She'd reach out to the network, even if she had to go a little further afield.

'Oh no,' he said. 'You don't understand. I don't want you to take it. I just came in to make sure it was okay. I want to look after it.'

'You?' She blinked, before shock gave way to good sense. 'No, it's okay, that won't be necessary. We have carers in the community trained to look after orphaned wildlife.' She'd find someone, though it might take a day or two. 'It'll be in good hands, I promise.'

'But I don't want that,' he said again, and this time there was a note of steel in his sing-song voice. 'I mean, her mam might have been daft for thinking she could win a race with a car, but I still feel responsible for leaving this little tacker alone in the world.'

'But you've taken care of it by bringing it in, and while I applaud your intentions, you've clearly got no idea what's involved.'

'Like what?'

She cuddled the pouch closer to her chest. It was a common mis-conception that looking after an infant kangaroo must be as easy as looking after a kitten or a puppy. So often people came upon orphaned joeys on the side of the road and thought they'd be doing the right thing by taking them home to raise them, and treating their kids to a special kind of pet at the same time, but then they'd mistakenly feed them cow's milk or bread and the joeys would weaken and become ill or just be stressed from too much handling. The lucky ones would be brought into the surgery before that happened, but plenty enough didn't make it. 'Joeys are just like human infants,' she explained, 'they need special care twenty-four hours a day. A joey like this has to be kept warm and quiet and has to be fed three-to-four-hourly with a special formula, and it'll need bottle-feeding until it's around eighteen months of age, and that's probably an entire year from now. It's a huge commitment, not to mention expensive for all the formula and bottles. Plus, you'll need to get a licence to care for native animals. They don't just let anyone take them.'

He shrugged. 'I can manage all that, sure enough.'

She frowned. 'It's not that easy. The joey also has to be toileted after feeding,' she went on, hitting him with the big guns because he was clearly mad, 'which involves stimulating its vent to ensure it urinates and defecates—otherwise it can end up with kidney disease or worse.'

'All right.'

She frowned. 'That wouldn't bother you?'

'If it's got to be fed, I figured the other end might take some looking after, too.'

Was this guy for real? Most men would run for the hills after being told they had to do that. 'And it's not going to work if you have dogs, of course. Or children who might treat it as a plaything and tire it or make too much noise.'

A spark lit up those midnight-blue eyes as he grinned, revealing long dimples that bracketed his mouth. A seriously good-looking mouth. 'Sounds like I'm just the man for the job.'

She shook her head. 'Look, Mr Cummins—'

'Declan,' he said. 'If you're going to be teaching me what I have to do to look after the little tacker, we should be on a first-name basis.'

She held up one hand. 'Hey, I never said—'

'Teach me, and if it doesn't flourish under my watch, you can find it another carer.'

She looked up at him, this man who seemed so sure of himself and so determined to look after the joey he'd left orphaned. Could she trust him to do the right thing? He certainly sounded confident enough, and right now, after a sudden influx of animals and a shortage of carers, what choice did she really have?

'All right,' she conceded. 'But I'm keeping it for a couple of nights for observation, and if it's doing well, I'll bring it by after work with everything you'll need to start, along with some more detailed instructions you can refer to and some phone numbers you can call if you're worried.'

'That'd be grand,' he said, reeling off his address. 'I'll be waiting.'

'It's a trial,' she stressed. 'Purely a trial. If the joey doesn't thrive or you find you can't take care of it, I'll have to place it elsewhere.'

He put out his hand. 'Deal,' he said, his dark eyes twinkling while his long dimples played around his mouth. 'Thank you, Doctor.'

She placed her hand in his, felt his long fingers wrap around hers and gently squeeze, and experienced a simultaneous rush of heat up her arm that swirled uncomfortably in her breasts and down further, to lodge heavy and warm in the pit of her belly.

Ridiculous, she thought, though she left her hand right where it was, encompassed by his inexplicable heat, for just a few seconds longer. 'Hannah,' she told him, resisting the urge to smile back at him, because first-name basis or not, this was still business. 'If I'm going to be teaching you how to care for an orphaned joey, you can call me Hannah.'

Two days later, she passed the roo's body on the side of the road, clearly marked with a giant X, and Hannah felt the sadness she always did when she encountered native animal road kill. She reached a hand over to the pouch she'd slung over the headrest as if to console the joey, when it was she who was looking for reassurance. It wasn't all bad. With any luck, this little one would now get to grow to full adulthood, instead of dying in the pouch, where it could have if Mr Cummins—*Declan*—hadn't noticed it wriggling.

The gravel road crunched under her tyres, the candlebark gums standing tall and proud in the bush either side of the road, their white bark reminiscent of wax flowing down a lit candle. The bush was thick here, the houses few and far between, settled on hilly acreage that bordered the dramatic cliffs and waterfalls of the Morialta Gorge. Beautiful country, and a long way from home for an Irishman, and in spite of herself, she couldn't help but be curious as she turned into his driveway. What was he doing here, on the other side of the world?

The track followed a creek bed before winding around the back of a grass-covered hill, the driveway ending near a wall of stone and windows, which is when she realised it wasn't a hill after all, but the roof of the house burrowed beneath the earth. On one side of the house, straight rows of vines marched up the hill while on the other, beyond the creek, was a stand of gums and bush between which a flock of black cockatoos screeched across the sky. Pretty much idyllic, she figured, negating the question she'd asked herself earlier. Who wouldn't want to live here?

'How are you?' she heard, and she turned to see him emerge from an arched door in the middle of the house, smiling as he approached the car with an easy denim-clad stride that was hard to ignore.

'Hi,' she said, nodding towards the house as she pulled open the passenger-side door to retrieve the joey. 'I like your house. Very *Lord of the Rings*.'

He grinned, and those brackets either side of his mouth deepened. 'Welcome to Hobbitville.'

Not to mention sensible-ville given the fire load in the national park nearby, she thought, trying to think rational thoughts, rather than how she was rapidly becoming a fan girl of long dimples of the masculine kind.

'How's the wee joey?'

'Doing well,' she replied, as she slung the pouch across her body, happy to be on firmer territory. Animals were her business. All she had to do was think about the joey and not get herself sidetracked by an Irish lilt and easy smiles. 'She's taking a bottle and we had a good night last night. She only woke for a feed at two and five.'

'Through the night?'

She raised an eyebrow at him. 'Having second thoughts, Mr Cummins?'

'Not a one. It'll be no trouble at all.' He grinned. 'And I thought I told you to call me Declan.'

'We'll see.' She got him to fetch the box in the back and followed him into the house, which was simple and homely, but the biggest surprise was that the interior was so light and airy. She looked around, admiring the use of timber and stone, and the big pot-belly stove that stood in one corner and no doubt made the entire home more than cosy come winter. 'Wow,' she admitted, stroking the baby joey through its pouch. 'I didn't expect it to be so light inside.'

'It's the aspect,' he said, depositing the box on a timber table that looked like it had been carved from a tree with a chisel and hammer. 'I designed it so it catches the winter sun but keeps out the summer heat.'

'You designed it?'

'And built it, sure, that too.' She looked at the table and chairs and figured he'd probably also made those himself. Clearly, he was a man who was good with his hands.

'So,' he said, and she looked around to see his gaze fall to the pouch slung around her neck. 'Are you going to be teaching me what I have to know about looking after the little tacker?'

Hannah blinked and felt her cheeks burn that she had to be reminded of why she was there. 'Let's get started,' she said.

She went through the contents of the box first, showing him the bottles and teats and the Wombaroo powder especially formulated for feeding baby marsupials. She'd brought spare pouches, too, and a heat mat in case the joey got too cold, and she explained how and when to use it. Next, she showed him how to make up the milk, stressing the importance of hygiene and making sure the equipment was thoroughly sterilised.

To his credit, the man listened, nodding his understanding, encouraging her to believe he could do this, and despite her first doubts, she found herself wanting him to succeed. For the joey's sake, she told herself, because there was no other reason than that for wanting the joey to thrive.

Then, when it was time to feed the joey, she showed him how to get the infant to take a bottle and had him feed her, offering him advice from the seat alongside, the bottle looking miniscule in his big hand. She watched him as he nursed the tiny kangaroo, its paws resting on his fingers as it drank, while it looked up at him with big dark eyes.

'Aye,' he said, looking down at it with abject adoration on his face. 'She's a right little sweetheart.'

And all Hannah could think was he was the one who looked adorable. Curiosity once more got the better of her. 'What are you doing out here?'

'A bit of a tree change. I've got rid of all the blackberries in the creek and then I planted myself up some vines. Some chardonnay. A bit of savvy blanc. I'll see how I go with that.'

'No,' she said, shaking her head and unable to suppress a smile. 'What are you doing so far from home? From Ireland?'

'Oh, you noticed, then?'

She smiled. 'It's hard not to.'

'Funny,' he said, 'when I go home, all me mates say I sound like an Aussie.'

Her smile widened. Not even close. 'Anyway, I didn't mean to pry.'

'I didn't think you were prying. I thought you were making conversation. Mostly, I get to talk to myself out here, so it's nice to have a conversation with somebody else every once in a while.'

She knew she was being nosy, but still she pressed on. 'There's no Mrs Cummins?'

'There was, but she wasn't a fan of the heat and had a hankering for the emerald green of home.'

'Oh, I'm sorry.'

'Don't be. I didn't stop her goin' and we're both happier now that we've gone our separate ways.'

'Any kids?' she felt compelled to ask.

'No kids, thank Christ, that made it easier.' He studied her for a moment, his brows drawn together. 'What about you, then? Do I need to feel guilty about keeping you out after hours when you have some nice fella waiting for you at home?'

She felt a zing in her stomach that made her toes curl in her boots, a zing she was so unfamiliar with, it was hard to think straight. But he was just making conversation, too, she told herself. It wasn't like he was hitting on her. She looked up at him. 'There's no need to feel guilty.'

He smiled. 'Grand,' he said, before he turned his attention back to the kangaroo.

As soon as the joey had been fed and toileted, Hannah figured it was time to leave the new carer with his charge. 'If you get into any trouble, or you have any concerns at all,' she stressed, 'call one of the numbers on the help sheet. They're all experienced carers and they're used to fielding queries from novices. They'll be able to help you out.'

'I'd rather ask you, if you don't mind, that is.'

She shook her head. 'I'm working most days. I can be hard to get hold of.'

'I'd sure be wanting to try, in the first instance, I mean.'

That was ridiculous, when she was so busy, but his blue eyes were imploring her and she found herself licking her lips and saying, 'Sure. It could save time, I guess, given I know the joey's history.'

He grinned. 'My thoughts exactly.' She wasn't sure if she was imagining it, because Hannah Faraday certainly wasn't the dreamer in the family, but she got the strangest impression that they hadn't been his thoughts at all.

10

Nick

It was Penelope's week to have Minnie, so it was a whole week before Nick had to go pick her up from school. A whole week to steel himself against the inevitability of seeing Sophie once more. A whole week in which he'd just about talked himself into believing it would be a doddle. He parked the Colorado on the road outside the school where he usually did and took a deep breath before climbing out. He'd walk in to meet Min like she expected, collect her bag from her locker, and wait outside her classroom until she ran out with all the day's art and craft looking for a hug like she always did at the end of the school day.

For one selfish minute, though, he'd actually considered asking her to pack her own bag and meet him in the car park, like Penelope got her to do so she didn't have to mix with the other mums, but that after-school hug, that was pure gold. He wasn't about to miss out on that.

He closed the door of the ute. So it might be a bit awkward seeing Sophie that first time, but after that, it'd be a doddle.

He greeted the mums who said hi to him, like he usually did, his obligations in that department well and truly acquitted—they knew he wasn't one for small talk—and stepped inside the tiny school that had been established more than a century and a half before. He looked down the corridor. And bugger feeling like it usually did, it felt weird.

It looked the same, the same corridor lined with lockers filled with kids' bags, the same corridor hung with decorations for the latest celebration, Special Person's Day. He saw Minnie's picture of him on the wall amongst all the other mums and dads and grandies and smiled in spite of his edginess. Because he had black hair and two arms and two legs for sure, but as far as he was concerned, that was pretty much where the similarities with what his daughter had painted ended. Not that he wouldn't be sticking it on the kitchen wall when the artwork got cleared away and sent home to make way for the next big thing. The siren sounded and he jumped, as if he hadn't heard it a thousand times before.

Yeah, it looked the same all right, but it just felt different, the air all but crackling. First time, he reminded himself. Next time he saw Sophie would be better. The next time would be easier.

He collected Min's bag and stood with the other parents outside the classroom and tried to calm his thoughts. Stupid to worry about it. If Sophie had wanted to get in touch with him, if she'd had a rethink about their one night, she'd had an entire week to do so. She could have called him any time. One night between consenting adults. That's all it had been to her. That's all it had been to him. That's all it should be to him.

Even if he couldn't sleep at night for thinking about it.

Get over it.

The corridor suddenly erupted with noise, milling with kids piling out of classrooms either side, parents calling for them to wait, did they have their hat, their lunchbox, their jumper. And all the while Nick's nerves strained to breaking point.

There was sweat trickling down the back of his neck by the time the door to Grade One/Two opened and kids started pouring out. Lots of kids. Mobs of kids. And in the middle of it was Minnie. Brilliant, he thought, they'd be out of here in thirty seconds flat. Piece of cake. It wasn't like he was avoiding Sophie at all, but if he didn't happen to bump into her ...

'Dad!' His daughter barrelled into his legs with arms flung wide, both hands full of whatever it was she'd constructed today out of the cereal and tissue boxes he duly bagged up every couple of weeks to send in.

'Hey, Minnie Mouse,' he said, leaning down to give her a hug. 'How was your day?'

She let go of him and looked up at him all serious. 'Penelope says you shouldn't call me that.'

'What?' he said, not for the first time cursing a mother who insisted her child called her by her name and not simply 'Mum'. 'And why does Penelope say that?'

'She says my name is Min-yon,' she said, sounding out the syllables he knew she would have been schooled to do, 'and that's what you should call me. Not Minnie or Min or Minnie Mouse anymore.'

'Yeah, well ...' Penelope-don't-call-me-Penny would say that. He did his best to clamp down on the oily scum of aggravation that always floated to the surface whenever he heard that his ex-wife had been laying down the law. 'What do you think?'

She screwed up her face. 'I like being called Min and Minnie. And Minnie Mouse. But only when you call me that.'

'Well, that's good. I figure it's your name. You decide how you want to use it.'

She nodded, seemingly satisfied, and he thought there was a chance he might gently usher her into the flow of foot traffic, but, 'Look,' she said, not going anywhere, holding up the mess of boxes she'd taped and glued together for his inspection.

'Wow,' he said, trying to make sense of the arrangement and drawing a blank. But he knew way better than to ask what it was, even when he had no idea. 'That's great. Did you make that?'

She nodded. 'Uh-huh. It's a truck. I made it for you, so you can take all the apples to market.' She held up what was in her other hand. 'Only the engine keeps falling off.'

'Ah.' Now that she mentioned it, it could be a truck. Or a rocket ship. Or even a giraffe, for that matter. 'That is the best present ever,' he said, standing up and putting a guiding hand to his daughter's slim shoulder. 'But we'll definitely need that engine. Let's get going, and I'll give you a hand fixing it at home.'

'Min, you forgot—'

A sizzle went down Nick's spine as Sophie Faraday emerged from the classroom.

'Oh,' she said, stopping dead, even though most of the congestion had cleared, looking at Nick across the corridor. 'Um, Nick. Hi.'

God, she looked gorgeous. She was wearing one of those spotted fifties-style dresses all cinched in at the waist with the scoop neck and a big skirt, with her hair pulled back in a ponytail. She looked fresh-faced and innocent, and he really wished he wouldn't get a hard-on just looking at her. But then she didn't look unaffected, either. If he wasn't mistaken, there was a distinct blush creeping up her face. 'Hello, Sophie.'

She sent a brief nod in his direction before she recovered, turning her attention to Min as she made her way across the corridor. 'Min, oh, sorry, Mignon, you forgot your reader.'

'Oh. Thanks, Ms Faraday.'

But Min's hands were full of truck, so Nick stepped forward and took the folder, careful not to go anywhere near Sophie's hands. It was bad enough to be within range of her perfume, the same one she'd worn that night. As if he didn't have enough reason to be pissed off. 'You can call her Min.'

She looked back at him, uncertainly. 'We had a call, from—'

'Penelope,' he finished for her, slipping the reader into Min's backpack. 'I know. But Min wants to be called Min and I reckon it's her decision.'

'Of course, it's just—'

'So I reckon we'll follow Min's lead on this, don't you?'

Her chin ratcheted up a notch, and he saw the movement in her throat as she swallowed. That flawless throat he'd had his mouth and tongue and whiskers all over. And he realised he was searching for evidence …

'Yeah. Thanks, Nick. I think I got that.'

He dragged his eyes from her throat and met her gaze. 'Right. Thanks for the reader.' And then to his daughter, 'Come on, Min. Let's get this truck home.'

He was still in a snit when he stashed Min's latest creation and her backpack on the back seat and climbed in. But at least talking about his ex-wife had taken care of his hard-on.

'Why were you so mean to Ms Faraday?'

He turned to his daughter as he clicked his seatbelt. 'Was I?'

'It wasn't her fault.'

No? So whose fault was it? She was the one who'd looked so bloody tragic in that posh hotel room and made him want to hold her and put all manner of carnal ideas into his head. She was the one wearing the perfume today that had transported him straight back—do not pass go, do not collect $200—to that night.

'If you don't like Min-yon either, why did you call me it?'

Ah! She was talking about that. Perhaps she was right, maybe he had been a bit gruff back there. It wasn't Sophie's fault that he had issues with his ex. Mignon definitely hadn't been top of the pops on his list, but he'd learned long before the time Min had come along to pick his battles, and Penelope had been deadset keen on it. And then, because he'd wondered …

He shrugged, putting the past firmly back where it belonged, and concentrated on the sanitised version of history. 'Your mother loved it and I didn't hate it, and I wanted to keep her happy.'

He saw Min's nod of acceptance in his rear-vision mirror and he thought he was home free.

'You still didn't have to be mean to Ms Faraday.'

He sighed, knowing there was no point telling Min it was more complicated than that. 'You're right,' he said, as he checked his mirrors and put the ute into drive.

Yeah, seeing Sophie the first time since that night had been exactly like he thought it would be. A complete doddle.

11

Beth

Beth was so late getting away from work that she didn't stop at the supermarket like she wanted to, and still got to school too late to do a drive-by pick-up. She cursed under her breath when she saw the student-collection point empty, knowing that by now Siena and any other uncollected children would have been ushered back inside the school building to sit on the blue mat awaiting pick-up by their parents. Which, after about the third time this month of Beth being late, was the equivalent of the parental walk of shame.

She sighed as she unclicked her seatbelt. Her job as a paramedic helped work around school times a lot, but when shifts ran long, as they seemed to be doing lately, not having a partner who could share parenting responsibilities put her out on a limb.

Tough. There was not a hell of a lot she could do about that.

Beth was halfway up to the school when she met the groundskeeper coming around a corner of the building, carrying what looked like half a shed full of equipment. He looked a bit taken aback when he saw her, but then his face lit up with a smile. 'Hey, Beth.'

'Hi, Harry,' she said with a wave, in the midst of mentally checking her pantry for a quick butter chicken recipe for tonight's dinner as she headed for the glass doors. Bugger—basmati rice. She was all out. She had enough other rice, though, didn't she? She'd be thoroughly pissed if she had to venture back down the hill to get some.

'Oh, and Beth?'

Head full of ingredients, she wheeled around to see the man waiting, a blower-vac in one hand, the hose rolled in loops around the other. He'd always struck her as a gentle giant, a bit like Hagrid from the Harry Potter movies, with his wild hair and bushy beard. She'd always liked Hagrid. 'I was wondering,' he said, before he stalled, his teeth gnawing at his bottom lip.

She tilted her head. 'What?'

'Well, I was wondering if you might like to come for a drink at the pub one night. Maybe this Friday night? Or Saturday?'

She blinked. A drink at the pub? Nobody asked her for drinks at the pub. She hadn't done drinks since forever. 'Oh, I don't …'

'Just a drink,' he said with a shrug. 'A chat. That's all.'

Slowly, she shook her head. 'I have Siena,' she said, gesturing towards the building, seizing on the excuse.

'Oh, of course,' he said suddenly. 'Fair enough, then.' And he turned and trudged towards the shed.

Beth shrugged and went on to get her daughter.

'You're late again,' accused Siena five minutes later, on their way back to the car.

Beth sighed. 'Sorry, love, I got held up at work.'

'So what did he want?'

'What? Who?'

'Harry. I saw you talking to him through the windows.'

'Oh. He was just chatting.'

'What about?'

'About stuff. Why do you ask?'

'I don't know,' she said with a shrug. 'I just got the impression that he likes you.'

Beth looked down at her daughter, a little miffed that she didn't have to look down as far as she once had, and more than a little miffed that Siena might have picked up signals from Harry before she had. 'What on earth gave you that impression?'

'Because I know he likes you.'

Beth arched a challenging brow as they climbed down the steps heading for the car.

'He does,' Siena said in her own defence. 'He's always asking how you are.'

Her challenge morphed into surprise. 'Since when?'

'Okay, so he asked today when I was waiting for you at the steps before.'

'Probably just making conversation in that case.'

'Maybe. But he didn't ask anyone else.'

Beth thought about Harry's unexpected invitation despite the fact she'd never once given him a word of encouragement—never given anyone a word of encouragement, for that matter—and wondered why he'd bother. Because he thought she might be lonely? Gawd, she didn't have time to be lonely. 'Like I said, probably just making conversation.' And she turned her mind right back to the rice situation—because hadn't she made rice pudding just a couple of nights back ...?

She pressed the automatic unlock button on her key.

'Mu-um?'

'Yeah?'

'If someone liked you, and you liked them, would you go out with them?'

She stopped, her hand on the doorhandle, looking over the roof of her small car to her daughter. 'What?'

'I mean, if say Harry asked you out, you'd go on a date, wouldn't you?'

Beth sent her daughter a death stare, except it didn't have the silencing power she was hoping for. 'It's just you never go out,' Siena continued inside the car. 'Everyone else's mums go out to the movies or dinner all the time.'

'I'm not everyone else's mum. I have you to worry about.'

'I'm ten years old! I'm not a baby.'

'And that's not the only consideration.'

'Do you like Harry?'

Beth rolled her eyes. God. Yes, she liked Harry, she guessed. Or rather, she didn't dislike him. But then, she hardly knew him, and she certainly hadn't planned on getting to know him any better. What was the point? 'Hey, did I tell you we're having butter chicken tonight? Your favourite.'

Siena crossed her arms and pouted. 'Are you changing the subject?'

Beth snorted as she turned the key in the ignition. Kids grew up way too fast these days.

❧

Crap. No rice. Beth chewed on her lip as her daughter continued the hunt in the low shelves. Then she hit on a brainwave that would save them both some time and picked up the phone.

Pop answered a few rings later. 'Hi, Pop, it's Beth. I wanted to ask if I could drop over to grab a cup of rice. Have you got some to spare?'

Pop grunted. 'You'd have to talk to Joanie about that.'

'Okay, can you put Nan on?'

'I would, only she's not here.'

'Oh, where is she?'

'Gone for a walk.'

Beth checked her watch. Getting on for five-thirty. She would have thought it was dinnertime at Nan and Pop's by now, the way they liked to have dinner early. Nursing-home hours, the sisters all joked about it. But why not go for a walk when it was such a beautiful spring day?

'So you didn't go with her?'

'I was busy with my plant. Plants, I mean. Um, and feeding the chooks. That's right, I was feeding the chooks.'

Beth shook her head. And there was Hannah worried about Nan losing the plot. She had no idea what Pop was talking about. 'Okay. I might as well come over and check—'

'Hey, Mum, I found some,' yelled Siena in her ear, brandishing half a bag of rice that must have been tucked away in some dark corner of the pantry. And who knew how long it had been there, but hey, it was rice, and did rice even have an expiry date? Then again, who cared?

'Forget that, Pop,' Beth said. 'Apparently we're good.'

'Forget what?'

Beth wasn't sure if he was joking or not. 'I'll see you Sunday,' she said. 'For your birthday lunch. Just in case you've forgotten, that is.'

'I'm hardly likely to forget that!' he said, taking umbrage, and Beth laughed.

'Give my love to Nan. We'll see you Sunday.'

12

Hannah

Hannah refused to make anything of the fluttering in her belly as she turned into Declan's driveway two days after she'd dropped off the joey. She'd skipped lunch, that was all that was. She was only here to check up on the joey. She'd been wrong to imagine he might call, just because he'd got her number. She'd be mad to imagine anything into Declan's words or his deep-blue eyes or those damned dimples. She didn't do flirting, and with good reason. She left that up to the likes of Sophie, who'd win gold if flirting were an Olympic event.

No, Irish charm or not, if the joey wasn't doing well, she'd be relieving Declan of his charge. And just because he'd hadn't called her didn't necessarily mean he was coping. She'd seen would-be carers overconfident in their abilities before, which is why they always followed up novices closely in the days following adoption.

The sun had begun its slow track down in the west as she pulled up outside the house he called Hobbitville and applied the hand-brake. A movement caught her eye and she turned towards it, totally unprepared for what she saw. Because there was Declan striding down towards her between the rows of vines, wearing his well-fitting jeans with a grin that split his face and a pouch slung over his neck, looking like it was the most natural thing in the world.

And for a moment she resented the fact that he looked so supremely confident and like he didn't need her at all. And she almost wanted to find a reason to take the joey away.

For a tiny baby that had been through one hell of an ordeal only four short days before and a change of carers in between, the joey was in disgustingly good condition. Hannah finished her examination before rolling the joey back into its pouch, torn between relief and bewilderment. 'Is there anything you can't do?' she asked, hanging the pouch up on a stand Declan had told her he'd fashioned from a few stray bits of timber.

He cranked those twin dimples up to devastating as he checked whatever it was he had cooking in the oven that was driving her empty stomach wild. 'Sure, my ex could probably give you a long list. But you're happy then, with the little tacker?'

'Couldn't be happier,' she said, as she washed her hands at the sink. 'What can I say, you're a natural.'

'Aye, that's grand. She's a good little one.' He pushed the oven tray back in and closed the door, straightening before her, his proximity making her skin tingle. 'Have you eaten, Hannah?'

'Me?' she practically squeaked. There was something about the way he said her name with a long A that stroked her senses. 'No.'

'Only I've got a stuffed chicken in the cooker and there's way too much for one. I'd love you to stay and help me out with it, if you don't have to rush off, I mean.'

She didn't have to rush off as it happened, but still she wavered, a long-held practice of saying no not allowing her to follow her first impulse.

'It'd be my way of thanking you for all you've done,' he went on. 'And I'm sure there's a lot more wisdom about looking after wee joey here that you can pass on.'

Well, if he put it like that … 'Sure,' she said, her stomach rumbling its applause, 'it would be my pleasure.'

She helped him prepare some beans and carrots, and soon they were sitting down to a meal of pancetta-stuffed chicken, with roast potatoes and steamed vegetables. Hannah couldn't remember when she'd eaten so well on a weeknight, as she was more used to making something out of leftovers or microwaving a boxed meal from the freezer. 'Don't tell me,' she said, only half kidding, 'you must have been a chef in a former life to put something like that together.'

He laughed. 'No. Nothing like that. The bird comes already trussed up. All I did was bang it in the cooker and turn up the heat.'

It was the joey's turn to be fed next, and while the world outside glowed red under the setting sun, Hannah watched Declan handle the bottle warming and feeding like a practised pro rather than the novice that he was, the tiny joey staring up at him with what looked like adoration in her big dark eyes as she drank from the teat. 'I think she likes me,' he said, gazing down at his charge.

Hannah wanted to ask what female wouldn't, when that face was staring down at you, but instead she asked, 'Have you decided what to call her?'

'I've been giving that some thought. I was going to call her Lucky, but then, she wasn't lucky to lose her mam, so I decided to call her Seans Eile.'

She frowned, the name meaning nothing to her. 'Shance Ella?'

'It's Irish,' he said with a grin. 'Seans is "chance", and Eile means "another", which is what she's got now, a second chance. I'll probably shorten it to just Eile, but what do you think?'

She nodded, and said with a smile, 'It's perfect.' She shifted her gaze to study him as he finished feeding and confidently but gently toileted the infant. 'Do you miss Ireland?'

'Sometimes. I miss my hometown, a little town on the west coast, on a road called the Wild Atlantic Way. I miss the boiling sea and the wind that whips around you searching for a way in, but then I look out there,' he said, gesturing to the sunset-painted gums, where the cockatoos screeched high up in the trees, 'and I can't think of a more beautiful place on God's earth where I'd rather be.'

Wow. She blinked at the poetry in his words as he tumbled the weary joey back into her pouch before turning his blue eyes on her, and for a moment—one heart-stopping moment—she thought he was going to add something else. Something else a whole lot more personal, a whole lot more threatening.

Uh-oh. She swallowed hard and sprang to her feet, wiping suddenly clammy hands on her jeans. 'Anyway, I should be going.'

'Hannah?' he said, also standing up. 'Is something wrong?'

'No, nothing,' she said, but she made the mistake of looking at his eyes. Wild Atlantic eyes, she registered, that's what they were, the colour of the ocean, wild and storm-tossed and dangerous. And she knew she was in danger if she stayed …

'Thanks for dinner,' she managed, feeling off balance and tongue-tied as she collected up her things and headed for the door.

'Will you be back to check on Seans Eile at all?'

'She's doing fine. You're doing a great job. Call … someone on that list if you have any concerns. Someone's sure to be able to help you out. I'll let them know to follow up on you.' She spared a glance in the direction of the pouch where the baby kangaroo slept, and doubted he'd need to call anyone, the way he was looking after her, before she looked back at him, with the briefest nod. 'Goodbye.'

13

Hannah

Hannah pulled up outside her nan and pop's cottage in Uraidla half an hour late for Pop's birthday party, relieved to see that the guests of honour hadn't arrived yet. No sign of Sophie's car, either.

She checked her phone—nothing—but then she wasn't expecting any calls. Still … She retrieved the potato salad she'd made from the back seat of her Subaru, and made her way through the small house, the comforting scent of all her grandparents' belongings wrapping around her like a hug. But it was that kind of house, full of Nan and Pop, carved chairs and lace tablecloths, and framed cross-stitch sayings on the wall like, *Home is where the heart is*, and Hannah's personal favourite, *You'll always be my friend, you know too much*. She always smiled at that one, unlike the one that said, *Sometimes the wrong choices can still lead us to the right places*. She wasn't so sure about that one. Sometimes wrong choices were just that. Wrong. There was no coming back from wrong.

She left the salad on the dining table with the rest of the food under the net cover, and joined everyone sitting outside on the back verandah, enjoying the mild October weather. Winter in the Adelaide Hills liked to hang on, so warm spring weather sent cooped-up indoor dwellers outdoors.

'About time you got here,' said Beth, as Hannah did the rounds of hugs and kisses, wincing at the big wad of photographs on the table. She would've liked to reach for them now and have a flick through, but she knew the drill. Nan would hand them out one by one with a detailed explanation of who was in them, along with a not-so-potted history of how this person came to be connected to the Faradays, whether or not this was common knowledge. The digital photo revolution clearly had bypassed Nan and Pop.

'Not that late, am I?' she said, pouring herself a glass of water and pulling up a chair. 'I beat Sophie and I see Lucy and Dan aren't here yet.'

'Dan and Lucy are newlyweds,' Nan said with an indulgent nod of the head.

'Does that mean they can be late?' protested Siena, fiddling with a game on her phone. 'I'm starving.'

'No,' Hannah said with a wink at her niece. 'Nan just means they might be so busy making goo-goo eyes at each other, they lose track of time.'

'Yuck. I am so never going to fall in love.'

'Excellent policy. And, for the record, you're always starving,' said Beth, offering her daughter a plate of carrot and celery sticks. 'Have some veggies if you're so hungry. They'll all be here soon, don't worry.'

Siena sniffed, but settled for a carrot stick, crunching on it as noisily as she could before she declared, 'This is boring. I'm going to visit the chooks.'

'Mind you don't go behind the shed,' said Pop.

'Why not?' challenged Siena with the bolshie attitude of a ten-year-old who didn't like to be told where not to go.

'Because there're spiders back there,' Pop growled, holding up his hands like claws. 'Big black ones, with fangs.'

'Eww,' said Siena, running off towards the chook house.

Beth laughed as the bells rang out from the Anglican church right behind. Through it all, Hannah thought she heard the front screen door open and close, but then came the sounds of cupboard doors banging inside and she went to check it out. She found Sophie at an open kitchen cupboard with a packet of painkillers in her hand. 'You okay?' she asked, as her little sister popped open a couple of blisters.

Sophie managed a weak smile though her face looked drawn, like her ponytail was pulling the skin back from her face. 'Just cramps,' she said, as she tossed the pills back and followed them with a glass of water. 'But it could be worse, I guess. It sure beats being pregnant.'

Her sister's words were like a cheese grater against her skin, opening old wounds, exposing old memories. Stinging so much it was hard to keep the snark from her voice. 'I thought you wanted kids.'

'Yeah, I do, but not just yet, if it's all the same to you.'

'You shouldn't joke about it. You don't always get a say in when something like that happens.'

'Relax, Han,' said Sophie, stashing a quiche she'd brought into the oven to warm. 'Why do you always have to take everything so seriously?'

'Somebody has to.'

'Lucky we've got you then, eh?' she quipped, as she wiped her hands on a towel. 'Come on, let's get this party started.'

'Lucy and Dan aren't here yet.'

'I'm sure they won't mind if we get a head start.'

Hannah followed her younger sister out the door, silently bristling as she watched her wishing Pop a happy birthday and greeting everyone like she didn't have a care in the world. Did she think Hannah wanted to be the one who always took things seriously? Did Sophie think that she liked being the serious one? Hell no. But sometimes you didn't get to choose. Sometimes life made you that way.

She picked up her phone, saw there were no messages and turned it back over on the table with a sigh.

'Yay,' called Siena, running across the lawn. 'Sophie's here! Can we eat now?'

'Not until Lucy and Dan get here,' said her mother, and Siena groaned and headed back to the chook house.

'Eighty-two years old,' said Sophie, pulling up a chair and sticking a celery stick into the dip. 'So how does it feel, Pop, being another year older.'

Pop grunted, leaning back in his chair, resting his interlaced hands on his pot belly. 'Well, it's not all bad, when all is said and done.'

'Yeah? That's good.'

'Yup, it beats the hell out of the alternative.' He laughed so hard at his own punch line, he gave himself a coughing fit. Beth sprang to her feet while Nan slapped him on the back, everyone else holding their breath until Pop spluttered and wheezed his way back down.

'Serve yourself right, Clarence Faraday,' said Nan. 'You'll be off to meet your maker sooner than you expect, if you keep that up.'

'Settle down,' Pop growled, reaching for his beer and taking a swig. 'Laughter's supposed to be the best medicine, don't you know?'

'It's not supposed to kill you,' Beth said, winking at Hannah and Sophie as she sat back down.

Hannah rolled her eyes.

'Oh, Pop,' Sophie said, 'I put a bottle of champagne in the fridge for later on, if we want to have a birthday toast with lunch. French champagne.'

Pop sniffed and jiggled the half-drunk bottle of Coopers in his hands. 'Well, I don't go much for the fancy stuff. You reckon it's as good as this?'

'You try it and see,' Sophie said.

Hannah arched an eyebrow. 'Nice of you to leave some champagne for somebody else, sis. How was your hangover the morning after the wedding?'

Across the table Sophie sighed and Hannah congratulated herself. Direct hit. Had she been hoping they'd all forgotten? She watched Sophie pick up another celery stick from the plate. 'I don't recall having one.'

'God, there's a miracle on par with the virgin birth.'

'Ha-ha,' she said drily. 'How about we change the subject?'

Beth was quick to oblige. 'So, what's the goss on the absentee boyfriend? Have you heard from Jason at all?'

'Not a word and that's fine by me. I'm over him. Over all men, for that matter.'

'What?' said Beth.

Hannah scoffed. 'You mean, until the next guy you hook up with on HEA-dot-com.'

Sophie shook her head. 'I've cancelled my subscription. I've decided I don't need a man.'

'What? Not at all?' asked Beth.

'You're not gay?' said Hannah.

'Of course she's not gay!' said Pop, having conniptions.

'The very idea is ridiculous,' added Nan. 'Call me old-fashioned if you like, but I don't know, I still really like the idea of a bride and a groom at a wedding. It's a funny old world, this one.'

'Times have changed,' agreed Beth. 'But there's nothing wrong with change.'

Pop snorted and shook his head. 'Well, be that as it may, not our Sophie, thank you very much.'

Sophie held up one hand. 'Relax, both of you. I just decided to enjoy being single.' She looked to her twin sisters. 'If you like, I'm taking a leaf out of your books. I've decided I'm not going to rely on some guy to make me happy. I'm going to stand on my own two feet a while and enjoy life on my terms, and my terms alone.'

'Wow,' said Beth, carrot stick in one hand, her eyes narrowed in appraisal. 'That was some speech. That break-up with Jason must have really shaken you up, huh?'

'I guess that's part of it,' Sophie said. 'I just got to thinking afterwards that it was time I took my independence a little more seriously while I have the chance, before the right guy does happen along and messes it up.'

'That all sounds eminently sensible,' said Nan, fidgeting with her marquisette watchband. 'And I know you all say times have changed, but I for one am very glad I don't have to admit to the girls on the community bus that one of my granddaughters is, well, you know, that way inclined.'

All the sisters smiled at that, knowing 'the girls' on the community bus Nan took to the nearest supermarket once a week were all, like their grandmother, at least eighty not out. Sophie patted her nan on the back of her papery-skinned hand. 'Glad I saved you from that, Nan. But I'm sure you'd still love me anyway.'

'Of course I would,' Nan conceded, 'but I'd rather pretend you'd fallen in love with some lovely fellow.'

'You expecting a call, Han?' Beth asked. 'You keep checking your phone.'

Hannah jumped. 'Just checking,' she said, trying not to sound flustered, 'in case anyone needs me.'

'Animals don't know our Hannah's got the day off,' Pop said.

'That's right,' she agreed, forever grateful to her grandfather. She slipped the phone into her bag. There was no point checking it. Declan had taken her at her word and he wasn't going to call. That was good, wasn't it? That was what she'd wanted?

The screen door behind them squeaked open. 'Hi, everyone! Happy birthday, Pop!'

'Hey, y'all!'

Dan and Lucy appeared full of smiles, both looking tanned and relaxed and supremely happy. From where Hannah was watching, waiting to give the returning couple a hug, it looked like they were almost glowing, and she was happy for them both and that they'd found each other. It said something about her brother that he'd been desperate to sire a new generation of Faradays whom he could one day pass the orchard to, as his father had done to him, and Clarry had done before that, and yet he'd put that aside for love, choosing Lucy first and foremost. There couldn't be too many men who would do that.

It was a long round of greetings and welcome homes before everyone fell on lunch, especially Siena, who loaded her plate like she hadn't eaten for a week.

'So maybe you lovebirds can finally fill us in on where you ended up going for your honeymoon,' Beth asked between forkfuls. 'We all had bets. The winner gets a free pass from hosting Christmas lunch this year.'

'There's a lot riding on it,' stressed Hannah.

'I want to go first,' said Sophie, 'because I reckon I'm going to win this. Given how you both look fabulous, like you've been lying around on a sun lounger alongside a pool or a beach somewhere gorgeous, I bet you went to Hawaii, right?'

'No, my money's on Broome,' said Beth. 'Those camel rides at sunset on Cable Beach. I know Lucy would love that.'

'Lord Howe Island,' said Hannah, butting in. 'Remote, lots of tropical mountain walks and amazing food, by all accounts. No contest.'

'What about you, Pop?' said Dan, smiling widely. 'Did you and Nan have a bet?'

The old man grunted, his clasped hands once again resting on his stomach as he leaned back in his chair after a big lunch. 'Gold Coast. Joanie and I saw a program about it on the telly, and you'd be mad to go elsewhere, we reckon.'

Dan looked at Lucy and smiled. 'Shall we tell them?'

'Hey,' interrupted Siena. 'You haven't heard my bet.'

'You're right, we haven't,' said Lucy. She grinned at her new niece. 'Where do you think we went for our honeymoon?'

'Where anyone who knew anything would go,' Siena said, rolling her dark eyes. 'Disneyland, of course.'

'Aw, dang,' said Lucy, turning to Dan. 'How come you didn't think of that?'

'Next time,' he promised with a smile.

Dan put his hand around Lucy's shoulders and pulled her close for a kiss, and Hannah half suspected that aliens must have kidnapped her grumpy big brother and replaced him with a clone, because ever since Lucy had turned up, he was a different person. 'So,' she said, because there was only so much lovey-dovey she could bear. 'Did any of us guess it right?'

'Nan and Pop were closest with the Gold Coast,' Dan said, 'but you were all kind of right.'

'Yeah,' Lucy chimed in, counting off on her fingers, 'we had beaches and walks and romantic sunsets and awesome food and a lot of lounging around.'

'So where did you go?' Beth prompted. 'Spill.'

Dan laced his fingers with Lucy's. 'Port Elliot.'

'What? You are kidding me,' said Hannah. 'You were an hour away at the coast, this whole time?'

'We could have come down and visited!' protested Siena. 'Couldn't we, Mum?'

Beth snorted. 'And wouldn't that have made your day, bro?'

Dan smiled and somehow managed to look suitably repentant. 'Sorry, Siena. I didn't think.'

'But seriously,' Sophie said, 'you really went to Port Elliot for your honeymoon?'

'Why not? We spent a day down there last cherry season when I had to do a delivery to Victor Harbor and we had a magical day and we thought, why the hell not? So, I rented us a house close to the beach with amazing views but totally private.'

Hannah chuckled. 'Handy.'

'Well, I think it sounds perfectly lovely,' said Nan. 'We celebrated one of our wedding anniversaries down there with the family, didn't we? Which one was it again, Clarry? Our fortieth?'

Pop grunted. 'Hundred and tenth?' he said, earning himself the evil eye from Nan. 'Well, it's just there've been so many, how's a man supposed to remember the details of each and every one of them?'

'We can soon put a stop to them,' Nan warned, 'if it's a problem for you, Clarence Faraday.'

Pop patted the back of her hand. 'Get back in your box, Joanie. Just a bit of harmless ribbing. I do recall that day as it happens. Bloody good spot down there, too. Glad you kids had a good time.'

'It was totally gorgeous,' said Lucy. 'We went body boarding at Boomer Beach and had fish and chips on the deck watching the sunset, but the best thing, the really best thing ever was the dolphins.'

'You saw dolphins!' said Siena, eyes wide.

Lucy nodded. 'Heaps of them right by the shore. They were catching the waves and surfing, and sometimes you'd see five or six of them in the wave and then leaping out the back of it before the wave crashed. It was awesome!'

'Can we go, Mum?' pleaded Siena. 'Please? I want to see the dolphins.'

'Maybe.'

'It was whales we saw that day,' said Pop. 'Remember? Biggest damn things I've ever seen, like dirty great black bricks floating on the sea.'

'I'd forgotten about the whales,' said Nan, blinking, 'that's right, we did too.'

'Can we go?' said Siena. 'Can we have a holiday there?'

'We should all go,' said Dan. 'Make a day of it.'

Siena clapped her hands together. 'Yay! When?'

Dan shrugged. 'How about Christmas Day? You guys were all right about where we went in a way—why can't we all have a day off for Christmas this year?'

Pop grunted. 'What about the cherries?'

'I was thinking the season's shaping up like last year, so might be done by then. Otherwise, we can still slide down to the coast for the day,' Dan said, 'order some barbecued chickens and salad for a change and make a day of it at the beach. The cherries will still be there when we get back.'

And that's when Hannah knew for certain that aliens had abducted her workaholic brother. 'Lucy, what have you done with the real Dan? This new improved version is all well and good, but I'm missing the grump.'

'Lucky we've still got you, in that case,' said Sophie with a grin.

'Miaow,' said Beth, but she was smiling too, and so was everyone else at the table, so there wasn't a hell of a lot Hannah could do about it.

Nan picked up her pile of photographs then, and it was just as Hannah had predicted. Each photo had to be pored over and the family connections of everyone in it dissected and analysed before they could move on to the next.

Hannah joined Sophie and Beth in the kitchen to help prepare the dessert and birthday cake when Sophie remembered the champagne still chilling. 'What do you reckon?' she said, holding it up for her sisters' inspection.

Beth's eyebrows headed north when she checked out the label. 'Real champagne? I thought you were kidding. Hell, why not? We've got plenty of reason to celebrate today.' So, Sophie popped the cork and half filled glasses for everyone and took them out on a tray to have with dessert.

And they toasted Pop's birthday, the happy return of the newlyweds and Christmas Day plans. Pop seemed to be acquiring a taste for French champagne despite the fact that it didn't bear the Coopers name. 'Have mine,' said Sophie, pushing her untouched glass his way. 'I dropped some painkillers before—I better not.'

'Thank you! This is a French drop, you say?' he said, holding up the glass. 'It's not bad for froggy stuff.'

Hannah sniffed, straightening in her chair. 'Pop, you can't say stuff like that anymore.'

'What stuff? That it's not bad?'

'No. Enough with the "froggy", all right?'

He looked taken aback as he looked at his glass. 'It's French, isn't it?'

'Yes, it's French.'

'There you go. Froggy. I rest my case. There's nothing wrong with a harmless nickname. It's just the same as calling someone a Pommie bastard or a septic tank. It's not being rude. Just ask our septic tank mate here.'

'Clarence Faraday!' Nan shrieked. 'God love us!' And even Hannah didn't know whether to laugh or cry as the table erupted into a discussion of political correctness.

'Before you all finish your glasses,' Lucy interrupted, standing up, her smile wide. 'This septic tank proposes one more toast.'

Everyone stopped bickering and pricked up their ears. She joined hands with Dan, who was beaming up at her like the sun shone out of her, and given the way she was smiling, it could very well have been. 'Today is a day to celebrate a very special birthday. The oldest member of the Faraday family.' She nodded towards Clarry. 'And Dan and I just wanted to share with you that there'll be another Faraday birthday to celebrate, too, this time the youngest in the Faraday family, so I'd like to propose a toast ...' Lucy picked up her glass.

Water, Hannah realised, her eyes opening wide as the shock reverberated through her body. Lucy hadn't touched her wine.

'To the Faradays,' she continued. 'Who have made me feel at home from the moment I arrived. It gives me the greatest pleasure to let you know that the next Faraday will be arriving in ooh, about six months from now.'

Dan stood up next to his new wife and pulled her to him for a kiss that rivalled the one they'd had when they'd been pronounced husband and wife.

'You're pregnant?' everyone seemed to say in shocked unison— everyone but Hannah—she was too blindsided to speak. But nobody noticed because the table erupted with congratulations and another round of hugs and kisses. 'I'm so happy for you,' said Nan, with tears streaming down her face. 'I told you this is what every woman truly wants.'

'I'm proud of you, my boy,' said Pop, clapping his grandson on the back.

Meanwhile, Hannah found herself lassoed into a posse of the sisters forming around Lucy. 'This is the best news,' said Sophie, pulling her into a hug. 'I'm so happy for you both.'

'Congratulations,' said Beth, when it was her turn, the smile on her lips tempered by the concern in her eyes and the lines drawing her brows closer together. 'I'm so excited for you both, but please, please tell me that big brother of ours didn't twist your arm about this, or there will be words, I promise.'

Hannah wanted to be thrilled for her new sister, but her heart wasn't one hundred per cent in it. She was happy for them, sure, but she couldn't help but feel almost … *betrayed* by the shock news. Because she'd thought she wasn't alone, she'd thought she wasn't the only one, and now … 'I thought Dan had given up on having kids,' she said. 'I thought you didn't want—'

'Oh, come on, Han,' said Beth. 'What's wrong with you? It's great news.'

'I know, but—'

Lucy smiled and gripped Hannah's hand. 'It's okay, I know you're only worried about me. But Dan's been the best. He told me it didn't matter if we never had kids and there was no pressure, and for a while that was enough. It was my decision to try. In the end, I just know I love him so much, I want to have his babies.' She sucked in a sudden breath. 'Or at least to try. But neither of us expected it to happen so quickly and that I'd be ten weeks gone by the wedding.'

'And you're okay?' Beth asked, ever the medico. 'You've seen a doctor?'

Her smile wavered at the edges. 'Yeah, because I'm scared, of course I am. But the doctor said that's normal and that there's no reason to think I won't carry this baby to full term. Fingers crossed, hey.'

'And toes,' said Beth.

'Of course you'll be fine,' Sophie added, pulling Lucy into a hug. 'Congratulations, sister. You were already the best thing to happen to this family in years. This news is the icing on the cake.'

'It is too,' Hannah said, doing her best to share the joy, even if she felt her emptiness more keenly in this moment than she had before Lucy had broken her news. Because it wasn't like that for Hannah. She couldn't just change her mind. And no matter how much she told herself that she didn't care that she would never have children, would never be a mother, she had to think that way or risk being swamped by regrets, and the heavy weight of guilt at what she'd done.

At what she'd brought on herself.

Siena stood by watching, taking it all in. 'Am I going to be an aunty?'

'No,' Hannah said with a sniff, trying to snap out of her funk and inject a degree of enthusiasm for the news. 'You're going to have your very first cousin. How cool is that?'

'A girl cousin or a boy cousin?'

'We don't know,' Lucy offered. 'We might have to wait until the baby is born to find out.'

Siena thought about it for a moment or two before she sighed. 'Yeah, pretty cool, I guess. Though I'd rather have a pony.'

14

Beth

Beth drove home later that afternoon, working out what she had to get done today, while Siena prattled on beside her about what Lucy and Dan should call the baby. She made sure she inserted the appropriate noises every now and then so it sounded like she was listening, while she was busy sorting the list. First off was getting the washing in and sorting Siena's school uniform, and hers, for the coming week. Next was getting stuck into a batch of meals and snacks for the freezer, because she knew for sure that if she didn't cook ahead, they wouldn't eat, unless it came out of a can or a jar or courtesy of the nearest drive-through.

And then it was probably time she ran the vac over the floors again. Maybe give the bathroom a quick once-over as well. She couldn't remember the last time she'd paid it too much attention. So long as she could find some time to escape to her studio and get some 'me time' in, although with the stuff that needed doing, that might require a raincheck.

Bugger this concept of work–life balance that people banged on about. People who had time to talk about it had way too much time on their hands. She blinked as she turned into their street. Something was wrong with the skyline ahead. It looked different somehow, like something was missing.

'Mum!'

'What?'

'You're not listening. I asked you a question.'

'Sorry, I was thinking. What was it?'

'Do you want another baby?'

'What?' Beth turned to her daughter, a bubble of laughter beneath her words. 'Why would I want to do that?'

'Why not?'

'Because I've got my hands full juggling everything as it is.'

'But it would be kind of cool, though, wouldn't it? If I had a little sister, I mean.'

'What? Cooler than having a pony?'

'No way!' Siena's face lit up like Sydney Harbour Bridge on New Year's Eve. 'Could we really get a pony?'

Snort. 'No!'

The fireworks on her daughter's face snuffed out. 'Then I guess a sister will have to do.'

'Siena,' she said, turning her eyes towards her daughter as she changed down gears on the approach to her driveway. 'It's not going to happen.' But Siena wasn't looking at her, she was looking ahead, her eyes as big as plates.

'Stop!' she screamed. 'Mum, stop!'

Beth looked. 'Shit!' she said, and slammed on the brakes. Because the driveway was all but gone, disappeared under a fallen tree.

'Well, crap,' she said, 'that's just perfect. And here I was wondering how to spend the rest of the day.' She reversed a little and parked on the side of the road. 'Looks like this is as far as we go, for now.'

'Are you going to call Pop to help?'

Not likely, thought Beth, not after watching him consume half a bottle of bubbles on top of a couple of Coopers. Which he was more than entitled to on his birthday, even if at the same time it disqualified him from a call for help. 'I'll try Dan.'

Unfortunately, Dan was about to take Lucy out to look at some baby furniture that had been advertised and that she'd arranged to see. 'I'll be there,' he said. 'But it'll be an hour or so.'

'No rush,' she told him, 'the tree's not going anywhere,' and turned her mind to attacking her to-do list.

Sure enough, an hour or so later, she heard the buzz and rip of a chainsaw out front. She wondered that Dan hadn't come up to tell her he'd arrived, but then he probably guessed she'd figure it out with that racket. She pulled a batch of raisin and oatmeal cookies from the oven that were almost a meal in themselves, letting them cool a few minutes while she made coffee for them both, because after dealing with the washing and putting on some chilli con carne sauce to simmer, she was ready for a break, too. She slipped a couple of cookies onto a plate for her brother, and the rest into a bag for him to take home. It was the least she could do for tearing Dan away from such a good news day.

The clear blue October afternoon had turned out warm, so Beth added a big glass of water to the tray before she headed down to see her brother. He was on the other side of the tree from her, she could see the back of his head with his orange ear protectors bobbing up and down as the chainsaw powered through the wood. She looked again. At least, she thought it was him.

And then the limb he was working on fell away, and he stood up straight and tall to stretch his broad back. When he looked around and saw her coming, her eyes opened wide, because it wasn't her brother at all.

Harry?

'Afternoon, Beth,' he said as he peeled off his earmuffs and protective glasses, surveying the tray and her as she drew closer.

'I made coffee,' she said, holding out the tray, feeling like a fool. Not to mention wary. In the forefront of her mind was the fact that he'd asked her out and she'd said no, but now he'd turned up here. What was that about? 'But I was expecting Dan and I don't know if you'll like it. It's white with one.'

'Spot on,' he said, 'just the way I like it,' and he put down the chainsaw and reached out a big paw of a hand to wrap around a cup.

She smiled weakly, feeling stupid, feeling trapped there with him because she'd brought her own coffee down, too, and it would have been churlish to walk back to the house with it untouched. She offered him a cookie and he took it, his free hand wrapping around it like it was an afternoon-tea-sized macaron instead of a thumping great cookie.

She put down the tray and perched herself against the trunk of the tree where he'd cleared the boughs, just a little disconcerted when he plonked his solid frame next to her. Not that there was anywhere else to sit, she told herself. 'So how did you get roped into this? I thought Dan was coming.'

'He called me up,' Harry explained, halfway through the next cookie. 'Said whatever he was doing was going to take longer than he thought, and asked if I could help. I owed him a favour, so here I am. I hope you don't mind.'

'How could I mind?' she said, sipping her coffee. The man was clearing a tree fallen across her driveway. It was no surprise that Dan knew Harry. It was a small community up here, neighbours helping out neighbours. And Harry was being neighbourly, that was all.

'Nice view you have from here,' he said, and Beth couldn't help but agree. The patchwork of the wide Piccadilly Valley spread out before them, fields sown with vegetables for the Adelaide markets, before the land rose to the gum-studded heights of Mount Lofty. The sun would be going down soon, the shadows and the night-time chill would descend, but for now it was still bathing them in spring's promising warmth, and it felt good.

'So how do you enjoy working at the primary school?'

'I like it, though it's only part-time. But then I do a bit of snake catching as well, come summer—that's starting to pick up a bit, with the weather warming. Mmm,' he said, as he devoured the cookie. 'These are good.'

'There's more. Help yourself.'

'Seriously?'

'And there's a bag full to take home after if you like. I really appreciate you coming, especially on a Sunday.'

'Not a problem,' he said with a shrug. 'One day's much like any other. And it's not like I'm abandoning anyone at home to come here.' He said it all in such a matter-of-fact way that he wasn't inviting sympathy. He was just stating how it was.

Harry demolished a third cookie, before he pushed himself from the fallen tree trunk and tugged his earphones from around his neck. 'I should be getting back to work. I reckon the sooner this lump of tree is gone, the easier it will be to get your car up your driveway.'

There was no arguing with that logic. 'Can I give you a hand?' she found herself asking, as she tossed away the dregs of her coffee and collected the tray. 'You chop off the branches, I'll drag them clear of the driveway.'

He gave her a quick once-over, taking in the spotted skirt and blouse and sandals she'd worn to lunch today. 'Nah, you don't want to do that. I'll be right.'

Because the job would be finished quicker with two, and Beth didn't want him thinking her some princess who was afraid of hauling a few branches or working up a sweat, she said, 'I'll be right back.'

She was too, wearing boots with jeans and a checked long-sleeved shirt to keep her from getting scratched to pieces. He looked up at her return, nodded his approval and kept on working the chainsaw.

They worked side by side with him cutting and her clearing for the next two hours, until the tree had been reduced to a series of logs and the branches were stacked in two big piles alongside the driveway.

'Phew,' she said, arching her aching back. She turned to Harry. 'Fancy a beer?'

He smiled his Hagrid smile and this time Beth saw mischief in it. 'I thought you'd never ask.'

A few minutes later, they were sitting on her verandah, looking out over the valley as they sipped from their longnecks.

'I'll be back during the week to tidy up all the bits,' Harry said.

'You don't have to do that,' she said.

'A job worth doing ...' he started.

'I'll pay you for your time.'

'No, like I said, I'm repaying Dan a favour. Though, I'd happily settle for another batch of those cookies.' There was a twinkle in his eye that made her smile.

'Deal,' she said.

Siena had her nose in one of her pony books and Taylor Swift singing on her iPod when Beth headed inside. 'Has he gone?'

'Yup,' she said from the kitchen, wondering what she'd been up to when Harry had arrived. Siena trailed in after her, sitting up on one of the stools under the breakfast bar Beth had had put in when she'd knocked out the wall between the kitchen and lounge room and turned her tiny two-bedroom cottage into something more open plan. 'He seems nice.'

'He does,' Beth said, the smell of chilli reminding her. Now she just needed a salad.

'You going to see him again?'

'I guess so. He's got a bit more work to do, cutting down the branches for kindling, that sort of thing. Should keep us going through winter, that's for sure.'

There was silence for a time as Beth checked the sauce she'd left simmering on low on the stove, and sniffed her approval. Perfect. She turned to see Siena staring at her. 'What?'

'That's it?'

'Yep.'

'Why? You said you liked him.'

Beth poked out her tongue. 'No, I didn't, cheeky. You said he seemed nice and I agreed with you.'

Siena rolled her eyes. 'So, what's the problem?'

'There is no problem. Harry's coming to do some work finishing off the tree. End of story. Okay?'

'But, Mu-um, don't you want to have a boyfriend?'

Beth was suddenly struck by inspiration and ducked into the pantry, seizing on a packet of corn chips and holding it up for inspection. Corn chips were a rare treat. 'I think, given what a special day it is, we should do the whole nachos thing, what do you reckon?'

Siena groaned. 'You're hopeless, Mum,' before she stomped away and turned Taylor up till the walls shook. Beth put the chips on the bench and sighed, before turning to the fridge, fishing out the cheese, tomatoes and lettuce.

Siena was right, she was hopeless. And, as it turned out, she did like Harry, and that had surprised her. Although not how Siena wanted, but in a companionable kind of way. They'd fallen quickly into a routine today and worked together well, and if the mischief in his eyes lent a spark to his grizzled face, why shouldn't she notice it and like that, too?

But that was all it was, whatever fantasies Siena was spinning in her head. Being flower girl at Dan and Lucy's wedding clearly had a lot to answer for. The girl was becoming an incurable romantic.

Beth sliced tomatoes, grated cheese and shredded lettuce. She could understand it of course. She'd been a romantic herself once. How could she not with an Italian boyfriend who'd exuded romance from his every pore.

God, was it really more than ten years? She could still remember Joe being in her life like it was yesterday. But how could she not, when every time Siena looked at her, she could see Joe in her eyes?

Beth sniffed as she gave the chilli another stir. They'd have been an old married couple by now. And there would have been more kids. Probably another one or two to keep Siena company, and Joe would be teaching them how to ride minibikes and taking them camping up the river.

They'd be a family.

And Siena thought she should date and find someone else to take the place of her father? Nobody could replace Joe. Nobody ever would. Not after what she'd done.

Siena wandered back into the kitchen, took one look at her mother and said, 'Are you crying?'

'Bloody chilli,' Beth lied, swiping at her cheeks. 'Gets me every time.'

15

Hannah

'Oh, you're back,' the vet nurse said, looking up as Hannah walked through the door after a house call. 'How's Boo?'

'Poor little thing,' said Hannah, joining Verity in the small office space to write up a few notes about the small Maltese terrier, before checking the appointment book to see what tomorrow had in store. Saturdays were always busy. 'I don't know what she ate, but it didn't agree with her. Fingers crossed, she's on the mend.'

'That's good. Mrs Jennings was in such a state. She'd be lost without Boo. Hey,' Verity said, picking up a scrap of paper, 'how do you pronounce this? Mind you, not sure I've spelled it right.'

Hannah peered over Verity's shoulder at the scrawled note with the botched name and felt a sizzle down her back all the way to her toes.

'I mean,' Verity continued, 'what kind of name is that for a kangaroo? Shinella?'

'It's pronounced Shance Ella. It's Irish, it means "second chance".' She looked up at the nurse, torn between fear and a secret thrill. 'Why did Declan call? Is something wrong?'

Verity screwed up her face. 'It was a bit weird, he was pretty vague. Asked for you, mentioned the joey might need a check-up. He didn't say it was urgent, so I didn't call you on your mobile, but I thought I should mention it.'

'Yeah, thanks, glad you did. He's not an experienced carer, I might drop in on the way home, see how the joey's going.'

'Probably a good idea,' said Verity, going back to her end-of-day accounts. 'I heard we lost one of the other joeys today, the little pinkie euro, so Jeanette has a vacancy, if you need to move it.'

'Oh, that's sad. She'll be gutted. I'll keep that in mind.' She reached for her bag and her keys. 'I'll get going.'

'See you tomorrow. Give my love to Mr Sexy Voice, won't you?'

'Who?'

'That Declan fellow with the joey. Got the sexiest accent over the phone, I'll give him that.'

'Really? I hadn't noticed.'

Declan didn't seem surprised at all to see Hannah. Just raised an eyebrow as he opened the door and ushered her in. 'How's the joey?' she said, wishing he'd given her a little more space at the door so she didn't have to brush quite so closely past him. Really, the man was infuriating.

'See for yourself,' he invited, pointing towards the stand where the joey's pouch hung.

'I will. There's a carer who lost an infant euro today. If you're having problems, I can hand it on.'

She heard his swift intake of air and imagined him bristling behind her. Good, she didn't want him thinking he was the one calling all the shots.

She lifted the pouch from the stand. 'How long since she had a feed?'

'About three hours.'

She nodded. The joey would be waking shortly anyway. She wouldn't be disturbing her too much, if she was feeling poorly. She sat down at the roughly hewn table with the pouch on her lap and peeled back the sides past the long legs pointing out until she could find its head. 'How are you going, sweetie?' she said, her hands gently traversing the infant's fur as she examined it.

But her eyes were bright and Hannah's seeking fingers were coming up blank so far. 'What seems to be the problem with her?' She turned and was surprised to find Declan at her shoulder. He crouched down alongside her chair and she could damn near smell the man's musky scent intermingled with the faint hint of coffee on his breath. Seriously beguiling. Seriously infuriating.

'Did I say she had a problem?'

Her hands stilled, her patience at breaking point. 'You called the surgery. You mentioned the joey might need an examination.'

'How else did you expect me to get you over here?'

She stroked the kangaroo, her massage an apology for waking it when there was no reason. 'There's nothing wrong with the joey, then? You got me out here under false pretences?'

'Not at all. It's actually me who's got the problem.' She felt the air shift as he spoke softly, his scent wrapping around her, and fought to ignore the impulse to lean closer. 'Because, for the life of me, I can't seem to get you out of my head.'

She swallowed. He looked so earnest, his dimples replaced by the furrowing between his eyebrows. 'I'm sorry, that's not something I can help you with.'

'No?' he said, putting his hand over hers where she stroked the joey, sending heat spiralling up her veins. 'But I need you to help me with it, because it's like this.' He took a breath as his eyes sought hers, storm-tossed blue eyes she could drown in. 'You see, I like you, Hannah. And I'd like the chance to know you better.'

She shook her head, unable to respond in any other way. She'd thrown herself into her work, purposely avoiding showing any interest in the opposite sex. She wasn't sure how to deal with it when it found her. So she turned to her usual defence.

'You're being ridiculous,' she snapped, finding a shred of armour plate to hammer back on, even if she couldn't do much about the faint tremor in her voice, or the fact that she'd made no attempt to pull her hand out from under the delicious warmth of his. 'I don't know what you're talking about.'

'No? Because I kind of got the impression you liked me, too.' He curled his hand around hers, and she had to swallow to keep her frantically beating heart from leaping right out of her chest. He coaxed her to her feet and wound his free hand around her neck to draw her closer, his eyes on her mouth. And then his lips met hers, a brush, a breath, before his arms held her close and his lips claimed hers.

Heat engulfed her, a sudden burst of heat that seemed to spring from some untapped well deep inside her, and it was all she could do to cling to him while his mouth made magic on hers. She'd never kissed a man before, not a real man. There'd been Ethan of course, who'd taken her to the Year Twelve formal, and who'd kissed her so hard his braces had cut her lip. Then sweet Sanjay in her first year of university, with whom she'd shared laughs and games of Canasta over cheap ciders at the uni bar, and who'd disappeared one summer holiday and came back married the next. And lastly there'd been James of the tall, dark looks, whom she'd fancied herself in love with—so much in love with—but in the end he'd been the biggest kid of them all.

Not one of them a real man. This kiss was different. Confident. Assured.

'There,' he said, putting her away from him. 'That wasn't so bad, was it?'

She was trembling, shaken, her cheeks burning up at the knowledge that he'd pulled out of the kiss before she'd been anywhere near ready to. Her tongue found her lips, tasting him. Liking it.

'Can we be friends?' he asked gently, putting his lips to her hair, breathing deeply of it before giving her space. 'Do I need to invent a reason to see you next time?'

Hannah's blood fizzed. She'd always been a good girl. Sensible. Apart from one major stuff-up, she'd been focused and on task, and who could blame her for one stuff-up when their world had been falling apart with their father's death and then the tragedy of losing Beth's fiancé not long afterwards?

She'd paid the price for that, and she'd go on paying the price forever. Was it any wonder she was cautious? But she was older and wiser than the vulnerable, hurting university student she'd been back then. And Declan was no teenager, either. Maybe it was time for her to rejoin the human race. God knows, she was twenty-nine years old. She'd gone without sex long enough not to want to try.

'If I kiss you again,' he said, as if sensing her wavering, 'will you run this time, or will you stay?'

And from a place she'd thought buried forever, Hannah found the courage and the boldness to smile. 'Stop talking and kiss me already.'

This was not normal, Hannah thought, as she sipped a glass of chardonnay from Declan's first-ever vintage in bed, while the naked man beside her fed a joey milk from a tiny bottle. She watched the pair of them gazing adoringly at each other, while he whispered soft words of encouragement to the animal, and outside the day slipped into night.

'How's the wine?' he asked.

'Good,' she said, and it was, the golden liquid dry but laden with fruit.

'You sound surprised.'

'Pleasantly surprised. If this is your first vintage, I think you might be onto something.'

'It's been my dream,' he said, as he eased the joey's mouth from the empty bottle. 'I'm going to have a little cellar door, get people up here to appreciate the beauty of the area and sell direct to customers.'

An expensive dream, Hannah couldn't help but think, and asked, 'What did you do before?'

Declan confidently and gently toileted the infant kangaroo, and Hannah watched on, impressed with how quickly he'd come to terms with being an adoptive mother to an orphaned joey. 'I bought and sold shares. Seems I've got a knack for it. I worked in Dublin with one of the big banks there before I was offered a job down here. 'Twas too good to miss, I thought, so we moved down and I threw myself into that.'

'But your wife didn't like it.'

He shook his head. 'To give her credit, she tried to make a fist of it. I think she imagined we were heading out on a holiday, and that things would slow down, but I was working stupid hours just like I'd been doing at home, and the writing was well and truly on the wall. And one day she decided she'd had enough and wanted out, and it took me a good couple of years to work out that maybe she had a point.' He shrugged. 'Not that she would have enjoyed it up here. The bush gave her the willies.' He rolled the joey into its pouch and slung it from the doorknob before washing up in the en suite. 'What about you?' he asked from the bathroom. 'Ever been married?'

'No.'

'Any significant others left in your wake?'

'Nope,' she said, suddenly feeling uncomfortable, hoping he wouldn't press further and wishing for a change of subject.

'Their loss,' he said, climbing back into bed and wrapping his arm around her shoulders. 'You won't be passing her on, will you?'

'Who?'

'Eile. Now that you know she's all right, there's no need to pass her on, right?'

She pretended to be shocked. 'Is that what this is about? Did you sleep with me as a bribe?'

'No, but that's not a bad idea. You reckon it might work?'

'No,' she said with a grin, 'but maybe we should give it another shot, just in case.'

'I like the way you think,' he said, as he pulled her into his arms, his lips descending on hers.

'It's been grand having you here,' he said, after they'd made love again and she was getting dressed. He watched her from the big bed, his arms crossed behind his head.

And Hannah smiled and decided that her new favourite word was 'grand'.

16

Sophie

Sophie was halfway across the city scanning the shelves of the seven-day pharmacy when someone asked if she needed help. She jumped, her heart in her throat, not expecting to hear a familiar voice so far from home. She looked up and sure enough, it was the mother of one of last year's final-year students looking right at her.

'Oh, it's you, Sophie,' the woman said, 'I didn't realise. What are you doing all the way down here on the flat?'

Sophie blinked, a kangaroo caught in the headlights of a much too brightly lit pharmacy. 'Oh, hi, Jenny, I was just—hey, I didn't know you worked here.'

'New job,' she said proudly, taking the bait. 'It's a bit of a drive from home in the hills, but it's great hours, and during the week I can drop Kristen off at high school on my way to work and she catches the school bus home. A Sunday shift like today is the bonus. Neat, huh?'

'Congratulations,' Sophie managed, wondering how far she'd have to go before she could find a pharmacy where she'd be anonymous. 'How's Kristen coping with high school?'

'She's settled in really well. Made some great friends.' Jenny looked over Sophie's shoulder and scanned the shelves stacked with feminine products behind her, frowning a little as she turned her attention back on Sophie. 'So, what can I help you with today?'

'I was just looking for some—nail-polish remover.'

'Oh. Then you're in the wrong aisle for a start.'

'I know,' Sophie said, shifting down the aisle a way and picking the first packet of tampons she could find. 'I just wanted to grab some of these while I was here.'

Jenny laughed. 'God, don't you wish you didn't need those for once?'

Sophie did her best to laugh along with her. *Actually, no ...*

By the time she got back to the unit she rented from her mum, she'd visited three different pharmacies across town before she'd finally had the courage to purchase what she'd gone looking for. She upended the bags on her bed and out spilled the nail-polish remover, multiple boxes of tampons, soft soap, ibuprofen, nail clippers, cotton buds, and three different shades of nail polish.

All useful stuff when it came down to it, not that she needed most of it right this minute. She dived for one of the boxes—because she'd bought two in case the first was faulty and she needed to do it again—and heart pumping, her fingers fumbled with the packaging, struggling to unfold the instructions, anticipation sending her thoughts into a hundred frenzied directions.

Fibroids, she'd talked herself into while consulting Dr Google. Or ovarian cysts even. Something innocent and out of the blue that explained why, despite cramping up a storm for the best part of a week, her period still hadn't put in an appearance. Something that might be annoying, without being life-shattering.

Something that might mean she hadn't just wasted money on three boxes of tampons today.

But of course she hadn't because it wouldn't be positive. It couldn't. She'd been on the pill—she'd only missed one because being dumped had thrown her and she'd forgotten, but she'd only missed one—and Nick had used condoms.

No way could it be positive.

All today's little exercise was about was ruling out the option.

That was all.

'Fuck!'

Sophie stared down at the stick in horror. Two bright-pink lines screamed up at her. One line to be sure the test worked. The second to confirm pregnancy.

No. No. No. Not possible.

'Stupid, pathetic, useless test!'

She slammed the stick down on the bathroom cabinet and snatched up the instructions. She'd done something wrong. After all, she'd resorted to this test to rule out the pregnancy scenario, not to lock it in. There was no way she could be pregnant.

She re-read the instructions and was none the wiser. It was only a store-bought test, after all. It wasn't like it was a laboratory confirmation. And it was early—only three weeks since that night—maybe it was too early for the test to be conclusive. She reached for the second box.

Shaking now, her throat desert dry while her palms were damp, she crouched over the loo. Although she'd only just gone, she was going to squeeze enough out of her bladder if it killed her. Anything to prove that damned test wrong.

But when she pulled the test away and waited the required period, those two pink lines were screaming at her again. Screaming that she was pregnant.

The bottom fell out of Sophie's world in the same moment that hope died. Shock and fear bubbled up inside her into a tidal wave of panic that roiled and seethed and churned, until with hot tears coursing down her cheeks, she dropped to her knees beside the toilet bowl and let her gut speak for her.

17

Nick

'Are you going to say sorry today?'

'Hmm?' Nick was dropping Min at school on Monday morning, and had just handed over her backpack. While she liked being met outside her classroom after school, before school was all about playing with her friends, and he was turning his mind to what he had planned for the day. The neglected cherry orchard he'd bought less than a year ago from one of Dan's neighbours had taken more time than he'd had to nurse it into some kind of shape. Most of the trees had put on an encouraging show of blossom, which proved the quality of the root stock, but he still needed to keep an eye out for evidence of disease. Now that he was back to juggling apples, pears and cherries, he needed to head off any potential problems before they turned serious.

'Are you going to say sorry to Ms Faraday?'

Nick sighed. He'd had a week of his daughter banging on about apologising for 'being mean' to her teacher before she'd gone off and spent the next week with Penelope, leaving him in peace, and he was hoping that by the time she came back, she would have forgotten all about it. Apparently not.

'Well? Are you?'

He looked up at the school, where he guessed Sophie would already be inside preparing for the coming day's lessons. 'You really think I need to?'

'Yes.'

He cocked an eyebrow at his daughter. That was decisive.

'Penelope thinks you should apologise too.'

'Oh, is that right?' he said, thinking he'd never get used to his daughter calling her mother by her name.

Min shrugged her *Frozen* backpack over her shoulders. 'She says if you have a problem with her telling the school something, you should talk to her, not take it out on the teacher.'

The growl started low down in his throat. For as much as he didn't like his ex-wife, he liked her a whole lot less when she was right. He had taken his aggravation with his ex's high-handed behaviour out on Sophie, he knew it. What he'd been hoping was that the incident would slip silently into the past and be forgotten, just like the night he'd spent with her at the hotel. Forever consigned to history, never to be spoken of again.

But then he hadn't counted on Min. She was like a terrier when she wanted to be. No question where she'd got that from.

He heaved another sigh. Might as well get it over with. 'Yeah, Penelope's right. Come on, then, let's go.' Nick felt Min's hand slide into his before she practically dragged him up the small hill to the school.

'She's not there,' said Min, poking her head into the classroom. 'She must be in the office.' She looked up at him gravely. 'You will go and see her, won't you. You will say you're sorry.'

He nodded just as gravely and put one hand over his heart. 'On my honour.'

She left him then, after placing her backpack in the lockers and giving him a quick kiss before running off with her friends to play outside. Nick watched her go, wishing things could be different, that Min had a mum and a dad who loved each other so she didn't have to do this week-around shuffle, and marvelling at how resilient she was under the circumstances. It didn't seem normal to him, because he'd grown up in your typical family unit with a mum, a dad and a couple of siblings. But then, this was what Min had grown up with and he knew for a fact there was another half-dozen kids in school living with the same kind of switcheroo arrangements. It was all Min knew. It was her normal.

He waved hello to a couple of the mums and his neighbour, Amy Jennings, who was dropping off a grandee, but without making enough eye contact to invite conversation, and made for the office. There was nobody behind the counter and he could hear the principal, Mrs Innstairs, talking on the phone in her office. That's when he happened upon Sophie emerging from the staff bathroom, holding a bunch of tissues to her nose, her eyes glossy, her dark eyelashes clumped together. Hayfever, he figured, guessing she'd been sneezing. It could be a killer this time of year. She stopped when she saw him, blinked and made a sharp left, marching towards her classroom.

'Sophie,' he said, and her footsteps halted. He saw the rise and fall of her shoulders as she took a deep breath, before she turned slowly around to face him. 'We need to talk.'

A flash of panic filled her eyes—and he did a rethink on the hayfever diagnosis because they were eyes that looked more like she'd been crying—before she looked to the ceiling, almost like she was praying for divine intervention. Around them kids milled through the main doors, boisterous and full of early-morning energy, at complete odds to the woman standing before him. Gone was the retro fifties princess he'd fronted up to a couple of weeks ago. Today she was dressed simply in jeans with a long-sleeved t-shirt and canvas shoes, and looked so brittle she'd snap if she caught so much as a puff of wind.

'Is this a bad time?'

She glanced at her wristwatch, took a moment to deliberate before she shook her head, her lips glued tightly together. 'This way,' she said, steering him into the staffroom with its empty chairs and table. She closed the door and stood with her back to it, blocking out the sounds of a school morning so the hum of the refrigerator took centrestage. 'What do you want?'

There was a quaver in her voice that didn't belong, but that slid seamlessly together with her puffy eyes and washed-out face and the way she looked ready to bolt out that door the first moment she could. 'Are you all right?' he asked.

'I'm fine.'

'Only you don't look so good.'

She sniffed. 'Thanks for that. That makes me feel a whole lot better.'

'Something is wrong.'

'Nothing is wrong, okay? And I've got a class to take in less than five minutes. What did you want to see me about?'

Okay, so it was going to be like that. It was no more than he deserved, he figured, after the way he'd treated her the last time they'd met. 'I came to apologise.'

'Oh?' She looked like it was the last thing she'd expected. Maybe she had forgotten, or maybe she'd just assumed it was never going to happen and moved on. Whatever, he was here, and he was going to go through with it.

'Yes, I need to apologise for the way I treated you that afternoon in the corridor. I'm afraid I took the frustrations I have with Penelope's fixation on moulding Min into some kind of mini-Penelope out on you. I was rude and it was unfair of me to dump that on you. I'm sorry.'

She blinked, confusion replacing the fear he'd witnessed before in her eyes. 'That's all?'

He rewound the words he'd spoken in his mind, searching for what he'd missed and coming up blank. 'Isn't that enough? I mean, of course I'll do my best not to let it happen again.'

She put her hands to her cheeks and nodded. 'Yes, of course it's enough. Thank you. Apology accepted. And now, if you'll excuse me—'

'Sophie …' She paused, her hand primed on the doorhandle. 'Are you sure there's nothing wrong?'

'Nothing is wrong. Okay?' She was out the door and swallowed up by the sound of the siren and one hundred kids yabbering at once on their way into class.

18

Sophie

Everything was wrong, that was the problem, but Sophie told herself that if she thought about it long enough, she'd find an answer eventually. Or better still, if she fretted about it long enough, nature would take care of the problem. She'd read that an astonishing percentage of early pregnancies were lost in the first few weeks. Maybe that might happen in her case. She really wanted it to happen in her case, and then she felt guilty and horrible that she could even think such a thing.

She loved children, after all. That's why she'd become a teacher. She'd always imagined herself with a clutch of her own kids one day—she'd just imagined she'd find the right man and do the marriage thing first. It wasn't supposed to happen like this. It wasn't supposed to happen now.

She got to her class and clapped her hands, the signal for all her students to sit down in a circle at the front of the room, and waited for them and the late arrivals to settle down so she could begin the day's lessons.

Boldly coloured artwork hung from the ceilings, shaded in silhouettes of the class members' heads. Paintings of rainbows and bushland and the koalas that sat in the forks of the surrounding trees and delighted the children at recess and lunch. Everything bright and happy and completely at odds with the storm of turmoil going on in Sophie's head.

Because everything was wrong. God, she was all kinds of a mess. After last night's discovery, she should have taken a sickie to get used to the idea, but she hadn't wanted to stay at home and fret. But fretting was apparently all she was good for. And she'd been in such a state when she'd come out of the bathroom and seen Nick standing there, and never once suspected he'd come to apologise. She'd walked out that door, taken one look at Nick and felt a thunderbolt of panic that somehow he knew.

Madness.

She made it through the school newsletter without her voice breaking, listened while four children delivered their show-and-tell, and worked her way through her pile of flash cards, before it was time for silent reading while she listened to today's lot of readers one by one. Cameron Jones closed his reader and went back to his seat, her praise for his improvement in his reading puffing him up like the winner he was. Usually, she took delight in seeing her students learn and become more confident with their reading. Today, however, nothing could permeate the dark shroud of numbness blanketing her.

Min Pasquale was the last reader before recess. The child sat next to her and opened her folder, turning to page one. She read a page haltingly, stopping at words to sound them out, and turned the page, then she looked up wide-eyed at her teacher. So much like her mother—Penelope—Sophie thought, with her heart-shaped face and fair skin, but the dark hair must have come from Nick.

'Ms Faraday,' Min said, her little face creased with concern. 'Was my daddy mean to you again? Did he make you cry?'

Sophie broke every rule in the book and put her arm around the girl's shoulders and held on tight to her fragile composure. 'No,' she said with a smile she'd prised from somewhere deep inside. 'Your father and I had a nice chat. It was good of him to come and clear the air.'

'So why do you look so sad?'

'Do I?' she said, fighting against a sudden wave of despair. 'Oh, I've got a bit of a headache today, that's all. Actually, I might go take something for it. Will you excuse me a moment?'

She told the class to carry on with silent reading and that she'd be right back so no talking while she was gone, retrieved her phone from her bag and stepped into the corridor, pulling the door shut behind her. The corridor was empty, only a muffled hum coming from the other classrooms as her phone beeped into life. She pressed a number, praying that her sister was on late shift, or better still, a rostered day off. What had happened was too big for her to deal with on her own. If she didn't talk to someone about this soon, she was going to explode.

'Hey, sis,' Beth answered on the third ring. 'What's up?'

Sophie clung onto her sister's voice like a lifeline. Beth would understand. Beth more than anyone would understand. 'I really need to talk. Can we meet somewhere—alone?'

Visiting Beth at her cottage usually made Sophie feel good, the bush, the views over Piccadilly Valley and Beth's colourful art-works all conspiring to engender a happy mood. Not today, when her gut churned with fear and panic.

Sophie bypassed the front door and headed straight out back to the studio. Beth waved when she looked up and saw her coming. 'Hey,' she called, 'come right in. I'm just in the middle of something.'

She stepped inside the old timber garage that had been converted into the studio. Beth hunkered over whatever she was working on atop the central bench, while Madeleine Peyroux's smooth voice spun magic sounds from an iPod dock.

It was all so calm and serene and in stark contrast to the turmoil of her panicked thoughts, and Sophie felt like a tangle of steel wool scraping its way out of a cloud.

'What are you making?' she said, leaning over, trying to make sense of it.

'Something for Dan and Lucy for Christmas,' Beth said, without looking up. 'Inspiration hit me in the middle of the night and I had to come play. It's such awesome news about the baby, isn't it? There's nothing like baby news to put a smile on your face.'

'Oh yeah,' she said tightly. 'Nothing at all like baby news.' Other than news of her period miraculously appearing, that is.

Whatever she'd loaded in her voice alerted her sister. She looked up, a quizzical expression on her face. 'What did you need to talk—' Her eyes opened wide. 'God, Sophie, you look like shit. What's wrong?'

'Where's Siena?' Sophie said, looking around, the comment about her appearance so unsurprising it slid straight off. 'She's not home, is she?'

'I told you, she's at a friend's place till dinner. It's okay, we're alone. Now, are you going to tell me what's going on? You seemed fine the other week at Nan and Pop's.' She looked closer into Sophie's face as she put an arm around her shoulders. 'Have you been crying?'

Sophie sniffed and started blinking, wiping the moisture away with her fingers. 'Oh God, don't get me started.'

'Oh no, wait, wait a minute,' Beth said, steering her backwards towards the sofa, plopping her down before sitting alongside her and passing her a box of tissues. 'What's happened?'

'I can't stop crying today,' she said, swiping at the tissues. 'I mean, I try to, but they just keep on coming. I just don't know what to do.'

'There has to be a reason for it.'

Sophie twisted the tissues into pretzels. 'Did you cry a lot,' she asked, 'when you found out you were expecting Siena?'

'No. But God, I couldn't stand the smell of—' Her sister halted mid-sentence. 'Oooh, back up a minute, sister, what are you saying? Surely you're not ...? Are you?'

Sophie turned her eyes beseechingly to Beth. 'I'm not sure. How reliable are those home-test kits, do you know? I mean, it says they're reliable on the packet, but they would say that, wouldn't they, or nobody would buy them.'

Beth nodded slowly. 'And you got a positive result?'

'Yeah. Two, actually, because I thought the first one must be faulty.'

'Oh.'

'That's bad, isn't it?'

'Well, it probably depends on your point of view and your circumstances whether you think it's good or bad, but I think you can safely assume you're pregnant.'

And the floodgates opened again and it felt to Sophie that she'd never stop crying, except this time they weren't just tears of despair but also mixed with tears of relief that she could tell someone, the burden of a secret too big to deal with alone finally shared.

'Bloody Norah,' Beth said, wrapping her arms around Sophie. 'It's turning into baby season in the Faraday family. First Lucy and now you.'

Sophie sniffed. 'But I didn't *mean* to get pregnant.'

'I hope that means you used some kind of protection.'

'Of course! We had condoms and I was still on the pill. Kind of.'

'You can't "kind of" be on the pill. It's like you can't be a little bit pregnant. You either are or you aren't.'

'I may have forgotten to take one ...'

'Good grief,' Beth said, rubbing her back. 'How do you think Jason will take it—after all that's happened, I mean?'

'It's not his.'

Beth's hands stopped for a moment and Sophie could just about hear the questions spinning around in her sister's head. 'You're sure of that?'

'It's been weeks since Jason and I were together, and I had my period since ...' She shook her head, twisting the tissues in her hands. 'It can't be his.'

'Well, that's a relief. The news is getting better already.'

Sophie attempted a laugh, but it came out sounding like a hiccup instead.

'So, who is the father?'

'What does that matter? He's not the one people are going to look at and whisper about behind his back.'

'Times have changed, Soph. Unplanned pregnancy doesn't have the baggage it once did.'

She sniffed. 'Maybe not for the rest of the planet. But I'm a school teacher. Parents expect me to be a good influence on their kids. They don't want to have to answer awkward questions about why Ms Faraday suddenly looks like a watermelon. They'd prefer to believe I don't know what sex is.'

'Come on, it's not that bad.'

'I don't know about that.' She chewed her bottom lip, thinking about some of the parent–teacher nights she'd had and knowing that not all of her parents were as open-minded as Beth. And if it got out in their tiny community that it was Nick who was the father … Oh no, that could never get out. 'Oh, Beth. What am I going to do?'

Beth hugged her close. 'I can't answer that, but there is one thing I can tell you.' She lifted Sophie's head from her shoulder with both hands and swiped back the damp hair that had stuck to her face. 'Whatever happens, you're going to get through this. You're going to be okay.'

Sophie sniffed. 'You mean it?'

'Hey, I've been there. I know it. Seriously, there are worse things in life than having a baby. I mean, didn't you always want to have kids?'

'Sure, but not yet! I was planning on doing the romance and marriage thing first.'

'What's that line in the song, about life happening when you're busy making other plans?' Beth squeezed Sophie and let her go long enough to make her a pot of tea and grab a packet of chocolate biscuits she'd hidden from Siena. Then she was back to hug her some more, and Sophie was grateful for the tea and biscuits and the comfort. Whatever happened from now on, at least she knew she wasn't alone.

'Were you frightened?' Sophie asked a little while later, her head on her sister's shoulder as the tea and comfort and demolishing three Tim Tams in a row worked on soothing her fractured psyche. 'You know, when you found out about Siena? I can't remember.'

'What do you think? I was eighteen years old and I was shit-scared. Joe and I both were, for that matter, and the last thing anyone wanted was to suck you into all of that. I didn't even confide in Hannah until I'd told Mum. But Joe and I were in love and planning on getting married one day, and we figured it just brought our plans forward a little. Still, it was terrifying the day we faced up to Mum and Nan and Pop to give them the news.'

'God, I can't imagine.' Sophie was almost seven years older than Beth had been back then, and even now the prospect of having to front up and admit she was pregnant was terrifying.

'But then once Mum got over the shock, she was one hundred per cent supportive. Nan and Pop too. I think after losing Dad not long before, everyone was happy to focus on the future. And of course, they all loved Joe. Everyone loved Joe ...'

Beth's voice trailed off and Sophie knew she was thinking of all that she had lost when Joe's motorbike had hit black ice on the road two months before Siena was born. That bit, she had no trouble remembering. 'Do you still miss him?' she asked.

'Every day,' her sister said on a wistful sigh. 'Every bloody day and every bloody night, for that matter. I miss him and I curse him for leaving me like he did, and I don't think I'll ever stop loving him. But I have Siena, and she's Joe's gift to me, and she's a pretty damned special gift if I do say so myself.'

'She's awesome.'

'That she is,' she said, shaking her head as if ridding herself of sorrowful thoughts. 'Anyway, that's all history. You need to work out what you're going to do. You have choices, you know that? It's not like the olden days when there were none. I mean, I would never have gone down that road, given I loved Joe so much, but maybe it's something you need to think about.'

Sophie blinked. 'You mean abortion.'

'It's an option.'

Sophie exhaled a long breath. Her thoughts hadn't got that far yet. She was still at the stage of hoping for a miracle. 'I read that a lot of early pregnancies take care of themselves. I was kind of hoping ...' She licked her lips. 'Only then I felt bad for wishing it away. I mean, Lucy's miscarriage really shook her up, didn't it, and there was me wishing for the same.'

'Welcome to mother guilt,' her sister said with an ironic laugh. 'It kicks in early and it'll never let go. But never try to compare your circumstances to anyone else's, and believe me, you wouldn't be the first woman to wish her little problem would just vanish. I can one hundred and ten per cent guarantee you won't be the last. Just don't go pinning your hopes on that eventuality because there are plenty more pregnancies that go the distance.'

'Great,' she said, 'just great.'

'You know,' Beth said, reaching for the pot to top up their tea. 'I know you don't want to tell me who the father is, and that's fine, but sooner or later, if you decide to keep this baby, you're going to have to tell him.'

Sophie stiffened. That was another place she hadn't wanted her thoughts to go. Especially when she thought about her meeting today with Nick, about how uncomfortable it had been already, even without confessing their one night together had ended with consequences. She swallowed. 'How long before I need to tell him? I mean, if it doesn't take care of itself.'

'That's a tough one. He's the father, so he has a right to know this has happened. Besides, sooner or later he's going to be able to tell you're having somebody's baby and he's bound to wonder, so you might want to give him a heads-up before that happens.'

'What if he doesn't want to know?'

'That's his problem. Maybe it'll teach him to keep his dick in his pants.'

'Beth!'

'Hey, that's what got you into this mess! Anyway, you need to tell him, in case you need help with medical expenses and the costs of raising his child, should you go down that route. You could be looking at twenty years of child-raising expenses, after all.'

Sophie's head spun. She was little more than three weeks out from conception with another eight months to go before the baby was even born—and Beth was talking twenty years of expenses after that.

And they said a puppy was for life.

'I don't know if I can do this,' she whispered, her tears drying up, leaving her bereft and empty and floundering like a fish on the beach searching for rescue. 'This wasn't the way it was supposed to happen. I don't think I'm ready.'

Beth covered Sophie's hand with her own. 'Hey, you don't have to decide today, you know. There's no rush. Maybe you should talk to someone—a professional at the Pregnancy Advisory Centre— maybe that might help you work through the issues and help you decide.'

Sophie nodded, staring straight ahead through eyes that couldn't see beyond the banner-sized twenty-year sentence in the forefront of her mind. Because right now, it felt like a sentence. It felt like her life had been hijacked while she hadn't been looking. 'Yeah. That sounds good.' She turned her eyes up to her sister's then. 'Would you come with me, Beth? I don't know if I can do this alone.'

Beth squeezed Sophie's shoulders and smiled. 'Of course I will.'

19

Nick

Nick served up the spaghetti bolognaise while Min found the grated parmesan in the fridge and jumped onto her chair. He'd never call himself a chef, but he had learned something over the years, especially once Penelope had walked out and he'd had to pay more attention to his mamma's recipes, and he liked to think his bolognaise was the real deal. It was Min's favourite, too.

'Eat up,' he said, 'and then we can get stuck into your reader before bath time.'

'I'm bored of that one,' she said, sprinkling on the cheese and sucking a forkful of saucy pasta into her mouth, the tails of her spaghetti slapping wetly against her cheeks.

'Why are you bored with it? Didn't you get a new one today?' Lord knows they'd spent hours on Sunday night hammering out each and every word until he'd thought she had it down pat.

'Ms Faraday had to go before I finished reading and then the siren went and it was recess and then we had library and I didn't get a new reader.'

Nick was still hung up on the 'Ms Faraday had to go'. 'Why did Ms Faraday have to go?'

'She said she had a headache,' Min said between mouthfuls, 'except she looked like she'd been crying.'

Nick thought back to their encounter this morning. He'd worked out it was something more than hayfever that was bothering her. But she hadn't wanted to talk about it and he hadn't hung around long enough when he'd picked up Min, to see how she was faring at the end of the day. He'd figured he'd made his peace and she'd accepted his apology. It wasn't like she'd wanted him inquiring about her welfare, anyway. Then again, it wasn't like she'd wanted anything to do with him since that night—but that was a good thing, wasn't it? 'Maybe it was a really bad headache.'

'Maybe. She said it wasn't you that made her cry.'

'Oh? And why would she say that?'

'Because I asked if you'd been mean to her again.'

Nick put his fork down. 'I might have snapped a bit at our last meeting ...' He caught Min's wide-eyed accusation, and amended that to, 'So I did snap at Ms Faraday, but that was an exception. I'm not in the habit of being mean to people, Min.'

She shrugged her six-year-old shoulders. 'I know. I was just checking. Just in case you needed to say sorry again.'

He grunted, picked up his fork and stabbed it into his spaghetti. Nobody said he couldn't be mean to that. 'So I'm off the hook, then? No other intervention required?'

'Inter-what?'

'Doesn't matter. Eat your dinner. And then, after the dishes, you can read your boring book to me.'

'Da-ad.'

'Yeah, I know. But that's what you get for thinking I upset your teacher.' Because Min was completely out of order. Whatever was bothering Sophie Faraday had nothing to do with him.

Nothing at all.

20

Hannah

Pop's lawnmower stood abandoned on the back lawn, a rough strip carved behind it, when Hannah dropped by lunchtime Friday. She found Pop out in his shed and muttering to himself while he rummaged around in his toolbox. 'Hey, Pop,' she said, giving him a quick hug around the shoulders and a peck on the cheek. 'Where's Nan? I was hoping to pick up some eggs.' She didn't cook a lot, but she was planning a chocolate cake for Declan, who was turning out to be a man with voracious appetites, in and out of bed. She figured the least she could do was supply him with a few calories.

He shrugged. 'She was inside mucking around in the laundry, when I came outside.'

'She's not there now. I couldn't find her anywhere.'

'Well, don't ask me what she gets up to when I'm not looking,' he said, gnarled fingers burrowing through a lifetime's collection of bits and pieces. 'The woman's a law unto herself, that one. Ah,' he said, frowning as he pulled out a spanner. 'I reckon this is the one. Blades are too bloody low, wouldn't you know it?'

'I better go look for Nan,' Hannah said.

'You do that, girlie,' said Pop, wandering back towards the lawn-mower. 'And tell her someone out here would kill for that cup of tea she promised me. My stomach thinks me throat's been cut.'

Hannah headed back inside, feeling a bit concerned, and it wasn't just that nobody should be able to just open the front door and walk through the house unchallenged. Nan and Pop weren't getting any younger. Summertown was hardly the crime capital of the world, but they'd be an easy target for any passing opportunist.

The fact that Nan was nowhere to be found was more troubling. 'Nan,' she called, when she got inside. No answer. She switched on the kettle—at least she could get Pop a cup of tea—and checked the house again. It didn't take long. It wasn't a big house.

Hannah leaned on the kitchen cupboards, chewing the inside of her lip while the kettle boiled. There was no need to panic, she'd probably just gone to the post office to collect the mail. Still, she might have said something to Pop.

She was just pulling the tea bag from the mug when the front screen door slammed and her nan appeared, still wearing her dressing gown and slippers although it was almost one.

'Hello, Hannah. What brings you here?'

'Where've you been in your pyjamas?' Hannah demanded. Surely she didn't go to the post office like that? 'I couldn't find you anywhere. Pop said he didn't know.'

'Well, no need to call in Inspector Barnaby.' She chuckled. 'I took half a dozen eggs to dear old Maggie Jones across the road.' She plonked herself down on a dining chair and looked at the cup of tea steaming on the bench. 'Is that for me, you darling girl? I'm gasping for a cuppa.'

'Sure,' Hannah said, relieved, passing over the cup and reaching for another mug to make one for Pop.

'Ooh,' said Nan, when Hannah came in from outside. 'We got a postcard from your mother. Where is it now?' She used her hands to push herself up from the table, and her knobbly fingers scanned the cards stuck by magnets to the fridge until she found one of some ancient ruins with a mountain rising behind. 'This one.' She prised it from under the magnets. 'Wendy and Dirk had a lovely weekend in Rome and they spent a day visiting Pompeii, imagine that.' She clucked her tongue as she handed the card over for Hannah to read. 'The plaster's off and she said her leg's holding up very well. She even managed to hobble nearly all the way around by herself.'

'That's good,' Hannah said, thinking it was about time she skyped her mother again. She'd been a bit distracted lately. And then she thought about why and remembered the eggs. 'Oh, I brought you back some egg cartons. Do you have any spare I could take?'

'Dozens. The girls have been busy lately.' But when she pulled open the fridge, she looked confused. 'Well that's odd,' the older woman said, rummaging around the contents of the fridge.

'What is?'

'I thought I had dozens, but all I could find were these.' She stood up, a stack of empty cartons in her hand. 'I was looking for some cartons, though, I was running short.'

'Don't worry, Nan, I have to go to the shops anyway.' She swiped up the empty cartons she'd brought together with the ones from the fridge. 'I'll put these in the cupboard, then I'd better get going.'

Nan was still standing by the fridge, looking confused. 'Are you all right, Nan?' Hannah asked, feeling the flutters of concern again.

'Oh, right as rain,' she said, going to fill up the kettle. 'Now, I promised to make Clarry a cup of tea.'

Hannah rolled her eyes and headed for the laundry. There was a basket of dirty washing on the floor by the cupboard and another basket of what looked like clean washing on the bench. She shook her head as she tipped the dirty washing into the machine. It was getting time her grandparents got some help in. She pulled open the cupboard only to be confronted by a wall of egg cartons. And there, in the midst of it all, were perched half a dozen closed cartons full of eggs.

'I found your eggs,' she said, as she carried them back to the kitchen. 'They were in the cupboard.'

Nan just shook her head and gave a little-girl laugh. 'Well, how on earth did they get there?'

$\sim$

'So you think she's okay?' Hannah asked Beth, while the scent of baking chocolate filled the air in her tiny flat. She'd recounted her visit to their grandparents' house, and the niggling concerns she had about Nan.

'She's eighty-one,' said Beth, sounding tired. 'She's getting forgetful, that's all. They all do. God, I forget half of what I'm supposed to do all the time.'

'But wandering around the neighbourhood in her dressing gown?'

'I'd give my eye teeth to waft around in my pyjamas all day. Wouldn't you?'

Hannah had to admit, the idea had some appeal. 'Sophie hasn't said anything to you?'

There was a pause at the end of the line. 'About what?'

'About Nan,' said Hannah, wishing her sister would keep up. 'What else?'

'Oh, no. Nothing.'

The timer on the oven beeped. 'Okay, then,' Hannah said, checking the cake through the oven door and reaching for a skewer and her oven mitts. 'But if you do notice anything, it might be worthwhile someone taking her to the doctor to get her properly checked out.'

Another pause. 'You mean I should, I take it.'

'I just meant somebody should. And you work shifts so …'

'No, if you think there's a problem and you want Nan checked out, *you* organise it. I've taken on two extra shifts and I'm slammed next week. I haven't got time to fart.'

Hannah sniffed. 'You can do two things at once, you know.'

'Try doing five or six. Let me know what you decide,' and Beth was gone.

'I was only asking,' Hannah muttered, as she pulled the cake from the oven to test it before letting it rest for ten minutes. She took herself off to get changed, still cranky with her sister's tone when all she was doing was looking out for their nan. But grumping over her sister could wait. Right now, there was a cake to deliver to a man with a very big bed.

21

Sophie

'I liked her,' Beth said, as she walked Sophie from the counselling session outside and into the late October afternoon, heading for her car.

'Me too.' Sophie had spent the last few days panicking, and gone into the Friday-afternoon session with her sister a bundle of nerves, her brain still a tangle looking for a resolution, but right away the counsellor had put her at ease. She'd been warm and non-judgemental, and she hadn't tried to influence her or Beth. 'At least it's clarified what my options are and how to go about the two difficult ones. All I have to do now is work out which way I want to go.' She shrugged. 'Piece of cake, really.'

Beth threw a soft smile her way. 'Nobody said it was going to be easy.' The car beeped as she hit the remote. 'Do you have a feel yet for which way you want to go?'

Her hand on the passenger-door handle, Sophie said across the car roof, 'I'm still trying to process it all. If I have the baby and keep it, it's going to turn my world upside down. I'll have to tell the father of course, and everyone else is going to find out about a one-night stand that went wrong. But if I go that way, I'll just have to pull up my big-girl panties and deal with it.' She opened the car door and climbed inside.

'Sounds like a fair assessment of option number one,' said Beth, sliding in behind the steering wheel.

'And then, if I have the baby with the intention of putting it up for adoption, I'm still going to have to tell the father, and everyone else is going to know anyway, and when it all comes down to it, I don't know that I could go through an entire pregnancy only to give the baby away. It would be too real then, too hard.' She put her hands low over her belly. Already, this pregnancy was becoming more real. Talking with the counsellor, acknowledging the fact that she was pregnant, discussing the possibility that inside eight months she could have a baby, that she would be a mother—how could it be any more real, unless it was when her waistline disappeared under a bump? 'It would be better—well, it would be easier not to get that far if I'm going to give the baby up.' She sucked in a breath. 'Which is where the abortion option comes in, I guess. Nobody need ever know. Nobody but me and you. And it neatly takes care of the problem, except ...'

'Except what?'

'Except it's the timing that's the problem, not the actual baby,' Sophie said. 'Along with the whole order of things, I mean. It's not how I planned it to happen.'

'Yes,' Beth said, taking advantage of a break in the traffic to pull out of the car park. 'I get that.'

Sophie realised what she'd said. 'Oh, I'm sorry, Beth. It's just, you never think this stuff is going to happen to you, and when it does, it blindsides you.'

Her older sister nodded with the wisdom of one who'd been there before. 'That's definitely one word for it.'

Sophie looked out at the passing parade of industrial buildings along the busy road before she turned misty eyes to her sister. 'And it's tempting to think I can make it go away, but I don't know if I can justify it, Beth. I mean, an unplanned pregnancy is inconvenient and life-changing, sure, but it's not like it's life-threatening. And I've got a good job and I can take leave and go back to work. And I get what you said about supporting a child, but it's not like I can't afford to have a baby. And then I can't help thinking it's not the baby's fault. It didn't ask to be conceived.'

'Mother guilt,' Beth said, as she deftly changed lanes around a parked bus. 'I did warn you.'

'I know you did, but it's more than that. Because I look at Siena and I see a child who was unplanned but who is all kinds of wonderful, and I think maybe, just maybe, she might never have been given a chance. And what a tragedy that would have been.'

Beth swiped a tissue from the box in the car, blinking rapidly. 'Jeepers, Soph, you'll have me started next. I told you abortion was never an option for me. This is your decision. You have to choose what's right for you.'

'I know, but it's so hard to choose. I can't do nothing and I can't go back. I can't just undo being pregnant. Even if I did have an abortion, I don't think I'd be able to forget. I don't think I could pretend it never happened.' Sophie shook her head. 'It just seems that no matter what I decide, it's not straightforward.'

Beth nodded. 'That's the trouble with choices. They come with consequences.'

Sophie blinked. Wasn't that the truth?

She sat back in her seat as Beth weaved her way through the busy city traffic and towards the foothills fringing the suburbs, where her unit was. The hills were starting to brown off, losing their green winter coat under the dry sunny skies. Soon it would be summer and baking hot, followed by the colours of autumn. Her hands rested on her tummy. Hers would be a winter baby if she went ahead with the pregnancy. The days would be cold, the hills shrouded in fog.

Her baby.

Would it have Nick's olive skin and dark hair, or would the baby be fairer, more a mix of the two of them?

If she decided to have a termination, she would never know. Would she ever stop wondering then? Would she ever stop asking, what if?

She turned to her sister. 'What would you do?'

'You know what I did. But my circumstances were different.'

'But if you were me?'

'I honestly don't know, Sophie. I can't answer that because I'm not you.'

'But you coped. You're a single mother—a good one.'

Beth shook her head. 'I wouldn't wish single motherhood on anyone. It's hard, Sophie. It's hard and exhausting and there's nobody else to lean on when you get tired, nobody else to get up for a crying baby two or three times a night or to help pay the mortgage or buy the groceries.'

'But you've got Siena. She's worth it, right?'

Beth pulled up at a red light and looked over at her. 'Yeah. Of course she's worth it. But it's not easy, and if you're thinking about going ahead with this pregnancy as a single mum, you need to know that it's going to be the hardest thing you've ever done.'

Sophie took a deep breath, the advice the counsellor had given her slotting into place around her own needs and thoughts, finding a fit she never thought would be there. 'Yeah. I kind of figured that.'

'Good.'

'I'm going to have it, Beth.'

Her sister's head snapped around. 'What?'

'I'm keeping the baby.'

'What? Are you sure? Look, you don't have to decide today.'

'No. I've decided. Let's face it, I'm hopeless at finding a man who's going to hang around long term, so why am I waiting for the impossible? I'm keeping the baby.'

A horn tooted behind them, and then another. 'Bugger,' said Beth, taking off when she realised the lights were green. 'Sorry,' she said, with a wave to the cars behind, before she pulled over on the side of the road and turned towards Sophie, her expression disbelieving. 'Are you sure about this? I mean, really sure?'

For the first time Sophie felt light, the decision made removing a smothering weight from her shoulders. She nodded. 'I am. I've decided to have this baby, Beth. I hope you don't mind.'

Her sister pulled her into her arms and hugged her.

'How could I mind, you daft woman? It's a huge decision, but you've done it. Wait till everyone finds out there's going to be another Faraday baby!'

'Don't tell anyone yet, please, Beth, not even Han. I want to do what the counsellor suggested if I decided to go ahead with the pregnancy—I'm going to have my seven-week scan next week and make sure everything's okay before I break the news to anyone else.' Her heart was tripping over itself at the prospect, but she knew there was somebody else who deserved to be told. 'And I want to tell the father first. I think that's only fair.'

Beth smiled approvingly as she squeezed Sophie. 'Sounds like a plan.'

22

Beth

Beth pulled up in her driveway to find Harry there before her, busy converting another mound of branches into a neat stack of kindling ready for next winter's fires. Arriving home to find Harry had been tackling the fallen tree remains was starting to become a habit, and Beth wasn't sure whether to be grateful or annoyed. What was the man playing at? Nobody could be that nice.

'You should ask him in for dinner,' said Siena unhelpfully from the back seat. 'I bet he loves chicken and chips.'

Harry looked up then and gave them a wave and a smile, before putting his head down again, the chainsaw reducing the branches into neat, thirty-centimetre lengths. Okay, so maybe Harry was actually that nice.

'I'm going to have to start putting you on the payroll,' she told him as she climbed out of the car.

He grinned at that. 'Just being neighbourly,' he said. 'Nice to have a bit of time to help people out.'

'I appreciate it,' she said, the beguiling scent from the bag of chicken and chips in her hand reminding her of Siena's idea. 'Hey, I picked up a chook on the way up the hill. How about you stay for dinner—unless you've got plans, I mean?'

Harry's eyes twinkled in appreciation. 'That's very hospitable of you.'

'No trouble. Siena and I are just going to rustle up a quick salad. Come in and wash up when you're ready.'

Which is how the three of them came to be sitting around Beth's small dining table ten minutes later, feasting on chicken and chips. And even though Beth could see from the way Harry demolished what was left of the chicken that her plans for leftover chicken sandwiches the next day would have to change, she didn't mind a bit. Not after the work the man had done for her. He'd saved her hours of time that she'd much rather spend out in her studio than cutting up a fallen tree.

When Siena turned on the television to watch a rerun of *Master-Chef* and Harry surprised them both by saying it was his favourite program, it would have been rude to expect him to leave right then. So, they all ended up watching an hour of television together. Even Beth sat down for the program, rather than take herself out to do an hour's work in her studio—because even though Harry seemed a nice bloke, she'd hardly be a responsible parent leaving any man with her child. And despite Beth not understanding the details of how the show actually worked, it turned out being enormous fun listening to Harry and Siena encouraging their favourite contestants through the challenges.

She'd rarely seen her daughter more animated. It made Siena's night to have someone to watch her favourite program with, and Beth felt a sudden stab of guilt that she'd had to grow up an only child with a parent who liked to hole herself up in her studio to think. Mother guilt again, she recognised; it had a lot to answer for, because no single parent could be expected to spend every waking moment devoted to their child. Her mosaics were her outlet and her sanity. But still, it was so unfair for Siena that she had nobody else to share things with.

And so, when the final credits of the show rolled, Beth found herself asking Harry to drop in next week for dinner and another episode. Because if he could be neighbourly, she could too.

23

Sophie

If there was one advantage of being a school teacher, Sophie figured, it was knowing when kids doing fifty-fifty shared parental arrangements were with one parent so you had a decent chance of catching the other one alone.

Not that it stopped your palms sweating on the steering wheel any. Nick's simple stone cottage looked welcoming enough as she slowed, with its central door, a window either side and a veran-dah wrapping around the old place. Probably the only kind of welcome she was going to get today, given the bombshell she was about to drop. But she'd put it off long enough and it was time. Last week's seven-week scan had confirmed it. A viable pregnancy. She'd actually felt relief when they'd told her. That was a turn-up after wishing it away. She'd been glad of a couple of days to absorb it.

But now, Min was spending the week at Penelope's and there were no excuses not to tell Nick.

She sucked in a breath. Eight weeks. More than halfway through her first trimester and her body was doing all the things the online pregnancy advice forums said it should be doing. Her breasts were undeniably tender and the smell of her morning coffee left her feeling queasy. Sophie had a feeling this baby had taken control of her body and wasn't budging anytime soon.

She pulled up in Nick's driveway behind his ute and took a deep breath as she looked up at the house. He was home. Might as well get this over with.

Before she got there, the front door was flung open and Nick burst out, a bundle of basket and fur in his arms. He stopped and frowned when he saw her, a flash of panic in his eyes. 'Sophie? What's wrong with Min?'

'Nothing,' she said, 'Min's fine.'

The mound of fur in the basket stirred and gave a plaintive mewl and Nick sprang back into action. 'Sorry, I've got to get to the vet. Bloody cat's been bitten by a snake.'

'Not Fat Cat?' Sophie had never met the feline, but she'd heard plenty of stories about him from Min during show-and-tell and seen his likeness in Min's oversized drawings. From the size of the bundle in the basket, Min hadn't been exaggerating.

'Yeah, Min'll kill me if he dies. He's not supposed to be outside.'

The mountain of cat writhed in its basket. 'Oh God, can I help?' She looked back at her car blocking his. 'I'll move my car.'

He nodded and said thanks before taking a look at his tyres, one of which was flat. 'Bloody hell, no time to change that, now. Sorry, we'll have to take yours.'

She pulled open the passenger door for him, but Nick had other ideas. 'You take Fat Cat. I'll drive.'

And before she knew it, Sophie was sitting in the passenger seat of her tiny Mazda 2 with a lapful of the fattest, hairiest cat she'd ever seen spilling over her legs, while Nick was cursing, pulling levers and probably already regretting his snap decision, as he attempted to shoehorn himself into the driver's seat.

Sophie sympathised. She didn't have a whole lot of room, either. She had one hand under the basket and with the other she stroked the cat's shaggy head. 'What kind of cat is he,' she said, wondering what breed could possibly be hiding under that long coat.

'Some kind of ragdoll variety,' Nick said as he reversed out of the driveway and sped down the road, managing the gears like a rally driver. 'Penelope gave it to Min for her birthday, only she'd had it six months already. I reckon she couldn't stand the fur all over her furniture and Min's birthday was the perfect excuse to get rid of it.'

'Poor Fat Cat,' she said, stroking the cat behind his ear. 'Did you see the snake?'

'Yeah, it was out by the clothesline. I saw the tail end of it disappearing with the cat following it.' He shook his head. 'Min's going to kill me for letting him out. At first I thought he was okay, but then he took to his bed and started acting strangely. I rang the vet and the nurse said to bring him straight over. The sooner they get the antivenene into them, the better.'

'He'll be okay, then, won't he?' She'd bet her life on it with her sister on the case, but she'd hate to be wrong and for Min to lose her precious pet.

'He should be.' He glanced over at the basket. 'How's he going?'

'He's panting.'

'Probably struggling to breathe. The venom attacks the organs.' He changed down gears to take a sharp bend, making the tiny Mazda hug the corners in a way Sophie didn't know was possible. 'Come on!' he urged the little car.

She was leaning over, trying to check out the speedo and running her hand down the cat's side when she felt something, and promptly forgot all about how fast they were going. She looked down at the mountain of fur on her lap and ran her hand down his side once more. Yep, there it was again. The cat mewled, a cry of distress, and stretched out long and straight onto its back. Sophie blinked down at it as the whole of its hairy stomach suddenly clenched tight and there, as the long, dense fur parted, she saw it. Something that looked one hell of a lot like a nipple.

Uh-oh.

'You did say this cat was a boy, right?'

'Yeah, of course he is.'

'Um, that's really interesting because, unless I'm terribly mistaken, Fat Cat's about to have kittens.'

'What!'

He stared in disbelief at her and the car veered across the centre line. 'Keep your eyes on the road!' she said, and he hauled the car back into their lane.

'But he can't be having kittens. Fat Cat is a male. Penelope said.'

Fat Cat panted and his belly constricted, and from under his tail bulged a slick black face.

Sophie's eyes widened as Fat Cat bent himself in half to welcome the kitten with a ready tongue as it emerged. 'Then he's had a sex change,' she said. 'Because Fat Cat is well and truly a female.'

'What the—!' Nick said, as he looked over.

'Oh wow,' cried Sophie. 'And there's another one coming!'

'Bloody hell.'

By the time Nick pulled up outside the vet, Fat Cat had very much removed any question of sex and was sitting in her basket on Sophie's lap contentedly licking her six kittens.

'You clever cat,' said Sophie, watching the new mother dote over her litter.

'Do you think she's finished now?' asked Nick, waiting by the open passenger door.

'How can you tell?'

'Don't ask me,' he said, 'I didn't know she was female let alone pregnant.'

Sophie figured that Nick was about to discover bad news really did come in threes. 'At least she's looking a lot better.'

'She is looking better,' he said, and smiled down at her like they'd shared something amazing, and Sophie felt the warmth of his smile zing all the way down to her toes. Damn. She blinked and broke eye contact.

'Come on,' he said, 'might as well get these checked out seeing we're here.' Nick leaned down to scoop the basket from her lap and Sophie pressed herself back into her seat, but it was impossible to get away from the stroke of his hands on her legs or the accidental brush of his fingers against hers. Impossible not to be reminded of a night of sin and the feel of his naked skin. Impossible to stop her heart from tripping and her tender nipples turning to bullets.

By the time he'd successfully juggled away the basket and new family, she was breathless from the effort of trying not to breathe in air filled with Nick's signature scent.

'I—I'll wait here,' she said, climbing out after him and stretching her legs, needing clear air and headspace and a Nick-free zone. Because any minute now she'd be thinking there was something in his smile or in his eyes that spelled out happily ever after, which was exactly the sort of thing she did, making something out of nothing, imagining meaningful things that were never there. This was exactly why she ended up making a fool of herself every time over men and what she'd promised herself she'd stop doing.

Now, it was more important than ever that she keep a level head.

Nick shrugged and would have gone in without her, but it would have been churlish of her to expect him to juggle both the cats and the surgery door. Suddenly, the vet nurse descended on them. 'Is this our snake bite?' she asked, her expression moving from concern through surprise to delight when she registered the tiny kittens lined up attached to their mother's nipples.

'Maybe not the medical emergency I thought it was,' Nick confessed, as Hannah came scurrying from a backroom and Sophie was sprung. The vet nurse clucked while Hannah looked from Nick to Sophie with questions in her eyes. Questions Sophie knew she'd have to answer later, after Hannah had taken care of her patient.

'Let's get them into an examination room,' Hannah said, all businesslike, as Sophie made a tactical withdrawal to wait by the car, 'and we'll take a look.'

Sophie chewed on her lip as she waited in the car park, knowing things were getting more complicated by the minute. There wasn't a snowball's chance in hell her sister wasn't going to ask Nick what Sophie was doing there, and he was going to be struggling to answer. The only upside was she hadn't told him yet. And please, God, he hadn't guessed.

He emerged from the surgery, looking like he was still in a state of shock.

'How's Fat Cat and Co?' she asked, nervous about what Hannah might have asked and wanting to get in first before he did.

'Good. No more kittens, but your sister says she's showing no signs of snake bite, though she'll keep her in overnight for observation.'

'Excellent,' she said, holding out her hand, not giving him a chance to speak. 'Give.'

He looked at it. 'What?'

'The keys,' she said. 'I think I'll drive us home, Fernando, if it's all the same to you.'

'Who?'

'Oh, sorry. Fernando Alonso. He's a racing driver, too. Easy mistake to make.'

'Ha,' he said, but he handed over the keys. She took them, determined to drop him home and get away. There was way too much breeding going on today to add any more to the mix. She'd go home, regroup, and work out another angle of attack. She snapped on the radio, feigned interest in the five o'clock news, and blessedly, he didn't say anything all the way home.

'Well,' she said, as she pulled up outside his house. 'That was an exciting afternoon.'

'It was,' he said, infuriatingly not making a move to get out of the car.

'I'm so relieved it doesn't look like snake bite.'

'Me too.'

'Though I'd be worried about having a snake in my backyard with Min around.'

'That's the problem with living in the Adelaide Hills. They're bound to be nearby. Most of the time we just don't see them. I've put some netting around to see if we can catch it. Meanwhile, I'll tell her to watch out, all right?'

'Yeah. Best do that.' *Meanwhile, go already.* This model car was far too small with a man whose scent invaded every square centimetre. A scent that reminded her of a night of tangled legs and tangled sheets, which is what had got her into this tangled mess. She slid her driver window down.

'I will.'

'So,' she said, licking her lips when still he hadn't budged, her hands a knot of fingers in her lap. 'Have a good evening, then. Bye.'

24

Nick

Nick wasn't sure what was up with Sophie, but he was enjoying the way she suddenly seemed so nervous, wanting him out of her car like she was afraid of something. After being the one on the back foot for so long, it was a good feeling. He just needed to give her a bit of encouragement to spit out why.

Why had she shown up out of the blue?

Why was she so reluctant to speak up?

'Sophie,' he said, angling himself the best he could towards her in the tiny space given his knees were already butting up against the dash.

'Yes?'

'Did you have something you wanted to say to me?'

Her eyes opened wide. 'What?' she said, in little more than a squeak.

'Well, you came here for a reason and you said it wasn't about Min, and unless you're clairvoyant, I figure you didn't drop around to give me a hand getting Fat Cat to the vet.'

'No, um, I—' She took a deep breath and exhaled on a sigh, the droop in her shoulders looking like resignation. 'Oh God, actually, there was something I wanted to talk to you about.'

'Spill.'

The look she sent him was pure panic. 'Actually, Nick, I can't talk about this in here.' She reached for her handle and pulled her door open. She was out of the car gulping in air, one hand on her brow, the other on her hip, by the time he managed to unfurl himself from the tiny car and join her.

Her features looked haunted as she watched him approach, her arms suddenly wrapping around herself like she was scared. What the hell was that about? 'Listen, Sophie, do you want to come inside? Have a beer or coffee or something?'

'No!' Her eyes darted to the house and back. 'I'd rather stay outside.'

He shrugged, his patience wearing thin. After today's developments, he really could do with an ice-cold beer. 'So, what's this about?'

She looked away then, and when she turned back, a blush was flaming her cheeks, her eyes darting sideways, downwards, anywhere but at him.

'I'm sorry, Nick. This is so hard for me to say. I know it was just one night we spent together and that's all it was meant to be …'

And for the first time, Nick's confusion and impatience gave way to an unexpected glimmer of hope, that he wasn't wasting his time listening here, and that she couldn't erase that night from her mind, either. The flush of her cheeks, her coyness at approaching the topic—what else could it mean? 'It's okay, Sophie. You don't have to apologise.'

Her eyes flicked up to his, framed with a frown, before darting away once more.

'Look, I get that we're both responsible for what happened,' he went on. 'But we're both grown-ups. Where's the problem?'

'What?' she said, shaking her head. 'What are you talking about?'

'The night we spent together,' he said, 'I had a good time that night. I seem to recall you having one, too. Why wouldn't we both want to revisit that night? Isn't that the reason you're here?'

'No! Why would you think that? That's not why I came at all.'

'What?' He didn't care if he sounded like an echo, because her words made no sense. Her denial that she wanted to resume their relationship made even less sense. 'Then why did you come out here today and at a time you knew Min conveniently wouldn't be around?'

She lifted her chin and poked her finger into his chest. 'Because, you fool, Fat Cat being a female and having kittens isn't the only surprise in store for you today. I came to tell you that I'm pregnant, Nick. And you're the father.'

Blood roared in Nick's ears, every last drop of it curdling and clotting with the same message. No way could this be happening again. *No way!*

'It's not mine,' he said. Because he damned well knew that much and he wasn't about to smile and pretend otherwise. 'Don't try pinning that on me.'

'I'm sorry, I didn't realise there was anyone else there that night.'

'Who says it happened that night? You had a boyfriend, right?'

'A boyfriend I hadn't seen for weeks! There's no question it's yours.'

'I used protection.'

'And I was on the pill—mostly. It still happened. It's still yours.'

He snatched up her confession like it was a lifeline. 'What do you mean "mostly"?'

'I forgot to take a pill that day. It's irrelevant. The condom had to fail before my lapse made any difference.'

'Condoms don't fail. That's an urban myth.'

'Is it? So how do you think we're in this mess? Maybe when you went all ape on me that night and tore the foil open with your teeth—remember that?—maybe you damaged it, I don't know. When it all comes down to it, does it even matter how it happened? Isn't it more important that it did?'

'I'm not marrying you.'

She snorted, an exceedingly unladylike snort. 'Did I ask you to marry me? I don't think so. That's not why I'm here. I came to tell you the baby is yours. That's all I came to do. And now I've discharged my duty in that department, and I'll let you get back to your life. Thanks for listening.'

She headed back to the car she'd left idling in the driveway and panic set in. 'What do you think you're doing?'

'I'm leaving.'

'But you can't just drop a bombshell like that and walk away. You can't just leave.'

'Watch me.'

'No!' he called behind her. 'Sophie, wait!'

Her back stiffened. 'Why?'

'Because you're pregnant. And, if what you say is true, you're having my baby.'

She turned her head, giving him a withering stare that defied him to doubt her, one more time. 'You're not actually telling me anything I don't already know.'

He raked a hand through his hair. 'For God's sake, Sophie. If this is true, there are things we need to discuss. What are you going to do? What do you want?'

She shook her head. 'That's simple. One, I've decided to have the baby. And two, for the record, I don't want anything. So, if you'll excuse me?'

She slid in behind the wheel. He watched her reverse down the driveway and followed her drive down the road until long after the little car had disappeared from view. He was still standing there rooted to the spot when his phone buzzed. Penelope's number. Great, that was all he needed. But when he answered, it was Min, fresh from her piano lesson.

'Fat Cat had kittens!' Min squealed. 'He's a girl! When can I see them?'

Min chattered on so excitedly Nick only had to make monosyllabic responses, which was just as well, because his brain was still too busy processing everything that had happened today to be able to form a coherent sentence. So much for Min's supposedly male desexed cat. And soon, Min wouldn't only have kittens to keep her occupied, but a new brother or sister. And Nick would have a new son or daughter.

Bloody hell, and he'd talked himself into believing Sophie had come around to tell him she wanted to renew their affair. But she'd wanted nothing from him, especially not that witless confession that he'd like to sleep with her again. God, had he really admitted that?

She was having his baby and she wanted nothing from him. Nothing at all.

He thought about another time and another woman presenting him with the news that she was pregnant and his gut twisted.

There was a reason he never wanted to get married again.

And women were a big part of it.

25

Sophie

Well, that went well. *Not.* Sophie gave a sigh of relief as she flopped on the sofa, never more grateful that her mum had left her this place to use after her marriage to Dirk. 'Just in case things don't work out,' she'd joked, and it had been a joke because she and Dirk were rock solid, and Sophie had known that her mum only had her welfare at heart. She'd never otherwise be able to afford a place on her own on her teacher's salary.

Her mum's two-bedroom townhouse would be perfect, so long as her mum didn't mind her turning the second bedroom into a nursery, and given Dirk had scored an appointment to Geneva for two years, Sophie couldn't see her objecting.

She rested a hand on her still flat belly, the concept that deep inside her a baby was growing still too overwhelming to comprehend. No wonder they gave a girl nine months to get used to the idea.

But she'd done the right thing, in spite of the headache she'd brought home with her. She'd told Nick. At least that should get that problem off her back.

Her phone buzzed, interrupting her quiet. 'So, what's going on between you and Nick?'

Sophie put a hand to her head. Even if it didn't get another problem off her back. 'Hi, Han. How's Fat Cat going?'

'Don't try to change the subject. What were you doing with Nick?'

'He had a flat tyre so I was doing my good deed for the day and loaning him my car. What do you think?'

'I don't know. I called Beth because you weren't picking up your phone—'

'I was driving. I couldn't pick up.'

'—and told her what happened, and she just said, "I can't tell you."'

'She said that?'

'Yeah. Just this big pause and then, "I can't tell you."'

Sophie's head started thumping. This was how it worked when you had sisters like hers. Even when they didn't tell someone something, they did, and then they extracted information piece by piece, and before you'd worked it out yourself, they'd put together an entire jigsaw puzzle.

Hannah clearly couldn't wait for an answer. 'So you tell me—are you and Nick an item?'

'No, we are not an item.' Pregnancy was not an item.

'Only you were dancing with him at Dan and Lucy's wedding.'

'I saw you dancing with Pop.'

'I don't think that's quite the same thing.'

'Well, thanks for calling, Han, but shouldn't you be saving some animal's life or something?'

'I'm good. All the animals that needed saving are safely tucked up in their beds dreaming about chasing cats or mice.' She paused. 'Are you going to tell me what's going on?'

Sophie sighed, but it was too late to slow it down. Now Beth knew, Nick knew and Hannah had figured something out, and already the snowball was off and rolling. The news would gather speed throughout the district and by the time the new school year started, every parent at the school would have heard the news or would have figured it out themselves from her telltale bump.

'All right, I was going to tell you soon, anyway. Apparently I'm pregnant.'

There was a full five seconds of silence, and Sophie was beginning to wonder if she'd been cut off, before her sister said, 'Fuck.'

'That's certainly a valid response. It sure crossed my mind a couple of times. But then, that's what got me into this mess, I guess.'

Her attempt at black humour was met with deaf ears. 'And Nick's the father.'

She paused. 'I didn't say that.'

'Ooh, I think you just did. So, what are you going to do?'

Sophie ground her thumb into her throbbing temple. Was there no way to keep a secret longer than ten minutes in this place? She'd have to go and tell Nan and Pop today, before there was a chance they heard it from anyone else first. 'Nick doesn't factor into this. And for what it's worth, I've decided to have the baby.'

'What? By yourself, you mean?'

'Yeah, as a single mum. I'm going to do it on my own.'

'Are you serious? Why wouldn't you ask for help from the father?'

'Beth did it on her own, didn't she? And she even went back to uni. I'll cope.'

'She didn't choose to be a single parent, you twit—she lost Joe. And for the record, she didn't do it on her own. She had Mum to help and Nan when she went back to uni, and now Mum's overseas and Nan's in her eighties—are you really expecting she's going to be minding your baby while you're at work?'

'I'll take time off or work part-time or something. I'll manage.'

'You're mad, Sophie. It's going to make life bloody difficult if not stuff up your career for years if you try to do it alone. Why would you do that?'

'What choice do I have?' Because wishing it away sure hadn't worked, and the only other option was something she'd thought long and hard about while she'd tossed and turned at night after talking to Beth, trying to find a solution. 'I did think about having an abortion,' she admitted.

'You what?'

'I went to see a counsellor,' she shakily confessed. 'And we talked about abortion. But in the end, I couldn't do it. I realised that having a baby now might be inconvenient and costly, but it wasn't enough reason for me to go down the termination route. It's not this baby's fault it's there, it's my responsibility and I have to step up. And I know it's going to be hard and people are going to gossip behind my back, but I didn't go back. I couldn't do it, Han. I just couldn't bring myself to do it.'

'When was this?'

'A couple of weeks ago. Beth came with me.'

'You told Beth and you didn't tell me?'

'I had to tell someone.'

'But not me.'

'I thought Beth would understand. She had an unplanned pregnancy, too.'

'Whereas I haven't.'

'It's nothing to get huffy about.'

Sophie heard her sister sigh at the end of the line. 'Yeah, I know, I know. Just, Sophie,' Hannah said, her voice breaking up on her name, and if Sophie didn't know her hard-nosed sister better, she'd almost think she was crying. 'I'm so glad you chose not to do that.'

26

Hannah

Hannah held onto the phone long after her sister had said goodbye. Sophie was pregnant. First Lucy, now Sophie. Well, it was bound to happen sooner or later, wasn't it? There was no reason why her sisters wouldn't want to have children. And even though Lucy had fears after her earlier miscarriage, there was no physical reason to stop her. All Hannah needed was for Beth to get pregnant, and there'd be a trifecta of babies and the yoke of her infertility would hang around her neck heavier than ever.

She was still sniffing when the phone in her hand buzzed and Hannah looked at the caller ID. 'Hi, Declan,' she said, never happier to hear his voice.

'I know we agreed to catch up on the weekend, but I just got to thinking. Are you busy right now, because the weekend feels a mighty long time away, and I was wondering ...'

She smiled as she thanked God for sexy Irishmen who seemed to have perfect timing and know the perfect thing to say.

'I'll be right over.'

27

Sophie

'You're having a what?' said Pop.

'A baby,' said Sophie, when she dropped in to their little cottage the next day after school on the pretext of picking up some eggs. The warm November afternoon sun filtered through the lace kitchen curtains lighting up the dust motes, while a pot of corned beef simmered on the stovetop. Such a normal everyday scene into which to drop a bombshell. Now, she just had to wait for the fallout. Sophie stared blindly at the carton of eggs Nan had placed in front of her a few moments ago and attempted a smile, trying to keep it light, as if she was talking about getting nothing more significant than a haircut. 'In a few months' time.'

'Oh, we already knew that,' said Pop, waving his hands in dismissal. 'Lucy's having a baby. Dan's going to be a father.'

Sophie put her cup down on her saucer with only a mild clatter. She'd known it wasn't going to be easy telling her octogenarian grandparents about the baby, but she couldn't afford to have them hearing her news from anyone else. 'Not Dan and Lucy's baby, Pop. I'm having a baby, too.'

Pop's cloudy eyes lit up in surprise. 'Is that so? When's the happy day?'

'The baby's due around late June. About eight weeks after Lucy's baby.'

'Not that day,' he growled. 'The wedding day! We'll have to get that suit of mine off to the drycleaner's again, Joanie.'

'Uh, Pop, before you go making plans—there isn't going to be a wedding. I'm not getting married.'

'Why not? This baby must have a father. Surely he's going to do the right thing?'

'It's okay. It just doesn't suit either of us to get married.'

Pop grunted and clambered to his feet, scraping his chair across the lino floor. 'That's not how we did things in my day,' he said, and promptly announced he was off to his shed. The screen door slammed behind him and Nan, who'd been sitting quietly contemplating her cup of tea the whole time, sighed.

Sophie felt the weight of that sigh heavy on her heart. 'I'm so sorry, Nan. I feel like I've let everyone down.'

Nan lifted her gaze and looked at her through watery eyes, and simply patted the back of her hand, before she said, 'Go and make a new pot of tea, lovey. I think it's time I showed you something.'

Sophie half-heartedly took herself off to the sink to fill the kettle, wondering if she'd made the right decision in keeping the baby, after all. It was so different to how Dan and Lucy's baby news had been received. Everyone had been thrilled for them, and full of congratulations. She didn't have a problem with that, she was over the moon happy for them, too, but all her news seemed to bring was shock or disappointment, and it was hard to believe she was doing the right thing in going ahead with this pregnancy.

She heard Nan muttering as she rummaged around in the linen closet, looking for whatever it was she was looking for, heard the doors bang shut, and met her bearing an old hat box back to the table. 'It's in here, I'm sure it is,' she said, as she lifted the lid to a treasure chest of old photographs and papers, spreading them one by one on the table.

'What is?' asked Sophie, scanning through the photographs. Some she'd seen before, the old sepia photographs stained and curling at the edges, containing images of great aunts, uncles and great grandparents long gone.

'This one,' Nan said, putting a black-and-white photo down in front of her granddaughter.

Sophie recognised it. 'That's you and Pop, on your wedding day.' There was a blown-up version of it in an oval frame on the mantelpiece in the lounge room. 'You both look so beautiful.' Her nan was wearing a calf-length gown with a short veil fixed to her dark hair by a band of flowers, a bouquet of white gardenias in her hands, while Pop stood tall and upright beside her in a smart double-breasted suit, a spray of matching flowers in his buttonhole.

Nan took back the photo, running her fingertips across the faded image as if trying to erase the years and connect with the girl she once was. 'I was so young. Just eighteen years old. Much younger than you are now.' She took a deep breath, as a single tear rolled down her wrinkled cheek. 'So young.'

She sighed and put down the photo, continuing to dig through the contents of the box with her knobbly-jointed fingers until they paused at a folded paper. She nodded as she unfolded it, ironing out the creases with the side of her hand on the table.

'Here,' she said, sliding it in front of Sophie.

'Your marriage certificate.'

Nan nodded. 'And what do you notice about it?'

Sophie could find nothing out of place. It all looked perfectly unremarkable. There was the name of the minister who'd married them and the names of her grandparents, the bride and groom, and there were their signatures, written in beautiful copperplate script.

'The date,' Nan hinted. 'Twenty-fifth of August, nineteen forty-nine,' Nan said, spelling it out. 'And when was your father born?'

'First of—' Sophie blinked as the tremor slid down her spine. 'Oh my God. February first, 1950. That's only—' She peered into her grandmother's face. 'You mean …?'

Nan nodded. '"Large for dates" the nurses all said when he was born, but back then, everyone knew what that meant.' She looked at the wedding photo again. 'I was barely eighteen.'

Sophie took her grandmother's hands in hers. 'Oh, Nan, you must have been so scared when you found out.'

'You have no idea how much. I was sick with fear at the thought of telling my parents. Sick with fear at what would happen if I tried to hide it. My father was a very strict man, you see, and highly respected in our church. He threatened to tear Clarry limb from limb when Mum broke the news to him. Shouted the house down and said he'd skin him alive if he didn't do the honourable thing. We were married inside a month.' She shrugged world-weary shoulders. 'That's how things happened back then. Nobody asked you what you wanted, a girl was expected to get married, like it or lump it. It's not like they gave you any say in it.' She shook her head. 'I'd sinned against God, my father told me. I'd pay for it, he said. I thought he meant by having to get married. I thought that was punishment enough. But he was right, because after your father, I never had another child.'

It sounded so harsh to Sophie, and so very cruel. 'But wouldn't you have married Pop anyway?'

Nan clucked her tongue. 'I don't know about that.' She blinked and turned her liquid eyes to Sophie's. 'I barely knew Clarry, and

I had such plans, you see. I was going to be a concert pianist. I'd already given recitals in the Adelaide Town Hall and I wanted to travel all over the world. London. Paris. New York, I had it all planned ...' She trailed off, her quaky voice softly wistful, her eyes staring into the past.

'I never knew that, Nan. You never told us you were a concert pianist.'

She screwed up her nose. 'Well, it's all water under the fridge, now,' and Sophie didn't have the heart to correct her.

'So you married Pop instead.'

Nan nodded as she blew out a breath. 'Yes. I married Clarry.'

'Yet you said you barely knew him. So how—'

'Oh, I know what you're thinking. But things weren't as different then as they are these days. Not by a long shot. Not when it comes down to the birds and the bees.'

She sighed and looked at herself in the old photo again. 'It was cousin Ivy who invited me up to the Ashton Hall for the Saturday-night dance. She was a good few years older than me and very sophisticated, I thought, and she did my hair and lent me her lipstick and I felt quite wicked. Ivy had a beau, a handsome young orchardist called Robert, who introduced me to his friend, your grandfather. Clarence was a good-looking young man back then, I can tell you, tall and sun-tanned from working outside, and he asked me to dance and I was smitten. I hadn't had much male attention up till then, you understand, I was always too busy practising my scales, and it went to my head. So, when he asked me to go out for some fresh air after Robert and Ivy had disappeared outside, I went. I suppose I was very naive, but I liked the attention and I wanted to seem more sophisticated than I was. I was off to Europe, or so I thought. I wanted to appear so very sophisticated.'

She shrugged. 'One minute I was a budding concert pianist and the next I was a housewife with a new baby who got to play the organ at Sunday church.'

'Oh, Nan,' Sophie said, leaning over to wrap her arms around her and hug her tight.

Nan patted Sophie's arms and pulled a flapping tissue from under her bra strap to wipe her eyes. 'So, don't you go worrying about Clarry and thinking you're letting us down. If anyone understands what you're going through, it's us old-timers, even though Clarry might not like to be reminded of it. And though I'd be lying if I pretended I didn't wish you had a lovely husband to go along with the baby, for my part, I'm glad you get some kind of say if you don't want to get married. I'm glad things have changed since my day.'

Sophie shook her head. 'I never knew any of this. Did any of us know? Did you tell Beth all this, when she was having Siena?'

Nan looked sad. 'I should have, I know. But we'd only recently lost your father, and I couldn't bring myself to admit the truth when it had been buried so long. I didn't want to go digging up the past when the present was still so painful. And call it a silly old lady's pride, but I was still so ashamed of what I'd done. And then Beth's Joe died and she didn't want to hear my sad story. She had more important things to think about then.'

She sniffed again into her tissue and Sophie gave Nan's shoulders another squeeze before letting her go. 'I'm sorry things didn't work out for you the way you would have liked back then.'

'I made my choice,' said Nan, clearing her throat and firming her shoulders, 'even if I was terribly naive. I had to live with the consequences. And mind, they're not all bad, if I had your father for as long as we had him, and I have four beautiful grandchildren, a great-grandchild and another two on the way.' She smiled, though her eyes were still clouded with the ghost of another life foregone.

'They're not all bad consequences, are they? I've had a good life and Clarry's been a good husband. A gem at times, if truth be told, but don't let him catch me saying that. I could have done a lot worse. And whatever happens, I know that it will work out for you, too.'

Sophie smiled at her nan, for her faith that things would turn out all right, her eyes falling on the framed cross-stitch on the wall above her head—the one that said, *Sometimes the wrong choices can still lead us to the right places.* And she wondered what her nan had been thinking as she'd stitched every letter of that herself.

They sipped their tea in silence, and for a while the generations slipped away and they were simply two women united by the common bond of an all-too-common misstep, a choice made and the repercussions that had spun their lives in different directions from what they'd planned.

Until through the screen door came the sound of a flock of screeching cockatoos descending into the line of pine trees outside, and the spell was broken. 'A shame about cousin Ivy,' Nan said at last, clucking her tongue, getting to her feet to check on her bubbling pot.

Sophie started collecting the cups and saucers. 'What happened? Did she marry the orchardist?'

'No. She broke that off. She ended up married to a banker from the city,' Nan said, now reaching into the fridge. 'Very well to do, he was too. Big society wedding. It was a huge scandal when the news broke that he already had a wife and two children tucked away somewhere over in Victoria.'

'He was a bigamist?'

'There's nothing new under the sun,' she said, coming back with another carton in her hands. 'The way people go on these days, you'd think this generation had invented everything, including, well, you know what. Here're your eggs,' she said, putting the carton down on the table.

'Thanks, Nan, but you already gave me a dozen.'

Nan looked at the two cartons on the table. 'No, I'd remember if I had. That one must be empty. Look,' she said, lifting the lid to find twelve eggs staring back at her. 'Oh,' she said, momentarily thrown, 'you should have told me you'd already helped yourself!'

28

Nick

Naturally enough, Min wanted to keep all the kittens the moment Penelope dropped her home and she laid eyes on them. 'Not happening,' said Nick as he watched his daughter stroking the tiny mewling creatures. 'You can keep one, but we have to find homes for the rest.'

'But, Dad …'

'But Dad nothing,' he said, putting his foot down. 'We're going to put an ad up in the post office and advertise them. Free kittens to good homes.' If he had his way, he'd hand them all over to Penelope as a not-so-subtle warning about gifting Min with any other supposedly male, desexed pets, but he knew they'd bounce right back when it was time for Min to come home again.

Min looked horrified. 'Free? You're going to give Fat Cat's kittens away for free?'

'Okay, how about we say five dollars each?' Damned if he was going to charge so much that he ended up stuck with them. 'You can have it for pocket money.'

Min clapped her hands. "'Cept we can give one to Ms Faraday for helping out, can't we?'

Now there was an idea. He'd been blindsided by Sophie's news—so blindsided that he'd let her walk away without considering probably the most important person in this equation. He watched his daughter sitting cross-legged on the floor, stroking Fat Cat behind the ears and thoroughly captivated by the kittens as they blindly stepped over each other in their quest to find and attach to a nipple.

But there was another important person in all this. Sophie's baby. *Their baby.* Who would grow up with no input from his or her own father, like he couldn't be bothered or simply didn't care. Like some deadbeat dad who turned his back and simply walked away.

He watched his daughter petting Fat Cat and cooing over the kittens. He wasn't the kind of man who could do that.

No, Sophie hadn't thought this through at all.

'Good thinking, Minnie Mouse. I think that's an excellent suggestion.'

Min beamed.

'How about we keep it our little secret,' he added, 'until the kitten is old enough to leave its mother? We'll give Ms Faraday a big surprise.'

Min grinned some more and Nick found himself grinning with her. After all, given the surprise she'd bestowed on him, it was the least he could do. Not that he'd be waiting that long before he talked to her again. Not by a long shot.

29

Hannah

'Penny for them?'

Hannah looked up as Declan put two coffees on the small table between them on the verandah, before sitting down in his chair. 'Sorry?'

He smiled, the brackets around his mouth deepening. 'I was wondering what you were thinking about. You looked miles away.'

'Oh,' she said, giving the pouch on her lap filled with the sleeping kangaroo one more hug before she slung it over its stand. 'Not much. Just some family stuff going on.'

'Like what,' he said, blowing over the top of the coffee cradled between his big hands, before taking a sip.

She shrugged. She'd been feeling unsettled since Sophie had revealed the news about her pregnancy. But that was only half the truth. She'd been feeling unsettled ever since Lucy had dropped her unexpected bombshell at Pop's birthday party, Sophie's news had just compounded it. There was nothing like ripping a plaster off to make a wound sting. 'Nothing much. Just the usual.'

'Ah, you see, I wouldn't know about that.'

She knew he was divorced with no kids, but no more than that. 'You don't have any family?'

'My folks, yeah, there's them. I had an older sister, Niamh, but she died when I was six. Leukaemia.'

'That's sad.'

'Aye. She was only ten years old.'

'Do you see your folks much?'

'They've been out a couple of times to visit. They loved the sunshine, so I suggested they move out and join me. But they can't do it. Mam can't leave Niamh behind. It'd be a wrench for her, for sure.'

Hannah sipped her coffee while the black cockatoos screeched their way home. 'I get that. My mum lives in Zurich.'

'But not your da?'

She shook her head. 'He died twelve or so years ago in a quad bike accident. Mum remarried a couple of years ago and Dan, my brother, runs the orchard. He's the eldest, recently married to Lucy. They're expecting their first baby in April. Then there's Beth and Sophie. Beth's my twin, Sophie's the youngest.' She paused. 'She's just found out she's pregnant, too.'

'Twins, eh? You and Beth must be close, then.'

Hannah screwed up her nose, not sure how to tackle that question. They had been close once upon a time. Inseparable. But then Beth had met Joe and Hannah had taken off for Perth to study to be a vet, and everything had gone belly up. 'We're not identical.' She put her empty cup down on the table. 'Thanks for tonight. I better get going, I've got a big day tomorrow.'

He stood and clasped both her hands in his, pulling her chest to chest with him, a frown knotting his brow as he leaned down and kissed hers. 'Have I made you sad? I didn't mean to.'

Lord, no, he was the one thing in her life making her happy. 'I'm tired,' she said, rising to her tippy toes to press a soft kiss on his lips, 'that's all.'

'Then I'll see you again.'

She smiled. 'Nothing surer.'

30

Beth

The latest *MasterChef* episode's credits had rolled and Siena had dragged herself off to bed, deciding it the lesser evil between that or doing the dishes.

'She's a credit to you, that girl,' said Harry, following Beth into the kitchen and picking up a tea towel.

'What are you doing?' said Beth, filling the kettle, not wanting to touch his compliment.

'Helping you with the dishes, what else?'

'I was going to do them after we had coffee.'

'I can't leave you with this lot.' He gestured towards the mountain of dishes and pans stacked by the sink. 'You wash, I'll dry.'

She had to hand it to him, he knew how to appeal to a weary woman. She'd been on the run all day at work before stopping at the shops on the way home. She wanted to make something a bit more substantial than her usual, so she'd picked up gravy beef and a bag of potatoes and carrots and frozen peas, and the meat had cooked to perfection, rich and full of flavour, but now all she really wanted to do was sit outside and relax for ten minutes.

Though if she did that, she had no doubt the dishes would still be mocking her at six tomorrow morning when she had to start all over again, and then at four when she finally got back home, and the last thing she'd feel like tackling would be a crusted-on mashed potato saucepan, when she'd much rather spend some time out in her studio.

So instead, she said thank you and together they got to work. So many dishes, so many more than when she did a quick one-pot meal, like tuna mornay or a casserole with leftover barbecue chicken. But Siena had loved it. She really should make the effort to cook something different more often.

'That was a delicious dinner, Beth, thank you.'

'My pleasure.'

She slotted a dish into the rack the same time Harry reached for the next, and their hands touched. 'Sorry,' she said, pulling hers back at the jolt. Harry looked equally uncomfortable.

'Thank you,' she said, snapping on the kettle when the last of the pots and pans was washed and dried and put away. 'How about that coffee, now?'

'I might take a raincheck, if it's okay with you, Beth. I really should be going.'

'Oh, okay.'

And as she watched his taillights head down the driveway, Beth couldn't help but feel a little disappointed.

31

Nick

Nick parked his ute at the far end of the school behind the pine trees and watched from a distance as Min ran down across the asphalt to meet her mother parked at the other end. It was her week with Penelope. He hated the fact that he couldn't call out and say hello, but he didn't need Min around to witness what he had to say.

He waited another ten minutes in his car while the car park emptied before he climbed out of the car and took the path across the oval to avoid any stragglers. He wasn't in the mood for small talk.

All but deserted now, the hallway was already strung with colourful chains and lanterns in preparation for Christmas. The librarian darted out of one room carrying an armful of books, nodding a quick hello, before disappearing just as quickly into the library. He snuck a glance in Sophie's classroom and found her there alone, stacking puzzles in the open shelves lining the walls.

'Hello, Sophie,' he said, closing the door behind him, suddenly feeling like Gulliver in a world of tiny chairs and desks so low, there was an entire ocean of airspace above them.

Airspace that crackled into life as her brown eyes flared in recognition. 'Nick. What are you doing here? I thought—'

'You thought it was Penelope's week to have Min? It is. I'm actually not here about Min.'

She blinked and licked her lips, her eyes looking towards the door and escape. 'Sorry, this isn't a good time. I have to go—' But she couldn't go anywhere because he stood between her and the door, and damned if he was moving. Besides, he got the distinct impression that it was a desire to flee that was behind her need not to hang around, rather than any pressing appointment.

'We need to talk, Sophie.'

She kicked up her chin and crossed her arms with the puzzle box held against her chest like a shield. 'About what?'

'About this baby. If, as you say, it's really mine—'

'It's yours.'

'Then I want to be involved.'

She turned her back to him, shoving the box in a space. 'No.'

'That wasn't a question.'

She spun back around, tossing her head and making the ends of her hair flick out. 'My answer's still no.'

'Listen to me, Sophie, you don't get to decide that.'

'I already have. I'm not going to rely on you or anyone else. I'm not asking or expecting you to help. I'm going to stand on my own two feet for once.'

'Christ Almighty, Sophie, this is a baby we're talking about. Not some high school personal development program. So you can stand on however many feet as you like, but you can't have this baby in a vacuum.'

She sniffed, but still he sensed that he was getting through to her. 'I want to be involved, and given this baby is half mine, don't I have that right?'

She closed her eyes and when she opened them again she'd found a bucket load of defiance from somewhere. 'God, Nick. It was a one-night stand. We don't mean anything to each other. I thought once I told you, that would be the end of the matter.'

'Then you thought wrong. You can't tell me you're having my baby and then slam the door in my face. It doesn't work that way. Just because we're not together, doesn't mean we can't share the responsibility for a child. Nobody expects you to do this on your own.'

'Beth did.'

'From what I know, Beth didn't have a choice. You do, and I'm offering my help.'

'But, Nick—'

'No. This is my baby, too. I want to be involved and I want to be kept informed. I want to come with you for your doctor's appointments and scans.'

Her eyes skidded sideways. 'I already had a scan. There's nothing to worry about.'

'What? When were you going to tell me this?'

'It was at seven weeks! Of course I wasn't going to tell you about it. I wasn't telling anybody I was pregnant until I'd had the scan and knew for certain.'

'Well, given that we know for certain, I want to be involved.'

'I honestly didn't think you'd be interested in a child you didn't want to believe was yours.'

'Come on, Sophie, you drop a bombshell like that when you know we used protection, of course it's going to be hard to swallow. So, give me some credit for being here now and stop trying to freeze me out.'

She swallowed against a desert-dry throat, the action kicking up her chin. 'Okay, for the record, it was all very routine and the baby is doing all the right things it's supposed to be doing. I'm ten weeks along and the baby is due in late June. Satisfied?'

He blinked. She might as well have been delivering a half-term report. *Johnny is a pleasant child who has performed to a satisfactory standard in all areas of the curriculum.* 'Thank you for that dispassionate report.'

'Look, I'm sorry, Nick, I didn't think—'

'You keep saying that. I'll tell you something else you haven't thought about. This baby is Min's family, too, and Min should grow up knowing her half-brother or sister, not just as some kid in another classroom, but as family. So, spare a thought for her when you seem content to cut the both of us out like we don't matter. Spare a thought for Min if you don't give a shit about me.'

A look like panic skidded across her eyes. 'What have you told her?'

'What do you think? I figure it's a bit early to go round broadcasting the news far and wide, least of all to Min, but sooner or later she's going to have to be told the truth. Which means we have to work out how we're going to deal with this.'

'You know you're making this so much more complicated than it has to be.'

'No. It's already complicated. I'm just trying to be grown up about how we deal with it. You might try being the same.'

Okay, he thought, as he marched back across the oval towards his car, Min would probably accuse him of being mean again, and maybe he could have left off the crack about being grown up given how she'd bared her soul to him that night. But how else was he supposed to get through to her except to put it in language she understood?

She hadn't left him a whole lot of choice.

32

Sophie

Sophie was shaking on her way to her car, still rattled from her encounter with Nick. He'd stood there barring her exit with his feet apart and his arms crossed, looking like a thundercloud with eyes. Scowling eyes. Damning eyes. Eyes that skewered into her soul and made her resolve waver. The same eyes that once had looked at her with hunger.

There was no hunger today, the air fairly crackling with electricity as he'd stood there all gunslinger in a black hat ready, trigger fingers itching for the big shootout. He'd looked larger than life, dangerous. And something must be seriously wrong with her, because he'd looked sexy as all get out. She really didn't need Nick in a classroom full of supercharged air looking sexy.

She didn't need Nick anywhere looking sexy, for that matter.

She zapped the car lock and slid into the driver's seat, starting the engine before dropping her head down onto crossed arms over the steering wheel. What a bloody mess.

Why did he want to be involved? She didn't need all that sexy shoved in her face every time she turned around. She didn't need the visual reminder and she certainly didn't need the proximity. Because she knew what would happen and next thing she'd be imagining rainbows and happily ever afters, which is what had got her into this mess in the first place. It was what she always did and she'd be damned if she was going to let it happen this time.

Why couldn't he be one of those loser fathers who were happy to sow their wild oats and walk away?

Okay, so clearly Nick was no deadbeat, or he could have walked away from being a father to Min, but it would make things a heck of a lot easier if he was.

There was a tap on her window, and Sophie jumped. She looked up to see the principal peering inside, looking concerned. 'Yvonne,' Sophie said, rolling down the window. 'You gave me a fright.'

Mrs Innstairs frowned down at her, not the least bit apologetic. 'Are you all right? You've been sitting there for ages.'

'It's nothing,' Sophie said, 'just a bit of a headache.'

'Are you okay to drive?'

'Thanks. I'm fine, really. I think all the end-of-year stuff is getting to me.'

'Well, that's understandable,' the principal said, 'I think we're all counting down the days. Less than three weeks to go, Sophie, hang in there.'

'I will,' she said, 'see you tomorrow.'

She gave a cheery wave that she didn't come close to feeling, jammed the car into gear, and bunny hopped her little Mazda down the road. It might be coming up to the end of the year, but Sophie knew her problems were only just beginning.

33

Hannah

Hannah dropped in to Nan and Pop's place after work to find Beth and Siena already there busy assembling the Christmas tree. It was late November, the Christmas Pageant had rolled down Adelaide's streets a week ago, and for Nan, that meant it was high time the decorations were up. 'Hi,' she said, feeling a little stab of guilt as she leaned down to give Nan a kiss. Was it her imagination or was her nan shrinking?

Nan, on the other hand, beamed with delight. 'Well, this is a pleasant surprise. First Beth and Siena drop by, and now you, too. I'll make us all some tea.'

Hannah blinked, wincing when she saw Siena sitting on the floor and sorting through a box of tired handmade decorations that dated back to when the girls were in primary school, and were way past their use-by date. 'You called me,' she said. 'You asked me to come and help put up the Christmas decorations.'

Nan snorted. 'I did no such thing. You must have dreamed it. But now that you're here, you might as well make yourself useful.'

Nan took herself off to the kitchen, while across the lounge room, Beth rolled her eyes sympathetically. 'She phoned me, too. Don't ask, I have no idea.'

Hannah turned on her sister, keeping her voice low. 'And you still think there's nothing wrong with her?'

'Hey, she's fine. A little absent-minded, maybe.'

'Come on, Beth, surely you can see she's not right. She rang us both and forgot—seriously? Who does that?'

Beth frowned, throwing a glance over her shoulder at her daughter, who was still sorting, oblivious to the conversation. 'Do you really think something's wrong?'

'I think we should at least get her checked out.'

'Hey, Aunty Hannah,' said Siena from across the room, 'did you see *MasterChef* the other night?'

'No, I missed it,' she said, picking up a tangle of tinsel to try to find the ends. She didn't feel the need to add that she'd missed it because she'd been tucked up in Declan's big bed recovering from some pretty dynamic sexual gymnastics. Or that watching the evening light paint the bush and the vine-planted hillside in a golden-red wash as her body hummed its way back down to earth was really the only thing she'd been capable of.

'It was really good,' the girl continued, 'only Harry's favourite team got eliminated. He thinks they might come back, though.'

Hannah's ears pricked up. 'Who's Harry?'

'Nobody in particular,' said Beth.

'Harry comes for dinner,' Siena offered, 'and we watch *Master-Chef* together.'

Hannah looked at her sister. 'Since when? Something you're not telling me, little sister?'

'Only by ten minutes,' Beth reminded her. 'And there's nothing to tell. Harry's the groundsman at school. Dan got him to do some cleaning up when that tree came down in the driveway. That's all.'

'And so now you have him over for dinner and a spot of telly? That sounds cosy.'

Beth was shaking her head. 'Don't go making anything of this. I'm a rusted-on spinster, same as you.'

'He is nice, though,' said Siena, sorting through baubles.

'And that's the end of it,' said Beth.

Nan bustled back with a tray of tea and rattling cups and saucers. 'Isn't this nice,' she said. 'Clarry's out in the garden, I'll tell him to come in for tea in a moment.'

Nan was pouring the tea when there was a knock on the door and Sophie poked her head inside. 'Wow, what is this? A little Faraday family reunion?'

'Don't tell me,' said Hannah. 'You got a call to come around, too?'

'No,' said Sophie, brandishing an egg carton and looking confused. 'I just dropped around to get some eggs.'

'You see,' Nan said. 'I told you girls you were dreaming.'

Nan was barely out the back door when Sophie looked from one sister to the other. 'What's going on?'

'Hannah thinks something's wrong with Nan. She thinks we should get her checked out.'

'Really?'

'Yeah, I was worried,' said Hannah, recounting her earlier visit. 'But Beth said I was imagining it and she's the paramedic, so—'

'Hey, don't use me as an excuse. If you thought she needed to be checked out, you should have done something about it.'

'Do you think something's wrong, too?' Sophie asked Beth.

'I don't know, but it just seems odd that she'd call us both and not remember.'

'Alzheimer's?'

'God, I hope not.' Beth shook her head. 'I didn't think she was that bad, but ...'

'What are you whispering about?' Siena called from across the room, where she was lining up decorations on the floor.

'What you're getting for Christmas,' Beth replied. 'So stop listening or you'll jinx it.'

The girl huffed, muttering something about grown–ups as she flounced out of the room. 'I'm going to get the eggs.'

'So, what do you want to do?' said Hannah. 'I can make an appointment for her, but I can't see us getting her into a specialist before Christmas.'

Beth nodded. 'Make an appointment, doesn't matter if it's not until the new year, and meanwhile we'll all enjoy Christmas. I mean, she might be getting a bit forgetful, but what can happen between now and then?'

34

Nick

'Can you make Sophie see sense?'

It had taken more courage than Nick had imagined possible to front up to Sophie's big brother to enlist his help. But apparently, sheer frustration with a woman could blind a man to any risk of personal injury.

'So, let me get this straight,' Dan said, sitting at his kitchen table, a frown dragging his brows together. 'Sophie's having a baby and you're the father.'

Nick's risk-assessment meter rapidly escalated into the red zone. 'You didn't know?'

'Well, I'd heard Sophie was expecting and your name was being bandied about by Han and Beth. I didn't want to pay too much attention to gossip.'

Nick swallowed. 'It's true.'

Dan crossed his arms, his eyes firmly fixed on the table. 'And so, I guess it's also true that this all happened the night of our wedding?'

'Yeah.'

'So,' Dan said, on a long sigh, his eyes rising from the table to meet Nick's, 'not to put too fine a point on it, I ask you at the wedding to look after Sophie—'

'I was looking after Sophie.'

'Right, because the next thing is, she's pregnant.'

'Okay, so it happened. I'm not backing away from that. I'm not pretending we didn't spend the night together. But I'm trying to be the responsible party here.'

Lucy put a coffee in front of each man before she unpeeled Dan's arms and found herself a seat in his lap. 'I think it's great. Our kids will grow up together. They'll be cousins and best friends.'

'That's just it,' Nick said, wanting to hug Lucy for changing the direction of the conversation to something positive. 'Our kids will grow up together, but she hasn't thought about Min at all, hasn't thought about anything beyond raising this child as a single parent—as the only parent. I thought you might be able to talk some sense into her.'

'You're expecting me to talk some sense into one of my sisters?'

'Somebody has to,' Nick said. 'Somebody has to make her see that she can't have this baby in a bubble, that it doesn't work that way.'

'And you have no long-term plans with Sophie that you might have this conversation yourself?'

'After Penelope you'd think I'd be making long-term plans with anyone? Are you kidding me?'

'Well, Sophie might have one or two things to learn, but as far as I can tell, she's no Penelope.'

Nick knew that for a fact. He had first-hand experience of the differences, not to mention a pretty fair idea of who'd come out on top in a contest. But that didn't mean he was about to jump headlong into another permanent relationship on the basis of a coming child. He'd made decisions about hanging around once before on the basis of an unexpected pregnancy, and while he loved Min to death, he'd learned that love for a child didn't depend on him sharing the marital bed with the mother. In fact, it could be a whole lot healthier for everyone if you weren't.

'Sorry, Dan, I like Sophie, but I'm not about to offer marriage, even if I thought she'd say yes.' And given she was on this independence kick and that she'd seemed appalled when he'd actually confessed he wouldn't mind a replay of their night together, that was hardly on the cards. 'But that's not to say that we can't sort out this shared parenting thing between us and make it work—if she just gives me a chance to be involved.'

Dan grunted. 'See how it goes—who knows, she might come round to thinking the right way all by herself—but if not, I'll talk to her,' he promised.

35

Beth

The *MasterChef* finale didn't disappoint, with Harry's favourite contestant—who'd been reinstated, just as he'd expected she would be—up against Siena's in the final challenge.

Beth's living room might have been mistaken for a showdown at the Adelaide Oval that night, the whoops and cheers loud and no doubt ringing across the valley as each competitor completed their challenges, the tension palpable before the final, drawn-out, nail-biting reveal.

Beth was the most torn of all. She didn't have a horse in this race, but she wanted both Siena and Harry to win, because they both had so much emotion invested in it, and the excitement was contagious.

In the end, it was Siena's champion who triumphed, sending Siena to her feet, cheering.

Harry cheered with her and then they slapped hands as the champagne corks popped while the credits rolled. 'Your favourite deserved to win,' he said. 'No doubt about it.'

'But yours was so good,' said Siena. 'She made the best Bombe Alaska ever.'

Beth was impressed. She was pretty certain her daughter would never know what a Bombe Alaska was, if it weren't for shows like *MasterChef*.

They had ice-cream (without the flamed meringue topping) for dessert to celebrate, spilling out onto the verandah to enjoy the warm December weather, Siena and Harry taking a long time to perform a post-mortem on the finale. Beth listened to the to and fro, thinking how nice it was that there was another voice here, and that she didn't have to be the one paying attention to what her daughter said every minute of the day.

She didn't even miss her studio on nights like this. It was just so nice to be.

The conversation changed direction. Something about school finishing up soon and the summer holidays being upon them, and was Siena going away.

Beth pricked up an ear, heard her daughter say they never went away for holidays, but they were having Christmas at the beach this year.

'I can't imagine anything nicer,' Harry said, 'it sounds perfect.'

Beth felt a sudden stab of guilt, because he lived alone and, as far as she knew, had no family. She was suddenly compelled to sit up and say, 'It's just a picnic, really. Something different for Nan and Pop.'

'They'll love it,' he said, without a hint of expecting to be invited to join their family Christmas. But why would he expect an invitation, Beth rationalised. And why should she feel guilty? It wasn't like he was family.

'It'll be different,' she said, trying to make light of it. 'We'll probably all come home sunburnt and itching with our bathers full of sand and determined never to do it again.'

'I won't,' declared Siena. 'I think we should go to the beach every year.'

'No,' Harry said, 'your mum's no doubt right. If you went every year, you'd soon get sick of it.'

Beth sent a smile of thanks to this big bear of a man, who seemed to instinctively know the right thing to say to Siena. And unexpectedly, she wished that she could invite him to join their Christmas, if only so he wouldn't have to spend it alone. But knowing that if she did, it might give him the wrong signals entirely.

He was far too nice a man to do that.

36

Sophie

Sophie was determined to manage this pregnancy her way, but she wasn't completely heartless. If Nick was serious about being kept abreast of the baby's progress, then okay, she could live with that. Her upcoming twelve-week scan would soon put how serious he was to the test.

He didn't answer the phone, so she kept her message brief and businesslike and left it up to Nick if he wanted to attend or not. He'd be busy in the orchard this time of year, she knew, so she'd understand if he couldn't make it, but she would meet him at the clinic if he could.

He called back within five minutes saying he'd be there.

He even offered her a lift. But no, she didn't want to be picked up. It was enough that she was agreeing that he come, surely? She didn't want them to look like a couple any more than they already would.

On the day, she arrived five minutes early for the scan. Nick was already there, seated in the crowded waiting room, half-heartedly leafing through a women's magazine. He stood but she waved him down, doing her best to put a lid on the irritating buzz she felt at seeing him, and went to the counter to register. This wasn't exactly a date. It wasn't like he was here to see her.

There was nowhere she could sit but beside him, which started her wishing she was here alone, after all. 'Hi,' she said, feeling strangely nervous. Which was daft when she'd slept with the guy, but this was a whole new experience and she was pretty sure that no dummies guide to the aftermath could have prepared her for this.

'How do you feel?' he asked.

'Horrible, if you must know. I've drunk the equivalent of Sydney Harbour. So if they're not on time, this waiting room is going to be awash with yachts and ferries soon. You might want to grab a life jacket while you can.'

He had the nerve to laugh.

'Believe me,' she said, 'it's not funny from where I'm sitting.'

'Ms Faraday?' a clinician called.

'Bingo,' she said, wincing at the need to pee as she got to her feet. 'We're on.' She sensed Nick's hesitation. He was still sitting down. 'Are you coming?'

'Are you sure? You don't want me to wait?'

'Don't you want to see your baby?'

He was up in a heartbeat, his smile so warm and real she had to look away, because it wasn't about her and it wasn't for her. 'Thank you,' he said, and she was beginning to understand how much this meant to him, and guilt piled on guilt that she'd ever imagined she could exclude him.

Ten minutes later, she was lying on the table with Nick sitting by her side.

'First off, I'll do the measurements,' the sonographer explained, lifting up Sophie's shirt to expose her bump, 'and then I'll turn the screen around so you can both see. Okay, here comes the gel, it might be a bit cold.'

It was, but it was Nick who said, 'Wow,' his eyes firmly fixed on her belly. 'That's coming along.'

'Almost one-third along,' she replied, feeling exposed and trying not to feel vulnerable. The last time he'd seen her this undressed, she'd been at her slimmest, and she'd thought, her hottest. It was wrong to worry what he thought about how she looked now. It was pointless to crave his approval, but she already felt unusually big and awkward, her body doing all kinds of things according to a pre-set plan she had no control over.

But she saw no revulsion in his eyes, only something that looked like wonder as they traced the clinician's hand across her bump.

It seemed to take forever, the sonographer turning the trans-ducer this way and that, frowning a little as she concentrated hard on her task, clicking on her keyboard here and there to take measurements. All the while, the silence in the room stretched out. Sophie just wanted her to be done so they could see how the baby looked, grab a picture, and she could go pee, but the sonographer kept going, asking Sophie to move position a couple of times to get a clearer shot.

Finally, she looked up from her screen. 'Will you excuse me a moment? I just have to consult with the doctor.'

Chills went down Sophie's spine. 'What's wrong?'

'Don't worry. I'll be right back, I promise.' The door closed behind her and she was gone.

Sophie blinked up at Nick. 'Something's wrong.'

'You don't know that,' said Nick, but he didn't look too confident.

'Then why would she go? The last time the sonographer didn't go out to consult with anyone, she just turned the screen around after ten minutes to show me. Lucy said the same thing happened at her scan a few weeks back. This is a test for abnormalities. They don't go out of the room to consult with someone else if there's nothing wrong. There's something she doesn't want us to see.'

'She said not to worry.'

'How can I not worry?'

'Hey,' he said, and he wrapped his large hand around hers, squeezing her fingers. 'We're in this together, okay? Whatever it is, we'll deal with it together.'

He had no business to be holding her hand. No business at all. But she felt shaky and afraid, and his hand was warm and strong and she felt secure with her hand in his. Safer, and so she left it there.

And something about that connection made her need to confess. She looked up at him, trying to put on a brave face but knowing she was failing miserably. 'When I first found out I was pregnant, I wanted it to go away. I willed it to go away. But what if something's wrong, now? What if I wanted it so bad, I made something happen?'

'That's not possible,' he said. 'Don't think like that.'

'How do you know?'

'Because it doesn't work that way. You can't make bad things happen just because you wished for something different.'

She sniffed and confessed something she'd never have expected to. 'I'm glad you're here.'

He nodded, his jaw set hard. 'So am I.'

'I'm sorry to keep you,' the sonographer said, returning with a similarly white-coated woman. 'This is Doctor Jameson.'

'Ms Faraday,' she said, before turning to Nick.

'Nick Pasquale,' he said. 'I'm the father.'

'I just need to have a look at some pictures here,' she said, as the sonographer got back to work on Sophie's tummy. 'It won't take a moment, I promise.'

'Is everything all right?' Sophie asked.

'Oh, I expect so. I just need to confirm something.' And she promptly turned her attention to the screen.

Sophie looked at Nick, despite everything, never more grateful to have him here, with his warm hand cradling hers, lending her his strength.

After what felt like another interminable delay, the doctor nodded and turned to them both. 'I'm so sorry to make you wait, but there was something that wasn't picked up on your seven-week scan that we just needed to check to ensure everything was in order.' She smiled apologetically. 'It happens sometimes, but it can come as a bit of a shock, I hope not an unpleasant one. You're expecting twins, Ms Faraday. Congratulations.'

Sophie was too dumbstruck to do anything but blink.

'Twins,' she heard Nick say, from what sounded like a long way away.

'Like I said,' the doctor continued with a knowing smile, 'it can come as a bit of a shock. Now if you'll excuse me, Jenny will introduce you to your babies. Enjoy.'

'Twins,' he said again as the doctor departed and Jenny turned the monitor around so they could see.

'I'm sorry I couldn't tell you straight away,' she said, working the transducer over Sophie's belly to find the best angle. 'I know it's awful waiting.'

'My sisters are twins,' said Sophie, her short-circuited brain starting to kick back in.

'It must run in the family,' said the clinician. 'Ah, here we go. They're lying next to each other, so it's hard to make them both out clearly, but right about here ...'

Nick looked at the screen, saw the black-and-white images zoom in and out, all weird circles and shapes and nothing that looked like anything to him, until the sonographer found the right spot and whoa, there they were, two tiny heads and two rows of tiny white beads that could only be their spines, and then the babies rolled over and there were tiny arms and even tinier fingers and toes.

'Oh my God,' said Sophie, 'look at that. Can you believe there're two of them?'

He couldn't believe it. And it didn't matter one iota that he'd been present for Min's scans and that he'd seen this kind of picture before, because this kind of miracle didn't get old. He lifted Sophie's hand in his, her gaze locked on the moving images on the screen before them, and pressed his lips to the back of it.

Two babies.

Bloody hell!

Fifteen minutes later they sat shell-shocked together in the coffee shop, his long black coffee and her lemon-and-ginger tea sitting untouched as they both stared disbelievingly at the picture on the table between them. 'What are you going to do?' he said.

'I don't know. I'd only just come to terms with having one baby. Now, I have to come to terms with having two.'

'I think I know the feeling.'

She managed to drag her eyes up to look at the man opposite, appreciating the fact that he would be a bit blindsided by the latest revelations. 'Nick—I want to thank you for coming.' She licked her lips. 'I really thought something was wrong. I'm so, so glad it wasn't, but I'm glad you were here.'

'Me too,' he said, and she had to look away, because his slate-blue eyes were altogether too warm for her to feel comfortable.

'What will you do about work?' he asked. 'With two babies, I mean?'

'I don't know. I'll have to take leave, I thought at first just for a few months, but now ...'

'Surely you can't think about working with twins. Not full time, at least.'

'Says who?'

'Says common sense. You're not working and putting our babies in care. They deserve better than that.'

She blinked. 'Oh, and just because I invite you along to a scan, you think you're running the show?'

'I'm just trying to think through the logistics. One baby would be challenging enough, but twins changes things, Sophie. You must see that. There's no way you're going to be able to cope by yourself. We have to make suitable arrangements.'

'Suitable for whom?'

'Suitable for the babies, of course. Like where are you going to live?'

'Where do you think? I'm not planning on moving just because I'm pregnant.'

'You and two babies, in that flat?'

'I'm converting the second bedroom into a nursery. It's no big deal. Babies are small.'

'Yep, they start out small and they come with a lot of shit. Before you know it, you'll have play gyms and baby rockers and lambskins and bouncers all over the place, and you won't have an inch of floor space left in which to scratch yourself.'

'We'll manage!'

'By yourself?'

'Of course by myself.' She put her cup down against the saucer with a decided smack, sending her cooling tea sloshing over the side. 'You know, if you really wanted to be involved with these babies, you might try supporting the decisions I make a little more. I am their mother, after all.'

'I'd like to do that, except you don't seem to have a clue what's in store. What are you proposing to do when you go into labour— drive yourself to hospital? Have you thought about that?'

She put her hands to her head. 'Enough, Nick, do I really need to have that worked out already? It's months away. I'll sort it. I'll manage.'

'Sorry, I know,' he said, holding up his hands. 'I know you will.' He sighed. 'It's just, there's so much to think about.'

'So give me time to think about it.'

He blew out a breath in a rush as he sat back in his seat. 'Yeah, okay, point taken. But twins, eh?'

'I know,' she said, feeling similarly stunned. 'Twins.'

⁓

Sophie stepped from the bright December sunlight into her unit, still shell-shocked at the news. Immediately the sofa beckoned, and it was all she could do not to plonk herself down and put her feet up. But that would have to wait, there was something she needed to do first.

Babies came with a lot of shit, Nick had said, and she didn't doubt it. But she'd been counting on one baby, not two. She looked around the combined lounge/dining room with its neat kitchen behind an archway, mentally measuring the space, filling it with highchairs and play mats and a double stroller that had to be parked somewhere.

She flicked on the light in the second bedroom, reassured by the size. It would easily take two cots, and in time, two small single beds, and surely she'd need only one change table?

Her own bedroom was larger and north-facing, cool in summer and filled with winter sunshine. She nodded, a plan already forming in her mind. She'd swap rooms, she didn't need all the space for herself, and then it could double as a toy room, too, when they grew older.

Heartened, she grabbed a glass of iced water and let herself flop onto the sofa at last.

Nick had nothing to worry about. It was going to work. She would make it work.

37

Hannah

'It's coming up to Christmas,' Declan said, nuzzling sideways into her throat. 'How about I take you out one night for a meal. The local does a great schnitzel.'

Hannah thought about all the people that knew her in this area, that she'd either grown up and gone to school with, or had tended their pets or livestock at one time or another, and said, 'Probably not a good idea. I know so many people around here, we'd hardly get a chance to talk.'

'We could go further afield,' he suggested. 'I don't mind travelling.'

'It's so close to Christmas, though, and I'm so busy. Isn't it easier if I just come here? It's so perfect here.'

He smiled at that. 'I'm glad you like Hobbitville, but I'd like to take you out somewhere for a change.'

'You have Ella to think about. You can't just leave her.'

'You know she's perfectly happy in her pouch, wherever I am.' He raised himself up, pressed his lips to her naked shoulder and leaned over to kiss her cheek. 'Wouldn't you like to come out with me?'

She turned in his arms. 'Of course I would. But if word got back to my family before I told them—'

'So, tell them you have a boyfriend.'

'I will, but can't it wait just a little longer?' Her fingers splayed in his sandy hair. 'We've only been seeing each other a few weeks and there's so much going on this time of year. Let's get Christmas out of the way. Things will be quieter then.'

'I'll still get to see you Christmas Day, though?'

'Didn't I already promise?'

He grabbed her hand, brought her fingers to his mouth. 'Okay, have it your way, then. I'll wait. Though, I don't know why your family knowing you've got a fella who's crazy about you would bother them.'

It bothers me, thought Hannah, her blood pressure spiking at the prospect of going public, and that was enough to want to keep this to herself.

38

Sophie

Christmas Day dawned bright and beautiful with the promise of low winds, warm temperatures and clear skies, pretty much idyllic beach weather. Sophie squeezed into her old one-piece, and it was a squeeze, but there was no way she was going to wear a bikini and she was grateful to find something to wear to the beach today. She'd put on the weight she'd lost before the wedding and then some. More than she was supposed to have put on, according to all the online forums she'd been reading. These twins of hers sure had a lot to answer for. She was going to end up being the size of a bus by the time the babies came if this kept up.

She was checking herself out in the mirror, thinking she didn't look too bad if she didn't look at herself sideways, when the doorbell rang.

Random callers on Christmas Day? That was weird.

Quickly, she threw the sundress she'd chosen for today over her head and opened the door. 'Surprise!' said Min, standing next to her father. 'Merry Christmas, Ms Faraday.'

'Min,' she said, 'happy Christmas to you, too.' Her eyes stole up to Nick, who was looking decidedly sheepish. She hadn't seen him since the scan two weeks ago, but he was up to something, she could tell. 'Merry Christmas, Nick. To what do I owe this pleasure?'

'We brought you a present,' said Min, grinning from ear to ear, 'didn't we, Dad?'

'It was Min's idea,' he warned. 'Just in case you're not too thrilled. Though, I checked with Dan and he ran it past the girls and they thought it was a good idea, so ...'

'Hurry up, Dad,' urged Min.

'Okay,' he said, 'just so you know. We left it in the car in case you'd already gone out. Be right back.'

A few moments later he returned holding a big cardboard box with red Christmas ribbon tied around it. She ushered them into the living room, by which time he'd passed it to Min, and she duly and with due gravity handed it to Sophie. 'Merry Christmas,' she said again, lisping a little on the Christmas.

'This is for me?' She shook her head as she took it, surprised it weighed a lot less than she'd expected. 'But, Min, I haven't got anything for you.'

'That's okay,' Min said, her grin refusing to let up. 'Open it.'

The tiny mewl gave it away before she'd got the ribbon undone. Min got the giggles and Sophie stopped. 'Is this what I think it is?'

Min giggled some more before she said, 'Open it.'

Sophie put it down in the centre of the sitting-room floor, undid the ribbon and eased off the lid. The tiny cat blinked its big blue eyes at her and mewled again, and Sophie felt herself melt. The kitten was mostly cream-coloured with a black-and-grey nose and black-edged ears with a grey tail. 'It's gorgeous,' she said, as she reached down into the box to pick it up, holding the soft, fluffy kitten to her chest.

'You like it?' said Min. 'It's one of Fat Cat's kittens. He's a ragdoll cat, or kind of, anyway.'

'And so much bigger now than when I last saw it,' she said.

'You don't mind?' said Nick. 'It's a boy, I guarantee it.'

She pressed her lips to its head. 'It's the best Christmas present I've ever had. Thank you!'

Min clapped her hands. 'Yay!'

'We've got some more stuff in the car for you,' Nick added, 'just in case you said yes. Figured you might need a basket and food and litter tray et cetera. They kind of need a bit of baggage and we figured it might be a bit hard getting set up on Christmas Day.'

'Thank you. What were you going to do if I said no?'

'Keep it,' said Min.

'Sell it,' Nick said at the same time.

Sophie laughed. 'Now, you won't need to do either. What should I call him, do you think?'

'Well,' Min started. 'I was calling him Whiskers, but you don't have to.'

'Oh no, I think Whiskers is an excellent name for a cat this handsome.'

Min beamed.

'I'll get that gear for you,' Nick said.

'I'll give you a hand. Min, can you look after Whiskers for a minute?'

Min was already on the case, making shadows on the floor with her hand that the kitten tried to jump on and catch.

Sophie followed Nick out, wondering how long it would be before she'd be immune to the sheer masculine poetry of the man. Or was it hormones getting in the way of forgetting him? That would be right. Whatever it was, watching his denim-clad hips reminded her of that night they'd spent together, while his open-neck navy-and-white check linen shirt showed off his olive skin to perfection.

Too damn good-looking to ignore—and now he was dropping in with his cute little daughter to give her an equally cute little Christmas present. Couldn't he see what he was doing? It would be his fault if she got the wrong idea.

Nick pulled the cover back on the ute, and Sophie saw the mess of kitten stuff hidden below and forgot about being annoyed.

'Wow, you got me all this?'

'Figured you were going to need it, and seeing as you hadn't actually asked for a kitten ...'

'It's very generous of you.'

'Hardly. You're taking an unexpected kitten off our hands. I probably should have got you one of those serious vacuum cleaners while I was at it, the ones that are supposed to be good with all that cat fur, but I didn't want to overdo it.'

'No,' Sophie said, smiling, and started to pick up stuff from the pile in the car. 'Glad you didn't overdo it.'

'Oh, and don't worry, I checked up with the doctor on whether it's okay to have a cat while you're pregnant, and he said so long as you're past your first trimester and you make sure you use gloves to change the cat litter, there's no risk to you or the babies from toxoplasmosis. I got a box of disposable gloves, too.'

She blinked at him. 'You asked the doctor? Did you tell him why?'

She saw him swallow. 'I said I was asking for a friend.'

Sophie smiled again. She would have loved to have been a fly on the wall at that consultation. 'Well, good to know.'

He hauled out a box containing cat litter, tray and food and turned to her. 'So, how are you, Sophie.'

'Yeah, I'm good.'

'And ...'

'The babies are good by all accounts, too. No change there, except to my waistline.' She tried to be annoyed about his line of questioning, but her heart wasn't in it. After all, it was Christmas Day and already it was proving to be too special a day to ruin, and why wouldn't he want to know?

'Dan says you're having lunch down on the South Coast.' He looked up at the clear blue sky. 'Thirty-five C in the city so probably a few degrees cooler down there. Looks like a good place for Christmas lunch.'

'It's going to be a nice change. What are you doing?'

'Min and I are going down to my sister's family's place for lunch. And then I'll drop Min off at Penelope's to have dinner there, but she's going away early in the morning so I'll pick her up after.'

'Gosh, I guess it makes Christmas Day hard, juggling like that.'

'Yeah,' he said, his brows drawn together, his eyes on hers. 'It does.'

She took a deep breath. This kind of sharing arrangement was exactly the sort of thing she'd been trying to avoid, but it would be churlish to say that, now. Besides, she could hardly argue that Min didn't seem well enough adjusted to her turnaround living arrangements. Which didn't suit her to think about at all. 'Well, let's get this lot inside, then.'

Min got Sophie organised and showed her how to set up the kitty-litter tray and how much food she needed to give the growing kitten, before Sophie went off to make coffee and get a water for Min.

Nick was lying on the rug, his back towards her and his head resting on his hand, his long legs stretched out. Sophie was struck by the father–daughter–kitten dynamic going on in her living room, the young daughter bubbly and brimming with excitement with the kitten's every antic, the father engaged and involved but calmer, a steadying influence.

Something sharp stabbed her then. A pointed accusation that this cutesy family scene could be hers for more than just one day, if only she forgot about wanting to do this parenting thing alone and let Nick in. And she could almost picture it—her and Nick, Min and two tiny babies, lying together in the living room and needing nothing more.

The trouble was, she wanted that for real, not like this, feeling like an intruder, gatecrashing someone else's family. And the pain was so intense she put her hand over her belly to protect her unborn children from it. Because no, this wasn't happening. This scene before her was as shallow and artificial as the emotions that had bound her and Nick the night their babies had been conceived.

On autopilot she found a tray for the coffees, water and a plate of shortbread she'd made to take to today's picnic. She'd just filled the tray and turned to return to the living room, when she heard Min say, 'But do I have to go to Penelope's?' And she stopped in the archway.

'Of course you do,' said Nick. 'Because it's Christmas Day and she's your mum and she wants to see you.'

'She doesn't want to be a mum, though,' said Min, picking up the kitten and cradling it in her lap. 'She just wants to be a Penelope.'

'I know, Minnie Mouse,' he said with a sigh, reaching out a hand to ruffle her dark hair. 'I know. But that doesn't change the fact that she is your mum and she deserves to see you on Christmas Day, too. Why should I have all the fun?'

The girl gave a theatrical sigh.

'Tell you what,' he said, 'how about after I pick you up tonight, we head down to the beach for a swim?'

Immediately her mood brightened. 'Can we?'

'Don't see why not. It'll still be Christmas Day when I pick you up, I figure we can fit another treat in before bedtime.'

'Anyone for shortbread?' said Sophie softly from the archway, not wanting to intrude but feeling guilty for eavesdropping on a private conversation.

'Me!' said Min. 'I love shortbread.'

39

Beth

The Faraday family travelled down to the beach in three cars, Dan and Lucy picking up Nan and Pop on the way, while Beth took Siena and Hannah picked up Sophie in her Subaru. The convoy bypassed the busy Horseshoe Bay where the car parks and the lawns were full, and headed for the quieter stretch of surf beach that ran all the way from Port Elliot to Victor Harbor, finding a spot on the firm white sand while the waves crashed and pounded just a few feet away. Dan put up a sunshade for Nan and Pop, a couple of umbrellas and some folding chairs, and when they joined up a few picnic rugs, they had an entire makeshift living room at their disposal.

Nan took up residence in one of the chairs, her gaze swinging from the rocky foreshore at one end of the beach to Victor Harbor's famous Bluff, while the women unpacked the lunch. 'My mother caught the train with me down to Victor when I was just a girl,' Nan said. 'She was your great-grandmother, girls, except to Siena here,' to whom she said, 'she was your great-great-grandmother.

Your mother's mother's mother's mother, what do you think about that?' Siena blinked at the older woman, lost in the generations of mothers when Nan had always been just that—Nan.

'And then,' Nan continued, locked in the past, 'we waited at the station to be picked up by Mr Summerfield's horse and dray for the trip to Encounter Bay. They had a lovely stone house near the beach, but back then, the rest of it was all paddocks.'

'It's sure not paddocks, these days,' said Sophie, scoping out the march of the suburbs up the hill away from the beach.

'How old were you, Nan?' asked Beth.

'Ooh, I must have been all of seven or eight.'

'What's a dray?' said Siena.

'It's a wagon or a cart,' Beth said.

'And it was pulled by an old draft horse,' said Nan. 'Dear old thing called Thunder.'

'Why didn't they pick you up in a car?'

'Nobody had cars in those days. Unless you lived in Adelaide and were very rich. The roads in the country just weren't good enough.'

'And it wasn't just cars,' Beth added. 'Nobody had TVs or computers or the internet. And certainly no *MasterChef*.'

'Yuck,' said Siena. 'What did people do?'

'They read books or listened to the radio or they sang around the piano for entertainment.'

'That's when they weren't working.'

'They're all gone now,' said Nan, sounding wistful for the old days. 'Mr and Mrs Summerfield and dear old Thunder, of course.'

Pop snorted. 'We're still here. Outlived the lot of them, we have.'

'Though it was touch and go there for a while,' Nan said, 'wasn't it, Clarence Faraday?'

Pop grumbled and scratched at the zipper-line scar on his chest with one hand, swiped up a piece of buttered French stick from a plate with the other and shoved it in his mouth. 'Got to hang around for these new young'uns,' he said between chews. 'The next crop of Faradays is coming on thick and fast.' He nodded as he lunged for a chicken leg and waved it in the air. 'Got good reason to hang around.'

They feasted on roast chicken with devilled eggs and salads, shortbread and Nan's famous Christmas cake that no Christmas would be complete without, before they exchanged presents. Small gifts mostly, pretty stationery from Siena, homemade treats from Sophie and tinkling wind chimes made from spoons from Hannah. Beth had made crystal sun catchers for everyone to hang in a sunny window, all except for Siena that is, who was delighted to unwrap a body board. But it was the gift Beth gave Lucy and Dan that raised the most sighs of appreciation. Made of shards of tiles, mirror and mottled glass, it was a mosaic wall hanging for the nursery featuring a sliver of silvery moon with a star dangling from the top and a plump yellow teddy lying fast asleep in the curve of the moon below.

'It's the most beautiful thing I've ever seen,' said Lucy, pulling Beth into a huge hug. 'You guys are the very best, you know that? I love being part of this family.'

'Hey,' said Beth, 'we think you're pretty cool, too.'

Hannah agreed. 'Especially since you managed to turn our brother into a functioning member of the human race.'

'Do you mind?' said Dan, aggrieved. 'I am within hearing range.'

'Oh, don't worry,' said Lucy, with a grin towards her still-new husband. 'Dan's a fully functioning member of the human race. I can swear to that.'

Dan just put his head in his hands and groaned, making the girls laugh. Dan then decided it was time to take Nan, Pop and Siena off in search of bathrooms and hopefully ice-creams, leaving the four sisters to soak up the sun by themselves.

Hannah watched them leave. 'Nan and Pop seem to have taken news of these babies of yours remarkably well, Soph. Sounds like they're looking forward to the birth as much as they're looking forward to Lucy and Dan's.'

'They need something to look forward to at their age,' said Beth. 'Why wouldn't they get used to the idea?'

'True,' Sophie said, 'but there's another reason they're not as upset as you might think. Something Nan shared with me. I know she won't mind me telling you guys.' And she told them the story Nan had confided in her, of a young woman and a handsome man and one night with consequences.

'Poor Nan,' said Beth. 'How unfair, to be forced into marriage like that.'

'And yet none of us would be here if it hadn't happened.'

'I know, it just all seems so wrong to be trapped that way.'

'Women didn't have a choice back then, though, did they? They couldn't work, not with a baby. And without a husband to support them, there was no way they'd be able to look after themselves and a child.'

The four women lay on their towels on the sand, looking up at the endless blue sky through dark glasses, thinking about families and secrets and skeletons rattling in the closet, while the waves rolled and crashed in the way they'd always done. And it seemed that suddenly everything had shifted somehow, so it was the same but different.

'I just can't believe we never worked it out ourselves,' said Sophie. 'We all knew Nan and Pop's anniversary was in August. And we always celebrated Dad's birthday in February. How is it that we never put the two together?'

'I guess we never thought about the actual years,' said Beth. 'Not back before Dad died, and that's nearly twelve years ago, now. We would have been too young to think about it back then, let alone make something of it.'

'And nobody else made a big deal of it,' Sophie added. 'It was just there all the time, hiding in plain sight.'

Lucy idly stroked her twenty-two-week belly that was still little more than a slight curve. 'There can't be too many families that have spotless histories,' she said. 'But nobody's going to advertise the spots, are they? And most children and grandchildren will assume that their parents and grandparents fell in love and got married and had babies in the right order, and everyone's happy to let them.'

'We sure did,' said Beth. And then added with a chuckle, 'God, you don't think it runs in the family?'

'How do you mean?' said Lucy.

'Well, me having Siena for a start, and now Sophie getting pregnant, too.'

'And Lucy got a head start,' added Sophie, earning a grin from Lucy.

'Yup,' she said, patting her tummy, 'sure did.'

'You'd better watch out, Han,' joked Beth. 'You'll be next.'

Hannah sprang to her feet, wiping sand from her legs. 'I'm going for another dip.'

Beth watched her sister's back as she marched purposefully down towards the waves between the walkers and kids building sand castles, and looked sideways at Sophie and Lucy. 'What's wrong with Han?'

'Probably just afraid of being left on the shelf,' said Sophie, sitting up.

'You mean the shelf she's padlocked herself to?'

They all watched the eldest-by-ten-minutes Faraday sister being embraced by the crashing waves and foam.

'So, she just hasn't met the right guy yet,' said Lucy.

'Hey, this is Han we're talking about,' said Beth. 'Her right guy doesn't exist.'

Sophie snorted and slapped at a fly on her elbow. 'Or he better have four legs.'

They heard Siena whoop behind them. 'We found ice-creams,' she said, running across the sand. 'Drumsticks.'

'Excellent,' said Sophie, patting the space beside her on the blanket. 'Come and sit down next to your favourite aunty.'

40

Hannah

Hannah was lying on her beach towel, everyone else dozing, while the thoughts in her mind tumbled over and over. Why hadn't she told them, the people closest to her, what had happened to her? Why, when Nan and Beth and Sophie and even Lucy, had all experienced unplanned pregnancies? Why, when she had never had a better opportunity to share?

But the answer kept coming back the same, so she kept repeating the question, while the slot-machine windows rolled again and again, still coming up the same.

She didn't want their pity. She'd gone so long holding her secret close to her, she didn't know if she could reveal it. Unless she was as old as Nan and it didn't matter anymore. Yes, she could do that. When it didn't matter anymore. When everyone her age around her had long ago stopped having babies and she could dote on their grandchildren instead.

Her phone buzzed. She seized on it and read the message, feeling the welcome smile on her lips. 'I have to go,' she said, springing up to dust off the sand and pull on her beach cover-up.

'What? Seriously, who would bother someone on Christmas Day?' asked Sophie, lifting her head up.

Hannah shrugged. 'Sophie, you'll have to get a lift back with Beth, sorry.'

Beth lifted her sunglasses and peered suspiciously at her. 'You don't look too cut up about being called in. You're smiling.'

'It's been a great day,' she said, immediately dropping the telltale smile.

'It's the best Christmas ever,' declared Siena. 'I don't ever want to go home.'

Hannah could let herself smile at that. 'Anyway, I really need to get out of the sun. I'm burning up here.'

Beth let her sunglasses drop back down with a sigh. 'Such a shame, though. There was me thinking you must have a hot date or something. A secret Santa you're not telling us about.'

Hannah tried to laugh, and hoped it didn't sound too brittle and false. If only they knew … 'Yeah, right.' She stuffed her things in her beach bag, gave a quick kiss to both Nan and Pop, who were softly snoring in their beach chairs, and waved her goodbyes to the rest.

She felt a little stab of guilt that she hadn't been entirely open with her family, but she was still getting used to the idea of having a lover herself, without sharing her secret with all and sundry. She didn't want her family probing and prodding for information. She didn't want them offering opinions and advice and making long-term plans, not when Declan had come out of a failed relationship and was hardly likely to jump into another.

So she wasn't being unreasonable. She was just being cautious. Wise.

41

Sophie

Sophie was inclined to agree with Siena; their untraditional Christmas was proving to be a huge success. After Hannah left, they played in the waves some more, before Dan suggested a game of Rounders. Pop was keen to umpire and Sophie was happy to let everyone else exercise while she plonked herself dripping wet in the sun with a still-dozing Nan.

'Soph, you awake?'

Sophie cracked open one eyelid and held up a hand to shield her eyes against the sun. 'Dan?'

'Yeah, you got a minute?'

'I thought you were playing Rounders.'

'Everyone's having a cool-off.'

She looked up and saw them all in the surf, Lucy standing next to Beth, who was holding onto Siena on her new body board waiting for a wave, and Pop, holding up the legs of his shorts while he paddled in the shallows. 'I'm supposed to be looking after Nan.'

'She's asleep. Come on, this won't take a minute.'

Sophie looked across at her nan, who was sitting with her head to one side and her mouth open, still snoring. Yeah, she was out for the count all right. 'Okay,' she said, mildly curious as she got to her feet. 'What's on your mind, big bro?'

He led her down towards the shore, where the waves crashed and turned to foam that lapped at their feet as they walked in the shallows. Before them in the distance sprawled Victor Harbor, ending with the mountainous Bluff that fell abruptly into the sea.

'Nick asked me to talk to you. I didn't do anything before, I wanted to stay out of it, but given we're here ...'

Wet sand squeezed between her toes while aggravation lapped at her brain. Nick had gone bleating to her brother? 'What are you talking about?'

'Nick. He feels like he's being cut out of this whole baby thing.'

'He told you that?'

'Well, I am his friend—and your brother.'

Any warm feelings she'd had for Nick about hand holding at scans and gifts of kittens evaporated in that moment. 'He's got a bloody nerve.'

'He is the father of these babies, isn't he?'

'Of course he is. So?'

'So he has responsibilities. He wants to be involved.'

She scowled across at him. 'Nick came to my twelve-week scan. Did he tell you that? I've agreed to keep him informed. What more does he want?'

Her brother shook his head. 'I didn't realise. That's good. Sorry, Soph, maybe I shouldn't say any more.'

'Maybe you shouldn't.' She kicked at the lapping water. 'And then maybe you should. What else did he say?'

'Sophie—'

'No, Dan. Spill. What else was Nick banging on about? What else does he want?'

Her brother rubbed the back of his neck, and she had a pretty good idea it wasn't sunburn making him uncomfortable. 'He wants to help.'

'Really? He's got a funny way of showing it.'

'Sophie, try to see it from his point of view. He's not shying away from his responsibilities, he's stepping up to them. He wants to be part of what's happening. He wants to be a father to these babies.'

She held up one hand. 'Look, Dan, it's really nice of you to look out for your friend, but it's not that easy.'

'Nobody said it was going to be easy. But if you don't mind hearing my opinion, you don't have to go making it more difficult than it has to be.'

She stopped, her feet being sucked deeper by the ebb and flow of the waves like she was being sucked deeper into a place she didn't want to go. 'You set him on me that night, didn't you? You set your watchdog onto me, only to have it backfire, big time. That's what you're worried about. Because whatever happened that night, you had a hand in it. That's why you're taking his side. Because you feel guilty and you think you owe him.'

'That's utter bullshit, Soph. I'm not wearing that and I'm not responsible for you getting banged up. I asked him to look after you and after that it was you and Nick who decided what to do next. And now, you guys have to sort it out for yourselves. Nick is trying to. I can't see that you're doing a lot to help.'

'It was a one-night stand. It didn't mean anything.'

'Great,' he said, rolling his eyes towards the clear blue sky. 'Because a big brother really needs to hear that.'

'Maybe you do. So you understand where I'm coming from and why I want to do this by myself.'

'Can't you understand where Nick's coming from? Have you thought about why he cares so much?'

'Because he's a control freak? I don't know.'

'No. Because these are his babies we're talking about, Sophie, his flesh and blood, just as much as they're yours. And Nick knows what having a child means. He could have turned his back and walked away, but no, he stepped up to the plate because he knows what it is to be a father. If you don't get that, then maybe you don't have any concept of what having a child really is and maybe you're not ready to be a mother.'

'How dare you!'

'I dare because I'm your brother. So stop being so selfish. Don't shut Nick out, and don't throw him breadcrumbs and expect him to be satisfied with that. He doesn't deserve it. Think about it, and talk to him and work out something that's fair and that's going to go some way to satisfy you both.'

Sophie wanted to tell her brother where to go. To tell him that he was wrong and that it was none of his business and she'd decide what was right for her babies, but she didn't get a chance, because between the rolling thunder of the waves she was sure she heard someone calling.

She turned to see Beth waving frantically in the distance, surprised when she realised how far they'd walked. 'Something's wrong,' she said. 'We better get back.'

Sophie took off across the beach, jogging through the soft sand back to their camp so she was breathless by the time she arrived. 'What is it?' But she looked at the empty chair and already knew. 'Where's Nan?' she said.

'I was hoping you might know that.'

'She was right there,' Dan said at her shoulder, 'fast asleep a minute or two ago.'

Beth had her hands on her forehead. 'Well, she's not there now.'

'Maybe she woke up and wondered where everyone was.' Sophie looked up and down the beach, hoping to catch a glimpse of Nan's navy-and-white spotted dress among the few scattered groups along the shoreline, but there was no sign of it or her. She wanted to rule out the possibility that Nan might have wandered the way she'd gone with Dan, but she couldn't. They'd been so intent on their conversation, the sky could have fallen and they wouldn't have realised. 'Where the hell could she be?' Sophie hadn't been gone that long, surely Nan couldn't be too far away. One by one the others came back from the water and gathered around dripping wet.

'What's that Joanie gone and done this time?' grumbled Pop, the bottoms of his shorts soaked through from paddling and getting caught out by the unpredictable waves.

'It's okay,' Sophie said, because there was no reason to panic, even if the thought of her eighty-one-year-old Nan wandering off by herself didn't exactly thrill her. 'She's gone for a walk, that's all. She can't have gone too far.'

'Silly woman,' said Pop, adding a grunt for good measure as he dropped into a chair and swiped sand from his shorts. 'She might have left a note. She never leaves a bloody note.'

They all looked at Pop. 'What?' Dan said. 'When doesn't she leave a note?'

'When she goes off on one of her walks. Never tells me she's going and I never know when she's coming back, and most times she can't even remember where she went.'

'Why didn't you tell us this?' said Beth.

'I did, that day you came around and she wasn't there and I said she'd gone for a walk. Why does nobody ever listen to me?'

Beth's face turned white. 'I thought it was just a walk. I didn't know ...'

Sophie felt a cold ooze of fear dribble down her spine, and by the look in her siblings' eyes, they all felt it, too. 'How long's this been going on?'

'I don't know. She does it all the time. She was in the middle of making lunch the other day and I heard the screen door slam, and I ended up having to make my own bloody sandwich.'

'Oh my God,' said Beth, her eyes wide as she exchanged looks with Sophie. 'It's worse than we thought.'

'I'll go this way,' Sophie said, pointing down the beach towards the rocky point. 'There're a few people around today, someone must have seen her if she's gone by.'

Beth nodded. 'Then I'll go the other way. Siena, come on, we'll check up the stairs first, in case she's headed back to the car,' and the young girl dumped her new body board on the sand and sprinted off across the beach towards the stairs.

'What's all the bloody fuss?' said Pop, opening a Tupperware container and helping himself to another piece of shortbread. 'She always wanders back when she's good and ready.'

'You,' Sophie said, 'you stay right here, promise me, Pop?'

'I'm not going anywhere. Not while there's any of your short-bread left, girlie.'

'I'll stay with Pop,' said Lucy and Sophie smiled her thanks, setting off down the beach towards the rocks and so busy beating herself up for leaving her nan that for a minute she didn't realise Dan was right there, at her shoulder.

'I wanted to talk to you, about before.'

'God, Dan, enough already. I get that you think Nick should be involved.'

'No, I wanted to apologise for taking you away from Nan. She looked sound asleep to me.'

'Gawd,' she said, her eyes scanning the undulating golden sands of the beach for some hint of Nan. 'Sorry for jumping down your throat. And for the record, I thought she was dead to the world, too.' She shuddered, replaying her words. 'Shouldn't have said that, sorry.'

She peeled her eyes away from the beach and the waves crashing on sand and stone and looked at him. 'Did you have any idea Nan had been going off on these walks?'

'None at all.'

'You don't think …' she started.

'I don't think what?'

'You don't think Han's right? She's been worried Nan was starting to lose it and wanted her to get checked out, but she couldn't get her in to see anyone before Christmas.'

'You mean Alzheimer's or something?' He shrugged. 'I hope not, but they're both getting on. And Nan seems kind of forgetful sometimes.'

'I'm forgetful. Everyone I know is forgetful.' Seagulls standing on the shore scattered before them. 'But wandering. I don't like that.'

'No,' Dan said, sounding grim, 'neither do I.'

A bunch of teenagers sat on the sand at the top of the beach sharing a bag of hot chips, and Dan went to ask if they'd seen a woman walk by.

Sophie surveyed what was left of the beach, more rocky outcrops than sand from here on, ending with the granite boulders of the jutting headland and the tide was coming in. Surely there was no way Nan could have come this far. Beth had probably found her up in the car park waiting by the car, thinking she'd been deserted, poor love.

She turned her head towards the group when Dan hadn't returned, and saw one of the boys pointing, and didn't know whether to feel relief or fear when Dan came sprinting back across the ankle-deep sand.

'One of them saw an old lady in a spotted dress walk by a few minutes ago, although he thought she was walking a dog. She went round those rocks that way.'

Sophie looked at the waves that crashed on a stone platform and whooshed in towards the jutting rocks above in a seething, foaming rage before being sucked out again and swallowed back into the sea. The tide was coming in, but if you timed it right, you could make it around the rocky outcrop to the narrow stretch of beach beyond, but if you got it wrong, you'd end up knocked off your feet. 'Are they sure they came this way?' she said, the sand patches between the rocks wiped clean of any trace of footprints.

'Wait here, I'll take a look,' Dan said, watching for a break in the waves.

It was worth a try, she supposed, the chances it was Nan were pretty slim, even if she could have made it this far.

She pulled out her phone, frustrated by its ongoing silence, toying with the idea of calling triple zero if she didn't hear from someone soon that they'd found her. Then above the crash of waves and the cries of seagulls she heard Dan shout. And she dodged a path between waves and rock and ran.

She found them under a curve of rock, a semi-cave dug out by the relentless tide with a high sand shelf at the back, where Nan was perched. Dan was helping her up, and Sophie could see her legs and the bottom of her dress were already soaked from the incoming tide. 'Nan,' she said, relief at war with fear, because this was so not like her nan. 'What are you doing here?'

She looked a little perplexed as she blinked up at Dan and Sophie. 'I needed a sit-down,' she said, 'and it was nice and shady, but then I got splashed.'

'Oh, Nan, where were you going? Everyone was frantic.'

'Were they? I was just looking for the whales. There were whales, weren't there. We saw whales here, didn't we, Clarry?' She searched for Pop, looking bewildered and confused and utterly fragile. Sophie bundled Nan in the crook of her arm and looked at

Dan. Even though she half suspected the answer, she asked, 'What's going on?'

'I don't want to think about it,' Dan said, his jaw set, as the next foaming wash of wave wrapped around their ankles, 'but let's get her out of here.'

Between them they negotiated Nan out of the cave and around the rocky outcrop, and found a higher spot with a flattened rock where she could safely sit and rest. 'It's too far to get her back. You wait with Nan, and I'll bring a car closer.'

'Bring back a nice cup of tea while you're at it,' said Nan, suddenly sounding more like her old self by the minute. 'I'm dying of thirst.'

And in spite of the cannonball of fear weighing heavily in her gut, Sophie felt a spark of hope as she pulled out her phone to let the others know they'd found her. Maybe she'd just had some kind of turn, because if Nan was still barking out the orders, they hadn't completely lost her yet.

42

Hannah

'Merry Christmas,' Declan said with his dimpled smile as he came to greet Hannah at the car. Her heart gave a little leap, and any thought of guilt at her secret tryst evaporated right there. He really was the most gorgeous man and she wasn't ready to share him with anyone.

'Happy Christmas yourself,' she said, reaching for her bag. 'I hope you don't mind, but I came straight from the beach.'

He wrapped his arms around her and pulled her into his kiss. 'Mmm,' he said, releasing her a good half-minute later. 'Salty, like a mermaid. Just the way I like them,' before he kissed her again.

Hannah's knees were weak from his kisses by the time he hoisted her bag over his shoulder and took her hand to lead her inside. They were weaker still after he peeled off her beach cover and her sandy swimsuit and stepped naked into the shower with her. His mouth kissed its way down her body until he was on his knees before her and his head between her thighs, his clever tongue turning Christmas into fireworks day.

'I thought you said you liked your mermaids salty,' she said, clinging onto his head, gasping from the sensations his hot mouth inspired that threatened to consume her.

'And sweet,' he said, lifting his head the tiniest of fractions, 'salty and sweet, so long as they taste like you.'

The water rained down on them as his words and his hot mouth tipped her over the edge, and she would have fallen, but he was there to save her, urging her useless legs around his waist as he surged into her.

'You're beautiful,' she heard him say, as she burst apart around him. 'So beautiful.'

And Hannah knew Siena had been one hundred per cent right.

It was the best Christmas ever.

Propped up between two pillows as they exchanged presents, sat Ella, watching on as she nibbled on a long blade of native grass. She'd grown a lot in the last few weeks, progressing to short stints outside the pouch, where she hopped after Declan as he worked on the vines, scratching on his leg and hopping back into the pouch when she'd had enough. She sat wide-eyed and content as Hannah opened her present from Declan.

She found lingerie inside, no more than scraps of silk and lace in a midnight blue that were exquisitely sheer and no doubt extravagantly expensive. 'You have something against my Cottontails?' she joked, while secretly thrilled.

'Nothing at all,' he assured her, 'so long as you're taking them off. But still, a man doesn't mind a little fantasy.' He wouldn't open her present until she'd put them on, and so she did, never before feeling so utterly decadent sitting there in glamorous underwear and nothing else.

'My present is nowhere near as personal,' she said, wondering if she should have made more of an effort as he tore away the paper. The chunky pipes inside sounded out a clue as he unwrapped, and she waited with bated breath. She'd thought she'd struck on the perfect present for everyone, the spoons for the girls tinkling light and pretty, and Declan's the warmest and deepest tones, but should she have found something more intimate for him?

He held up the wind chime and the pipes bounced off each other, the mellow notes making music together. Ella stopped nibbling for a moment, suddenly on alert, her long ears up and swivelling at this new sound, before she relaxed, going back to chewing on her grass.

'Do you like them?' she asked, because it was suddenly important that he approve. 'I thought you could hang them outside to catch a breeze.'

'It's the most perfect present ever,' he said, pulling her close. 'And every time I hear them, it will remind me of you.'

As he swept her up into his kiss, Hannah for once wasn't blaming herself for the mistakes of the past and wishing that things could be different. Because right now, the repercussions of a choice she'd made back when she was twenty didn't seem so important. She had Declan, a man settled and happy in his own skin, just willing to be and not asking her for things she couldn't give.

Declan put his hands to her shoulder and eased her away. 'Your phone,' he said, 'did you want to answer that?'

Hannah blinked. She hadn't even heard it. She turned and snatched it up, frowning when she saw who it was from. She got out of bed and walked to the wall of windows overlooking the bush, the warm air like a whisper over her skin. 'Beth, hi.'

'How was the emergency? All okay?'

Oh, yeah, that. She turned and looked at Declan, looking sex-rumpled and gorgeous, his sandy hair askew, and sent him a smile. 'Um, all good. Is everything okay?'

'It's Nan,' her sister said. 'We thought you should know. There is something wrong.' And Hannah listened while Beth recounted what had happened at the beach.

Hannah's hand flew to her head. 'God, I'm sorry. I knew something was up, but by the time I booked, I couldn't get her in before January.'

'Forget it,' Beth said. 'I'm supposed to be the one with medical expertise here, and I didn't pick it. To be honest, I don't think I had the headspace to deal with it. I'm just sorry I didn't listen to you earlier.'

Hannah went back to bed after the call, perching on the side, one leg folded beneath her. 'It's Nan. She went missing at the beach, and now they're worried it's Alzheimer's. And I knew something was wrong but I didn't do anything.'

Declan pulled her against him. 'And you think having it diagnosed earlier would have made any difference?'

'We would have known. We wouldn't have done something crazy like go to the beach for Christmas.'

'No? And what do you think your nan would have preferred? Being out in the fresh air with the sand and the surf, or stuck inside somewhere where it was safe but dull?'

'You don't know anything about my nan.'

'No, that's true enough. But then, you haven't exactly invited me in to your world, Hannah Faraday. You seem to be content to let me live on the fringe.'

She lifted her head from his shoulder, suddenly thrown off balance. They'd been sleeping together since October, more than two months, and yet still this affair with Declan felt new and fragile. She didn't feel ready to share it with anyone yet, let alone her family. It wasn't as if she was the only one with secrets, after all. Beth hadn't exactly volunteered that she was seeing this Harry fellow. 'Are you criticising me?'

'No. Just stating a fact and expressing a wish at the same time. I'd like to meet your family, Hannah. I'd like to think I was that special in your life that you'd want me to meet with them.'

'You are special, you know that. Do I make chocolate cake for anyone else?'

He laughed, and pressed his lips to her hair. 'You'd better not. But I'd still like to meet your family. Unless you're ashamed of me, of course.'

'Of course I'm not ashamed of you!' She knew he was kidding, but there was no harm in kissing him to convince him.

Her family would be stunned, of course, that the Faraday least likely to actually had a love interest. It would be worth telling them just for the shock interest.

'All right,' she conceded on a sigh, her lips tingling from the brush of his whiskered jaw. 'But give us time to work through what's happening with Nan first, before I inflict my family on you, okay?'

He put his fingers under her jaw and lifted her mouth to his smiling lips. 'It's a deal.'

43

Beth

Lucy had taken Nan and Siena out for coffee and cake at a local cafe when the GP uttered the words no family wanted to hear. 'I'm sorry,' he said. 'There's no cure for dementia. What we can do, now that the test results are back and we have a clearer picture, is work out a way to manage the progress of the illness as best we can.'

Pop slapped his palm against his leg and looked away. 'Well, that's that, then.'

Beth could see he was blinking back the tears and she rubbed his bony shoulder, willing him to be strong, before she turned to the doctor. 'Does this mean Nan will have to go into a home?'

'God, not that,' said Hannah.

'It would kill her to have to move into a nursing home,' Dan added.

'It would bloody well kill me,' said Pop. 'Might as well shoot us both and be done with it.'

'Not at all,' the doctor said, holding up his hand. 'There's no need for that kind of talk, Clarence. In Joanie's case, where she's still managing at home, there's no need to rush a move into a nursing home. And with assistance with meals and cleaning, hopefully that won't be necessary for some time.'

'How much time?' asked Beth, still beating herself up for not being the one to notice Nan's decline and brushing off her sister's concerns. 'What are we talking—months or years?'

'That's a harder question to answer. Every case is different. For some patients the disease can move quite rapidly, while in others the change over time might be quite imperceptible to the casual observer. But in either case, it can't be stopped or the symptoms reversed.'

'It's awful,' said Sophie.

'It's the pits,' said Beth. 'Half my day is transporting oldies between nursing homes and hospitals. Some of the old dears don't even know their own names, or they think they're back in the nineteen forties.' She sniffed back a tear. 'I'm sorry, everyone, you'd think that I, more than anyone, might have noticed something was wrong.'

'Don't blame yourself,' said the doctor. 'It's often only when something major happens that the pieces suddenly add up.'

Beside her Dan nodded. 'So how much of this do we tell her? Or do we not tell her at all and we just pretend everything is normal?'

The doctor nodded. 'Not even that's easy. Some patients are actually relieved to have a diagnosis, because it explains things they've been secretly worried about for a while but afraid to share with anyone. Others might not take it so well. But you're her family and you know Joanie better than anyone. What would she want? And ask yourselves what you'd want to know in the same circumstances.'

'Oh God,' said Hannah, 'I'm with Pop. I'd shoot myself if I had a diagnosis like that.'

'Or you might,' said the doctor, 'just decide to finally go on that world cruise you'd been promising yourself all your life.'

They all looked aghast, but the GP just shrugged. 'It might take a little more organisation and a few more precautions, but it can be done.'

Pop nodded. 'Joanie always loves going up the river to Mildura. I reckon she might fancy a bus trip up that way.'

The doctor looked levelly at them all. 'So, maybe this is something you want to plan sooner rather than later.'

44

Sophie

'And I still say there's nothing wrong with me!'

'It's not up to you, though, is it?' said Pop, sitting in his chair opposite Nan on the verandah as Sophie put mugs of tea and a plate of Yo-Yo biscuits on the table between them. 'It's what the doctors say, and they all say you've got old-timer's disease.'

'Rubbish,' said Nan, puffing out her chest. 'I'm not having it.'

'You don't get a bloody choice, woman! And the sooner you get that through your head, the better.' He snorted. 'And to think I thought you deserved a weekend away!' Pop gave another snort and said he was heading off to the shed, while Nan appealed to her youngest granddaughter. 'It's not true, is it, Sophie. It's all a load of codswallop. I'm perfectly fine.'

Sophie's heart was breaking. It was exhausting. The debate had been raging for a week, ever since they'd got the results from the tests the specialist had ordered and the diagnosis delivered. As a family they'd battled with the question of how much to tell Nan,

but in the end it had seemed unfair to pretend to her that all was
well, and impractical not to tell her when Dan had been making
the house more secure.

But now, Nan was in denial and Pop was frustrated and determined to shake her out of it. Though, Sophie thought, he could
have handled it slightly less combatively.

'You are fine, Nan, most of the time.' And that was the problem
right there, because nobody knew when she'd wander again or
something else would come unplugged from her brain. 'It's just,
there are times when you forget where you are or what you're
doing, and those are the times we're worried about.'

'But I don't want to be locked away inside one of those nursing
homes.'

'And there's no reason why you should, not if we can help it.
Which is why Dan's been busy this week fixing things up. You
won't be able to wander off without a bell ringing, so Pop will
know you're outside, and we'll know you're safe.'

Dan had been busy doing more than that, though. He'd put bolts
up high on the doors so Nan couldn't reach them and get out at night,
and he'd put a new lock on the gate so that Nan couldn't slip away
if she went out the back to hang up the washing or feed the chooks.

Nan was even sporting a pretty MedicAlert bracelet that should
help her get home if she somehow did manage to escape.

Nan was topping up their tea when Sophie felt it, a fluttering in
her belly, like the beat of butterfly wings deep inside. She put the
pot down and put a hand to her belly. *Oh my …*

'What is it?' said Nan. 'You've come over all strange-looking.'

'I felt something,' she said, struck by this new sensation. 'I felt
something move.'

Nan smiled and patted her arm. 'It's the quickening, that's what
it is. The first tiny flutters of your baby moving.'

Sophie smiled, feeling a mix of wonder and awe. It was really there, this new life she'd inadvertently created. It was there and it was moving and she could feel it. 'I'm only fifteen weeks. I didn't expect to feel anything so soon.'

'Your baby's just saying hello to you,' Nan said with a sigh. 'Letting you know it's there and that everything's going well. I remember the first time I felt your father move, and I knew right then, I knew at that very moment that everything would be all right. And it was too—for the most part.' She sniffed and searched for a tissue up her cardigan sleeve, before she turned watery eyes on Sophie. 'I miss your father every day, you know. I think of him and I miss him terribly.'

'Aw, Nan, I know.' Sophie reached over to hug the older woman, noticing how slight her nan felt under her hand when she'd always thought her soft and ample, and pressed her lips to Nan's forehead. 'I miss him too.'

'It's not right, you know,' Nan said, her voice quaking as she blew her nose. 'No mother should ever have to bury her own child.'

Sophie rocked her nan while she had a little weep, and not for the first time, Sophie found herself cursing Nan's damned disease. For if dementia was going to suck your memories out one by one, it might at least take away the ones that hurt the most first.

45

Beth

Beth had initially been embarrassed when Harry had noticed the gutters on the cottage needed cleaning out, especially when it was so far into fire season and they should have been cleared weeks ago. But while she'd never had a fear of blood or spiders, heights had always given Beth the creeps. She'd never been like Sophie, who'd been clambering up and down cherry-picking ladders from the time she could walk, and so the gutters at Beth's place tended to get ignored for way too long.

But with a forecast of heatwave conditions on the way, embarrassment had swiftly given way to relief. She'd been grateful when Harry had offered to help, because there was no way she was getting up a ladder to do them herself, and it wasn't like she could ask Sophie to help in her condition.

A scant two hours after he'd started and with the gutters cleared, Harry now manned the barbecue cooking sausages and chops, while Beth whipped up salads, and Siena buttered bread and set the

outdoor table for three. Just a simple dinner to repay Harry a little
for all his hard work and save him from having to rustle something
up when he got home, that was all it was, even if he did have to
man the barbecue himself.

Beth sighed and took a sip of her cool white wine as she sat back in
her chair, still glowing from the satisfaction that morning of helping a
baby come into the world in the back of her ambulance. Watching a
new life be born definitely beat their usual battle to save lives; the first
cry of the baby had left her with a warm feeling that lasted all day.

And tonight was the perfect evening to be outside. The afternoon summer temperature had moderated, and the gentle hills
breeze kept any flies at bay. And her full-of-gum-leaves gutters
were finally cleared.

For all its warts, and there were plenty of those, life was okay. And
that was before Harry asked, 'Back at school next week, Siena?' as he
reached for another sausage and a piece of bread to wrap around it.

'Bleh,' she said, rolling her head back theatrically. 'Why does
school take up your whole life? It's so boring.'

Beth was about to laugh, but Harry just said quietly, 'So what do
you want to do when you leave school?'

'Something with animals. I love animals. I'd love to be a vet like
Aunty Hannah.'

Beth, who knew Siena loved horses but had never heard her
daughter express anything about wanting to be a vet, sat up straight.

'So you need your schooling, then,' Harry said gently, as he laid a
line of sauce down his sausage sandwich. 'I hear they're big on that
for veterinary studies.'

'Ugh,' Siena said.

'But it's worth it,' Harry countered. 'I wish I'd known what I
wanted to do back then, rather than just leaving school and drifting
from one thing to another like I do.'

Siena blinked up at him. 'Don't you like what you do?'

'I do,' he said on a sigh, 'but it's not like I have any choice about things, because I never knew what I wanted to do and so I never went after it. You're lucky if you know what you want to do, though that comes with obligations, too because then you have to go after it. Isn't it worth a bit of schooling, even if it is boring at times?'

Siena looked up at him. 'I guess.'

❧

'Thank you, Harry,' Beth said later, as he was leaving with a container of potato salad and the leftover meat. 'I don't know what we would have done without you, lately. And not just about all the work you've done. Thanks for talking to Siena like that. She's much more likely to listen to you than me. Kids always take more notice of adults who don't happen to be their parents.'

Harry smiled his Hagrid smile and looked so endearing that Beth reached up and kissed him on the cheek.

A moment later she felt his big hands at her back. 'Oh, Beth,' he said, his gruff voice quavering, and suddenly his lips were on hers.

She should have stopped him then, but it was so unexpected and she was so shocked, and it felt kind of nice. It had been so long since she'd been held in a man's arms and kissed.

He tasted of his after-dinner coffee, his breath warm against her skin, the brush of his beard adding another dimension, and sensation rippled through her, heady sensation, and it was all kinds of wonderful.

But it was all kinds of wrong.

She went rigid in his arms and pulled her mouth away, her breathing choppy. 'You should go.'

'But, Beth—'

'Just go,' she said, knowing she'd overstepped the mark, guilt descending like a heavy cloud.

Siena was still washing up when Beth grabbed a tea towel and started drying up, furiously attacking each plate.

'So school next week, then? I suppose it's time we organised stationery and uniforms and stuff.'

'I guess,' said Siena, sounding deep in thought, her hands swishing in the soapy water.

'Hopefully, we can get another year out of your sandals and save that expense.'

Siena looked sideways up at her. 'Are you going to marry him?'

Beth's stomach lurched, her hands stalled on a cup. 'What? Who?'

'Who do you think? Harry. Are you going to marry him?'

Beth snorted to show how ridiculous the notion was. 'Whatever gave you that idea?'

'Because he's always here doing stuff or having dinner or watching telly with us.'

'He's just being neighbourly, and it would be rude not to at least offer him a meal.'

'And he likes you.'

'Like a friend.'

'And you like him.'

She shrugged, turning to the cutlery, not wanting to think too much about that kiss. It was a mistake. An accident. It wouldn't happen again. 'As a friend, sure.'

'You kissed him, just now.'

Oh, good grief, she'd seen that? 'Were you spying on me?' she said, trying to joke it away. 'That was just a thankyou kiss, that was all that was.'

Siena looked up at her mother like she was stupid. 'I wouldn't mind if you did want to marry Harry, in case you were worried, I mean.'

Beth put the tea towel down on the bench. 'This is crazy. I don't know what's put all this into your head, but it's rubbish, okay? You finish up here, I'm going out to the studio.'

Out there in her space, Beth sorted through pieces of coloured tile while she ran the conversation through her mind over and over, searching for a key, searching for whatever it was that had sparked Siena's foolish thoughts. Harry helped out about the place. So what? She invited him for dinner. Big deal. And it certainly wasn't Beth whom he shared an interest in television with.

And the kiss was nothing. A peck on the cheek. That's all she'd intended it to be, anyway.

It was laughable if it weren't so ridiculous. Joe was the only man she'd ever been going to marry, and he was gone. She tried to picture him in her mind, tried to recall the picture she had on her bedside table, of Joe lying with her on a sofa, his arm wrapped possessively around her, and his dark eyes looking up at the camera as if declaring to the world, she's mine.

Siena knew nothing.

It was Joe she'd been going to marry.

It was Joe she'd loved.

The clock ticked by and for a while the light through the windows glowed red over Mount Lofty as day moved spectacularly to night. Beth worked feverishly to organise the pieces before her, her hands moving fast, her eyes always scanning, selecting, to find the perfect piece for the perfect placement.

It had only ever been Joe. She had the hair right, she was sure. Black and thick and sexy as hell when she'd run her fingers through it. The hair was right, the angle of the chin almost there, but it was the eyes she was having trouble with. She shifted pieces around and still it eluded her. She squeezed her eyes shut and thought of the picture, forcing herself to remember, trying to work out where she'd gone wrong. It shouldn't be so hard to remember.

Only when she had it clear in her mind's eye and when she could see him properly again, she opened her eyes to figure out where she'd made a mistake. And the sizzle of recognition became a thunderbolt as she realised what she'd done.

That it was Harry's eyes looking back at her.

She gave a cry as she pushed away the unfinished work, staring at it aghast, her breathing coming fast and furious, before she snapped off the lights. Numbly, she walked back into the house. Siena was still up, the TV blaring in the lounge room beyond, even though it was after eleven and well after her bedtime. The moment Beth walked into the room, Siena sprang into action, the TV screen turning black.

'I was just going to bed,' she said, the worry that she was in serious trouble clear to read in her dark eyes. Joe's eyes, Beth thought with a smile. They were right there all along. She pulled her daughter into a hug and kissed her head.

'I love you, Siena, never forget that, okay?'

'Uh,' said her daughter. 'I love you, too.'

'I know.' Beth released her after one last squeeze. 'I'm going to bed. See you in the morning.'

'Mum,' Siena called after her, 'are you all right?'

She found what she hoped was a smile. 'Just tired.'

She undressed in the silvery light of the moon, and slid under the light summer bedcover to the cool embrace of her sheets, and whispered into her tear-dampened pillow, 'I'm sorry, Joe.'

46

Sophie

Sophie hadn't been thinking fond thoughts about Nick since Christmas, her conversation with Dan on the beach that day burrowed deeply in the back of her mind like a festering wound. Even petting the rapidly growing Whiskers on her lap couldn't soften the edges of her resentment.

The nerve of the man, going behind her back to her brother.

The nerve of her brother, insinuating she wasn't fit to be a mother, just because she wanted to prove that she could do this on her own. Her babies tumbled and kicked in her tummy. 'Damn right,' she said, giving them a pat before lifting the kitten from her lap, relieved to have at least that pressure off her bladder.

'Time to go, babies,' she said, collecting her things. School started back next week, so they'd agreed to doing her twenty-week scan one week early, and as much as she was looking forward to this latest peek at her babies, she wasn't looking forward to seeing Nick, or to baring her expanding belly to him. One thing was for certain, though, there would be no hand holding this time. No leaning on him for support. She'd show him she was strong enough to do this on her own. Let him go bleat to her brother about that.

'Your babies are looking very happy and healthy,' the sonographer said after the usual round of measurement and checks were performed. 'Do you want to know the sex?'

Nick looked at her. 'Sophie?'

She blinked. He was actually asking her? 'No,' she said, shaking her head. 'Why spoil the surprise?' And curse the man, but he nodded his agreement.

That's what got her sitting opposite him drinking tea in the cafe afterwards, she figured. If he'd disagreed or argued or insisted on knowing, it would have fed that simmering bubble of resentment, and she would have blown him off and headed straight to school to prep for next week's new batch of students. But he'd let her decide and he'd agreed with her decision.

Infuriating, really.

And she sure didn't want to see that goofy expression on his face when he looked at the picture of the babies, like he was already falling in love with them.

She swallowed, remembering her brother's words. *They're his flesh and blood, just as much as they're yours.*

Damn.

She glanced at her watch, seizing on the excuse. 'I need to go, Nick. I'm due at school to prep for next week.'

He put down the picture, shifting in his chair, his expression a little pained. 'Listen, Sophie, I've been thinking ...'

Instantly her hackles went up. 'Have you? About what?'

He clasped his hands together on the table. An entreaty? 'A couple of things. Like what name the babies have.'

She shook her head. 'It's too early to think about names yet. I haven't got that far ahead.'

'No, I meant their surname.'

'They have one. The Faraday name is a perfectly good name.'

'So is Pasquale.'

'You're not suggesting we hyphenate?'

He rubbed the back of his neck. 'God no, I hate double-barrelled surnames.'

'Fine, Faraday it is. Was that all, because I really have to go.'

'There is one more thing. I've been thinking, you're about half-way along now, and it's not going to get easier.'

'So?'

'So you really shouldn't be living alone.'

'I'm fine, really, I am.' She stood to leave.

'Hear me out, Sophie, please?'

She sat down again, sure she wasn't going to like it, whatever it was.

He exhaled, the knuckles on his clasped hands turning white. 'What about if you moved into my place.'

'What? Why on earth would I do that?'

'Because I've got the space.'

'Oh good grief, you mean you looking over my shoulder making sure I'm behaving myself? No thanks, I don't need to be micromanaged.'

'It's not about micromanaging anyone,' he argued, 'it's about ensuring you've got the support you need and that I've got access to the babies. They are half mine, remember.'

She rolled her eyes. 'How could I forget?'

'So, think it over and you'll see I'm right. We can share the parenting responsibilities and the expenses, and Min will help, I know she will. She'll fuss all over them.'

'Right. And what happens to my mum's unit while I'm shacked up with you?'

'You'll be in the spare room. It's not like we're shacking up together. And let the unit out. Make yourself some money while you can't teach.'

'This is crazy talk, Nick. What will your family make of it?'

'My sister lives an hour away, so it's not like she's going to be sticking her nose in every other day, and my folks retired to Melbourne a few years back to be closer to my other two siblings, but it wouldn't matter if they hadn't. They're Italian. They love big families. They'll be thrilled for me.'

'And what about Min? What are you going to tell your daughter when her teacher moves into the spare room?'

He sighed and rubbed the back of his neck. 'Yeah, well, I never said it was going to be easy, but there's no point underestimating Min. She's going to know sooner or later that she's got two new siblings on the way, and I reckon she'll be okay with it. Kids these days don't come with the same preconceived notions we did. Given every second kid seems to come from a broken or blended or collided family, they can't afford to, I guess.'

She nodded at that because it all made so much perfect sense. If you wanted to be railroaded into something you didn't want to do. 'I can't believe you ever imagined that was a good idea.'

'Sophie, think about it.'

'No.'

'What do you mean, no?'

'I mean, thanks for the kind offer, but I won't think about it because there's nothing to think about. I'm not moving in with you, Nick. I'm perfectly happy by myself. I'm sure the babies and I will be fine.' She picked up the photo and her bag as she stood. 'And now, I really have to go.'

'Think about it, Sophie and you'll see I'm right. You can't do this by yourself.'

'I have thought about it, Nick, and the answer's still no. Thanks for the tea.'

47

Nick

Min barrelled out of her first day in her Year One class full of excitement, colliding full force into Nick with a whump. 'Year One is so cool!' she said, holding up the picture she'd done for his approval and praise. 'Look!'

'You did this?' he said, only half paying attention, because he was keeping an eye on the corridor outside the reception room hoping to get a glimpse of Sophie. He was also hoping to get a word in, because the way they'd parted company after last week's scan was all wrong and he needed to mend some bridges big time, something he couldn't do over the phone.

'Uh-huh,' she said. 'Don't you know what it is?'

Now, she had his full attention. He studied the various blobs on the picture, all swirls of grey and white. 'That's easy,' he said, sure he was right. 'Clouds. It's a picture of a cloudy sky.'

'No! It's Fat Cat with all her kittens, before we had to give them all away.'

He nodded. Because now that he looked at it closer, he could just make out the odd eye or two and it could very well be a basketful of cats. And it definitely didn't look like a giraffe. 'Very good,' he said.

'Come on,' said Min, grabbing his hand, 'let's go show Fat Cat.'

'Sure.' Nick gave a wistful glance down the corridor, but there was no sight or sound of Sophie, and what was he going to say anyway with Min around?

They were halfway home in the car when Min said, 'Oh, Ms Faraday is having a baby.'

'Oh?' said Nick, trying not to sound too interested. Trying harder not to spill the beans that he knew she was having two. 'Did she tell you?'

'No. Someone thought she had a fat tummy from eating too much Christmas pudding, but Erin Thomas—she's one of the Year Seven girls this year—she told her sister Caitlin in Year Four that she's having a baby and Caitlin told Holly Hunter and she told Emily Hunter, who's in my class.'

Wow, he thought, the grapevine certainly started early these days. And that was the problem because it wasn't just the kids. Soon, it would be the entire community talking as kids went home from school and started telling their parents. Jesus, couldn't Sophie see what was in store? It would have made it so much easier if she'd agreed to move in when he'd suggested it. At least it would have put a full stop on the conjecture and the gossip.

'So, what do you think?' Min asked.

'Sorry, about what?'

'About Ms Faraday having a baby. Babies are so cool, just like kittens. Isn't it great?'

Nick found a smile to toss in his daughter's direction before he had to pay attention to the road to take a right. 'Yeah,' he said, 'babies are cool. Exactly like kittens.' Except he still had to explain to this girl that she was expecting two extra kittens in her own family. How was that going to go?

48

Beth

'You can't come by anymore.'

Harry blinked, the smile that had lit up his creased face when Beth had found him in the groundsman's shed sliding clean away, leaving a tangle of surprise and confusion in its wake.

'Beth, you can't mean that.'

'I'm sorry, Harry. That's the way it has to be.'

He frowned. 'Because I kissed you? Because, if that's the reason—'

She kicked up her chin, her lips tight. 'It doesn't matter why. It just doesn't make sense you coming around all the time. Not when I have a ten-year-old daughter who might get the wrong idea—and when other people might get the wrong idea.'

He shook his head, setting his shaggy hair moving like a rolling tide around his face. 'You think … You think I got the wrong idea.'

'I didn't mean you,' she said, although clearly something had him barking up the wrong tree. Somewhere along the line, he'd got the impression that having him over to share a meal and a program on the telly with Siena meant a whole lot more.

'I like you,' he said. 'I like you a lot.'

'I like you, too. But I'm sorry, it's best for everyone if you don't come over anymore.' She tried not to notice how crestfallen he looked, putting it down to the fact that he'd be missing a few hot meals. 'Siena's my priority,' she said tightly. 'I have to think about her.'

She left him standing there and went to pick up Siena from after-hours care, telling herself it was for the best, that she didn't want anyone thinking that she was leading him on or that there was something between them when there wasn't and when there could never be.

Siena chattered on all the way home about something; Beth didn't have the headspace or the will to pay attention. It was only when she pulled up the driveway next to the house and Siena shouted, 'Look!' that she saw it. The big bunch of flowers sitting up in a bucket of water. There was no mistaking who they were from, because they were right next to the Tupperware containers in which she'd sent the leftovers home with Harry.

'I told you he liked you,' said Siena, picking up the bouquet and sticking her nose into the blooms.

Beth walked past her daughter and unlocked the front door, turfing her bag on the bed before heading numbly straight out to her studio, and telling herself over and over that she'd been right to do what she had done and stop it, now.

It was for the best.

She knew it was for the best.

She just wished it didn't hurt so much.

49

Sophie

The first day back at school wrangling a new bunch of kids all still high on holiday spirit into a functioning obedient class unit was always an impossible task and always tiring, but Sophie felt exhausted by the end of this one. Her feet hurt, her back ached and there was a headache banging around her temples that she could really do without. It didn't help that summer had decided to kick in with a vengeance and the temperature outside was nudging forty degrees in the shade. Likewise, it didn't help that she had the equivalent of an internal combustion engine on board or that she'd had to pee what felt like every ten minutes. The end of school siren hadn't come soon enough.

It will get better, she told herself as she stashed the last of her things in her bag and retrieved her water bottle, while waiting for the noisy battleground that was the corridor outside to calm a little. Maybe not the peeing, but the first day had to be the worst. It would get easier, surely, or she'd never make it all the way to May, when her maternity leave would kick in.

The corridor was emptying fast by the time Sophie figured it safe enough to leave. Wearily, she slung her bag strap over her shoulder and headed towards the staffroom to fill up her water bottle. She couldn't wait to get home to Whiskers and collapse on the sofa under the air conditioner and put her feet up.

'Hello, Sophie,' she heard behind her in the corridor. 'Happy new year.'

She turned to greet the woman, who was looking cool and effortlessly stylish in a white linen shift dress and wedged sandals, and nothing at all like the limp rag Sophie must look in her stretch skirt and layered cami. 'Penelope, happy new year to you, too. Are you looking for Min … Mignon? She's probably already left.'

The woman shook her head and Sophie got a whiff of her perfume as they headed towards the office together. She smelled as fresh as she looked, and Sophie envied the way she could stay looking so cool when it was like an oven outside. 'I've just come in to talk to the principal. I want Mignon to start violin and piano lessons this year and they've told me she can only do recorder in Year One. Ridiculous! And I'm so sorry she's not in your class this year. She loved having you as a teacher.' Her eyes looked sideways up and down as she spoke, and Sophie knew her big shoulder bag and her floaty top were going to disguise nothing to a keen pair of eyes.

'I'm sorry,' she said, 'but unless I'm mistaken, are you …?'

'Pregnant? Yes.' *To your ex-husband, as it happens.* Sophie looked straight ahead and licked her lips. Because wasn't that awkward?

'Oh,' Penelope said, blinking. Then a moment later, 'Sorry, I should have said congratulations. It's just I didn't realise … I always had in mind you were single.'

Despite her aching head, back and feet, Sophie dragged out a smile. Maybe Nick was right about things not changing that much. 'I am.'

'Wow. And you're still going ahead with it on your own?'

Sophie placed a protective hand over her belly. 'That's the plan.'

The other woman nodded as they slowed near the reception area, the principal's office to the left, the staffroom to the right. 'Then at least see if you can get the father to share custody. I do love my weeks when Mignon's with her father.'

'Um, thanks for that,' Sophie said, more than a little discombobulated. 'I'll see what I can arrange.'

The weather conditions worsened that week instead of improving as Sophie had hoped, and the first week back at school was a nightmare. The heatwave locked itself in just shy of the conditions where the fire danger was declared catastrophic, so the school remained open for business despite the blistering heat. By the end of the week Sophie felt limp and wrung out and like she needed another six-week break to recover.

Whiskers climbed onto a space on her ever-diminishing lap and promptly flopped into his ragdoll self. He was three times the size he'd been at Christmas when Nick and Min had dropped him off, and he was utterly adorable. Happy to see her when she came home from work, happy to laze on the sofa when she was incapable of doing anything more. And in a few months, there'd be a couple of new babies in the place.

Sophie looked critically around at the space. The open-plan kitchen, dining and living area had been a nice space for her and her mum, when Wendy had been here, though she'd spent most of her time at Dirk's, even before their marriage. And it was fine for her and Whiskers.

Yeah, it was going to be a squeeze in here, and she might have to move out a lounge chair or two.

But this was a first-world problem, surely? Other cultures managed family groups in much smaller spaces and got on fine. And at least here she could be independent. She wasn't about to be subsumed into anyone else's life, just because of one night with consequences. And maybe this place did look small right now, but once she'd shed some excess furniture and redecorated, it would be perfect.

It had to be.

She glanced over at the pile of nursery designer magazines stacked up on the coffee table, and pulled the first one off the top. It was time to start planning.

That weekend Dan stood with his hands on his hips looking at both Sophie's bedroom and the spare room she was planning to move into so the twins could share her bigger room. Sophie had stripped the spare bed and cleaned out the contents of the cupboards in preparation for the move. 'Are you sure about this, Sophie? You reckon you're going to have enough room in here to set up two babies with cots and change table and all the other rubbish they need?'

'Hey, it's all vitally important equipment,' Lucy chimed in. 'You just wait.'

Dan grinned at his wife. 'Yeah? Well, be that as it may, you should see how much stuff Lucy's already accumulated, and we're only expecting one.'

'Watch out, big brother, you're starting to sound a lot like Nick.'

'So maybe he's got a point. Maybe you don't have enough room in this place for all three of you.'

Whiskers chose that moment to curl around Sophie's ankles and protest about not being fed. 'Make that four,' Dan amended.

Sophie picked up the growing kitten. 'I've got it all worked out. There'll be heaps of space, you'll see.'

Dan sighed. 'Well, okay. Have it your way. But don't be surprised if you don't have room to swing a cat when it's done.' He looked at Whiskers and gave him an apologetic tickle behind the ears. 'Lucky for you, eh?'

He tasked her and Lucy with making tea while he set about clearing a path through the living area to take everything out to the trailer he'd parked in the driveway. Sophie put the kettle on while Lucy found mugs for everyone. 'So how are you feeling?' Lucy asked.

'Tired,' Sophie replied, 'most of the time, lately. Work is killing me, not to mention the heat. If I ever have another baby, I'm definitely going to be pregnant through winter so I can make use of all this added heat.' And that was a joke when she was clearly so good at planning. 'How about you?'

'Okay. A bit unwieldy at times, but not too bad overall.'

'I can't believe you're eight weeks further on and we're the same size,' said Sophie, rummaging around in the pantry for a packet of Tim Tams. 'That's so unfair.'

Lucy grinned as she carried their tea to the table. 'Well, you will go buying in bulk. Now, show me this nursery decor you've decided on.'

'You girls carry on,' Dan said, puffing as he lugged the double mattress past them. 'Don't mind me.'

Lucy grinned. 'You want for us to help? Sophie and I could manage the bed between us.'

'Don't you dare,' he called as he headed through the door.

Sophie turned to Lucy. 'Do you think he means it?'

'Yes, I bloody well mean it!' he yelled.

'Yep.' Lucy laughed. 'I think he does.'

Her bedroom furniture was gone, the room empty but for a carpet in need of a shampoo, and the dust motes playing in the light slanting through the window. Sophie rubbed her tummy, feeling her babies flutter and tumble. 'This is it, kiddos, the makings of your new bedroom. It's going to be gorgeous.'

She'd decided on a misty-blue wall colour up to an animal frieze, above which the colour changed from blue to creamy clouds. It would look soft and pretty and it left plenty of scope to add splashes of pink or blue, or pink and blue, for that matter, after the babies arrived.

But before then, there was work to be done. She'd organised a carpet cleaner for Saturday morning, which meant she needed to get the walls dusted and cleaned beforehand and she'd have the non-toxic paint she'd found out about all ready to go by the time the carpet dried. She looked up at the light, switched it on and frowned. The inside of that could do with a good clean out as well. But that was one thing she could do right now.

The ladder weighed twice as much as she remembered, but it wasn't so much the weight but how awkward it was to carry. It clattered as she walked, waking Whiskers with a shock. He took one look at the silver monster tucked under her arm and darted under the sofa.

'Sorry, puss,' she said, a little breathless when she got the ladder into the spare room and opened it up under the light. She looked up at the light again and went off in search of a cleaning cloth, surprised to find herself puffing from the exertion. This was bad. She must be getting really unfit, she could even hear the drum of her heartbeat in her ears.

Armed with a cloth, she stood at the base of the ladder, giving thanks for low ceilings. About halfway up, she wagered, and she'd be able to reach the light shade. A quick dust-off and it would be done. Too easy.

Two steps up, she realised she needed to climb another. One more and she could just about reach. Damn. Lucky she'd always had a head for heights. She took another step up, leaning her legs against the top rail, and looked up. Perfect. She perched the cloth on top of the ladder, reached her arms up and fiddled with the shade until she could feel it unclip at the exact moment she felt the room tip and sway.

Whoa, that was weird.

She clung onto the loose shade with one hand, her other seeking the top of the ladder as her head reeled and her world spun. Her flailing wrist smacked hard against the top of the ladder and her fingers wrapped around the edge. She made it down one step, and then two, before her foot slipped past the next rung and she fell.

50

Hannah

'How's your nan?' Declan asked, hunkered down on his haunches alongside, watching Hannah give Ella her bottle for a treat. Big brown eyes stared into hers as the joey suckled on the teat, its little paws resting on Hannah's fingers as she held the bottle. It was no wonder Declan was besotted, Ella was adorable.

'She's good,' said Hannah. 'Last I heard anyway. Dan's put bolts on the doors and gate so she can't just disappear, and she seems to be coping all right.'

'That's good news, then,' he said. 'So, when do you think it would be a good time to meet your family? I was thinking maybe I should invite them over to Hobbitville for a barbecue one week-end.' Too late, Hannah realised the trap Declan had sprung. She looked up to see him grinning at her, the challenge clear in his eyes. 'What do you say?'

'That sounds like an awful lot of trouble for you to go to.'

'No trouble. I'll enjoy it.' And she knew he would.

She concentrated on easing the joey from the now empty bottle rather than look at Declan, her mind racing. 'Well, it's a lovely idea, but it could be tricky to arrange. Beth does shift work, often on the weekends. I'd have to check.'

'Ah, Hannah love,' he said, letting his head drop on a sigh. 'Why do I get the impression you don't want me to meet your family?'

'That's not true!'

'A man starts to feel like he's only good for one thing. Or maybe, you really have got a husband you run off to when you leave me?'

'No! That's a ridiculous idea. There's nobody else, Declan.' She tried to make light of it as she sat Ella on her lap to toilet her. 'I wouldn't have the energy, for starters.'

He laughed at that. 'Well, there's a relief.'

He watched her for a few seconds, reaching a hand over to tickle the joey behind its soft ears. 'What is it that makes you tick, Hannah?' he asked, his voice low and husky, his wild Atlantic eyes searching hers. 'What is it that I'm missing?'

She stiffened. 'What do you mean?'

'I don't know, only it feels like I'm only being allowed into a part of Hannah-world. I'd like to be let into the rest, only I don't know how to get there.'

Her throat achingly tight, she swallowed. 'God, I'm sorry, Declan. I'm not very good at relationships. I've not had much practice.'

He nodded, slipping an arm around her shoulders. 'Which is no doubt why you haven't been snapped up before now. Their loss is my gain.'

She lifted her gaze to his. 'Why are you so nice to me?'

'Maybe because you're someone special.' His thumb swept the line of her jaw. 'And because I like you, Hannah. I like you a lot.'

51

Sophie

If Nick was relieved to see that Sophie was okay, he sure wasn't showing it.

'What the hell were you thinking?' he said, when he got a chance to speak to her alone in the mechanical monster that masqueraded as a hospital bed. 'What on earth were you doing up a ladder?'

'Calm down,' Sophie said, wrangling with the heavy pillows at her back. 'This is supposed to be a hospital, remember.'

'But a ladder,' he said, waving an angry hand in the direction of the bump under the sheet, 'in your condition.'

'I had to dust the light cover somehow.'

'No, you didn't. You could have asked someone else to do it, if it was so damned necessary. You could have asked Dan or one of your sisters to help. You could have damned well asked me.'

Sophie closed her eyes, and took a deep, hopefully calming breath, but clearly the man wasn't done with her yet.

'Don't you realise, you could have hurt the babies with a stunt like that?'

She snapped open her eyes. 'The babies are fine.'

'No thanks to you. How could you do something so irresponsible?'

'Don't you think I feel bad enough already? How was I to know I'd get dizzy. Don't worry, it won't happen again.'

'Damned right it won't.'

She punched at her pillows this time, the waterproof protectors crackling under the pillow slips, the action strangely therapeutic. 'Okay, Nick,' she said, settling back into them. 'I made a mistake. I'm sorry. But you're not exactly helping my blood pressure here.'

He turned away, raking a hand through his hair, one hand on his hip. 'No,' he said, blowing out a long sigh before he turned back, his dark eyes remorseful. 'I guess not. You gave me the fright of my life, Sophie.'

'I'm sorry,' she said, because now that he wasn't coming over all alpha, she could see his point of view. She hadn't had to clean the shade herself. 'I'll be more careful, I promise.'

'No more climbing ladders?'

She shook her head, managed a weak smile and crossed her heart with her fingers. 'Promise.'

He returned an answering smile. 'Thank you.'

He looked almost endearing standing at the end of her bed in his crumpled work shirt and pants, concern, relief and the makings of a five o'clock shadow lining his dark features. He'd come straight to the hospital from the orchard, and God, could the man rock that outdoor look—almost as well as he'd rocked his best-man threads.

She blinked and shook her head. No point going there.

'Thanks for coming,' she said, thinking they had nothing else to say. But the man was going nowhere, apparently. He curved his hands around the bed rail at her side.

'Sophie,' he started, 'I know you want to remain independent, but what if something else happens? I'm worried about you being by yourself. Can you at least think about my offer to share the house?'

'Nick—'

He held up a hand to stop her. 'Hear me out, Sophie. It's a big house. I promise I won't get in your way. I promise not to micro-manage you. You'll have space, and you'll be closer to the rest of your family, too, up in the hills. Will you at least think about it?'

His dark eyes looked down at her, imploring, and all she could think was that her heart was beating too fast, even when he wasn't yelling at her. She shook her head.

'Think about it,' he said, his hand lifting from the railing. She thought he was going to touch her then, just a parting hand to her shoulder, a squeeze, but he pulled his hand back. 'That's all I ask.' And then he was gone.

Sophie lay back against her crackling pillows. This was not how she'd imagined it would be when she'd decided to go ahead with the pregnancy. This was not what she'd planned. She squirmed and punched her noisy pillows again. Why was it, that when you'd made a choice to do one thing, your life suddenly hurtled off into a completely different direction? What was that about?

'Bloody man,' Sophie grumbled half an hour later, as Beth topped up the water in her flowers. She'd told them about Nick, thinking she'd get it off her chest and get their agreement. 'Who does he think he is?'

'He's only trying to help,' Hannah said.

'No, he's not. He's trying to take over, that's what he's doing.'

'Hey, you're a first-time mum expecting twins and you live by yourself,' Beth said, now perched on the edge of the bed. 'And on top of that, you've got high blood pressure.' She patted Sophie's hand. 'This is not something to take lightly. First-time mothers of twins are more likely to develop pre-eclampsia and that's something you and these babies do not want.'

'Well, he's not helping my blood pressure one bit. You know he asked me to move into his place.'

Her sisters exchanged glances. 'Um,' said Beth, looking questioningly at her older sister.

'Is that such a bad idea?' Hannah finished.

'What?' Sophie crossed her arms over her bump, as well as the IV in one hand let her. 'It's a rubbish idea. I'm not moving.'

'Sophie,' Beth warned. 'The specialist said you shouldn't be alone if it could be avoided. And it can be avoided.'

'Nope. Not moving in with Nick. No way. I'll move in with one of you if I have to move anywhere.'

'Well that won't work,' said Hannah. 'Both of us do shift work and we're on call half the time. Which means if and when you need us, there's a chance we won't be there.'

'Then I'll move back home with Dan and Lucy.'

'Seriously? Your brother's been married a few short months and you'd go play gooseberry? That'd be a heap of laughs for everyone.'

'Besides, Lucy is pregnant, too,' Beth added. 'Don't you think that's a bit unfair? It's not like she's going to be able to do anything with you if you needed a hand when Dan wasn't around.'

'And don't even think about moving in with Nan and Pop. Not given their age, especially now with Nan's diagnosis.'

Sophie snorted in disgust. 'I am not moving in with Nick.'

'Why the hell not? It seems like the perfect solution for everyone.'

Sophie crossed her arms. 'Not for me it doesn't.'

'Why not give it a trial?' Beth suggested. 'A couple of weeks? A month?'

Hannah nodded. 'And then if it doesn't work out, we'll think of something else.'

She shook her head. 'That's crazy.'

Hannah and Beth looked at each other, then back at Sophie, before Beth ventured, 'He is the father, right?'

'And he wants to help. Wasn't he there for you at your scans?'

'Yes on both counts. So?'

'So, clearly you don't find him too repulsive,' said Beth. 'After all, you did sleep with him.'

'God, do you have to keep reminding me?'

'That's a joke, right,' said Hannah. 'With that bump, how can you possibly forget?'

Sophie sighed, and let herself flop back into her crinkly hospital pillows. 'I can't move in with him.'

'Can't, or won't?' Beth said. 'Seriously, what's wrong with the guy?'

'He's controlling, he thinks I'm irresponsible and he wants to call all the shots.'

Hannah's nose twitched. 'That's only two things, though, isn't it? Controlling and wanting to call all the shots—aren't they the same thing?'

'What does it matter?'

'And in his favour,' said Beth, counting on her fingers, 'he's a good father, he lives closer to the school than you do, which will ease your commute, and he's clearly hot enough to sleep with.'

'I was drunk!'

'Finally the truth comes out! But he is kind of hot, don't you reckon, Han?'

'I'll say,' she agreed, 'if you go for that hunky primary producer kind of guy, the kind with broad shoulders and dark hair and Mediterranean good looks—'

Sophie wanted to scream. 'Can you guys just quit it? You're not helping.'

'And you're not making any sense. What are you so afraid of? Because right now, Nick doesn't look anything like the monster you've painted him to be.'

'Exactly,' Hannah agreed. 'He wants to help and you're not letting him. What's with that?'

'Don't you see? I need to do this on my own. I want to prove I can stand on my own two feet.'

Her sisters looked blankly at each other, before Beth shrugged.

'It gets worse,' Sophie added, 'because the doctors are saying I can't work full time. They want me to cut my hours by fifty per cent. I mean, if I did move in with Nick on those terms, I'd never get away from him.'

Hannah rolled her eyes theatrically. 'Ghastly!'

'Come on,' urged Beth. 'Spill.'

'I've told you!'

Hannah cocked an eyebrow and both sisters waited.

Finally Sophie sighed, sagging on her bed. 'Okay, so maybe there is another reason. Maybe I don't want to fall for him.'

Beth and Hannah looked at each other and burst out laughing.

Sophie rolled her eyes. 'I knew telling you would be a mistake! I knew you wouldn't understand.'

Hannah was still chortling. Beth was swiping tears from her cheek. 'Yes, because falling for Nick would be the worst thing in the world, of course.'

'It would be,' said Sophie. 'Don't you see? Every time a guy looks at me, I fall in love with him, and then it all goes pear-shaped and ends up being a disaster because he never really loved me. Look at what happened with Jason and how that ended, and it was exactly the same with the guy before that. I've promised myself I won't let that happen again.'

'You really think there's a danger of you falling for Nick?'

'We'll be living under the same roof and I'm having his babies. What do you think?'

'Well, maybe that would be a good outcome? The perfect ready-made family.'

'No! Because he's only worried about these twins of his. They're the reason he rushed in when he found out I fell. He came in here shouting the walls down. You see, that's why he wants me to move in with him, because he doesn't trust me to look after them.'

'He may have a point,' Hannah said drily.

Beth nodded. 'You did climb up that ladder. You were very lucky.'

'But you see,' Sophie argued, because her sisters were sounding more and more like Nick and she needed to make them see that there was more than the babies at stake. 'I'd go falling in love with him, and he'd only be interested in the babies and I'd end up with my heart broken, only it would be worse than ever because now we'd be stuck together because of those babies. That's hardly a healthy way to bring up kids.'

'Wow,' said Beth, sitting down on the bed, plucking at the sheet. 'That would be a mess, huh?'

'See?' Sophie said, seizing on some agreement for a change. 'I can't afford for that to happen, it would be a disaster. That's why I can't move in.'

'Hang on,' Hannah said. 'We are talking about a guy who's controlling and thinks you're irresponsible. That was it, wasn't it?'

'Plus, he wants to call all the shots!'

'Same thing really, but yeah, let's add it in for good measure.' Hannah nodded sagely. 'In which case, I think I've got the answer.'

Sophie licked her lips, suspicious. 'What?'

'With a list of character faults that long, there's no way on earth you could possibly fall in love with the man. I reckon you're perfectly safe.'

Beth grinned. 'In which case, there's nothing to stop you moving in. Case dismissed.'

It was far from settled as far as Sophie was concerned, but apparently the juggernaut was off and racing, and there was no stopping it. Whenever she turned around over the next few days, she found one or other of her sisters invading her space and sorting out what to take and what to put in storage in preparation for renting out the flat. To help her, they said, but Sophie felt like they were delivering her up to Nick on a platter. All she needed was someone to stick an apple into her mouth.

Even Nan thought it was lovely that she'd be moving in with him. 'It's right that the father will be on hand to look after you,' she said, when she phoned one night after hearing the news.

'I thought you'd be on my side,' Sophie protested, stroking Whiskers' tummy as he lay collapsed on his back across her legs. It was too hot to have a furry hairball adding to her temperature, even with the air conditioner on, but Whiskers was on her side, she was sure. 'I thought you of all people would understand. I feel like I'm being forced into something I don't want to do.'

'Nobody's forcing you to marry him, are they?' Nan chuckled. 'Though Clarry here's sending his suit off to the drycleaner's, just in case.'

Sophie rolled her eyes, but the sound of Nan's chuckle had sent a shaft of pain straight through her heart. She was struck by how well Nan could appear on the surface ninety-five per cent of the time, while the dementia was working away behind the scenes, gradually chipping at her mind and her capabilities. It was all so unfair.

She sighed, because Nan wasn't the only one who could be irrational. 'Tell him not to bother, Nan.'

'I did, not that he'll listen to me,' she said. 'Shame though. I always did like that nice young man. Always so polite. Now, how are you off for eggs?'

52

Nick

Nick stood back with his hands on his hips checking out the guest room. He'd spent the last couple of nights turfing out all the junk that seemed to have been deposited in there over the years—junk with Min's name on it for the most part—and he'd stripped the bed and aired the room and given it a decent once-over with the vacuum cleaner. Now, with the bed made up and the floral curtains playing on the soft night breeze, the room looked fresh and inviting.

Probably wasted on Sophie, he figured, who had only agreed to this trial under sufferance, but at least she should be comfortable. He'd be happier once she was under his roof. He could keep an eye on her. Make sure she was not climbing up any more bloody ladders.

Women!

He heard a car pull up outside and checked his watch. Yup, that was another one and right on time. He sucked in a lungful of air. He knew Min liked Sophie as a teacher, and he had enough faith in his daughter that she'd soon come to accept this new arrangement, but he still had to cross that bridge and tell her. This was the moment of truth. A second later the front door opened and closed, and Min came barrelling through the house, calling for Fat Cat and Moe, the kitten. She stopped when she got to the guest room and saw him there, her *Frozen* backpack swinging in her hand. She blinked. 'Wow. What happened?'

He couldn't help but smile. 'I cleaned it up.'

'Why?'

'Because we're going to have a visitor come and stay, if it's okay with you.'

His daughter turned big eyes onto him. 'Who?'

'Come here,' he said, and took a deep breath as he sat down with her on the edge of the big old bed and put his arm around her shoulders. 'Sophie—Ms Faraday—is going to be coming to stay with us, Min, if you don't mind, that is.'

Min's eyes looked too big for her face 'Really? How come?'

'She needs a place to stay where she won't be alone, at least until she has her babies, and I'm going to be daddy to her babies and you're going to be their big sister. What do you think?'

She blinked those big eyes up at him. 'Is she going to bring Whiskers with her?'

He shrugged. 'Sure. I don't see why she wouldn't.'

'Yay,' said Min, jumping up from the bed and she was off. 'I'm going to tell Fat Cat. Whiskers is coming home!'

Nick sat there, hornswoggled. Yup, that went pretty well.

Sophie stepped into the room behind Beth, who'd offered to come with her and help her settle in, though she suspected it was more about making sure Sophie didn't run away. 'It's gorgeous, Nick,' gushed Beth, sitting down on the side of the big brass bed. 'Hey, comfy bed, too. Come and try it out, Soph.'

Sophie ignored the fact that her sister seemed to be overdoing it on the enthusiasm scale lately and looked around. So, this was to be her cell for the next however long. Okay, so it was a big cell and even with a double bed and a big old chest of drawers, there was still plenty of room for bassinets and a change table—if she was still here by then—but still she sniffed, trying to find something she didn't like beyond the fact that it wasn't her own room in her mum's house.

But all she smelled was beeswax polish and fresh air sweetly scented. Because God, he'd even put fresh flowers in a vase on the bedside table. 'I guess it'll do,' she said, knowing she sounded ungracious but unable to stop herself. She was still reeling at the speed with which all this had happened.

Somehow, Nick still managed a wry smile as he looked on from where he leaned his shoulder ever so casually against the doorway, with his thumbs stuck in his jeans and his light-blue chambray shirt open at the neck, revealing a slice of olive skin and dark chest hair. She'd raked her fingers through that chest hair, tracing the sculpted skinscape that lay beneath. She swallowed, cursing the fact that he looked like he'd just stepped out of some kind of menswear ad, and lifted her eyes in time to see his smile widen. But then, he would smile under that designer stubble, wouldn't he? He'd got his damned way, just like the annoying, railroading man had intended all along.

Maybe Hannah and Beth were right. Maybe there was no way in the world she could fall in love with someone like him, even if he did look kind of hot. Just a bit hot. It'd sure help the situation if he stopped wearing those open-necked shirts, for starters ...

Something beeped from the direction of the kitchen. 'It's ready, Dad,' called Min, who was busy reacquainting Whiskers with his family.

'I've got a quiche in the oven for lunch. Beth, you're welcome to stay.'

'Sorry, I've got to run. I've got a shift this afternoon, but thanks.' She turned to Sophie. 'And you, behave.'

Sophie rolled her eyes. 'Yes, Mum.'

Beth just grinned and gave her a peck on the cheek. 'Let me know if there's anything else you need.' Sophie was sure she must have imagined the shadows under Beth's eyes right then, because she didn't sound too down. Nick made way for her to leave and then she was gone and it was just the two of them in a room full of awkwardness. Nick recovered first. 'Right, lunch in five. I'll leave you to it.'

Sophie sat down on the bed in a daze and half-heartedly bounced up and down a couple of times. It was comfortable, damn it. She looked around at the high-ceilinged walls of the old stone house. It was cool inside and they didn't even have the air conditioner on.

Double damn.

Nick had served up by the time she made it to the round dining table a few minutes later and took a seat next to Min. 'Do you like your room?' asked the girl.

'It's lovely, yes,' she said, although she wouldn't have admitted that to Nick. 'I'm sure I'll be very comfortable.'

'It was really messy before. Dad cleaned it all up.'

'Oh.' She flicked her eyes up to his and then away again. 'I'm sorry to put your dad to the trouble. I could have done that.'

'Oh no, it was re-eally messy, wasn't it, Dad?'

'It was a bit of an archaeological dig with a few layers of Min's cast-offs to sort through, that's true,' he said, slicing up the quiche and putting a slice on everyone's plates. 'Help yourself to salad and bread,' he said.

Fresh out of the oven, the quiche sure smelled good. It tasted even better, rich with cheese and chunks of ham.

'It's delicious,' she said, remembering a snippet from her past. 'My dad used to say real men didn't eat quiche.'

'This real man does.'

'Dad makes the best quiche in the whole world,' contributed Min, busy picking off the pastry edge and munching on that first. 'And he makes the best pasghetti boganese.'

Sophie blinked, but not at Min's cute stumble over the name. 'You actually made this? You cook?'

'What did you think? That I had an ulterior motive? That I was going to chain you to the kitchen?'

'Well, no. I just didn't expect ...'

He shrugged as he helped himself to more salad. 'Maybe if it was just me, I wouldn't bother. But when you've got a girl like this one who enjoys good food, it would be wrong to dish up something like McDonald's every day, don't you agree?'

Sophie nodded, feeling dislocated as she sliced off a bite of quiche. Of course she agreed that a child needed a good and healthy diet, she just didn't know what she'd expected to find in Nick. He and Penelope had to be doing something right, but she sure hadn't expected to find a man who was such a dab hand in the kitchen. But then, she already knew he was a good dad. Not that it made up for all his other litany of faults, though.

And this was only the first day she was living under his roof, and he was bound to be on his best behaviour. He'd do something to blot his copybook soon, she was sure of it.

'Anyway,' Min said, licking her thumb. 'Dad makes better hamburgers than McDonald's.' She turned to her father. 'Can we have hamburgers again, Dad?'

'Sure,' said Nick. 'So long as you help make the patties.'

'Maybe Ms Faraday can help too!' suggested Min brightly, who had worked her way around the crust and was now attacking the actual quiche. She stopped then and stuck out her bottom lip. 'Do I still have to call you Ms Faraday?'

'I think you can call me Sophie,' she said. 'Unless we're at school. It might be best if you called me Ms Faraday there.'

Min nodded. 'I like Sophie, it's a nice name.'

Sophie found a smile, the easiest since she'd arrived. 'And I like Min.'

The girl agreed, loading her fork with quiche. 'I like Min, too.'

Nick watched the interplay between his daughter and their new guest. Sophie was still resentful of him—he'd expected that, moving in with them was a huge concession she was being forced to make, but one she'd soon see was the right decision—but he was relieved to see that she saved her rancour for him while she sent Min the smiles.

She had a good smile. A beautiful smile. It looked warm and real, and it was no wonder Min and her other students all loved her. He wouldn't half mind it if she wanted to send a smile like that in his direction every once in a while, but Sophie's smiles for him had all but dried up. That night should never have happened, she was reminding him, and she was only here under duress.

'So, when are we making these world-famous hamburger patties, then?' asked Sophie.

Min's head swung around to him. 'Dad?'

He'd had in mind barbecued lamb chops and veggies for dinner tomorrow, but there was something about the thought of Sophie and Min working together making hamburgers in his kitchen that moved hamburgers right on up the list. And selfishly he thought, it might even break down a barrier or two in the process.

'Why not tomorrow?' he said, making a note to run down to the shops after school drop-off to pick up the burger buns. The chops could wait.

53

Beth

It was another shitty day. Another shitty day in a whole string of shitty days and Beth had had a gutful. She slammed her locker door, the crash of metal against metal not the least bit as therapeutic as it damn well should have been.

And the trouble was, she couldn't put her finger on why it had been such a shitty day. They'd picked up and dropped off three old people for visits to Outpatients, attended a man who'd fallen off his bike and scraped off a fair bit of skin and was concussed, and done a school visit to talk about their job and show the kids exactly what was in the back of an ambulance. Totally unremarkable. She couldn't even blame her period for her foul mood.

So, what the hell was wrong with her?

She pulled up outside the school, late again, the pick-up area empty—*perfect*—and parked the car. The noise of the blower-vacuum didn't register at first, just so much more noise in her head, until she saw him. Harry, clearing gum leaves and bark from the path.

Her heart lurched. He looked up and saw her coming and stopped, the blower shutting down as he peeled the headphones from his ears. 'Beth,' he said, and even from a distance, she could see the hurt in his sorrowful eyes. 'How are you?'

'Good,' she lied, even though she felt like crap and knew she looked even worse. 'How've you been?'

He shrugged. 'Oh, you know.'

She had a fair idea. But that was hardly her fault, surely? She'd never promised anything, had she? It wasn't like they'd broken up—you'd have to be in some kind of relationship for that to have happened. All she'd done was tell him he couldn't come around anymore. 'Well, I better get inside, before the principal calls Family Services to take Siena away.'

'I guess.'

'See you,' she said as she walked on by. Harry just nodded as she passed, and a second later she heard the blower-vac start up once more, the noise feeding into the din in her head and blotting out the ache in her heart.

'You're late, again,' Siena snarled as they made their way back to the car. 'I was waiting ages.'

'I'm here now, aren't I?' Beth said, marching the long way back to the car, keeping a wide berth from the blast of the blower-vac.

'You're always late,' said Siena.

'I got held up.'

'And you're always cranky.'

'No, I'm not.'

'Yes, you are.'

Beth stopped and wheeled around. 'For God's sake, Siena, give me a break!'

'See! I told you,' and her daughter sprinted to the car.

54

Sophie

It was fun cooking with Min. The girl was passionate about her hamburgers and her enthusiasm was contagious. Min issued instructions and Sophie fetched and carried, and it was a great way, she decided, to find where everything lived in the cupboards.

Sophie chopped the onion while Min added the mixed herbs, pepper and an egg to the beef mince already in the bowl and started mixing. 'Oh,' she said, 'I forgot the mint.'

Sophie went to the cupboard, where she'd found the mixed herbs and spotted a jar of dried mint. 'Mint. Check.'

'No. Fresh mint.' Min clambered down from her chair.

'Oh, I'll get it. You tell me where.'

'Do you know where the clothesline is?'

'No, but I'm sure I can find it.' Sophie had been settling in all day and hadn't explored outside yet, but she figured a clothesline was a hard thing to miss.

'That's okay. I don't mind showing you.' And they went off in the quest for mint.

There was a brick paved patio outside the back door, complete with an outdoor table and chairs and a vine-covered pergola, and that ended in a low wall and a rosemary hedge set against the rising hill behind. 'Nice,' she said, liking the way the vine leaves filtered out the worst of the sun. 'Maybe we could eat outside tonight?'

'Yay,' said Min, looking over her shoulder. 'That'd be cool. Around here's the mint.'

The paving continued around the corner, this area not covered by a pergola and the perfect sun trap for the clothesline fixed to the wall of the house.

The perfect sun trap for a brown snake to be stretched out sunbaking on the hot bricks.

'Min!' Sophie screamed, her blood running cold. Min stopped, one foot in the air, and her face turned white as a sheet when she turned her head and saw what was lying across the bricks just a few short steps ahead.

The snake realised it had company. It slithered at speed into the garden, vanishing into the mint plants alongside the house as it headed the other way.

Sophie put her hands on the girl's shoulders and backed away, keeping an eye on the bushes for any movement. 'How about we use dried mint today in the burgers.'

Min nodded, her little shoulders trembling under Sophie's hands, although Sophie wasn't sure who was shaking the most. 'I don't think it will matter today.'

'It was enormous!' said Min to her father as they sat around the table eating their hamburgers. The dining table inside rather than the outdoor table, given the unexpected sighting of their visitor.

Nick looked across at Sophie, who nodded. 'It was a biggie, all right. A couple of metres, I'd guess. Could it be the one you thought had bitten Fat Cat?'

'Could be. I was hoping it had moved on, because I hadn't caught anything in the netting. I'll set up some more first thing tomorrow.'

'I almost stepped on it,' said Min, who was clearly over the shock and was now firmly in tall-tale territory. 'I would have too, if Sophie hadn't called out and made me stop.'

'We're just lucky it wanted to go the opposite way when it sensed us coming,' Sophie said. 'I don't know what we would have done if it had decided it wanted to come towards us.'

'Damn. Min, don't go out the back unless you have to and if you do, make sure you stamp your feet at the back door and give anything a chance to clear out. And make sure you keep those kittens inside, too.'

He turned to Sophie, his blue-grey eyes filled with concern. 'That goes for you, too. And thank you for staying calm and looking out for Min.'

'I sure didn't feel calm. Snakes give me the creeps, but I guess if you grow up around here, you get used to the odd sighting.' Sophie shivered, remembering the ice-cold chill in her veins when she'd seen it lying directly in Min's path. 'Though that one was way too close for my liking.'

Nick nodded grimly. 'And mine.'

All in all, the first week hadn't gone too badly, Sophie reflected, as she lay in bed waiting for sleep to claim her. Despite living in the same house, she'd managed to keep up a professional separation between herself and Nick, and the presence of Min was a constant reminder to keep it that way. She'd taken herself off one morning to have coffee with Amy Jennings, Nick's sixty-something-year-old neighbour, and gran to a couple of the school kids she'd taught, and she'd walked with her and her little dog, Boo, one morning before it got too hot.

And work had given her a very welcome couple of days' reprieve from being in Nick's domain, even though two and a half days with her young class was enough to wear her out. This twins caper sure wasn't for the faint-hearted.

It was just a shame it was time for Min to spend a week at Penelope's, and though she'd get to see her at school, Sophie would miss her bright face around the house, and not only for the natural buffer she provided.

Come to think of it, it was also a shame the house didn't have an en suite and they all had to share the same bathroom. She wasn't used to encountering a man wearing only a towel lashed low on his hips while she padded barefoot along the passage. Especially not one whose naked chest sparked off all kinds of memories she'd been trying to blot out.

But it had only happened the once, the morning after they'd had hamburgers when she'd headed to the bathroom at the same time he was heading out and they'd both been awkward and had to duck and weave around each other to the sound of muttered apologies. Since then, she'd made a point of making sure she didn't need the bathroom about the time he liked to get up, and so far it hadn't happened again.

And that's what this was all about. Control. This was how she was going to make it through these next few months of forced proximity, by continually being on guard and protecting herself against any situations where she might possibly get the wrong idea and start imagining things she had no right imagining.

At least there was no chance of that happening tomorrow.

Tomorrow, after he dropped Min down at her mother's, he was taking her baby shopping. She could think of nothing less romantic. She was sure it was too early and that they had months in which to prepare, but Nick had been adamant about getting it done while she was still mobile. He'd made it sound like she was going to become as big as a beached whale. Then again, given the size of her expanding belly, maybe he was right. She felt a prod followed by a kick in that region, and put her hands to her belly and thought, yeah, right on time. Because her babies seemed to love to come out and play just when she was tired and ready to go to sleep. She felt them swoop and tumble under her hands. She felt the magic of their existence. And she felt the bond between herself and her babies tighten another notch.

Her babies.

So, this was motherhood? She'd always wanted to be a mother someday, but nobody had told her it started so early, long before your babies were born. She didn't know what was in store. She was nervous about the whole birth thing and how that would go— whether it would hurt or whether she'd need a caesarean because she was having twins—but she knew she would do the very best she could for them. She'd be the best mother she could be.

And she wondered, as she drifted off to sleep with her hands still cradling her motion-filled belly, how she could ever have wished them away?

Sophie knew such things existed, of course, but she'd never actually ventured inside a baby goods shop. Only it wasn't a shop, it was an entire warehouse. On one side there was a huge section for prams, while behind it lay a section for cots and bassinets, and the other was filled with baby clothes. What looked like acres and acres of baby clothes. From speakers all around came the sound of music, happy, boppy music, interspersed with the business's ads and specials, and there was a signpost directing customers to sections further back for toys, car seats, manchester and bathing needs, and, to top it all off, a cafe.

'Right,' said Nick, a list of requirements he'd printed out from the internet in his hand. 'Where shall we start?'

Sophie was exhausted already. 'At the cafe?' she suggested, only half joking as she looked at the length of his list. 'We don't have to get everything on that list today, do we?'

'I know,' he said, 'it's daunting, but you see now why I wanted to tackle this sooner rather than later. At least we can check out what we like and arrange to have it delivered down the track.'

'I guess,' she conceded, as she glumly surveyed the warehouse filled with dozens of happy couples and women with bumps and more baby gear than she'd ever seen. And they needed two cots, two bassinets, two of just about every damn thing. Nick might have been right about her flat being too small, after all, and that made her glummer still, because at some stage she needed to get back into her own space.

It took the best part of two hours simply to check out and make some decisions about bassinets and cots and a change table—Sophie was adamant just one of those would do—before they moved on to manchester for a few basics and found themselves staring at prams, by which time Sophie's feet were killing her. Nick noticed her flagging and sat her down at the cafe, bringing a pot of tea and scones.

'I'm sorry, this was too much to do in one day.'

'No, you were right, I'm glad we came. I had no idea how much choice there was.' He poured them both a cup as Sophie asked, 'How much more do you think we need to look at?'

'We've seen enough. I think you need some looking after. We can take a catalogue and order the rest online if you like.'

'Thanks,' she said, sprawled back in her seat with her legs out, relieved beyond measure. 'I think I like.'

He smiled as he passed her the tea, and Sophie saw a flash of humour in his eyes.

'Are you laughing at me?' she said. 'Do I look that ridiculous?'

He broke open a scone and loaded it up with raspberry jam and cream and sent that her way, too, his lips still curved. 'You look adorable.'

'I look like a beach ball, more like it,' she said, pushing herself back in her seat so she could tackle the scone, because two hours of baby-equipment shopping sure left a girl with an appetite.

'An adorable beach ball, then,' he countered.

'Fine,' she said, trying to dredge up some remnant of grudge against the man, liking being looked after but telling herself he was only doing so because of the babies. He was only being polite. The smiles and the banter didn't mean anything. 'Just don't go sticking any pins in me and we'll stay friends.'

He chuckled as he bit into his own scone, and she was reminded of his laughter while they'd been sitting waiting for her scan. It had taken her by surprise then, too, because it was a side of him she'd never seen before, and damn him to hell and back, she liked this unexpected playful side to him. She liked it very much.

'Expecting twins?' the middle-aged shop assistant asked unnecessarily while she totted up the order of two of almost everything on the cash register. She looked over the few small items of manchester, the sheets and then wraps and bunny rugs they'd loaded in their trolley, and all in whites and pastel shades that didn't include blue or pink. 'And not sure of the sex, right?'

Sophie and Nick exchanged glances over their self-appointed Sherlock.

'Why spoil the surprise?' said Nick.

'My thoughts exactly,' the assistant asserted with a knowing smile. 'After all, it's not like you'll be having kittens.'

'No,' said Nick deadpan. 'We've already had those.'

'Did you see her face?' Sophie had made it all the way to the car before she couldn't contain it any longer and collapsed into a fit of giggles. 'After all,' she mimicked, in the woman's all-knowing tones, 'it's not like you'll be having kittens.' She laughed so much she snorted.

Nick chuckled as he climbed into the driver's seat. 'You liked that, eh?'

She nodded, tears squeezing from her eyes. 'Especially when you said, "Six of the damned things. We're so relieved this time there's only two."' She collapsed into another fit of laughter. 'You should never have told her these would go the same way if they didn't behave. You should never have told her you'd sell them on eBay and if you do, will they accept returns.'

'A bit much?'

'She's probably calling Family Services right now.'

He fired up the engine and smiled as he looked over at her. She looked at him still laughing, with tears streaming down her cheeks, and something snagged and pulled tight in the space between them. The laughter died in her mouth and the only sound in the car was her ragged breathing. She licked her lips and looked down at her lap, busying her hands with smoothing her tunic over her bump, while her blood fizzed in her veins and she wondered what had just happened.

Oh no.

No, nothing was happening.

She turned her head to look out her window, trying to calm the mad beat of her heart. She wouldn't let it.

55

Hannah

'So, how's it going with Nick?' Hannah asked when she dropped by after work one evening during the week. She perched her bum up on the kitchen counter and helped herself to a Golden Delicious apple from the fruit bowl. 'Mmm,' she said, looking approvingly at the apple as she started munching.

'They're good, aren't they,' agreed Sophie. 'Picked fresh this morning. Nick brought them in at lunchtime.'

'Very good. So, you have a man who supplies you with apples picked fresh from the tree? Clearly this trial is going well.'

'Oh, it's okay, I guess,' Sophie said, 'I'm settling in.'

'You haven't fallen in love with him yet?'

'No!'

'Wow,' Hannah said, her eyes narrowing. 'Do you need time to think about that? Only you seem pretty emphatic.'

'There's nothing going on, no.'

'There you go, Beth and I told you that you were worrying about nothing.' She crunched into the apple again, the crispy sweetness the perfect summer treat.

Sophie rolled her eyes. 'Is there a reason you dropped by, Han, other than to ask after my love-life, or lack thereof?'

Hannah laughed. 'There is actually. I was wondering if Nick could help me out with any windfalls. Only the local wildlife park would love some fresh produce. I dropped by Dan's before and he's already agreed to help, and seeing as they'll take as much as we can supply, I figured, since I was in the neighbourhood, I'd ask Nick.'

Sophie shrugged as she looked at the clock. 'He's still out in the orchard picking, but I can't see he'd have a problem with it.'

'Yeah? Tell him I'm happy to come collect them myself. Sunday morning would be good for me.'

'I could give you a hand, if you like.'

'Sure, you can help by picking apples off the ground,' Hannah said as she jumped off the counter and flicked her apple core into the bin. 'I'd give you about ten minutes of stoop labour before you'd collapse in a heap and we have to call an ambulance. How is the blood pressure going, anyway? Seen the doctor lately?'

'I've got an appointment next week. I feel fine, though, most of the time.'

'Most of the time?'

'Just the usual stuff. A bit dizzy if I get out of bed too quickly, that's all. And big. I'm starting to feel huge.'

'Ha,' Hannah laughed, looking at Sophie's growing baby bump, 'there's a reason for that.'

Sophie scowled at her, suddenly. 'Is something up with you?'

'Me? Why?'

'You seem different somehow. Happy.'

'I'm always happy.'

'No, you're not,' said Sophie. 'You're the sensible older sister, remember. The one who delights in telling her younger sisters off when they step out of line. Only for some reason you look happy all of a sudden.'

'That is such a crock, little sister.'

'Ah,' said Sophie, as she walked her sister out to the car, 'that's more like it.' And Hannah snorted.

'Have you heard anything about how Nan's going?' Sophie asked. 'I haven't seen her the last few days.'

'Good as gold, from all reports,' Hannah said. 'Pop said she's been great. Not a hint of wandering or anything untoward.'

'Good. You don't think we overreacted with all the security stuff Dan put in, do you?'

Hannah shrugged and leaned over to give her sister a kiss before she climbed into her four-wheel drive. 'It's that kind of disease, though, isn't it? Going to sneak up and catch you unawares. And given all the tests she's had, well, the doctors are sure about their diagnosis.'

'I guess,' Sophie conceded. 'It just sucks.'

'That it does. Makes you realise we have to appreciate her while she's still around, physically and mentally.'

Hannah headed straight over to Declan's after she'd visited Sophie. She nibbled on her lip, feeling a little bit guilty that she hadn't said anything to Sophie about Declan. She hadn't realised her joy was so evident to anyone else.

Maybe it wouldn't hurt to share the reason for her happiness with her family. A barbecue wasn't such a bad idea. Simple and informal and an outing for Nan and Pop. Nan would love that. Siena would adore Ella, too.

She pulled the car up out front and Declan came out and greeted her, as he always did. Open-armed and warm-hearted and making her feel more special than she'd ever been made to feel. They talked about her day's work and how Ella was growing and what was happening in the vineyard while they ate steak and salad. Then they settled in the courtyard with their tea to watch the black cockatoos screeching for their nests while the sunset painted the candlebark gums red.

Sitting there, with the ever-changing light as their entertainment, the koala grunting and bird calls, and even the way the wind played in the trees, their music, Hannah couldn't remember a time she'd been happier.

After her often batshit-crazy days, filled with examinations and injections, surgery and emergencies, there was the promise of calm and serenity and the simple joy of being with a man she could be herself with. Who didn't ask of her what she couldn't give.

She looked over at him as he sat with his elbows resting on his knees, nursing his tea in his hands, while he watched Ella hopping around his feet, busy exploring her world or reaching up to twist around and try to scratch her back with her short arms. He must have sensed her eyes on him, because he turned his head towards her and smiled, his dimples bracketing his gorgeous mouth, and she felt something unfurl inside her chest, something tentative but warm and wonderful. He put down his tea and took her hand in his.

'I've been thinking,' he said, and her whole body went on alert. If he was going to raise the question of when he'd get to meet her family, she was going to get in first.

'Me too,' she said, jumping in. 'I think it's time I let you out of the closet. Maybe we should organise that barbecue, if you still want to, I mean.'

'Oh, Hannah love, that'd be grand.' He nodded on a sigh, before smiling back at her. 'You know, I like spending time with you. I like having you here.' He squeezed her hand and she squeezed back.

'I like being with you, too.'

He nodded as he lifted her hand to his mouth and pressed his lips to it. 'That's what I thought. You're a very special woman, you know that?'

God, but the man knew how to make her feel good. 'Don't worry, I have my share of shortcomings. You just haven't known me long enough.'

It was Declan's turn to laugh and the joey looked up at the sound.

'What's so funny?' she said.

'That's what they used to call me, back when I was just a little tacker in school. Short Cummins.'

She sniggered. 'You are so not short.'

He laughed with her before he pulled her into his kiss. 'You know, I came up here because I needed time and space and I needed to be alone. And then you came along and I realised I'd been alone long enough. You fill something in me, Hannah, something that had been empty for a long time.'

Hannah held her breath, his words sending a sizzle from the inside of her all the way out.

'And while I love you coming around every evening that you can, I'd like to see you more. I'd like to see you coming home—to me.'

Her heart hammered in her chest. 'What exactly are you saying?'

He smiled and slowly shook his head. 'Something I never thought I'd say to any woman, ever again. I've fallen for you, Hannah, and I want to marry you. That is, if you can put up with an old codger like me. Maybe we could make an announcement at that barbecue, and turn it into a real celebration.'

Whoa. Marriage. Hannah was glad she was sitting down, the concept was so left field. The thought of coming home to Declan every day, to wake up to him every morning was beyond anything she had ever hoped for. But still, her commonsense brain told her to take it slowly. She'd been so careful since university, so cautious to avoid getting herself involved too deeply, only to find it had snuck up on her. She swallowed. 'This is kind of sudden.'

He shrugged. 'Yes and no. It's something that's been playing on my mind a while. You don't have to give me an answer today. Take your time. And meanwhile, let me try to persuade you.'

A little thrill sizzled in her belly. 'And just how do you intend to do that?'

He stood then, took her hands and pulled her against him, his hands kneading her denim-clad butt. 'Any number of ways,' he said, his mouth dipping to hers. 'And I warn you, I'm very persuasive.'

She smiled under his mouth. 'I was kind of hoping you'd say that.'

An hour later Hannah was thoroughly persuaded. *He loves me*, she thought in wonder, as she panted her way down from the heights he'd taken her. *He actually loves me.* And a little voice inside her chest told her that she'd been wrong to think this thing between them would blow over anytime soon, because she knew in her heart that she loved him, too.

But marriage?

He stirred and pulled her into his embrace and nuzzled against her throat. 'So, my beautiful Hannah, have I persuaded you yet?'

'Not quite.' She closed her eyes against the evocative rasp of his whiskers and the heat of his breath against her skin. *I love you*, she thought, although she was still too afraid to admit it out loud. He was offering her the world, but how could she take it, until she knew for sure that it could work. She swallowed. And there was only one way to find out.

'In that case,' he said, dipping his head to her nipple, 'I'll have to try harder.'

Hannah's breath caught at the electric pull of his mouth while her mind was in turmoil, knowing all she had to do was ask. Knowing that she couldn't.

Because now there was too much at risk.

Because a wrong answer would mean the end.

And Declan's love was too precious to lose.

56

Sophie

Sophie had always wanted more time to read. Now that she was only allowed to work two and a half days a week, she had it in spades. She had an entire box of books she'd brought from home, and she'd already read a couple of those, but she figured she might as well check out the contents of Nick's lounge-room library shelves while she was here. She found lots of the classics plus a range of thrillers, crime novels and blockbuster blokey books, plus an entire shelf devoted to Dick Francis novels. She'd never read a Dick Francis. She pulled out the first one, checked out the back-cover blurb and the first page and thought, why the hell not? And started reading.

She'd taken the book into the kitchen and made herself a sandwich for lunch, sitting at the table eating it, still reading, when Nick came in. He looked hot, sweat sticking his dark hair to his head where his hat had been, and she felt guilty because she had the air conditioner on and it was blissfully cool inside.

'Working hard?' he said, as he wiped his brow, though he was smiling with it.

She shrugged. 'Doctor's orders. What's a girl to do?'

But she felt guiltier when he started fossicking in the fridge and pulling out sandwich fillings, just as he'd done last week on her non-teaching days. It was starting to become an uncomfortable pattern. 'I should have made you a sandwich,' she said, the crumbs on her plate staring accusingly up at her.

'I don't expect you to do that. You're supposed to be resting.'

'I think I can make you a sodding sandwich without overdoing it.'

'No. You take care of you,' he said, being the ridiculous man he was, and went right on making his sandwich.

So, she surreptitiously took note of what he liked on a sandwich and the next day she had one already prepared when he came in for lunch. In case he was in any doubt whom the sandwich was intended for, she took a leaf out of Alice in Wonderland's book and wrote 'Eat Me' on a sticky note.

He came in and took one look at it, all wrapped up in cling film on a plate, looked at her, and grinned. 'Thank you,' he said. 'You didn't need to.'

'I know.' But she felt extraordinarily pleased that she had. After all, it was no big deal to make an extra one for him. It wasn't like it meant anything, it was just helping out.

By the end of the second week they were getting into the hang of coexisting under the one roof, and Sophie was pretty proud of the way she'd handled herself around Nick. There'd been no more laughs or meaningful exchanges and she'd made sure she wasn't around when he was going to and from the bathroom in the morning. If things got awkward, she could always head over to Amy Jennings's place next door for a circuit-breaker. And now, Min was due back from Penelope's and there was another week when she didn't have to worry about anything untoward happening. The mere fact that Min was around would see to that.

Nick was in the shower before heading down to pick up Min when the doorbell rang. Sophie hauled herself out of bed, where she'd been munching on a piece of toast. 'I'll get it,' she called out as she passed the bathroom door, her vegemite toast in hand as she walked to the door. She stuck her toast in between her teeth and tried to do up her robe, but it didn't go all the way around her anymore, so she gave up, letting it swing at her sides over her nightie. It was hot anyway and it was only Hannah they were expecting, to pick up some windfalls for her kangaroos.

Still munching, she pulled open the door and froze.

'Tell Han there's a couple of buckets already collected—' said Nick, who was flashing by with a towel wrapped around his waist. He stopped when he realised it wasn't Hannah at the door.

'Well, well,' Penelope said, looking from one to the other, the look on her face like the proverbial cat with the cream. 'Doesn't this look cosy?'

Nick straightened, lashing his towel tighter around his waist with a determined tug. 'What are you doing here, Penelope? I'm supposed to be picking Min up in twenty minutes.'

'I was too curious not to come after you told me you had a new house guest.' She turned her eyes on Sophie. 'A very pregnant house guest, as it happens. Now, why would a very pregnant school teacher be moving in with you, do you think?'

'Where's Min?'

'Mignon is in the car. I told her to wait while the adults had a little chat.'

'I've got nothing to say to you that I can't say in front of Min.'

'What? So she knows you're sleeping with her teacher?'

'We're not sleeping together,' said Sophie, her toast forgotten as she pulled the sides of her robe as far as she could over her nightie.

'Come on,' Penelope said, nodding in Sophie's direction, 'that little bundle didn't burrow its way in there all by itself. Why would Sophie be here if it wasn't your baby?'

Sophie felt like she'd been slapped, and was going to argue the point, but Nick held up his hand to stop her. 'You know what, Penelope? It's none of your damned business.'

Sophie saw Min edging around the car, clutching her backpack to her chest, her face white, and her heart went out to the girl for being caught up in the middle of this.

'Excuse me, Nicholas, but shouldn't I have a say in who you're going to play happy families with in this house with my daughter?'

He shook his head. 'No, you shouldn't.'

'But—'

'But nothing. You gave up any rights to what happens in this household, who I have living here and who I may or may not choose to sleep with, when you slammed this very door and walked away.' He saw Min and called, 'Min, come inside, sweetheart. Penelope is just leaving.'

'This isn't the last you're going to hear of it, Nicholas Pasquale. I'll be speaking to the school principal about this.'

'You do that,' he said, ushering Min inside before he closed the door on his ex-wife. 'And for the record, my name is Nick.'

'I shouldn't have said all that,' he said, when Min was off catching up with Fat Cat and kittens and safely out of earshot. 'Not in front of Min.'

Sophie put a coffee in front of him on the table outside and pulled up a chair. Things had taken a little while to settle down after cyclone Penelope had left, but Nick had made pancakes for brunch and Sophie had dressed, and Hannah had been and gone for her windfalls, and now, in the dappled light filtering through the glory-vine-covered pergola, there was a chance to breathe. A light breeze shifted the air, setting a wind chime tinkling intermittently. 'I honestly don't think you had much of a choice.'

He looked over at her. 'She'll do it, though. She'll talk to the principal like she threatened. She'll probably ring the department of education and her local member of parliament, for that matter. She'll complain to whoever she thinks will listen.'

'But what can she honestly hope to achieve? We haven't done anything wrong.'

'She could still make things uncomfortable for you at school.'

'Hey,' she said, sitting up straighter in her seat as she plastered a stern expression to her face, 'I'm tougher than I look, you know.'

He looked at her, and said, 'Yeah, you are. You moved in here with me and Min against your better judgement, and you could have made life hell for everyone if you wanted, but instead you're doing your best to make it work. I'm just sorry you had to get caught up in the crossfire between Penelope and me.'

'Given I'm having your twins, that was bound to happen sooner or later, regardless of where I lived.' He grunted his agreement as she took a sip of her coffee, almost glowing from his praise. She had tried to fit in. It was nice to see he appreciated it. 'How long were you married?' she asked.

'Five years. It wouldn't have lasted three, but then Penelope discovered she was pregnant ...' He blew out a long breath, twirling his coffee cup in one hand. 'You think sticking together is going to be better for a baby, but it's not, you know. It's hell on everyone.'

'What was the worst thing about being married?'

He pulled a face. 'That's easy. Getting divorced. The endless arguments and the lawyers, the property settlement and the custody battle surrounding Min. It was the ugliest and worst experience of my life.'

She nodded, filing his words front and centre of her brain. If they didn't give her sufficient warning not to go falling in love with the man, she didn't know what would. 'So, what was the best thing about being married?' she asked. 'If there was a best thing.'

'Min,' he said without hesitation. 'I wouldn't be without her for the world.'

Sophie nodded. 'She is pretty amazing.'

'I think so.' He pushed away his empty cup and clasped his hands, his forearms resting on the table. 'I always expected to have a few kids,' he started. 'But I didn't see how it might happen, I mean, with not wanting to get hitched again. I have to say, I'm pretty pleased about having more.'

'Even though the circumstances are less than ideal?'

'The circumstances are what they are,' he said, collecting up the cups to take them inside. 'I guess it's how we choose to deal with them that matters.'

She gathered that was exactly his philosophy regarding the shared arrangements with Min—dealing with circumstances as they existed, making the best of a bad situation. And she figured it was being through what he had been that made him so wise. You couldn't come through an experience like he'd done unscathed, or without either being bent completely out of shape or having learned a lesson or three along the way.

He was a good dad. A bloody good dad. Her babies' lives would be so much the richer for their relationship with him.

She was about to follow him inside when she remembered the washing she'd put on the line earlier that should be dry. She stomped her feet on the ground a few times to give anything warning so it could slither away if it was there, and peeked around the corner. Nothing. Perfect.

Halfway through unpegging the washing, she sensed a movement out of the corner of her eye and felt that cold sizzle of fear zipper down her spine as she spun, repulsed by what she saw when she turned. It was like a scene from a horror movie, a tangled knot of snake that rolled and writhed in on itself, its tail thrashing through the base of the netting as it struggled to escape, its power evident in every coiling twist.

Sophie dropped her bundle of washing and ran to find Nick.

⁓

'Got yourselves a decent brownie here, Nick. Reckon it'd be close to six feet long,' Harry said half an hour later as Sophie and Min ventured outside to watch, keeping a safe distance away.

The snake catcher glanced over at Sophie and Min, who was peeking out from behind her.

'Oh, hello, Sophie,' he said, and if he was surprised to see her at Nick's place, he didn't show it. 'Hello, Min.'

'I didn't know you were a snake catcher, too,' Min said.

'Jack-of-all-trades,' he said with a smile, 'master of none, that's me. I guess you don't need this hanging around any longer.'

Sophie watched as he gave Nick a bag to hold and got to work, locating the head amongst the mess of tangled coils and pinning the snake down while he grabbed it behind the head. With his free hand, he pulled a pair of snippers from a back pocket and set to work, delicately snipping away the netting from the captured snake.

'It's always good when people don't take matters into their own hands,' Harry said, nodding towards Nick as he snipped, the snake gradually being freed, twisting itself around the snake-catcher's arm. 'They're pretty easy targets once they're snagged up in the netting.'

'I figure it's got a right to exist as much as I do,' Nick said. 'Maybe just a little further away than where my kids live.'

'Dead right,' Harry said with a laugh as the snake came free. Still with his fingers at its neck, he pulled the coils from his arm and the snake dangled long and fat from his hand. 'Yup, two metres, I reckon. You got yourselves a goodie.'

'Aren't you scared it's going to bite you?' asked Min.

'Aw, I've been bitten four times,' he said, as he negotiated the snake into the bag Nick passed him, dropped the head with a flick of his wrist and twisted the bag around on itself several times, securing the snake at the bottom. 'But better to bite me than bite you, or your mum or dad trying to protect you, eh?'

Sophie looked down at Min, who was busy looking up at her, her little brows knotted together. 'Yeah, I guess.'

'Oh, Sophie,' Harry said, as he was leaving, 'you're Beth's sister, right?'

'That's right.'

'How is she?'

Sophie blinked. 'Um, okay, I think,' she said, trying to work out the last time they'd caught up. 'Why do you ask?'

'No reason,' he said, and headed for his car.

'He thought you were my mum,' said Min, after Harry had left with the snake and they'd gone inside.

'I noticed that,' Sophie said with a smile. 'I hope you don't mind. I couldn't see the point of correcting him.'

'Nope, I thought it was kind of cool. You'd be a cool mum to have,' she said, before running off to drape herself in ragdolls, leaving Sophie decidedly confused. Forget about falling in love with Nick, she told herself, right now she was in imminent danger of falling in love with Min.

Sophie put down the latest Dick Francis she was trying to read, distracted by the football game going on inside her belly, when Min came into the lounge room, ready for bed. 'What are you doing?'

'I should be in bed,' Sophie conceded, her hand on her bump, 'but now there's this AFL game going on in my belly and I'm waiting for the quarter-time siren to blow.'

Min looked at her t-shirt-covered stomach with wide eyes. 'Who's playing?'

'I think it's the showdown, Port versus the Crows. At least, that's how it feels.' Something moved under her hand. 'Oh, someone just kicked a goal—I think the Crows are in front.'

'Yay,' said Min. 'Go Crows. Can I feel?'

Sophie blinked, momentarily taken by surprise. 'Of course you can,' she said. After all, these were Min's siblings and why shouldn't she experience the magic of feeling them at play. 'Okay, so put your hands here and here,' she said, guiding them into position on her t-shirt where she was pretty sure she'd feel something.

Min waited, her face screwed up in concentration. 'I can't feel anything,' she said, disappointed. 'Is it quarter time already?'

'Just wait a second,' Sophie said, getting used to the program and the pauses between movements. And almost immediately she was rewarded with a fresh bout of prods and kicks and tumbles.

'Wow,' said Min, her eyes lighting up. 'I feel them, I feel them. Port tried to kick a goal, but it was marked by the Crows. The Crows are still in front!'

Sophie laughed, and the babies tumbled some more, adding to the girl's joy.

And suddenly, Sophie realised they had an audience. 'Dad!' Min squealed, 'the babies are playing footy and the Crows are winning.'

'I wondered what all the noise was about,' he said, but he was smiling and Sophie knew he approved.

'Come and feel,' Min said, 'it's the showdown.' And then a couple of seconds later when he hadn't moved, 'Dad!'

Nick apologetically raised his eyebrows. 'May I?'

Sophie breathed deeply. 'Sure,' she said, trying her best to sound cool, calm and blasé, rather than the scared shitless she felt about having his hands on her. They were his babies, too, why shouldn't he be able to feel them moving? And she was fully dressed, it wasn't like she was naked or anything.

How difficult could it be?

Except then Min knelt down on the floor and made space, and he sat down on the edge of the sofa and placed his hands on her belly. Large hands, so much larger than Min's, his fingers extending so much farther than her tiny ones had done.

Warm hands that had explored her body in exquisite detail.

Knowing hands.

She felt their heat sizzle its way through the knit of her fabric and into her skin. She felt it seeping into her veins and pumping through her body, only to pool heavy and insistent in that newly aching place between her thighs.

She felt his eyes on her face, but she dared not meet them when she was lying down and he was so close, his hands on her, so she looked at Min, instead, but she was looking expectantly at her dad. 'Feel it, Dad?'

His hands shifted, traversing her belly and sending shockwaves straight to her core, and her babies obliged and swooped and kicked under his hands. Min whooped. 'You see?'

'I do,' he said, and his voice sounded so full of wonder that she stole a glance up at him and saw him watching her, his dark eyes so rich with emotion that her breath caught in her throat.

This was intimacy without being intimate, sensuality without sex, his big, warm hands stroking her senses as much as they stroked her skin, and she trembled under the power of his touch.

'Amazing,' he said, still watching her face as she tried to mask her reaction.

'Another goal!' shouted Min at the next prod. 'Yay! The Crows are winning.'

Sophie laughed, the spell broken, never more grateful for the presence of the six-year-old. 'I think I need to get up,' she said, needing Nick's hands off her, grateful when he took the hint and offered his arm, making the ascent to vertical that much easier.

'Oh,' said Min, 'we don't know who won.'

Sophie stroked her hair. 'There'll be other games, don't worry.'

'Besides, it's past your bedtime,' Nick said.

'And mine,' Sophie said. Although, with her blood buzzing like high-voltage electricity wires, she suspected she would lie awake for hours.

Very, very awake.

57

Sophie

The doctor at Sophie's next antenatal visit was blunt. 'Your blood pressure's still too high.'

'White-coat syndrome?' Sophie offered by way of explanation, doing her best to counter Nick's frown.

The doctor was having none of it. She peered at Sophie over her reading glasses. 'I'm afraid it's a bit more serious than that.' She turned to her computer screen to input the test results. 'How much are you working at the moment.'

'Point five.'

'Days per week?'

'Oh, no, that's workload. Two and a half days a week.'

'And you're up on your feet those days with a classroom full of kids, right?'

'True, but only when I'm not sitting down with them, of course.'

'Hmm, you might need to think about cutting that.'

'But then I'll hardly be there at all.'

The doctor looked levelly at her. 'That's what I meant. I think you'd be wise to drop your work commitments altogether.'

'But—stop work? Already? The babies aren't due until June sometime. What am I supposed to do until then?'

'Live a quiet life for a few months, get a bit of gentle exercise, but basically put your feet up,' said the doctor, 'because I can tell you that if you don't, or won't, and your blood pressure keeps going the way it's going, you'll end up being assigned permanent bed rest, and I can promise you now, you're going to like that a whole lot less.'

It wasn't much of a choice, Sophie figured, as they left the surgery. In fact, it was pretty much no choice at all.

'It's not so bad,' said Nick as he opened the passenger door for her. 'It's only for a few months.'

'Months of doing nothing,' she said as she clambered awkwardly into the car. 'Would you like that?'

'I'll make it easier for you to enjoy, I promise.'

'How?'

'I don't know. I'll find a way.'

It was Sophie who worked out what she could do for fun the next morning. She was washing up the few bits and pieces that didn't go in the dishwasher, while Nick was doing the school run and dropping off Min.

She'd hung back from offering to help with the cooking, not wanting to get in Nick's way at meal times in the kitchen, or make him think she was taking over. This was his domain and he was good at it and she was a guest, after all—a temporary guest. But she remembered the fun she'd had with Min making the hamburger patties, and how the girl loved spaghetti bolognaise, and she thought about the pasta machine she'd been given on her twenty-first that she had tucked away in one of her boxes in the shed. She'd used it heaps in the first year or so, until she'd started watching her carbs and her weight, and it had been ages since she'd last used it. Min would get a kick out of it, she was sure.

Two minutes later she was out in the shed looking at the stash of boxes. But which box was it in? Damn.

That's when she saw it.

It was sitting on a shelf on the opposite wall, orange-sided with a bright-yellow lid. She recognised it because it was similar in shape to the one her nan had always used, though that had been green. Boxes stacked alongside were labelled 'Rings and Lids'.

An entire Vacola bottling unit was sitting here going begging.

How long ago was it that she'd bottled up fruit with her sisters and her nan? Too long to remember. Before they were all at university, probably. Long before. She had a hankering to return to those times, with her sisters slicing fruit and making sugar syrup, Nan issuing instructions and running the timer, and Pop dropping in with a wink to say Nan was a right little bottler. She smiled at the memories. Funny, but she'd never understood what that had meant at the time.

They were simpler times.

Good times.

And with the pears in the orchard ripening up, it was the perfect time to be thinking about bottling them. Nick had mentioned the Beurre Bosc pears were just about ready.

And surely he wouldn't have any issues with this idea, especially if she wasn't doing it alone but had her family involved. Maybe even Nan, for that matter. She thought about what Hannah had said about appreciating Nan while they could. This would be something they could do together. She'd probably love overseeing her grandchildren bottle up a batch of fruit.

She heard Nick's car coming up the driveway and went to meet him to help her get the set down.

Nick had to help her with this. Because otherwise, she was going to go out of her mind.

꩜

Nick had done more than help with fetching the pasta machine and the bottling outfit. He'd helped her clean out the boiler and stack and unstack the dishwasher with the jars to freshen them all up. He'd even run down to the local hardware store and topped up on lids and seals so everything was ready for bottling day. And he'd done it smiling. Not his smug 'I've got you now' smile that she'd witnessed when she'd first arrived, but the smile she'd seen unfurling slowly over the time she'd been here. Almost a smile of approval.

She thought about that smile and how good it made her feel as she and Min assembled the flour, oil and eggs they'd need for the pasta. Nick already had a big pot of bolognaise sauce simmering on the stove, and the kitchen smelled deliciously of tomatoes, garlic and herbs.

To make it easier and quicker this time, she used the food processor to prepare the dough, before resting it in the fridge for a few minutes while she clamped the pasta machine to the benchtop and put a pot of water on to boil. Then it was time to roll the pasta. Min was a fabulous apprentice. She divided the ball of pasta into three pieces and floured one, and Sophie showed her how to feed the smaller portion of pasta in between the rollers, at first on the thickest setting, and then progressively rolling the pasta sheet thinner and thinner, until Min had to use both hands to support it as it rolled out of the machine. Gingerly, she laid it down on a floured tea towel, reverently dusting it with more flour, before repeating the task with the other two pieces.

'It's just like play dough,' she said, squishing a portion between her little fingers.

'Exactly like play dough,' Sophie agreed, scratching an itch on her nose with the back of one floured hand. 'Only better, because we get to eat this kind. Next time, I'll get you to mix up the dough in a bowl if you like, now that you know how it's supposed to feel.'

'Yeah? That'd be really cool.'

Nick watched the scene from the doorway. Neither of them had heard him come in, both with their backs to him and one hundred per cent focused on their task. Sophie was in an old-fashioned pinny with frills around the sleeves and Min had an apron fashioned out of a tea towel around her waist. Cute. He watched them roll the final sheet and then Sophie switched ends or rollers or something and the next time it went through the machine, it came out in narrow strips.

'Look! Pasghetti!' Min said, beside herself with excitement as she watched, holding onto the counter with her fingers. His girl was having the time of her life and he couldn't stop himself from smiling along with her.

But Min wasn't the only one enjoying herself. The woman beside her was clearly having a good time, too. And whether it was because she was a teacher that she was so good with Min, or she was naturally good with kids which made teaching a good fit, he didn't know, but there was no doubt in his mind that she'd make a good mum.

Probably just as well. His gaze dropped to the region of where her waist once had been, and maybe it was because the babies she was carrying were his, but even now with her body bent out of shape and carrying a few extra kilos, he thought she looked sexy as hell. She was rounder. Softer.

He watched on while Min took a turn cranking the handle, and together they ran the other two sheets through the machine until the noodles were done. 'Right,' she said to Min as she wiped her hands with her pinny, 'now they have to be cooked, but they'll be ready in about three minutes so we don't want to start too soon. Where's your father, do you think?'

'He's right here,' he said, his voice a little thick.

She turned in surprise, her eyes wide. 'Oh.'

'We made pasghetti!' said Min excitedly. 'See!'

'You did,' said Nick, coming closer to inspect the noodles, putting his hand on her shoulder. 'Aren't you clever?'

'And next time, Sophie says I can mix up the dough, too.'

'Sounds like fun,' he said. 'Now, how about you go get washed up. Dinner sounds like it'll be ready in no time. I'll give Sophie a hand serving up.'

Min scampered off to the bathroom to wash her hands while Sophie added olive oil to the pot and brought it to a rolling boil. 'That was a pretty impressive display,' he said, looking over her shoulder as she sprinkled in a pinch of salt.

'It's easy really,' she said. 'I wondered if it might be a bit old hat, given Min's and your Italian heritage, but she told me she hadn't made fresh pasta before.'

'My nonna used to make it, but Mum's speciality is cakes. She still makes them for a local cafe near where they live in Melbourne. I haven't had fresh pasta for years.'

'I hope you like it.' She swung around to pick up the pasta, but he was right behind her and her belly was so big it brushed against him.

'Oh,' she said, looking up at him, and he could swear he saw her tremble as her eyes flared. 'Sorry.'

'My mistake,' he said, 'I shouldn't have been so close.' But he didn't move away, he stayed exactly where he was, his eyes intent on her face, with her belly so close he could feel her warmth and hear the sound of his pulse thumping in his ears. Even in a kitchen that smelled right now like something out of Tuscany, all he seemed to be able to smell was her signature scent. 'You have flour on your nose,' he said, and he lifted one hand to brush it off with the pad of his thumb.

Her eyes were wide, her pupils dilating, and as his thumb made contact with her skin, she trembled again, and without the distraction of the flour, there was nothing to stop his gaze dropping to her mouth. He saw her chin kick up as she swallowed and those pink lips parted on a sigh.

'Ready!' yelled Min, zooming back into the room, and they sprang apart, Nick to put the salad on the table, Sophie to scoop up the tangle of noodles and drop them into the pot. 'Oh,' she said, watching what Sophie was doing. 'I thought they'd be ready already.'

'We were waiting for you to get back,' said Nick.

'We didn't want you to miss anything,' added Sophie.

And Nick thought, with that remnant of his brain still working while most of his blood continued doing confused loop-the-loops in his veins, she almost hadn't.

'I think I'll have an early night tonight,' Sophie said half an hour later as she cleared the salad from the table, 'if that's okay with everyone.'

Nick looked up from where he was stacking the dishwasher.

'Already?' asked Min. 'It's not even my bedtime yet.'

'Are you feeling all right?' asked Nick, straightening.

'I'm fine,' she said, her hand on her belly, 'I just need to lie down and process all this delicious pasta a little before I explode.'

'You hardly ate anything.'

'I ate plenty. Shouldn't have filled up on bread beforehand, always a mistake. Night, all.' And with a wave, she fled.

She closed the door to her room and leaned her back against it. Because it wasn't her dinner she had to process. It was a touch, a look and an almost kiss. It was an inability, or more correctly, an unwillingness to make a move to avoid it. It was a yearning to know how it might have ended if Min hadn't burst in when she had, because she'd looked at his eyes on her mouth and she'd all but willed him to kiss her.

God, this was exactly the kind of thing she'd been worried about, that would get her thinking she actually meant something to Nick and that this arrangement might lead to something more permanent. The sort of thing that would get her thinking about those damned unicorns and rainbows and happy-ever-afters like she always did.

Damn.

She'd known moving in with Nick would end in disaster.

She'd already fallen in love with Min.

And now, she was in danger of falling in love with Nick as well.

What the hell was she supposed to do?

58

Hannah

Hannah still hadn't given Declan an answer. He didn't push her, but she caught him watching her sometimes, his gaze quizzical, as if trying to work out what was going on in her head.

There was too much going on in there, that was the problem. Too much second-guessing and too many what-ifs. Too much speculation and too many questions. He was forty-two, for heaven's sake. Surely he wouldn't want children at this stage in his life? Or maybe that was the time men thought about it, if they hadn't had them. Maybe he saw this opportunity as his last hurrah?

If she'd had more life experience, if she hadn't buried herself away after university, concentrating on her career and refusing to notice the opposite sex, she might have more of an idea of how to deal with this situation. But all she had were the bitter memories of James and his reaction to her news, and the knowledge that she didn't want to lose what she had with Declan. So, she put off the question and immersed herself in his love-making and his gentle, relentless persuasion, all the while falling deeper and deeper in love with him, so tempted to say yes, but knowing she risked everything.

She never expected Declan to be the one to raise the issue.

They were walking between the rows of vines under a cloudless blue sky, the growing joey hopping along beside them, when up ahead they saw the snake. Declan put out a hand to stop her and instinctively reached down and rolled Ella into her pouch, while the two of them stood stock still and watched the snake slither silently away into the bush. When it disappeared, Hannah found herself relating the story of Sophie and Nick and the snake catcher.

'Sophie's the one having twins, right?'

'That's right,' said Hannah, feeling a bit guilty that she still hadn't introduced him to her family. But, there seemed no point unless she said yes. She was so tempted to say yes. 'Lucy's baby is due in April and the twins are due in June.'

'And she's the school teacher?'

'Yeah, she takes the first-year kids at school. She's going to make the best mum.'

'You'd be a great mum.'

Hannah's heart missed a beat as ice clogged her arteries. It was all she could do to keep her feet moving. 'No, I'd be rubbish. I like animals way better than people.'

'You like me.'

'You're a rare exception.'

They walked on a while, Hannah hoping that was the end of the topic, feeling more relieved with every passing step.

'I never figured on having kids,' he said, and for a moment Hannah held her breath. 'Was always too busy with work and I was glad of it.'

'They're overrated, I'm sure,' she said, trying to keep it light and let the tiny flame of hope flicker in her heart. 'Unless you're going to be an aunty or uncle, of course.'

He chuckled at that and she thought for a moment she was home free. Until he said, 'Only I was thinking'—and this time it was fear that infused her veins—'I'm going to be forty-three next birthday—'

No. No. No!

'—and if I want it to happen …' He stopped and turned to face her, taking her hands in his. 'I know you haven't even agreed to marry me yet, but if you do say yes, then I would very much like you to be the mother of my babies.'

And Hannah felt the tiny flickering flame of hope in her heart get snuffed out.

59

Sophie

Sophie worked out that the best way to protect herself from falling victim to the happy family all around her was to keep busy. To keep her nose in a book, or keep herself occupied with anything that didn't involve Nick. The fruit bottling was a perfect example. She'd surround herself in female company and conversation, and be reminded there was a whole wide world out there. It would take her mind off Nick, completely.

Neither Hannah nor Beth could take time off at short notice, so it was only Sophie, Lucy and Nan who could front up for the bottling. It was a weekday and so Min was at school, but it was her week at Penelope's, and Sophie was determined to have another day again if it was a success. If she couldn't do anything else while she was in forced resting mode, she'd make sure everyone's pantries were filled up with bottled fruit.

'I'm so glad to have escaped,' said Nan, when Dan dropped off Lucy and Nan and unpacked Nan's old Vacola from the boot so they'd have two sterilisers working at the same time. 'It's like being in Stalag Thirteen at home.'

Lucy laughed as she gave Nan a hug, an awkward hug with Lucy getting so big. 'Is it really that bad?'

'I can't get out the door without a bloody bell going off! It's like trying to get over the Maginot Line with Clarry watching me like a hawk every minute of the day. I can't take a tinkle without him hollering out to me, wanting to know where I am.'

Sophie sympathised. She felt trapped too, though for a different reason, but at least Nick didn't holler at her through bathroom doors. 'Well, you're here now. And today we are going to have fun.'

Nan was in her element. She organised the set-up of the kitchen and bossed Nick into finding a table to set up the second outfit on an element outside because they wouldn't fit on the stove together. Then the three women donned aprons and got to work peeling and halving the boxes of long, brown pears Nick had supplied, while the clean glass jars sterilised in the oven, and they tossed baby names back and forth between each other because neither Sophie nor Lucy could decide.

'Two pounds of sugar to a gallon of water,' Nan said, in the midst of the deliberations, giving Sophie instructions to prepare the syrup.

'Huh?' said Sophie. 'How much?'

'Move over, sister,' Lucy said, flashing a grin, taking the sugar from Sophie's hands to weigh on the big scales. 'Imperial measurements? Nan and I speak the same language, I am so all over this one.'

Nan showed them how to stack the jars with the peeled and cored pears so they'd look beautiful as well as taste good, though their jars looked nowhere near as professional as Nan's. 'It's not as easy as it looks,' said Sophie, poking a recalcitrant piece of pear into place with the handle of a wooden spoon.

'I used to win awards at the Royal Adelaide Show,' Nan told them. 'Cherries, pears and apricots Clarry used to go pick up from the riverland. Oh, they're good.'

Sophie blinked. 'I remember having those with your homemade ice-cream.'

'You're making me hungry,' said Lucy, rubbing her belly.

'Not long now,' said Nan, slowly pouring syrup into the fruit-filled jars, while Sophie and Lucy set about slapping on the rings and lids and clipping them down to seal before they went into the steriliser.

'Phew,' said Sophie, when the first two batches were coming up to temperature. 'Let's take a break before we start on the next load of jars.'

'Wow,' Nick said as he took in the sight of the couple of dozen jars lined up cooling on the bench. He'd packed a lunch today because he hadn't wanted to come home in the middle of proceedings and get in everyone's way. 'So you had a good day?'

'It was amazing,' Sophie said, her hand buried in oven gloves and that cute little frill-edged pinny stretched tight over her bump again. She was wearing a sleeveless shift beneath so her lower legs were bare, and her toes winked glossy red at him from inside her sandals. 'We had so much fun, and Nan was so cool, she is such an expert at this. We even had time to give each other a pedicure in between. You can give me a hand getting the rest of them out.'

He raised an eyebrow. 'There's more?'

'That's only the first batch. The second batch just finished.'

He went to peek over her shoulder as she lifted the lid from the steriliser on the stove. 'Sure you're not overdoing it?'

'I had a nap. I only just woke up before you came in. Here, take these and give me a hand.' She passed him the tongs for removing the jars and spread out some tea towels to put the steaming hot bottles on. He helped her with the unit on the stove and then they tackled the one Nan Faraday had him set up outside, setting the bottles to cool on the bench with the others. Sophie was delighted with each and every one, cooing with pleasure as each bottle emerged.

'They look like Christmas baubles,' she said, her smile wide. 'Don't they look wonderful?' And Nick thought, yes, she does.

There was something different about her today. He'd walked inside and she'd been lit up like someone had flicked a switch, her face animated and her eyes bright. She was luminescent, glowing brighter than the pears in the jars. Even her toes looked cheerful.

And in that little frilly pinny, in the middle of his kitchen with a bottling outfit that was older than he was and dozens of bottles of preserved fruit, she looked like she'd just stepped out of the nineteen fifties.

She looked irresistible.

Scrap that, she was irresistible.

She looked up at him, still smiling, so supremely happy with herself and her world that she was almost vibrating with joy. Until a tiny frown marred her smile. 'What?'

'You're beautiful.'

She blinked. 'What?'

'I said, you're beautiful.'

'Oh.'

He put his hand to the spot where her neck met her shoulders, saw her lean into his touch, and knew he wasn't mistaken. 'And I would very much like to kiss you.'

Her eyes flared, focusing on his lips while the pink tip of her tongue found hers, as he curved his fingers and drew her closer.

She went willingly, the one, tiny solitary voice in the back of her mind telling her this was not a good idea, drowned out in the thumping beat of her heart insisting it was the best idea ever. She sighed when her lips met his, the press of his mouth so gentle, so exquisitely tender that a single tear squeezed from her eye. And when they moved over hers, their warm breath intermingling, it was with that same, magical delicacy.

It was Sophie who pressed for more. Sophie who needed more and wrapped her arms around his neck and pressed her aching breasts against his chest, never more conscious of her bump as she squeezed herself over it in her bid to get closer. It was Sophie who parted her lips and invited him to deepen the kiss, and welcomed him when he did.

And then her hands were in his hair and their tongues tangled and duelled, and his heated breath mixed with hers until she felt she was burning up with desire.

Still it wasn't enough. She took his hand and brought it to her breast and he growled, low in this throat, as his fingers squeezed her flesh. She arched against him as best she could, riding a wave of desire so strong there was no fighting it.

It was reckless and all kinds of madness, but it didn't matter in the least because she was here, now, feeling sensations she'd tried to ignore, and there was no ignoring it anymore because she needed this, so badly. She needed him.

'Make love to me,' she whispered.

He broke the kiss, his hands cupping her face. 'Is it safe?' he said, interspersing his words with butterfly kisses to her eyes and nose and mouth. 'Are you allowed?'

Nothing she'd read or been told said that she couldn't make love. True, her blood pressure might be higher than desired, but she knew one thing. 'I'll explode right here and now if you don't.'

'Hell no,' he said, swinging her into his arms as if she weighed nothing, thrilling her with his brute strength. 'We don't want that.'

He undressed her like she was made of glass. Slowly, reverently, he removed her sandals, kissing each painted toe and the inside of her ankles, before he pulled the bow that tied her apron and peeled it away.

And it was torture and joy in equal measure. She felt cherished as he slid the zipper down on her loose shift dress and glided it over her shoulders until she lay there in just her underwear, and he sat back and drank her in with his eyes. Worshipped.

Then even her underwear was gone, and she lay naked and fully exposed before him. He reached out a hand and palmed her bump, tracing the curve, his touch so tender but unleashing fireworks under her skin, before he leaned down and pressed his lips to her tummy and each dark-peaked nipple. 'Beautiful,' he said, before his mouth once again claimed hers as he undid his buttons and dispensed with his shirt.

'I should have had a shower,' he said between kisses.

'You smell amazing,' she countered, because he did. He smelled of hard work and heat and that increasingly familiar scent that was all his own, and she didn't want him going anywhere.

He stood to kick off his trousers and it was her turn to worship. He was magnificent. Broad-shouldered, lean and fit from a lifetime of working outdoors, his erection standing proud, and a sizzle of anticipation bloomed in her veins.

Skin against skin. There was no feeling like it in the world, Sophie vaguely registered as he joined her naked on the bed, the slide of his hand on her thigh, the press of her nipples against his chest, the rough of his whiskered jaw on her skin. Textures leading to sensations, building layer upon delicious layer. He took his own sweet time reacquainting himself with her body, but Sophie didn't mind. She wasn't going anywhere and there was no need to rush. She was floating on a fog of sensual pleasure.

Except when he turned her on her side away from him and slid his hand under the curve of her butt cheek and she felt the press of him at her core, she knew it was time. 'Tell me if I hurt you,' he said, as his lips and teeth worked magic on her neck, his hot breath stroking her skin, stoking the fire inside.

So gently, so tenderly he entered her. Filling her, until he was seated deep inside, and she gasped as stars burst behind her eyelids.

'Are you okay?'

'You feel amazing.'

She felt his smile as he pressed his lips to her shoulder and started to move. And she was lost in the slide and the friction as pleasure built upon pleasure, until she was cast adrift on a stormy sea that matched the eyes of the man she loved.

Her heart gave a jolt and she snapped her eyes open, a sudden panic vanquishing the humming goodness of her body coming down from the heights he'd taken her to.

Did she love him? Had she let the thing she most feared happen? Or was she spinning castles in the air the way she always did? But this was nothing like she'd imagined she'd felt before. This was bigger.

He stirred behind her and pressed his lips to her back, his hand stroking her belly.

'Okay?' he asked dozily.

She let herself relax against the warm body of the man behind her. This man was the father of her babies and he wanted her in his bed. This was not the same thing she'd felt with any man ever before. This was way better. This was real.

60

Beth

Beth climbed into the front seat of the ambulance, still stewing over an argument she'd had with Siena this morning. God, but the girl was developing an attitude, she was having the biggest sulk about something. 'What have we got?'

Her colleague turned on the siren and flashing lights, and slid the vehicle into a space someone made for them, and they were off, the road before them clearing as cars shifted sideways. 'Guy fallen from a tree. Head injuries and suspected fractures, sounds pretty serious. The rapid response car's already on its way.'

Beth nodded as the car cautiously ran a red light and swept out of the city and up Magill Road towards the hills. 'Where did it happen?'

'Up in the hills near Ashton.' He turned to her momentarily and rattled off an address. 'Don't you live up that way somewhere?'

Beth was already on the phone to her brother, relieved to hear his voice when he answered. Not Dan, then, she thought after a couple of words to explain, before pocketing her phone. But then, even though she couldn't pick the address, it could be any one of the people she knew from up that way.

She bit down on her lip as the ambulance screamed its way along the road, and headed into the cleft in the hills. Beth navigated, knowing the roads better than the GPS, instructing the driver to take a dirt road she knew would be quicker than the main one.

Barely fifteen minutes after leaving the base, they came upon the accident site with the SPRINT vehicle parked nearby, a couple of onlookers looking concerned.

'This is it,' she said, getting ready to jump out.

They pulled up in a spray of gravel and Beth was out. Their patient was lying awkwardly on the ground, a massive tree branch beside him, amidst a tangle of ropes and tackle that had clearly come down with him. The rapid responder hovered over the man, administering emergency aid. Something about the fallen form and the size of the patient, and the shaggy hair sticking out from under the strap of the goggles that had twisted around his neck, looked startlingly familiar.

And suddenly it hit her.

'Harry!' she screamed, breaking into a run and hurling herself down at his side. There was blood pooling beneath his head, so much blood, and one arm was twisted at a funny angle.

The rapid responder was too busy to look up. 'You know him?'

She sniffed. 'Harry Simpson. Aged around thirty-five or so. Harry,' she shouted. 'Harry! Oh God, don't you dare die on me. Don't you dare die on me. I love you!'

Harry's eyelids fluttered a moment, and Beth swore he was looking at her, trying to focus while his lips soundlessly mouthed her name.

'I love you!' she said again, before his eyes rolled back in his head and he slipped into unconsciousness. 'Harry!'

'We have to intubate him,' her partner said, his hand on her shoulders, edging her aside.

Beth let herself be shunted away, because she knew she was probably worse than useless, right now. She trembled with shock as the past and present collided.

The nightmare was happening all over again. She was going to lose the man she loved. And this time she hadn't even had a chance to tell him properly before it happened.

'Please don't die,' she willed him, her hands clenched together as her colleagues worked furiously on him. 'Please, Harry, please God, please don't die!'

Beth sat shivering in the starkly furnished waiting room, the harsh fluorescent lighting draining the room of any warmth, when Hannah brought Sophie to sit with her.

'I thought there must be something going on between you and Harry,' Hannah said as her sisters sat down either side of her.

Beth was hunched over on the seat, her head in her hands. 'Nothing was going on.'

'Clearly something was.'

'Go easy on her,' chided Sophie, her hand rubbing circles on Beth's back, her big belly jutting against her.

'Otherwise, why else would we all be here tonight?'

'He's a friend,' Beth said, her voice numb. 'He's been helping me out from time to time, that's all.' Because even she couldn't believe the admission she'd made at Harry's side. Had he heard her? Would he remember? Oh God.

'Just a friend and yet we all end up here tonight doing the vigil thing with you. Does that sound right?'

'Han!'

Her eldest sister was unrepentant, her tone suddenly strident. 'Sorry but no. Why can't you admit you have feelings for someone?'

'He's a friend, that's all!'

'Is it because of what happened to Joe? You have to let go of the past, Beth, or you'll never move on.'

'Stop it,' said Sophie. 'Can't you see you're hurting her?'

'Joe's gone, Beth,' Hannah persisted, her hand squeezing Beth's leg. 'You're allowed to move on. You're allowed to love somebody else. That's what Joe would want.'

'No!' Beth sat up bolt upright so quickly, both sisters had to jump away. 'Why should I be happy? Why should I be allowed to fall in love again?'

'But, Beth,' Hannah reasoned, 'he was speeding and his bike hit black ice. It wasn't your fault.'

'Yes, it damned well was.' And she crumpled down again as she burst into tears, the painful secret she'd held for so long now threatening to tear her apart.

'No,' her sisters both said above her, and she knew they were trying to help, but they were wrong.

They weren't there.

They didn't know.

'We argued.' Beth's voice was fractured and broken, sounding even to herself like it was coming from a long way away. 'I can't even remember what it was about, something pathetic, something that didn't matter, but Joe always had to win, and this time I wouldn't give in and he got angrier and angrier. And in the end, I told him he could shove his wedding ring. I told him it was over. I told him to piss off and never come back.' She gulped in air, before descending back into tears. 'And he didn't,' she wailed. 'He never came back.'

'Oh, Beth,' her sisters chorused as they leaned over to hug her tight, rocking together to comfort her. 'Oh, Beth.'

They stayed that way for what must have been minutes, while her tears subsided and her breathing slowed. 'And the hardest part of all is I didn't mean it,' she said. 'I didn't mean any of it. I was just sick of him always having to get his way. I just didn't want him to win for once.'

'We know,' Hannah said softly, pressing her lips to Beth's hair. 'We know how much you two loved each other. You didn't put that ice there and you didn't make him speed. He chose to do that.'

'Yes,' echoed Sophie. 'You have to stop blaming yourself.'

But could she after all this time? Beth sat up, wiping her tear-stricken face with her hands, and feeling strangely lighter now that she'd finally confessed what she'd never been able to tell anyone. Because in her head she knew what her sisters were saying was right. But she'd clung onto the truth for so long, she didn't know if she could let her heart believe it.

The door swung open. 'Ms Faraday? Beth?' said a white-coated doctor, her expression concerned.

All three sisters looked up. 'How is he?' whispered Beth. 'Is he going to be okay?'

The doctor gave a weary smile. 'He's had a major blow to the head, and he's fractured his arm badly, but the scans are all good, so yes, he's going to be okay.'

Beth felt herself slump with relief. 'He's asked to see you.' She glanced at the other women. 'Just one visitor, if you don't mind, and keep it brief. Harry needs to rest.'

Beth smiled and squeezed her sisters' hands. 'We'll wait for you,' said Sophie.

The doctor showed her to a small room, made smaller by the myriad bleeping machines and the bulk on the bed in between them all that was Harry. Beth squeezed her way to the head of the bed.

One of Harry's arms was shrouded in plaster, his other hand rising and falling with his chest. His eyes were closed and there was a big bandage around his head. She placed one hand over his, careful of the IV, and said, 'Harry.'

His eyelids flickered open, widening when they saw her.

'Beth,' he whispered roughly, and even that sounded like a struggle.

'Don't talk,' she said. 'I'm just relieved you're okay. I was so afraid.'

He smiled a wonky Hagrid smile up at her as best he could, and stroked the back of her hand with his big thumb, and Beth felt something breaking inside her. 'I'm sorry I hurt you, Harry. I wouldn't hurt you for all the world.' She would have stalled there but for the twinkle in his eye that urged her on. 'Because it seems I love you, Harry, you daft bastard, but if I ever catch you climbing a tree again, I swear I'll kill you.'

He tried to laugh but he winced instead. 'Ah, Beth,' he whispered after the pain eased. 'I was afraid I'd dreamed it. I love you.'

The doctor knocked softly on the door and poked her head inside. 'Harry needs to rest now.' Beth nodded before turning back to the patient on the bed. 'You'll have to come home with me so I can look after you,' she said, 'and make sure you don't get yourself into any more trouble.'

He frowned. 'Are you sure about this, Beth?'

She smiled down at him as she gently pressed her lips to his mouth. 'I've never been more certain of anything in my life.'

61

Hannah

Hannah called in to Beth's house after work to drop off some eggs from Nan a couple of weeks later. 'How's the patient?' she asked.

'Doing well,' said Beth with a smile. 'The cast should come off in about four weeks. And thanks so much for these. I reckon our food bill has just about tripled.'

'A man with a big appetite, eh?'

'You could say that,' she said, looking at her feet and coyly tucking the ends of her hair behind her ears, and Hannah saw the blush creep up over her sister's cheeks. Good, at least one of them was getting some sex. It had been twenty sex-free days and nights so far for her, but who was counting? Her phone buzzed and she checked it before shoving it back in her pocket. The man couldn't take no for an answer.

'You look good,' Hannah said, concentrating on her sister. 'Happy.'

'Yeah. I am. It took nearly losing Harry to realise I was allowed to be. Stupid hey, I could have lost a second chance and ended up even more miserable.'

Hannah pulled her into a hug. 'You carried that burden for too long. It's about time you had some fun. Sorry I gave you such a rough time in hospital over it.'

'Not at all,' she said. 'Thank you for badgering me the way you did. Somebody had to knock some sense into me. Who better than my older sister.'

Hannah smiled. 'Only by ten minutes.'

Beth frowned as they separated. 'I hope you don't mind me asking, but is everything all right?'

She stiffened. 'Why?'

'I don't know, but you just look a bit tired lately and you seem a bit withdrawn. We hardly ever get to see you these days.'

'I'm busy,' she said, and it was the God-honest truth, even if the bags under her eyes were the result of a far different reason.

'I know, but you'd tell us if there was something wrong?'

She gave her sister another hug. 'Of course I would,' she said brightly before waving goodbye. 'See you!'

It didn't make her feel good to lie to her sister, but there was no point trawling over the coals of her failed relationship, now. Declan was history.

Which is why, when she got to work the next morning, it thrilled her no end to see he was down as the last appointment for the day.

Crap.

She spent the day in a state of dread, never more aware of the clock and its changing hands, and the growing ball of anxiety rolling around in her gut. If the joey had a problem, it had to be treated. She just didn't want to see him.

Finally it was time. She ushered the penultimate client out the door with her two yapping chihuahuas and barely had a chance to steel herself against seeing Declan again before he was there, filling her space with his wild Atlantic eyes and his wide dimpled mouth.

'Hello, Hannah,' he said, and the sound of his voice stroked down her spine.

She stiffened it and tried not to look anywhere near his sorrowful eyes. 'Declan,' she said, matter-of-factly. 'What's wrong with Ella?' She could see by the size of the pouch he had slung over his shoulder that the joey had grown in the weeks since she'd last seen it.

He gently coaxed the joey to put out her head and Hannah almost melted to see her sweet face again. 'She's pining.'

Hannah took the joey's small head in her hands and looked into her big dark eyes, wishing away the beguiling scent of a man she'd tried fruitlessly to forget.

'She's missing you. As am I. Why don't you return my calls?'

She looked up at him, at his whiskery face and his wilder-than-she-remembered hair, and her heart went out to him, but that couldn't change anything.

'Why did you say no, Hannah. Why did you leave?'

She sighed, as she finished a rudimentary examination of the joey. 'Ella is fine. I think you're worrying about nothing.'

'Hannah, I love you.'

'It was a mistake,' she said with a lightness she didn't feel, stroking the soft fur of the joey and knowing it might be the last time she did. 'I'm not the woman for you.'

'Why not?' he demanded, his frustration clear in his rising tone.

And she knew that if she didn't tell him, he'd be back. 'I'm sorry, Declan. Maybe I should have laid my cards on the table from day one, but then you kind of crept up on me. And then the longer it went, the more I thought, at least I hoped that I might never have to tell you.' She dragged in a breath, concentrating on the joey so she didn't have to look at the man whose gaze she could feel searching her face.

'You see, I can't have children. I'm sorry I didn't tell you before, but I couldn't. I was afraid to tell you the truth because I feared this might happen.'

'But why?' he said. 'There must be a way. You're young, and there're all kinds of amazing things they can do these days. There's IVF—'

'No,' she said, cutting him off. 'Not in my case. There's no way I can ever have children, not of my own.' *Not now.* 'You need to find a woman who can give you children.'

The joey fidgeted and twitched under her hands, as if picking up on the discomfiting vibe in the room. Hannah soothed it with her hands, pressed her lips to its pretty head, saying one final goodbye.

'Hannah—'

'I'm so sorry, Declan. Look after Ella here, won't you?' She let go of the joey and turned to fill in her notes. 'You've done an incredible job with her,' she said, a solitary tear falling on her notes. 'There's no charge for today.'

He didn't budge. 'That day when you told me about your sisters being pregnant, I thought you were a bit sad because you wanted children yourself. I'm sorry, Hannah.'

'Yeah,' she said, when she heard the door softly close behind him. 'Me too.'

It wasn't until she knew Declan had left the surgery that Hannah allowed herself to slump into the corner chair, her heart in tatters. It was done.

She reached for her phone, found the number she wanted and dialled. It answered on the second ring. 'Hi, Beth,' she said, pinching her nose, 'you know how you asked me to tell you if there was something wrong?'

Half an hour later they met at Nick's place to save Sophie from travelling. The three of them sat outside under the pergola, the glory vine leaves turned gold and red, the occasional leaf fluttering down on the soft breeze. Sophie had made tea and a batch of Anzac cookies, and Beth had brought a bottle of Clare Valley Riesling in case Hannah needed something stronger.

Hannah told them about Declan and the orphaned joey, and how one thing had led to another, culminating in him asking her to marry him.

Beth turned to Sophie and said, 'Did you know about any of this?'

Sophie began to shake her head, before her eyes widened. 'Oh, I knew something was up, though. You seemed happy. That was because of him?'

Hannah nodded glumly. There was no feeling happy, now. She'd been living in a bubble, a perfect, blissful orb filled with happiness and love. But that was the trouble with bubbles, they were fragile. Easily popped, only to disappear into nothing, like they'd never been there.

'So why did you say no? He sounds wonderful, and if he made you feel happy like that?'

'He's older,' she said, feeling numb, operating on autopilot. 'Forty-three this year, and his first marriage ended before they had any children. He wants to have a child.'

'So?'

She looked bleakly at her sisters. 'When I was at uni in Perth, there was this boy—James. We hung out together, a lot. He said he loved me. I thought I loved him.' She shrugged. 'Well, you both know how the old story goes. I ended up pregnant.'

Both of her sisters gasped. 'You never told us that!'

She shook her head. 'I never told anyone. Dad had died the year before and it was just after Joe had been killed. We'd all had enough grief, I couldn't do that to everyone.'

'And so you ...'

Hannah sucked in air. 'So I had an abortion. I'm not particularly proud of the fact, but I could see no other way. Not without abandoning my studies and coming home. And James said he wanted to marry me, but the time wasn't right. He agreed with me, said it was for the best, and I believed him. But don't think I'm blaming him. It was my choice. I was a mess. I wouldn't have coped.

'And for a while afterwards it was fine, until I started having pain and cramps and I thought I must be dying. Instead, I was diagnosed with pelvic inflammatory disease. They told me the scarring to my uterus was so bad, I'd never have another baby.' She dropped her head. 'I'm infertile.'

'Oh, Han,' said Beth, putting her arm around her shoulders. 'I'm so sorry. You shouldn't have had to go through all that on your own.'

'How could I tell you when you'd just lost Joe? You had more than enough on your plate. Everyone here did.'

'Does it have to mean the end with Declan, though?' asked Sophie. 'Surely he'll understand.'

'He wants a child,' said Hannah. 'I can't give him one. It's pointless.'

'Why couldn't you adopt?'

Hannah sniffed. 'I looked it up. It's next to useless even applying. The process can take years and there are no guarantees.'

'Maybe he'll wait—'

Hannah slowly shook her head. 'You should have seen his face when I told him. He said nothing. He just walked away. And the sad thing was, I knew he would.'

'How could you know that?' said Beth.

Hannah gave a bitter laugh. 'Because after I got sick and I discovered I could never have children, James dumped me for a mutual friend. Last I heard, they're happily married and living in the Perth wheat-belt with three kids and another on the way.' Her face crumpled, her shoulders caved in. 'I knew Declan would leave me, too.'

'He's an idiot, that's what he is,' said Beth, gathering Hannah into her arms to rock her from side to side while she sobbed.

'What a family,' Beth said a few minutes later, as Sophie brought out a fresh pot of tea, 'with our secrets and our guilt.' She looked over to their youngest sister as she poured them all a fresh cup. 'Please tell us you don't have any other secrets, Sophie?'

Sophie glanced towards the house and almost looked like she was about to say something, when she shook her head. 'Sorry, guys, I'm all out of secrets right now.'

62

Nick

The valley was changing. The heat of summer had given way to the glorious colours of autumn. Now, it was leaves that twirled and spun on the breeze, rather than dust, and rains had soaked into the sun-parched earth and made everything look and smell fresh and clean.

It was Nick's favourite time of year. It was also the most labour intensive. But the Golden Delicious and the Galas were in, and soon it would be the turn of the Pink Ladies. It was a good season.

Min came running down from the house, calling him. 'We made pasghetti again and dinner's nearly ready.'

'Yeah?' he said, pulling the hat from his head and wiping his brow. 'I better come wash up.'

'And I made the dough again. Sophie said I was a natural.'

'That good, eh?' He smiled at his daughter, letting her small hand slip into his as they walked up the slope to the house. 'I get the impression you like having Sophie around.'

Min skipped alongside him. 'I do. Penelope's still saying mean things about her. She says she'll soon come to her senses.' She looked up at her father. 'What does she mean?'

'I guess she means Sophie will leave, like Penelope did.'

'But you don't want Sophie to go, do you? You want Sophie to stay?'

Nick didn't know what to say to that. 'I guess, in the end it's up to Sophie. But yeah, it's really nice having her around.'

They got inside and he hung his hat, before heading to the bathroom to wash the dust off his arms and face. When he fronted up to the kitchen, Sophie looked up from the stove and smiled; she was wearing that frilly pinny again, her hair tied up in a ponytail with the loose ends swinging free around her face like a halo, and he thought, yeah, it was a very good season, indeed.

Sophie was in that blissful place where nothing on earth could touch her. She had her head on Nick's shoulder, one of her legs curved over his, and her belly nestled up against his side, and that was as far as her world needed to go. She had everything she needed right here. She felt safe with his arms wrapped around her. Warm. Even loved.

She felt something sizzle down her spine, something that started in shock and ended in a warm bloom of recognition, and she knew she couldn't be wrong. This deliciousness of being was how love must feel, where nothing mattered outside of being here, in this moment.

So, the phone call was an unwelcome reminder that the rest of the world did exist.

'I'll get it,' Nick said, gently untangling himself from her limbs. She murmured something vague in protest but let him go, missing him already, wanting him back as she resettled herself into the mattress, hoping whoever it was wasn't going to keep him long.

He wasn't kept long at all, but he didn't slide back under the covers like she was hoping. Instead, he threw her robe on the bed. 'That was Dan,' he said, already pulling clothes out of drawers. 'Your nan's gone missing. I told him we'd join the search.'

⁎

The family gathered at Pop's a few minutes later, all except Beth, who was working, everyone keeping an eye out on the way but with no luck. 'I've checked outside and the chook house, and she's gone all right,' Dan said. 'We've called the police.'

'How did she get out?'

Pop sat at the table, looking downcast. 'I went out to get the paper. Normally, I go out the back and use the gate, but I thought she was asleep so I went the front way. Left the front door unbolted, didn't I, so I could get back in. I was only going to be out for a minute.' He dropped his head into his hands. 'Bloody old fool, I didn't think.'

Hannah patted Pop's back. 'Don't blame yourself. We'll find her.'

Sophie chewed her lip, wondering. 'She was complaining to Lucy and me about being locked up. You don't think she was waiting for a chance to escape, do you?'

'Is that possible?' Nick asked. 'In her condition?'

'Would you like being locked up, if most of the time you were perfectly rational? And she was rational that day, wasn't she, Lucy?'

'She was good,' Lucy agreed, her hand rubbing the small of her back, which was no surprise when she was due in a couple of weeks. 'Sharp as a tack.'

'Cunning bloody tack,' grumbled Pop.

Nick nodded. 'Right. She can't have gone too far.'

'Don't think that,' Sophie said, 'because I said the same when we lost her at the beach, so she must have taken off like a rocket to get as far as she had.'

Dan looked at his watch and Sophie knew what he was thinking, that Nan had been gone an hour or more. 'Tell me we're not waiting for the police to arrive to start searching,' she said.

'No way. Let's go.'

Hannah stayed with Pop to wait for the police, while Nick and Sophie, and Dan and Lucy set off in opposite directions to check the surrounding streets. And even though they were searching from a vehicle, it was harder than it had been looking for her at the beach. There were gardens and backyards and hidden places they just couldn't see into. 'It's worse than looking for a needle in a haystack,' Sophie despaired.

'Hey,' Nick said, squeezing her hand. 'We'll find her.'

And it struck her, with the strength of his warm hand leaching into hers, that he didn't have to do this. He could have let Dan pick her up on the way and stayed right out of it, but he hadn't. He'd known what her nan going missing had meant to her and he'd taken her himself. Because he cared? Because of more than that?

Oh boy.

'Thank you for coming to help look.'

Though his lips were tight, his eyes were filled with warmth and understanding, and they warmed her bone deep until she felt like she was back in that bed and there was only the two of them, before she turned her head to search out her window again.

It was another twenty minutes of fruitless searching before her phone rang and Dan gave her the news she so wanted. 'We found her. She's okay.'

'What a relief,' Sophie said, flopping back against her seat, as Nick turned the car back towards Summertown. 'She was halfway along

Swamp Road between Uraidla and Piccadilly, can you believe it? What the hell was she doing walking out there?'

There was a police car parked outside her grandparents' house when they got there. Sophie frowned. 'I hope Nan's not in any trouble. It'd kill her if she had to go to a nursing home because of this.'

'Hey,' Nick said, 'thank your lucky stars it's not an ambulance. She must be exhausted.'

But Nan was as bright as a button and busy in the kitchen making tea and a batch of scones for all her unexpected guests, and looking for all the world like they hadn't all been out searching for her half the morning. Hannah rolled her eyes. 'I told her not to bother, but she thinks this is some kind of excuse for a family party.'

Meanwhile, Pop was out the back being spoken to by two very stern-looking police.

'What's with that?' asked Sophie, bewildered as she peeked through the screen door and saw one of the officers taking notes. 'Can they charge Nan with making a nuisance or something?'

'Not Nan,' said Hannah, her eyebrows heading north as her face said you're not going to believe this. 'It's Pop. He's just been busted by the cops.'

Sophie shook her head. 'For losing Nan? Surely they can't do that.'

'Nope,' said Hannah, blowing on the cup of tea her nan had just handed to her. 'Of course they can't, but it seems our dear old pop's been caught red-handed growing weed.'

'What?'

But Hannah had swung into action helping their nan. The first batch of scones appeared plump and tall, their tops perfectly golden from the oven, and Nan began fussing over the supply of jam and cream. The police officers brought Pop inside to talk to the family, gently convincing Nan that no, they didn't need a plate and she should sit down with them at the table. 'Am I under arrest?' she asked, looking altogether too thrilled at the prospect for Sophie's liking.

'It must have grown by accident,' Dan said, after the police explained about the plant they'd found growing behind the shed while they were double-checking the premises for any sign of Nan, and how they'd imposed an on-the-spot fine for cultivation of cannabis. 'Pop would never do such a thing.'

The younger officer coughed. 'We found a watering system, and Clarence has admitted at length to planting it. He assured us it was for personal use, otherwise it's a much more serious offence.'

Dan, Sophie and Hannah exchanged glances, while Pop sat disconsolately sipping on his tea. Hannah spoke up first. 'Surely you can use a bit of discretion here, Officer? It's only one plant, after all and Pop—Clarry—well, he's in his eighties and Nan has medical issues. They both have medical issues, for that matter. Can't you just remove the plant and forget about it?' She sent a glare in the direction of their grandfather. 'We'll make sure it doesn't happen again, you can be sure of that.'

'I could issue a caution and leave it at that,' said the older officer, 'and we often do in these cases where we have a little discretion, but your grandfather was being uncooperative and so we've decided to issue him with a fine.'

'Uncooperative?' Hannah said, staring at her grandfather, who was looking more sheepish by the minute. 'What did he do?'

'He accused the neighbours behind of "sneaking it in when he wasn't looking".'

Sophie looked at her grandfather, aghast. 'Pop! That's the church!'

'Exactly. So we're charging him. What happens now is the plant will be removed and a sample taken in case the matter is disputed and needs to be sent for forensic testing. This sample will be deposited

into police property, where it will be kept until twenty-eight days
after the fine is paid or until such time as the matter is settled in
court. The rest of the plant will be destroyed.' He shrugged and
gave the briefest nod in Nan's direction. 'I'm sorry, I understand
what you're going through, but if Clarence pays the fine within
twenty-eight days, the matter won't have to proceed to court and
there'll be no conviction recorded. I have to tell you, it would be a
much more serious matter again if there was more than one plant
or we thought the plant was being cultivated for sale; the penalties
are much higher. But, as Clarence has assured us it was intended
for personal use, and we've found no evidence of bags or scales, it's
classified as a simple cannabis offence under the legislation. If he
pays the fine, that's the end of the matter.'

'He'll pay the fine,' said Sophie, watching her grandfather sitting
innocently at the table while he chomped into a scone laden with
jam and cream.

'We'll make sure he does,' agreed Hannah.

'He always was a silly old fool,' Nan said with a sniff, clearly not
impressed that her impromptu party had taken such a serious turn
and that Pop was getting all the attention. 'Now, perhaps I could
offer you nice officers some fresh eggs?'

The police car departed, the distinctive plant bagged up and taken
away, leaving the family shell-shocked in their wake.

'Well, that's that, then,' said Pop, slapping his hands on his legs.
'I'm off to the shed.'

'No, you're damned well not,' said Hannah, using an imperious
tone in her voice Sophie had only ever heard her use against Beth
and her. 'You sit right down and answer a few damned questions.'

Pop clutched his shirt over his heart. 'Don't upset me, I've got a dicky ticker. You know I have to worry about my blood pressure.'

'How about our blood pressure?' Hannah bit back. 'How do you think we all feel? What were you thinking planting marijuana in your backyard?'

'The copper said it was for personal use, didn't he? That's what it was for.'

'Since when have you used marijuana?' demanded Dan.

'He doesn't, does he?' said Nan with a sniff. 'He's talking codswallop.'

Pop snorted. 'Thank you very much, my dearly beloved, for sticking up for me.' He turned to his family. 'You all think it's so easy living on the pension, you try it.'

'What?' Dan said.

'You've never mentioned money problems,' said Sophie.

'We manage fine,' protested Nan.

'Well, all right, it's just there was this bloke in a pub—'

'You are kidding me,' said Hannah.

'A bloke in a pub?' squeaked Sophie.

Dan just groaned and put his hand to his head.

'—and I was thinking it might be a good little earner, that's what. He said it was failsafe and it was only one plant and the police won't charge you for one plant, and so I thought I'd give it a shot. So, he gave me this seedling and it looked harmless enough, and I stuck it behind the shed so it wouldn't bother anyone, and it didn't bother anyone, until Joanie decided to get herself lost and you lot called out the national guard.'

'I wasn't lost,' protested Nan.

'It was a beauty, too,' said Pop, ignoring her. 'Grew like billyo. It started getting all sticky and I thought it was ready, but I never heard again from the bloke.'

'Probably in jail,' said Sophie, and Hannah nodded.

'Where Pop could have been if the police had got wind of all this,' said Dan. 'Though come to think of it, that's not such a bad idea. Maybe we should lock you both up.'

'Calm down,' said Pop, 'you're all making a mountain out of a molehill.'

Sophie heard a noise like a gasp and turned to see Lucy pushing herself to her feet. 'Speaking of mountains,' said Lucy, a puddle pooling on the floor below her. 'You might want to start timing contractions, Dan, because I think this one's about to blow.'

And Sophie saw Dan's face turn white.

63

Sophie

It was a boy. A beautiful bouncing baby boy that weighed in at three-point-eight kilos, or eight pounds four ounces on the old scale.

'He looks like his father,' said Nan, cuddling the infant child in a chair, when the family came to visit at the birthing suite.

'How can you bloody tell?' said Pop, 'it just looks like a baby to me.'

'Have you decided on a name yet?' Sophie asked, thoroughly captivated by the baby, more impatient than ever to hold her two in her arms. Two months seemed an eternity, right now.

Lucy was sitting up in the hospital bed, glowing. She looked at Dan, who was holding her hand. 'We have decided. We wanted to call him after both Nan and Pop, but we couldn't work out how, so we're going to call him J.C.'

Dan added, 'He'll probably get called Jace, for short.'

Pop puffed up his chest. 'You know, the boy does look like his dad, doesn't he? A chip off the old block, all right.'

Nan rolled her eyes at her husband before smiling at the pair on the bed. 'I'm tickled pink you thought of me. Who else would like to give little Jace here a cuddle?'

'Me,' said Sophie, before anyone else had a chance to respond, and the swaddled baby was duly passed to her. There wasn't a lot of room on her lap so Sophie cradled the baby above her bump, breathing deeply of his sweet baby smell and marvelling at the dark eyelashes and perfect lips and the tiny fingers that peeped out of his bunny rug. 'He's gorgeous,' she said with tears in her eyes at this miracle of life, and pressed her lips to his brow, knowing that two months would never pass quickly enough.

⁓

Visiting time finished and they farewelled the new family member and made their way to the car park. Nick waited at his car as Sophie said goodbye to Nan and Pop, giving them a kiss on the cheek before they clambered slowly into Hannah's car. When Hannah closed the door on Nan she said, 'So what's happened to you, then?'

Sophie started. 'Nothing,' she said, trying not to sound too defensive. 'Why?'

Her sister's eyes narrowed. 'Only you look different, lately. Happier.'

'So I'm blooming,' she said, tucking stray hair behind her ears. 'That's what pregnant women do, isn't it? Bloom?'

'I don't know,' said Hannah, her eyes suspiciously on Nick. 'You said you had no secrets, but I'm beginning to wonder.'

It wasn't that it was a secret exactly, Sophie thought as they journeyed home. It was just that it was so new and she didn't know what it meant. And though she felt his passion and desire, Nick had said nothing of his feelings for her. He wasn't looking for a wife, she knew that much, but was she a convenient bed warmer? Would he expect her to stay after the babies arrived?

How did you tell your sister that you were sleeping with the father of your unborn babies, but you had no idea where it might lead? No, better to say nothing and not have to admit to this tangle of feelings that had no end.

She chewed her lip as the car left the flat land and climbed the windy road up the escarpment to Norton Summit, the wind sending a scatter of yellow leaves raining down from the autumn trees.

'You seem deep in thought,' Nick said beside her.

'Just tired,' she lied.

'Too tired?'

He sounded so disappointed she couldn't help but laugh. 'Never too tired for that.'

He picked up her hand and pressed it to his lips. 'I was hoping you might say that.'

❧

Later, when they'd made slow, languorous love and she lay with her head on his shoulder, her babies too active for her to sleep, she wondered if she should tell him how she felt, and if he was waiting for her because she'd already turned him down once before.

Because they couldn't just drift on this way forever. Sooner or later they were going to have to come clean with each other. Sooner or later she'd find out if she'd been building straw castles in the air again.

She squeezed her eyes tightly shut. Please God, not that. She couldn't be so wrong this time, surely? Beside her Nick slumbered, his breath slow in and out, his heartbeat a steady drum beat under her head.

She pressed her lips to his shoulder and tested the words in the soft night air. 'I love you.'

ᘓ

The weather turned unseasonably wintry, the nights so cold Nick put the combustion heater on in the living room to warm the house, and even Sophie, who'd been running hot the whole summer, had to pull out her ugg boots. They were tighter than she remembered, her ankles swollen with her advancing pregnancy and being stuck inside the last couple of days.

But at least the wet days had been a good excuse to prepare her room for the babies. The baby furniture had been delivered and she'd had fun unpacking the sheets and soft bunny rugs, and finding places for everything. Min had been beside herself, looking at the tiny clothes. So tiny, for her twins when they arrived would be much smaller than Jace had been when he was born.

But she'd had enough of being cooped up.

She'd woken this morning to a misty valley, but the mist had burned off and it was the most perfect autumn day, the sun blissfully warm as she sat outside enjoying a cup of tea. She remembered she'd been meaning to take a bottle of pears over to Amy Jennings across the road. With the weather better, it was the perfect time.

Ten minutes later Amy hobbled to answer the door. 'Oh, bless you,' she said, letting her in. 'What a lovely surprise.'

'What have you done?' Sophie asked, looking at the moon boot adorning one of Amy's feet.

'Such a silly thing to do. I slipped on some wet leaves in the garden and twisted my ankle. The worst of it is I can't take poor Boo out for her walk. She's missing it so.'

'My ankles could do with a walk, if you'd like me to take her. I've been getting cabin fever myself the last couple of days, and it's such a gorgeous day.'

'Would you? Oh, that would be wonderful. I'll just get her coat.'

It wasn't that cold a day that a dog would need a Driza-Bone, Sophie thought, but Boo was old and maybe she felt the cold in her aged joints, so a few minutes later, she set off with Boo in her smart coat on her pink diamante leash. Boo might be old and almost blind with cataracts, but she was still the cutest little white Maltese cross, her fluffy tail waving like a happy flag as she trotted along. She sure did love her walks.

So did Sophie. There was so much happening in the valley, the red apples on the trees in the orchards hanging like Christmas decorations, the russet-coloured pears ripening elsewhere, and old gardens filled with deciduous trees putting on a colourful show.

And it occurred to Sophie that she didn't miss her unit down in the suburbs at all, because there was something always going on up here with the change of seasons. She'd taken it for granted as a child growing up, but now that she'd lived elsewhere, it was like she was discovering how beautiful it was all over again.

She rounded a bend and saw a woman coming the other way walking two fierce-looking German shepherds, which began straining at their leashes from the moment they saw Boo. Sophie pulled Boo closer and uttered a nervous hello to the woman, but the woman didn't notice, all her attention focused on keeping her snarling dogs under control.

Good thing, too, Sophie thought, as the dogs kept growling long after they'd passed. She would never have walked this way if she'd known. The only positive was that Boo was too blind to have noticed, her white flag of a tail still wagging jauntily.

A flock of sulphur-crested cockatoos flew overhead, screeching in the mild air before descending into a pine tree, splashes of white and yellow amongst the green. God, it was gorgeous. Overnight rain had washed away any dust and turned the tiny creek to running, and she breathed in the clean fresh air and thought, there were worse places to bring up children. They'd grow up here with koalas and parrots as their neighbours, and knowing that apples and pears came from trees and not supermarket bins. They'd go to the local primary school where she'd gone with her sisters and where Dan had preceded them and Pop had gone decades before, a school where there was never more than one hundred kids and you knew every teacher and every kid in the school from Reception to Year Seven. A school where it was impossible to get lost in the cracks.

A kid could do a hell of a lot worse. A couple of kids, for that matter.

If she was still here.

Because Nick had yet to say anything and she had no idea how this would all pan out. All she knew was that she didn't want to leave.

She turned for home, thinking she'd walked far enough. The block was something like three kilometres around and so too far for her to walk all the way these days. She smiled, enjoying the mild autumn sun on her face, thinking she and Boo made the perfect couple, right now. But when she rounded the bend, there was the woman with the dogs again, stopped to talk to someone passing in a car, the dogs by her side.

Crap, she thought, thinking she'd have to turn around and wait it out until the dogs were gone. She had no wish to go anywhere near them. Except the dogs had already spotted Boo and her jaunty tail, and together they lunged for her, catching the owner unawares and yanking free of her hold.

Sophie's heart was in her mouth as the dogs came at Boo, their fangs bared, snarling, evil in their eyes, and there was no time for flight. There was nowhere to go even if there was. All she could do was pick up the unsuspecting Boo and hope the owner could get to the dogs and pull them off.

Sophie stooped down, but she was way too slow and Boo's little legs scrabbled the air awkwardly as the first dog sprang, cannoning into them and knocking the tiny dog from her hands. Boo screamed in pain and terror as it hit the ground, somehow managing to stay upright, darting this way and that on its short legs around Sophie's, frantically trying to get away while the big dogs snapped and growled either side of it. One of them grabbed her neck in its large jaws and Boo squealed in terror while Sophie screamed at them to let her go, trying to kick the dogs away. But she was caught in the leads and she and the dogs and Boo circled and spun on the road. The dogs wouldn't stop, they wouldn't let go, and Sophie knew they wouldn't stop until they killed poor Boo and there was nothing she could do, lost as she was in a spinning wheel of vicious, screeching dogs.

When suddenly, the ground was tugged out from under her feet and she fell to the road.

Hard.

Sophie opened her eyes in the sterile hospital room and instinctively she put her hands to her belly, reliving the panic she'd felt in the ambulance as the paramedics had checked the babies' vitals. But she and her bump were still intact, though she had an annoying belt around her tummy that was attached to some kind of monitor that kept beeping, along with a pain in her hip every time she tried to move.

'I hesitate to say this,' Beth said, 'but between work and this family I'm really getting over visiting this place.'

'I don't blame you,' Sophie said, pinching the bridge of her nose with her fingers. And then suddenly she remembered. 'How's Boo?'

'Lucky to be alive, according to Han. That Driza-Bone coat she had on protected her or it would have been a whole lot worse. She still got a couple of deep puncture wounds to her neck and legs. She's had shots and a stitch or two and she's pretty shaken up, like you'd expect, but she's getting lots of treats. Han thinks she'll come good.'

'Oh, poor Boo, it's a wonder she didn't have a heart attack. And poor Mrs Jennings. She didn't need a shock like that.'

'Poor you,' Beth said, sitting down on the bed next to her as a cleaning trolley clattered down the hallway. 'What a terrifying experience. You're lucky you weren't bitten yourself—or worse.'

Sophie shivered as she thought back. 'They wanted Boo.' She remembered finding herself on the ground, and someone calling for an ambulance—a man who'd managed to pull the dogs off. She remembered a panicked Boo whimpering, curled up and shaking next to her. She remembered the shock that had seen her throwing up on the ground where she lay and not giving a damn who saw her. 'It's lucky there was someone there to drag the dogs away.'

'Oh, that must have been the guy who spoke to the ambos. Thank God he was there.'

Sophie shivered. Yeah, thank God. 'Who was the owner of the German shepherds, did anyone find out?' Sophie said. 'I've never seen her or those dogs around before.'

'She's some woman from the city who likes to walk her dogs where it's quiet, apparently.' Beth rolled her eyes. 'And I can't imagine why she'd need to do that. Oh, and she complained about you screaming, by the way. Said you excited the dogs and caused a frenzy.'

Sophie put a hand to her face and almost cried in disbelief. 'I caused a frenzy? Those dogs were out to kill. Boo was screaming too—it was awful, Beth, just awful, she didn't have a chance. And I thought,' she cradled her bump, 'I thought, imagine what they could do to a child.'

Beth shuddered. 'Ugh, don't think about that. Stupid owner. Make sure you report her to the council. Aggressive dogs like that shouldn't be out without being muzzled.' She looked up as the door swung open. 'Oh hi, Nick. I might go grab myself a coffee while you guys catch up.' She gave Sophie a quick kiss on the cheek. 'Back soon!'

Nick didn't kiss her. He didn't hug her. He didn't make a move to come anywhere near her. Sophie noticed that as he stood at the foot of her bed, looking like a storm cloud that had rolled overhead, big, dark and threatening, and just waiting to drop, and totally at odds with the chirpy little beep of the machine alongside her.

'I heard you were awake,' he said, his voice sounding like it was coming from far away, like there was an ocean separating them rather than just a few short feet.

'I am,' she said, and tried to smile, but he looked so damned disapproving, and so very, very distant, and she realised it was control he was exercising that made his voice so flat. So emotionless.

'The doctor says the babies are all right.'

'I know,' she said, and found a smile. Surely he'd have to be happy about that. 'A huge relief. Apparently, they're tough little critters. Lucky, eh?'

'Lucky?' He flung an arm around at the room. 'You call all this lucky?' And whatever control he'd overlaid on his voice fractured.

She swallowed. 'Okay, maybe lucky was the wrong choice of word, but I meant fortunate or it's a relief. But I'm trying to hold a reasonable conversation here. I don't think you want conversation, though. I think you want some kind of argument.'

'I'm not looking for an argument. Right now, I'll settle for an explanation. Because I just can't help wondering what the hell you thought you were doing.'

She screwed up her nose. 'Well, I thought I was helping out Amy Jennings by walking her dog when she'd hurt her ankle.'

'And why would you do that, when you know you're supposed to be resting? What the hell were you thinking?'

'Okay, I was thinking that after a couple of days of being locked inside with the weather, that I'd get a little bit of fresh air and gentle exercise. I am allowed that. Walking is on the permitted list.'

'And being attacked by two savage German shepherds? That's gentle exercise? That's on the permitted list, too?'

'I didn't ask to be attacked. I was trying to avoid them!'

'Well, you didn't do a very good job of it, did you?'

Tears pricked the corners of her eyes. 'Why are you attacking me?'

'Christ almighty, Sophie,' he said, clawing one hand through his hair. 'Don't you see? You're the one who's supposed to be taking care of those two,' he said, pointing at her bump. 'And you could have gone into labour then and there. You could have haemorrhaged. You put our babies' lives at risk.'

'The babies are fine, the doctor sa—'

'No thanks to you,' he said, cutting her off. He shook his head, hands on hips, as he huffed out a long breath. 'Do you have any idea what it's like getting a phone call like that, saying you'd been attacked and were being carted off to emergency? I really thought that stunt you pulled climbing a ladder couldn't be topped, but this one, this one really takes the cake.'

The sheer injustice of his words slammed into her. Okay, so she'd decided to take the dog for a walk, but she hadn't invited the attack. She'd done her best to avoid it, and sure, it turned out she hadn't. But what was the point of arguing her case, when he was worried about the babies she was carrying. The babies and only the babies. It was obvious he didn't care about her. This was cold, hard truth and it hit her exactly the same way the hard road had.

And didn't that make it crystal clear what she had to do next?

She pressed her red call bell. 'Thanks for coming, Nick,' she said, 'it's lovely of you to drop by and see how I was going.'

A nurse bustled into the room. 'Something I can get for you,' she said, checking the monitor before plumping Sophie's pillows behind her.

'Yes, you can see this man out. He's just leaving.'

'Sophie—'

'Just go!'

She smoothed the sheet on her bed after he'd gone. The room was quiet apart from her beeping companion, and she swallowed back a hot-air-balloon-sized bubble of disenchantment and despair. But there was resolve mixed in with it, too, and a hard-edged realism that her way ahead was clear. Because at least now she finally knew where she stood. And in the depths of her disappointment, she found strength from a place she didn't know she had. Strength that Beth had bestowed upon her when she'd told her she'd get through this, strength from her nan, who'd told her things could be different these days. Strength from her amazing sisters, who did amazing things and who didn't need a man—and then she thought about Beth and her unexpected Galahad—well, who mostly didn't need a man.

Things were different these days. She didn't need Nick. She didn't need a man who wanted to control her, or who wanted to keep her close simply because she was carrying his babies.

She deserved to be loved and she'd never stop believing that, but in the absence of love, she was better off alone.

❧

'Are you sure about this?' said Dan, carting a box from his ute that was full of Sophie's belongings plus all the bassinets, prams and baby gear that he'd picked up from Nick's place. 'Before I unload the lot, I mean.'

Sophie was holding the back door open for him so it wouldn't slam, the autumn wind sending golden leaves scuttling along the path. 'Sorry, guys, but where else can I go now that the flat's let out?'

'No, are you sure about leaving Nick's?'

'Never more sure of anything in my life. It was a mistake all along. I should never have moved in.'

Lucy was sitting at the dining table, nursing a growing Jace. 'What happened? I thought it had been working out really well.'

'It was okay, so long as I didn't do anything wrong. And according to Nick, there was a long list of possible transgressions.'

'Maybe he's just worried about you,' said Dan. 'You've got his two babies on board and he wants to take care of you.'

'He wants to control me, more like it. He thinks he's in charge and he doesn't trust me to look after the babies. He practically blamed me for those dogs attacking Boo and being caught up in the middle of it.'

Lucy and Dan exchanged glances. 'No way.'

'Go ahead and ask him if you don't believe me, and then think about whether you'd want to live with him if he did the same to you.'

Dan scratched his head as Lucy lifted Jace to her towel-covered shoulder for a burp. 'It's a shame. We were all kind of hoping …'

Sophie didn't want to hear the answer, but still she couldn't prevent herself from asking. 'Hoping what exactly?'

'That things might work out between you guys and it might even be the start of something permanent.'

Sophie snorted, because she'd been stupid enough to believe that once-upon-a-time happy-ever-after shit, too. 'Sorry to burst that little bubble, but apple trees will be sprouting bananas before that happens.'

64

Hannah

Hannah stepped through the door that separated her flat from the surgery with a sigh of relief. It had been a long day punctuated by the panic of Boo's emergency and the news that Sophie had also been on the receiving end of the attack.

But Beth had messaged and assured her that Sophie and the babies were okay, so that was one thing less to stress about. She threw her bag on the kitchen bench and picked up her mail, and only then did she notice the huge vase of flowers sitting on the dining table. The huge vase of flowers that certainly hadn't been there when she'd stepped out of the flat this morning.

She approached it warily, the sunny yellow and blue of the lilies and irises looking altogether too happy for her mood. Who would be sending her flowers? Unless it was the woman whose dog she'd saved from a bowel blockage with emergency surgery last week?

She found the card, opened the envelope and slid it out, her eyes turning misty when she read the words.

H

I don't care. I want you, and only you (and Seans Eile, but let's not go there).

So marry me already and put me out of the misery of trying to live without you.

I love you.

Dx

And Hannah burst into tears.

65

Nick

Min loved Nick's spaghetti bolognaise.

Usually.

Tonight, she seemed happy to lean her head against her fist while she stabbed at her pasta with her fork.

'Are you missing having fresh pasta?'

'I'm missing Sophie.' She looked up at him with plaintive eyes. 'It's so lonely here, lately.'

'I'm here.'

Min huffed and looked back into her bowl. 'But you're always grumpy.'

'That's not true.' Though maybe he'd been a bit grouchy lately. Who wouldn't be after the week he'd had, having to box up all Sophie's stuff plus the baby gear that she'd be needing once the babies arrived.

The house seemed empty and cheerless without her and all the promise of the babies coming soon. Min had been devastated to come home from Penelope's and find Sophie gone. Even Fat Cat and the grown-up kittens failed to cheer her up.

Min sighed. 'Don't you miss Sophie, Dad?'

God, she might as well stick her fork right into his eyes; he had to blink hard enough as it was. When didn't he miss her would be more to the point. Her scent was on his sheets and his pillow, and he wasn't planning on washing the linen anytime soon. 'Yes, I miss Sophie, too. Now eat your spaghetti.'

Min stabbed some more at her pasta, eating nothing. 'Why did she have to go?'

'I don't know,' he lied. 'She wanted to be independent, I guess. The babies will be here soon. She didn't need looking after.' Not that he'd looked after her, exactly.

'So, why didn't she stay when we had everything ready here?' Min asked. 'Is she mad at me? Did I do something wrong?'

'No. Don't think that. Of course she's not mad at you.' He stabbed at his own pasta a few times for good measure. But he knew that merely telling Min not to think it was her fault wouldn't be enough. There was only one way she'd believe it hadn't been because of her and that was him coming clean. 'If she's mad at anyone, it's me.'

Min slammed down her fork and bits of tomato sauce splattered in all directions. 'What did you do this time?' She glared accusingly at him, a pint-sized warrior princess taking him to task. 'Were you mean to Sophie again?'

Nick thought about denying it, but realised he'd be lying, and what he'd really been grumpy about was how stupid he'd been. How he'd been so terrified when he'd heard Sophie had been attacked that he'd charged into that hospital and gone apeshit, when he should have been so grateful she was all right. He should have taken her in his arms and comforted her. He should have told her how mad he was at himself because he hadn't been able to protect her.

'I messed up,' he admitted, pushing away his unfinished plate because he wasn't hungry anymore. 'Big time.'

'Penelope said she'd leave,' Min said, before she burst into tears. 'But I didn't want her to. Please tell her you're sorry and get her back,' she cried. 'Please, Daddy, get her back.'

And Nick had tears in his own eyes and gravel filling his throat, and not the faintest idea how he might possibly achieve that, but he knew Min was right. 'I'll try.'

Dan answered the door. He had bags under his eyes and the baby was crying in the background. Nick could hear Lucy trying to soothe it, and he was reminded of Min as a baby and the witching hour. 'Is this a bad time?'

'We've had better. Baby's got colic. Fun times.'

'Oh. Anything I can do to help?'

Dan rubbed his brow. 'Let's cut to the chase here, Nick, because you definitely didn't come around to offer baby advice. So what do you want?'

He swallowed. 'I came hoping to talk to Sophie.'

'Look, Nick,' Dan said, leaning up against the door, 'don't think I don't empathise, because I do. I know how hard it is to get a woman to listen to you when you've majorly fucked up. But would it surprise you to learn that Sophie doesn't want to see you? She was pretty clear on that point when she saw your car roll up and took off into her bedroom.'

Nick let the accusation of majorly screwing up roll on by, not that he didn't think it was wrong, he just didn't need everyone else knowing what an arse he'd been. Though it sounded a bit late for that. Great. 'But I need to talk to her. It's important.'

Dan sighed, and rapped his knuckles on the doorframe. 'All right. I'll give it a shot. Stay here.'

It was the white-knuckle ride of his life, waiting there outside that door while Dan disappeared to talk to Sophie and the rest of Nick's future hung in the balance. It took an entire lifetime, or maybe it really was just the three minutes his watch told him it was, before Sophie appeared. He could do nothing to stop his heart giving a little leap when he saw her, only to be followed by a massive slide when he realised what he'd lost. Maybe forever. Please God, not forever.

Her body language was plain, her arms crossed high over her belly, her lips pressed tightly together, and there were bags under her eyes, too. He had matching ones, but he knew he was kidding himself and he had no right to even hope that she might have missed him half as much as he'd missed her. But even with the bags and the scowl she was wearing, she was still the most beautiful thing he'd ever seen, and the sheer dimensions of his stupidity rammed home.

'Hi,' he said, shifting uncomfortably from foot to foot, and he realised he hadn't been this nervous around a female since he'd asked Millie Anderson to dance with him at the Year Seven school social, but that memory was hardly a good omen. She'd told him to piss off and it had been a whole five years before he'd been game enough to approach a girl again.

'Dan said I probably should listen to what you have to say,' she said. Not coming outside, staying inside, leaving a screen door closed between them, though that was nothing compared to the walls he saw in her eyes. 'Even though I didn't want to. So this better be good.'

Bloody hell. No pressure there. He took a deep breath and began. 'Once upon a time, Min told me I needed to apologise to you. As so often is the case, she was right. And now I find myself needing to apologise to you again, only this time I screwed up so badly, I don't think words alone are going to cut it. But I need to tell you how bad I feel about the way I acted in hospital, Sophie.'

She blinked, her face emotionless, a blank mask. 'You should feel bad.'

He nodded. He deserved that. He deserved all she might dish out and more for the way he'd treated her. 'If it's any consolation, I feel like crap. I was wrong, and way out of line, and there are no excuses, but I need to talk to you, to explain. Only,' he looked around, 'not here. I came to ask if you'd let me show you something, to show you how sorry I am.'

'Show me what?'

'Not here. Somewhere it might mean something.' Somewhere there was a chance she might even believe it.

He could see the conflict in her eyes. See her wrestle with the possibilities, and he was even grateful for that, when she could so easily slam the door in his face and he wouldn't have a leg to stand on. 'Why should I?'

'Give me this,' he pleaded. 'At least give me this opportunity to show you how sorry I am. To try to explain.'

With troubled eyes and her teeth chewing her bottom lip, she agreed, and Nick felt a flicker of hope.

It was something.

66

Sophie

They drove in silence along the winding hills roads, the evening sun slanting red through the trees and the clouds. A light shower of rain sprayed down on the car, a scatter of leaves sticking to the windscreen until the wipers swished them away.

Soon the leaves would all be gone and the trees would stand bare-boned to the sky, and the air would crisp and her babies would be born. Their babies. She glanced over at him, taking in his grim expression, his shadowed jaw and his big hands on the steering wheel, before she looked away. What was he playing at?

She'd expected Nick would turn up at some stage, of course. He'd be sure to realise he'd overplayed his hand and want to negotiate access to their babies, once they arrived; to stake an ambit claim now to ensure he didn't miss out once they put in an appearance. And that might be a reasonable thing for a father to ask, but after his hospital visit and her departure, she'd expected him not to be reasonable about any of it. She'd expected him to be making demands and claiming his due as the father. Expected him to come out all guns blazing and tell her how it was going to be. Expected all of that and she'd been ready to argue back and tell him he could shove his demands.

What she hadn't expected was to see him looking so utterly devoid of fight. So defeated. So shattered.

And she knew she shouldn't care and she shouldn't give a damn, but her heart had gone out to him for just one moment, and it was one moment long enough to acquiesce with his request. Because it had been a request and not a demand and he'd looked so damned pathetic, and like it or not, he was still the father of these babies and she still cared, just a bit …

But when he turned up the road heading towards Mount Lofty House, she was suspicious and broke her silence. 'Where are we going?'

'Soon,' he said. 'You'll see soon enough.'

And soon enough she did, because he pulled up in the sunset-lit car park of the swish hotel, and everything but nothing made sense. 'Why have you brought me here?'

He killed the engine and turned to her and said, 'Because this is where it started, seven months ago. And if it's going to end, this is where it's going to end.'

'I thought it already had. You saw to that.'

'No,' he said, 'I can't believe that. Not until you hear what I have to say. Then you can decide whether it's over or not.'

She shook her head. 'This is crazy. I don't know what you've got in mind, but I don't want any part of it.'

He looked out the windscreen. 'Look. The sun's setting.' He turned to her. 'Walk with me?'

She looked at the sky then back at Nick, and she decided that being outside was infinitely preferable to being inside a car that was filled with the scent of him and she reached for her doorhandle.

It was annoying that he was there to open it for her and offer her his arm, and more annoying that it did make it easier, but once she was upright, she let him go and wandered to the lawns, where she could see the picturesque Piccadilly Valley stretched out below. It was higher here on Mount Lofty, the air a shade cooler, edgier, and she shrugged her jacket closer around her as she looked out over the patchwork fields and hills and trees all painted in the sunset's rays. And it was so damned beautiful it almost hurt.

'So,' she said, turning to him with a sigh, refusing to be swayed by the changing colours and the shifting scenery. 'What's so important that you had to bring me all the way up here to tell me?'

'Something that's taken me far too long to admit.' And he too turned from the view and looked down at her. 'I love you, Sophie.'

She snorted as a fuse shorted in her brain. 'What? You love me? Don't you dare give me that crap. Not after the way you treated me.'

'Sophie, it's true!'

'You don't give a damn about me.' She put a hand over her belly. 'All you care about is this pair in here. All you've ever cared about are these two babies. And now, you spin this line about love because you're afraid you've blown it? Well you have blown it, wide open. Take me home, Nick, I've heard enough.' She started marching to the car.

'Sophie,' he said, but she kept right on going.

'Sophie?'

Still she didn't listen.

'Min's not mine.'

Halfway to the car she stopped as his words registered. 'What did you say?'

'Min's not mine,' he said, drawing alongside. 'I mean, it's my name on her birth certificate and I love her to bits and I'll always be her father, but biologically, she's not mine.'

'But ...'

'Penelope was fooling around. I only found out about it after-wards, after we'd decided to stick together for the sake of the baby. When she was born, I wondered, but it wasn't until we argued one day and she threw it at me that I knew for certain.'

'But you still kept her?'

'By then she was mine, in all but one way. I wasn't giving up the one positive thing that had come out of our marriage.'

Sophie thought back to the conversation about marriage they'd had that day over coffee in the back patio, when he'd said, 'The circumstances are what they are—it's how we choose to deal with them that matters ...'

'I never thought I'd get married again,' he continued. 'I never thought for a moment there'd be another chance to have a child of my own—a biological child of my own. And I love Min with all my heart, and maybe there shouldn't be, but there's a difference in knowing ...' He turned his storm-filled eyes to hers and put his hand over his heart. 'To know they are mine is more special than I ever thought possible. Not more special than Min, but special to me. And I was so focused on them and the fact that they were mine, that I didn't see what was sneaking up on me all the time. I didn't see you. I didn't count on falling in love with you.'

She blinked into the fading light, trying to assimilate it all. Afraid to believe. Afraid not to.

'Please, Sophie, I love you and I'm sorry for being such a stupid bastard and treating you the way I did, and I hope that one day you'll forgive me.'

'You hurt me,' she said, remembering the pain and shock of his unwarranted attack, remembering the bitterness of having her dreams shattered once again, dreams she'd been so guarded against having, but which had grown up regardless.

'I'm sorry. When I got the call, I didn't know what I felt for you, I hadn't put it into words I wanted to admit. And when I found you were okay, relief turned to anger that I could have lost you—all of you—and I couldn't deal with it. I didn't deal with it. I didn't know what I was feeling, so I focused on the babies, because that bit I knew, that bit I understood.'

'I don't know,' she said, confused, stunned by his revelation, wanting to be swayed by his words but afraid in case she was wrong and the rug was once again pulled out from under her feet. 'I want to believe you, but ...'

'It's true,' he said, putting a hand to her neck, his thumb stroking her skin, stroking her senses. She leaned into his touch. God, how she'd missed his touch. 'I love you, Sophie. Can you forgive me? Can you love me back, just a little?'

Her battered heart lurched and kicked back into life as happy tears squeezed unbidden from her eyes. 'I wanted to hate you,' she admitted. 'I wanted to forget. But I couldn't forget. I love you, Nick.'

He made a sound in the back of his throat, half relief, half triumph, before his mouth joined with hers and they kissed long and hard under the fading colour of the sky.

Breathing hard, he drew away. 'I booked our room,' he said, his breathing as ragged as hers, 'just in case.'

'Our room?'

'It will always be our room.'

'You're mad,' she said, while secretly she was delighted. 'Do you know how much those rooms cost?'

'You're worth it,' he said. 'You're worth it a hundred times over.'

And he took her hand and led her back up to the hotel entrance while a rain shower drifted across the valley, and in the dying light from the sunset, emerged a rainbow.

EPILOGUE

Sophie was booked in for a precautionary caesarean at thirty-eight weeks, but her babies had their own timetable and weren't waiting that long. When Sophie got up to pee early one morning and felt something come unstuck, she knew that the babies had taken matters into their own hands.

Rose Marie and Evie Grace were born eight hours later and ten minutes apart, just as Sophie's sisters had been, and Nick was there the whole time to hold her hand and rub her back and welcome their new babies into the world.

And when visiting time came around, Nan fussed and clucked over the pair and said, 'I told you all that women want babies, didn't I? And there you go, I was right.'

'You did indeed, Nan,' said Hannah, smiling at Sophie and Beth to reassure them it was okay, while she firmly held the hand of Declan, who'd been the newest welcome addition to the Faraday family until these two babies had put in an appearance.

Pop looked as proud as punch with the two newborns. 'I told you this was worth hanging around for,' he said to anyone who'd listen. 'That's three great-grandchildren in the space of two months. Reckon that's gotta be close to a record,' to which Nan just rolled her eyes as if he was trying to steal her thunder.

Min was beside herself with joy with her brand-new baby sisters, fascinated by how tiny they were even though they'd each weighed in at just over two-point-seven kilos, or six pounds as Nan liked to tell everyone, bewitched by even tinier fingers and toes, and grinning proudly as she posed for photographs on the bed with a baby tucked under each arm, three dark-haired sisters together.

Dan and Lucy brought Jace in to visit, who looked huge now at two months old compared to the newborns, and was smiling up a storm for anyone who looked his way, and Beth came down with Harry and Siena.

'Twins are so cool,' said Hannah, with what looked like a tear in her eye, and Declan pulled her close and pressed his lips to her hair.

'You would say that,' agreed a smiling Beth, holding Rose in her arms as Siena enjoyed a cuddle of Evie. 'You've done good, sis.'

Then visiting time wound up and the family departed, Min going home for a sleepover night with Siena, leaving just the four of them. 'Tired?' Nick asked as he helped organise pillows to support the babies for a feed.

'I feel amazing,' Sophie said.

'You are amazing,' he told her. 'And you were amazing today. So unbelievably strong.' He leaned over and kissed her brow before he sat back and watched as the babies suckled at her breasts.

'I don't think I've ever seen a sight more beautiful.'

She smiled up at him, her arms full of their babies, her heart so overflowing with love in this moment that the air seemed to shimmer with it.

'Marry me,' he said.

She blinked, not sure what she was hearing. 'Really? I thought you never wanted to get married again.'

'I was wrong. I once told you the worst part of being married was the divorce, but that wasn't the worst thing at all. The worst part was choosing the wrong person to start with.'

'How do you know I'm not the wrong person, too?'

He shrugged. 'Maybe because I'm older and wiser and I've learned from my mistakes. Maybe because you're the amazing woman you are and I happen to be head over heels in love with you. But I know we'll last, because when I look at you, and when I'm with you, forever doesn't seem anywhere near long enough.'

She blinked. 'Wow. That was some speech.'

'So what do you say, Sophie, will you marry me?'

Sophie thought about the events that had brought her to this place, the foolish choices and the mistakes she'd made along the way, the missteps and her futile rebellion when things didn't go her way, and she realised that the old saying on Nan's wall was true, that sometimes the wrong choices could still bring you to the right place.

Like ending up here, with Nick and gorgeous Min, and their two tiny babies, along with the promise of forever.

But there was something else she knew too, because this time there was only one choice she could make—the right choice.

She looked up at Nick and smiled over the bundle of babies on her chest, and over a heart that had somehow quadrupled in size today. 'You better get over here pretty darn fast, because you're going to want to kiss me when I say yes.'

And, just as Sophie predicted, he did.

ACKNOWLEDGEMENTS

The Adelaide Hills is a very special part of the world, so close to the city, and yet an entire world away, a world of gum trees and orchards, of koalas and kangaroos, and hard-working people who are the salt of the earth. It was fabulous writing *The Trouble with Choices* to revisit the area that was our family home for nigh on twenty years.

It was equally satisfying to revisit my fictional hills family and tell the stories of sisters, Sophie, Hannah and Beth Faraday. It made such sense to interweave their stories together, all set against a backdrop of the trials, laughter and unexpected bombshells of family life. I hope you enjoy reading about the Faraday sisters as much as I enjoyed writing them.

It's an amazing feeling seeing a book of yours published and on the shelves in bookstores—a book with your very own name on it! It's probably no exaggeration to say it's one of the most amazing feelings on earth. But getting that book out there on those shelves is only partly down to the author, and I have to pay tribute to the fantastic team and the wonderful colleagues that helped turn a manuscript into the gorgeous book that *The Trouble with Choices* has become.

To my savvy agent, Helen Breitwieser, thank you for your sage advice, for always believing in this book, and for finding the right home for it. I don't think it could be in a better place.

Thanks also have to go to the fabulous team at Harlequin Australia. To Rachael Donovan, who loved *Choices* from the get-go, and who together with Julia Knapman shepherded the book through its journey to publication with such care, skill and enthusiasm, thank you from the bottom of my heart. To Alex Nahlous, who can edit the leg off a chair and yet somehow make it more comfortable to sit on, and the wonderful proofreader, Chrysoula Aiello, thank you muchly too ☺. It is both a privilege and a pleasure working with such awesome professionals who clearly love what they do.

Speaking of people who love what they do, thank you to the wonderful volunteers who care for our native animals in need, whether they be kangaroos, or koalas, possums or birds or wombats. Mum and my late dad were foster parents to something like thirty orphaned and injured kangaroos and wallabies over a period of about twenty years, and our girls grew up thinking it was normal to have kangaroos popping their heads up out of pouches, or hopping around the backyard. Hats off to all the native-animal carers out there, and thank you for all the amazing work you do.

To Abby Green, who kindly gave my orphaned joey an Irish name that made sense, thank you! I had oodles of fun writing a gorgeous Irish man—I admit I fell a bit in love with Declan myself—but readers, please note, any and all Irish bloopers are mine and mine alone.

Huge thanks also to the amazing Kate Cowling, who kindly filled me in on the legalities of how Pop's drug bust might happen here in South Australia with a cantankerous client and dodgy plant. Again, if there are any legal slip-ups, they're mine, and for story purposes.

Then there are the Maytoners to thank, the members of my writing tribe, all far flung but no more than an email away, who keep this writer sane when real life doesn't behave. With special mention to Fiona McArthur, who is a one-person smiling cheer squad and who makes anything and everything seem possible and is so often right. Port Barb is ready and awaiting your return!

And, of course, there is the family at home to thank; 2017 was a mad year of downsizing and weddings and removals left, right and centre, and at the core, it's always been about family and the love that binds us together. Thank you to our gorgeous gals for enduring and helping through all the upheavals, with once again, thanks to Gavin, for hanging in there all these years. It is some treat to find yourself on the other side of babies, school, driving lessons and school formals only to discover you still rather fancy the person you married. I am blessed.

Finally, to each and every one of you who pick up *The Trouble with Choices*, I say thank you for giving my story your time. There is no greater gift a reader can give an author. Thank you from the bottom of my heart.

And may all your choices be trouble-free ones …

Trish x